AMERICAN
BEAUTY

AMERICAN BEAUTY

Mary Ellin Barrett

E. P. DUTTON   •   NEW YORK

For information contact: Elsevier-Dutton Publishing Co., Inc.
2 Park Avenue, New York, N.Y. 10016

Library of Congress Cataloging in Publication Data

Barrett, Mary Ellin.
American beauty.
I. Title.
PZ4.B2738Am   1980   813'.54   80-15142
ISBN: 0-525-05285-2

Published simultaneously in Canada by
Clarke, Irwin & Company Limited, Toronto and Vancouver
Designed by The Etheredges

10 9 8 7 6 5 4 3 2 1

First Edition

For Marvin, again,
who had faith in me and
this book.

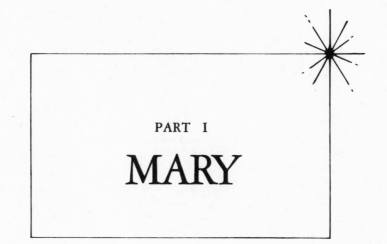

PART I

MARY

CHAPTER 1

1975

When the doorbell rang, Mary had just fastened the clasp of the necklace.

A few moments before she heard the unexpected summons, too late to be part of the day just past, too early for the evening to come, she had gone through a dressing-table ritual as familiar and studied as some savored piece of stage business in the longest-running show of her venerable career.

Caressing the soft blue velvet case, soft as her skin, once, velvety blue as the low notes of her voice, still, then opening the lid, she had stared for a while at the glittering contents as if she'd forgotten the strangeness and beauty of the ruby. "As big as an all-day sucker," her sister-in-law had once said, at the opera house bar, of the stone, which had a star at its center and was a rich milky crimson closer to mauve than red. If it had been true red and lacking the star, the same clever lady allowed, and the equivalent weight, some seventy carats, it would have been worth five times as much. But then it wouldn't have been her ruby. Mary's ruby. The famous Grace ruby. And at that, hung off a chain of perfectly matched diamonds, it had a value sufficient to give the family (not to mention the insurance company) fits whenever she removed the piece from the vault. As tonight.

Next she'd held the glittering chain with its glowing burden up to the light, between her eyes and the mirror, letting the great mysterious stone twist slowly to the right and the left . . . just as the man who gave it to her in the first place, one long-ago evening, had done and then with a quick gesture clasped the chain around her neck—that newly clipped nape, shingled like a boy's —murmuring, "I still don't forgive you for doing that." "But I was so bored, not working," she said. "I'll try from now on to make sure you aren't bored," he'd said. Shaking off the ghost, Mary felt for the clasp now herself, under hair that had never been bobbed again.

As she felt the click of the cunningly wrought safety lock (how she'd get the necklace off had always been a puzzle for later), she gave the face she saw before her a wry smile. So. For the space of an hour, interrupted only by two brief telephone calls, sitting at her dressing table, that raffish splash of color in a perfect pastel lady's chamber, concentrating on the earnest business of fixing her hair and making up, she'd quite forgotten the cream of the jest: that the occasion over which she'd taken such pains was not an opening night or a great charity ball but an affair she had often sworn she would never attend, would fly to the moon or drown herself to avoid . . . her own seventy-fifth birthday party.

"A joke in very poor taste," said Mary Gay, that distinguished resident of Manhattan, known to the world as the last of the old-time golden girls and in the daily rounds of her life sometimes as the saint of Madison Avenue, sometimes as the holy terror of the Upper East Side, more often simply as the amazing Miss Gay. She had another notable name also, her husband's name, which she used when the spirit or convenience moved her, but not too often.

Joke or no joke, seventy-five or not, the amazing Miss Gay, after one shrewd look at the line-tracked face that had once been indecently, heartbreakingly beautiful, had set to work and enjoyed the challenge, though some people would no doubt insist that to look at herself in the mirror these days must surely be as cruel as to hear herself sing. Mary could imagine her daughter-in-law, for example, the pure Serena, a few blocks south and east, also getting ready for the party.

"Poor Mary," Serena would say, who could find a reason to feel sorry for anyone so unfortunate as not to be herself. Well, poor Serena, who'd never understand that for a woman like Mary Gay there were no "shoulds" or "musts," no timetables of life. She made a face at the thought of Serena, and then smiled. . . . Poor Serena, dear Serena, the mouse who had become as sleek as a cat . . . her Serena . . . Lion's Serena.

Why, where else in the world . . . *dear Serena* . . . other than in her bed or at the golden piano in the drawing room downstairs, would Mary feel more comfortable, more herself, less of a relic (less aware that the year was 1975 and she turned seventy-five with it) than at that memory-charged dressing table, so much a part of her legend and eccentricity, such a Maryism, as her grandchildren would say. For look at that peculiar vanity more closely and you would realize it was nothing less than a sideboard, a fine Regency sideboard such as you might come across in a great London house, with its legs broken off midway for convenient sitting. But what else could hold all the paraphernalia that went into the composing of Miss Gay? "Such gall," said Charlie Grace— who had bought the piece at an auction, expecting to find it in their dining room when he returned from his annual trip abroad —anger fighting amusement in his voice. "So typical! To mutilate something beautiful to satisfy a whim. Someday I'll chop you down to size, my sweet, for convenient sitting."

Affectionately now she regarded the litter around her. The tubes, brushes, and rainbow pots, the orange sticks and pumice stones, the scissors and sprays, powders and masks. Mary's things. The boxes of patches, buttons, and coins, the perfume bottles with the grand old labels, Schiaparelli in the shape of a dressmaker's dummy, Matchabelli with its stopper like a crown, and the crystal vial square-cut like a jewel, holding the fresh and spicy scent that a famous couturier had named in her youthful honor La Gaieté. Mary Gay's things. The enameled dresser set with the diamond monograms (souvenir of a honeymoon) and the plastic-handled dog brushes she actually used on her time-defying hair; the bristling pincushion in the shape of a heart (handiwork of a loving daughter), and all the other good-luck and bon-voyage hearts, of gold, glass, clay, and ivory; the miniatures of her mother and father and Charlie's photograph in the little silver frame (gift of a son with his first earned money) and the old tin candy box where she kept her lipsticks, which had been her original good luck and bon voyage . . . a woman's things, baffling and disturbing to a man. How Charlie had laughed at the cluttered surface, mocked her inability to throw anything away, and at other times how cold the clutter had made him, how angry.

Yet that time she'd run away and then come creeping back the very next night. She'd found him sitting there in her place on the stool, touching her things as if they were precious to him, looking worse than she, as if he'd been crying. "Looking for something?" she said quietly. "Your checkbook," he answered, "if you'd left your checkbook, I would have called the police," an old joke between them though they had not laughed that night, only stared at each other till she looked away.

Oh, surely there was enough of a lifetime on that crowded glass-covered surface to make a sentimental woman weep or a superstitious one shiver before she'd ever faced the mirror. Not Mary. The only shivering she did was in bed, alone, in the black of the night, thinking about her death.

"I swear, you don't look a day over fifty-eight, darling!" Miss Gay had said aloud, finishing the job, a second or so before the doorbell rang, smiling at herself in the mirror and then at the cat that watched her from a beige velvet chair, a smile that in spirit was not a day over eighteen, whose charm was not spoiled by the old ivory color of the big strong teeth. Mary was proud of those teeth, all but two her own and only half a dozen capped, as she was proud of her hair, wiry, indestructible, not eked out by hairpieces, no pink scalp showing through its abundance. A fabulous family inheritance, that hair, held to its natural golden brown only by a weekly rinse; like her mother before her, she had not begun to go gray till her sixties. Unlike the stately Honora, however, always coiffed in later years in dowager dignity, Mary wore her own lively tresses as she had for decades, ever since the war, with bangs, and just slightly longer than chin length, softly curled under in the manner of a movie star of the late thirties. The effect on any other woman three-quarters of a century old would have been outlandish, like the effect of the patently false eyelashes that framed her expressive brown eyes. On the amazing Miss Gay it was just right. The dark eyes and pink-lipped smile, the enchantingly tilted nose and live golden-brown hair came at you, as though you and the whole world were photographers—flash—hold it, Miss Gay!—and you simply didn't see the wrinkles, the sags, the pouchings of the pale powdered skin.

"Not turned into a prune yet or a man," she added softly, "as long as you keep your temper and stay out of the sun." Thinking of something now that annoyed her—unfortunately something she'd done, just a half hour ago, and was already regretting —she stood up abruptly as she had promised herself she would not rise from a sofa or chair that night, no matter what. For in anger, so she had been told and knew, though fiercely denied to herself, she became ancient, without sex, ugly as sin. Yet when one of those flashes overtook her, she didn't care. Inside it was like being young again, worth it for the moment. But whatever happened later, and God knows, families being families and old friends being old friends, there'd be provocations, she was going to keep calm. Walk into Lion and Serena's apartment like the great lady she was. Charm everyone, handle everything, even ill-placed toasts and empty places, and at the moment when things were on the brink of going completely to pieces, get Mr. Harry Dresser to the piano and polish the evening off with a song or two, knowing she had them, that the magic could still happen. Having asked her politely, tolerantly, as if she were a child again and all the relatives were chorusing, "Amazing for her age!," they would stop being polite and be smitten. Because she was still an artist—the artist her father had prophesied when she was eleven years old—something these ones wouldn't know about, not even Lion though he wasn't a bad writer, and the devil with them.

"You will not take offense," she ordered. At that moment the doorbell rang. Queer. Was it so late, that the car was downstairs already?

Except it wasn't that late. The car was expected at ten to eight and the traveling clock on her dresser, which hadn't lost or gained a minute in thirty years, told her it was just seven. "What on earth," she said loudly. Cherubino the cat jumped down, as he always did at the sound of the bell, and ran silently out of the room. He'd be waiting below thinking that if he were clever when the door opened, he could escape; ungrateful creature, living in the lap of luxury, yet wanting nothing so much as to get out. Mary stood up and crossed the long bedroom, full width of a wide house, to pick up the speaking tube, unchanged since her mother-in-law's day. As she did so, she caught a glimpse in the mirrored closet doors of a plump old woman in a pink corset, a gaudy old woman with gold-dusted hair, wearing sturdy silver sandals and stockings held up by long garters that pressed against oozing white thighs, and a ruby albatross around her neck: an old woman she did not recognize.

"Who is it?" she shouted into the box.

"Flowers," came the reply. "Flowers for you, madame."

Flowers! Everywhere you looked the house already resembled an opening-night dressing room or a funeral parlor. There were long-stemmed yellow tea roses, stiff-necked in the vases as royalty, and tiny sweetheart roses that looked as though they were made of sugar icing; there were plants as big as trees and bright clumps of out-of-season tulips and hyacinths; there were sprays of rare white orchids, recalling the bygone days of corsages; there were scarlet anemones just revealing their black hearts. But the flowers she'd been looking for all day were still missing. "I'll be down in a minute," she called into the tube. She had to see, one last time. He hadn't forgotten, that secret admirer of hers. She, Mary Gay, who hadn't answered her own bell for more than half a century, was going to the door like a young girl on the evening of the ball.

She had been going to the door all day, up- and downstairs, for she was alone in the house. She did not generally live alone. Besides the cat, who sometimes thought he was a dog, there was Ninon, the maid, who sometimes thought she was a governess. But Ninon hardly counted these days. And this day she counted not at all. Over eighty, in bed all week with *la grippe* and a cheap novel, she had been taken late the previous afternoon to the hospital—on the eve of Mary's birthday too—where she could be looked after. Until recently there had always been a butler and a cook as well. But the last couple, Marcel and Marianne, bullies and cheats, though lucky Mary was to have them, Lion said, had left a month ago taking valuable silver and a paperweight of no value at all except it happened to be precious to Mary Gay, a relic from her Chicago childhood. Perhaps Marianne meant to kill Marcel with it. He would, Mary agreed, have provoked an angel, and Marianne was no angel. And the last dog was gone, princely Lord George, her standard poodle, run over a month ago by a sports car gunning through the block when he'd pulled the lead out of Ninon's tired old hands. Mary wanted no more to do with bad-tempered thieving couples who practically made you a prisoner, or dogs you loved that got killed, but Lion and Serena were up in arms, telling her she couldn't live in a house alone, that far uptown, at her age, in these times; though April said, "Why not, if that's what she wants."

Ninon was worse than useless and should be in a nursing home. Yet if Ninon left, or died, who would know where anything was? Who could find things in the closets without starting an avalanche? Or make the morning coffee so it tasted like Paris, and potpourri and sachets so they smelled like her mother's? Who else would understand how little her temper mattered, who would remember him, the ghost, remember the two of them together and the children when they were small? Who else knew her secrets? "Ninon!" she called out of habit, just up to the next floor, Lion and April's old floor, where long ago Ninon had moved in

—one room for herself, two rooms for Madame's clothes, and no guests. But there was silence. Of course. Ninon wasn't there.

On the closet door hung the dress Mary was going to wear, dark blue satin, traced with glinting embroidery, made to order some years earlier by the (then) unknown young designer she'd helped launch, for another less-special occasion, a dress designed to last for always. But now, hurriedly, she put on a high-necked dressing gown that would hide her nakedness and jewels. The bell rang again.

"Coming, coming," she said querulously, starting down the slippery curving stair, taking care to hold on to the banister, feeling as she went an unreasonable excitement. For even at her age, with shaky knees and a bad back and alarming variations in the beat of her heart, it was possible for life to hold surprises, sweet gifts. Life could still, in the space of a minute, change. She was, after all, wearing the ruby.

Peering through the Magic Eye in the kitchen door, she saw a man carrying a box, long and white as an infant's coffin, big enough to hold three or four dozen long-stemmed American Beauty roses, her favorite flower, however banal, above all others, for was it not her emblem? Even with the bloating effect of the peephole, which made every one look like Tweedledum, she recognized Mr. Mercier, the assistant to Mr. Bradley, the florist. A thoughtful touch, not to send at this hour a strange messenger, someone she might have hesitated to let in, but this familiar, slightly comical figure with his French beret and steel-rimmed glasses, his flowing scarf and beard, Mr. François Mercier, artist of arrangements, who dressed as if it were 1850, and upper Madison Avenue, Montparnasse.

To see him with that box, surely the one she was waiting for, made her happy. She would have him wait while she found five dollars, she thought, unhooking the chain.

For an instant, Mary did not believe what was happening. She opened her eyes so wide it hurt, a trick she'd taught her children long ago for waking up out of a nightmare, an expression she'd used onstage to convey wonder or perplexity. And found herself not upstairs in the softness of her Hollywood bed, struggling against the ambush of sleep, nor stage center with the curtain up and a thousand spellbound victims in front of her, but exactly where she had been, in her gleaming kitchen with a man pointing a gun at her—a man in a beret and beard with steel-rimmed glasses and an artist's scarf, who was not Mr. Bradley's assistant, not the pathetic Mr. Mercier, not at all, though he wore his costume, his glasses, his flowing beard and mustache.

In her arms Cherubino cried and squirmed and scratched. Fear—cold, gray, disgusting sheets of fear—assailed her body and another feeling, of unimaginable affront, at the sight of that gun, metallic, with a long menacing barrel that could not be mistaken for a toy.

"Drop the cat," the man said. "Anyone else in the house?"

Somehow the sound of a voice made her less frightened. A crisp, unslurred, efficient voice, like that of a director or conductor or police officer ordering you away from catastrophe; not the voice of Mr. Mercier, not at all, though she could have sworn it was Mr. Mercier's voice shouting, "Flowers, flowers for you, madame," over the intercom. It was a contact of sorts and freed her mind. She tried to remember what her friends said, what newspapers said, what would be the smart thing to do. She couldn't see the man's eyes; the steel-rimmed glasses had lenses that threw the light back at you; but from his expression and manner she judged him neither drugged nor crazy. The set of his face was unemotional, almost regretful. "I said, who else is here?" he repeated.

"Just my poor old maid who's sick on the fourth floor," she lied. "She has a bad heart."

"Don't make a noise and we won't bother her." He knew she was lying. He obviously knew everything about the house. His speech was educated and resonant, theatrical in its soft roundness, like that of a singer or actor or public speaker. His age, too, like that of a singer or actor or politician, was indeterminate. He was not a boy but seemed young to her, forty perhaps. Framed by that dashing mustache and a flowing beard, the mouth forming the words was attractive. The pleasant voice and the man's cheerful bohemian air distressed her. His was not the city face she feared, though she didn't like the blind look of those glasses; not the face of the young beast who'd mortally wounded her neighborhood jeweler, a friend of thirty years, when the old man reached for the alarm. Only then did she remember her own alarm button by the door. The man with the gun knocked her hand as she reached for it, hurting her. "Touch that and I'll shoot," he said. "I don't mind killing people. I killed plenty in the war once. I know there's no one else in the house. If there are any surprises, I'll use this." Not so pleasant after all.

"You hurt me," she said sharply, as she might have to an equal, a lover. Then, "In a half hour or so a car will be coming to take me to dinner."

"I won't be around. Get the animal." Cherubino was at the man's ankles now, a ball of snapping, playful fluff. "In there," pointing to the broom closet. "It won't smother in a half hour."

How pitifully the cat mewed as she shut the door. "Rotten thing to do to an animal," Mary accused.

"Take me to the safe."

"There is no safe. There's a little cash upstairs."

"I'm not here for money. Where are the jewels? The ones you took out for the party tonight."

So that was it. He was a thief, a professional jewel thief who'd done his research, who knew exactly who lived in the house and when the alarm signal was turned on, and who'd read the birthday piece about her in yesterday's *Post* . . . "Lady Ruby Turns Seventy-five." There was a visitor she should have never let through the door, Mary thought bitterly, that reporter with her long hair and tired face and brilliant eyes and feminist pitch. Then this smart fellow would never have paid her a visit, posing as a florist's assistant. Still she felt a certain relief. If I don't make any mistakes, she decided then, I'll get out alive.

"In the bedroom," she answered, remembering the piece that wasn't in the bedroom, that was there with them at that very moment. The one she cared about that he no doubt cared about also. Her heart beat frantically. If she was clever and lucky, though, she might fool him. She had deceived men before, after all. "Everything's upstairs," she said, and her voice was firm in the deliberate lie.

Tying her to the beige velvet chair with a piece of cord he'd brought, the thief was quick and graceful and sure of himself, his gloved hands as impersonal as a doctor's or hairdresser's. Next he cut the cord of the telephone by the bed, not knowing about the hidden one, the one in the drawer—not all that clever. There was something stagy about the way he moved. The illusion of Mr. Mercier dissolved into another impression, reaching much further back into the past, of a tenor she'd once known made up to play Rodolfo, though the tenor wouldn't have worn glasses. "Do you know you look like Amara in *Bohème*," she thought of saying, except you have a hard and sinister look and that man had trouble looking anything but saucy. Singing Rodolfo, that man winked at poor Mimi as she drew her last breath.

"Do you by any chance sing?" the lady asked the thief as he began going through the jewel cases on her dressing table. The casualness of her own voice amazed her. "You remind me of a tenor I once knew."

"Not your kind of music, Miss Gay," he said. For an instant he smiled, just the faintest smile. "Don't talk."

"What do you think my kind of music is? I've sung everything in my time. What do you sing?" It was almost impossible for Mary Gay to be with any human male and not attempt some sort of communication, even with a man as swarthy as she was fair, as poor as she was rich, a man who might be her executioner.

"I said don't talk." He worked quickly, taking, she noticed, just the pieces with the big stones. The sapphire ring, the sapphire and ruby bracelet, the pearls with the diamond clasp. His fingers were loving; his excitement visible. The pretty gold bangles, the amusing pins in shapes of birds and animals, or of geometric Art Deco design, the colorful flexible bracelets woven of tiny stones held no interest for him, no more than her gold wedding band or her engagement ring composed of many beautiful but small

[13]

diamonds, inlaid like mosaic in a square. His pose told her something more about him: beyond money, he had a passion for the gems themselves. "Where's the rest?" he said. The gun was on her steadily. She had never felt anything so steady in her life.

"You have me trussed up tighter than a turkey for Thanksgiving," she said. "Couldn't you put that thing away?"

"The rest?"

"I suppose you enjoy pointing it at me. Why?"

"Because it makes me feel powerful. The rest."

"Over there," nodding in the direction of the cloisonné box with its intricately decorated doors that opened onto a dozen gold-knobbed drawers—a box that had once belonged to a Manchu princess—another of Charlie's presents. Its workmanship was so marvelously strong and intricate that, locked, it was as difficult to break into as a small safe or the hidden clasp at the back of her neck. It was where she kept the best, the largest . . . the necklace when it wasn't in the vault. This night the coffer was open.

"I've felt powerful in my life," she said, "and equal. Without carrying a gun." It was as if even this experience had to be made special, hers, transformed into an encounter, a Mary Gay performance.

For an instant the man turned on her, not with the gun, but with his face and person, answering her challenge. "You carried your own weapons, ma'am. And used them, I'm sure."

Then he went to work, again picking through, rejecting everything but the ruby ring, the ruby and diamond bracelet, and the ruby earclips, items she'd decided against wearing, wanting nothing to distract from the necklace.

"You don't care for the tiara?" she asked ironically and thought she heard him reply, contemptuously, "That shit?" She felt her temper rise. She'd never let her fellow actors or singers, her children, even her lovers—save one—use coarse language in her presence. As for Charlie Grace, such words from him, almost never used, were bolts of lightning, flung grenades. How dare this fellow—but she caught herself. Steady, Mary. He seemed finished. Time was very slow. Five minutes seemed an hour. Young people had described to her the effect of marijuana as time running down like a slow-motion dance, a slow-motion film of a diver underwater. She had thought that sounded eerie but agreeable. She would not think so again.

"All right," he said. "Where's the ruby?"

From the walls and from surfaces they watched her, the ones frozen in frames. Her father. Her mother. Her singing teacher. Her husband and her children. Aware of the gun, she did not think large thoughts such as, Is this where it's going to end, my particular adventure, so far from its beginning? That the gun might go off had no more reality than that it might not go off. She only thought of the performance at hand, played to a gallery of photographs and paintings. "This is a room in which nothing happens except in memory," she had said, foolishly and not entirely candidly, to the young woman from the paper, not expecting her to poke around so, ask such uncomfortable questions so that, to distract her, Mary had told her something of the ruby, thinking such a girl of the seventies—such a new woman—would enjoy the way it had been handed down from one important woman to another, a passed torch so to speak, not just a bauble purchased by a millionaire for his darling. How it had been in the turban of a Persian caliph once, and had belonged to a famous French actress of the last century, and after that to her husband's mother, the actress Jean Archibald, and how Mary had worn it playing her finest role . . . herself. For *An Evening with Mary Gay* would have been incomplete without the ruby."

"You have the ring," Mary said.

"Not the ring. The necklace. The one with the history."

"It's in the vault," she lied. "I decided not to take it out after all." The high collar of her dressing gown concealed not only the necklace, but her hammering pulse. Yet the blue vein at her temple must be throbbing. How had someone—not Charlie —put it to her nearly a lifetime ago? "Your heart's showing." And touched the telltale spot.

"You have enough there to put my insurance company out

[15]

of business," she said bravely. "Enough to buy an island paradise, young man, or a life. Is that what you want, a life? A new life after your horrid war? I've known some wars."

"I want the necklace. The one you are wearing."

Then something rose in the old woman as it had risen, from time to time, throughout her life. Danger be damned. Risk everything. Defy everyone. She was Mary Gay, and she'd set a course for herself nearly sixty years ago, back in Chicago when she was still Mary Geylin, the day she walked out on that grave, studious girl and the hard and high life she was being prepared for, and followed Charlie Grace to New York and Broadway, not Broadway and Thirty-ninth Street with its diamond horseshoe and curtain of gold, but three blocks north to the Broadway known as the Great White Way.

From the wall now, in splendid Steichen chiaroscuro, Charlie looked down on her with a gaze impossible to read. Would he sit back and laugh? Would he say, "Serves you right, my dear, not so easy come, not so easy go," or would he try to protect her, as he had every now and then from herself, from life, from Mary Geylin, that odd little person who kept popping up, disturbing the surface of a triumphant career; would he vault out of the frame and stand between the gunman and the woman who had been his wife? And the man who was not Charlie? What would he have done?

At seventy-five, Mary was no more ready to die and join her ghosts than a middle-aged man she'd read about who'd lost his life to a street thief trying to save his father's gold watch; no more ready to die than her father had been in 1911 at forty-nine, or her mother a half century later at eighty, nor than she had been at nineteen or fifty-two; nor indifferent to death as she had thought herself at eighteen and thirty-three. Nonetheless.

"I want the necklace," the man repeated. "I know it's on you."

"No," said Mary Gay as she had said more than once in her life.

A rare ruby appended to a matchless diamond necklace, she thought, could have as much sentimental importance as a dented

[16]

pocket watch hung on a tarnished gold chain, or a lock of hair or a monogrammed handkerchief of yellowed linen, though the tabloid sob sisters might not agree.

That stone was alive, symbol of the good young days, the prancing golden days of Mary Gay . . . Mary Grace . . . before fate dealt her the unpardonable blow, that hardened her for always so that her beloved daughter could look at her with those narrow green eyes, so like Charlie's, and say in that soft hostile voice, "Young, I don't believe you were ever young, ever seventeen. I believe you were born old, born hard. . . ."

Never was Mary Gay younger—more Mary Geylin—than saying, "You can't have it," as the gunman came toward her, bringing into play her most powerful weapons—her fearsome glance, her commanding seductive voice—daring to think that she, a helpless seventy-five-year-old woman might win this last battle. "You have enough! Leave! Don't you come near me!"

CHAPTER 2

1911

"I want that ring," the mother said to the little girl on the evening her father died, just a fortnight after the child's eleventh birthday. "Are you going to give it to me?"

"No," said the little girl, her fist tightly clenched, her dark eyes wide. "You can't have it. Don't come near me!"

On Mary Geylin's eleventh birthday in January of 1911, the lake had frozen solid so that if you'd wanted you could have walked or driven a wagon and pair all the way from the Oak Street Beach to Gary, except it was so cold you wouldn't have wanted to. When Mary and her father, on the way to the opera house, bundled up and walked down to the shore, past the waterworks like an ogre's castle, past the brown dungeon turrets of the grandest private house in Chicago, cliffs of ice had risen monstrously along the beach and, looking north and south beyond the silver plumes of their own breath, there was no one else visible.

It was a walk father and daughter enjoyed in all seasons, the proximity of the water being one of the pleasures of their quiet section of the North Side of the city, a neighborhood as friendly in its narrow side streets to artists and musicians and the modestly genteel as to the millionaires who lived along the broad drive that bordered the lakefront. Mysterious, beckoning, limitless as some ancient sea, Lake Michigan was the lodestone of the child's life, whether spangled under the sun and dotted with racing sails, or angry white-capped green and perilous to ships, or an empty gleaming deathly expanse as it was that day, bone-white and prehistoric in formation. But she and her father were not meant to be taking the air that day; the man was not meant to linger in that icy cold, looking at frozen wonders, answering the child's questions as if he were a walking book of knowledge.

Afterward, in the trolley going downtown, as he answered more questions, about the performance ahead, the man had sneezed and coughed as if he were the one who needed warming. For that was her real eleventh birthday present, not the beaver muff she'd so proudly displayed on their walk, but this trip to the Auditorium to hear Nellie Melba and John McCormack sing *La Bohème* . . . the very first opera of a grave musician's child who enjoyed playing the piano and singing better than anything in the world except perhaps her father's company.

"God bless you," Mary exclaimed, frowning, looking at her father wth concern. *"Gesundheit. Dieu vous bénisse!"*

"Just an old New Year's cold on its last legs," Louis Geylin said, as he'd said to Mary's mother earlier when that good lady had questioned whether he shouldn't be in his bed with a mustard plaster and she shouldn't take Mary in his stead.

The child, already dressed in her crimson velvet party frock and high-buttoned kid boots, had made one of her wretched scenes. She loved her red-haired, bossy mother. Her mother was her friend and patient tutor, who had taught her to read before she ever went to school; who had given her piano lessons before turning her over to a "more important" teacher in the Fine Arts Building; who let her make fudge and stretchy molasses candy on rainy Sundays. But to go with Honora, who had at times the air of an ancient Roman matron, suitable to the name she had inherited

[19]

from her New England forebears—who was "the law"—that would not be the same . . . not fun, not special. To love was not the same as to adore; Mary adored her father. "He won't get sick," Mary said to Honora, pink and perspiring at the stove. "You always think people are going to get sick. You have to let him go. Who's going to cook dinner if you go?" "It's not up to your mother, though don't be impertinent," said Louis, who earned his living accompanying singers, sopranos one and all, and had no sons, and was weary of being fussed over and ordered about by women. Besides, he was as keyed up as Mary. He hadn't heard Melba since 1890, and that had been in Paris when he was still a young man.

So all her life Mary would remember that day, though it wasn't a memory she chose to share with anyone till Charlie Grace turned on her and said with a coldness that was at the same time kind, "Stop punishing yourself. I want to hear."

She'd remember the ride downtown through the glistening city, with even the black jets of coal smoke from chimneys appearing frozen against the pale blue sky. She'd remember the fine carriages and broughams and an occasional thrilling touring car with its side curtains buttoned tight, lined up on Congress Street and around the corner, for blocks up Michigan Avenue, and the excitement of mingling with the huge dressy matinee crowd that poured into the lobby of Chicago's great opera house. Outside, the Auditorium was forbidding, a gray stone fortress against the elements. But within, everything was golden, lit up like a merry-go-round at night, the curves and undulations of the interior, the arches of light bulbs and vaulted spaces, magical to the child. "Like Oz or At the Back of the North Wind or Camelot," said her father, who read to her evenings when she'd finished practicing and enjoyed conjuring up the illusions they had shared. Yet everything had its function, he added, for he also enjoyed puncturing magic with reason: every one of those curves, the very pitch of their seats (so steep where they sat, it made her dizzy) had been designed by the great Louis Sullivan to enhance the sound. And indeed, though the stage from where they sat seemed barely large enough for a troupe of marionettes, yet the voices of the tiny figures sounded closer and clearer than they did coming from the big morning-glory horn of the phonograph at home.

Even from that far away, how real it was—Paris! Love! Light talk and caperings in a garret! Street fair madness! Falling snow! Death in a garret turned cold!—and how those voices set her tingling, in melodies she knew as well as her school chums knew those of *The Red Mill*, for Honora and Louis had played the score at home and sung much of it in their imperfect though spirited voices. Now it was the silvery soprano of Melba twined around the golden Irish tenor of McCormack, middle-aged Nellie singing like a girl with the last young partner she'd bring along, making such musical romance of the first two acts, such sadness of the third and fourth, that father and daughter were caught on their high perch when the lights came up with the mist still in their eyes.

Always she'd remember that also: handsome, shaggy Louis, in his smart brown worsted suit, with his hair like a seal's winter coat, looking at her sheepishly with tired dark eyes, as if to say: A fine thing your father crying like a woman over make-believe. Then he'd put an arm around his daughter who had his eyes and full red lips and broad cheeks, though she was more golden than brown, stroking the thick mane of her tawny hair that escaped its velvet bow, telling her it was just a story. "I know," Mary said, and, ashamed of her emotion, wanting to puncture that emotion, added, "They were funny, weren't they? So fat."

On the way home (not in a trolley, but a horse-drawn hack, final birthday extravagance), Louis had said, "No one can sing that first-act aria like Melba." And then what he called later that evening "the amazing incident" had happened. Mary had begun to sing the familiar words—*Mi chiamano Mimì, ma il mio nome è Lucia*—quietly at first, then gaining power. Her voice was childish and wobbled at certain of those soaring Puccini rises and halfway through she became self-conscious and stopped, but what he heard gave Louis Geylin goose bumps. So he told Honora and Mary's sister, Isabelle, and all those self-important relatives of his —Uncle Boris Geylin, the cellist, Aunt Denise, the church singer, Danny and Walter Geylin, the prodigy cousins, not to mention his wife's sister, Margaret, the modiste—when they came by the apartment that evening to celebrate. Everyone talked freely about everyone else's talent, or lack of talent, in the Geylin family, and right to one another's faces. Walter had perfect pitch and remarkable endurance, and the profile essential for a star violinist. . . . Danny had fingers like Paderewski. . . . Belle was a lazy cow. . . . Mary a show-off. . . . But it was more than Mary's amazing ear, mimicking Melba, Louis said. There was something the precocious eleven-year-old added of her own, though it was difficult to say just what: something perilously adult, dangerous, and he used a French phrase Mary didn't understand.

Then Louis had made her do it all over again, with the score and himself at the concert grand that took up two-thirds of their parlor, stretching inward from the windowed bay that was curtained in dingy gold against the night: so exaggerated, like the Geylins' manner of speaking, that piano, those heavy stagy curtains. Everyone had been transfixed at the sheer prettiness of the sounds the child was making, except, that is, for her sister. Already, at fourteen, with blond ringlets and pansy-blue eyes, Isabelle was the obvious beauty of the family, yet its ugly duckling, for she had a tin ear, poor darling. While Mary sang, Isabelle sat cross-legged on the faded Persian carpet—her place, back to the piano—pointedly coloring in her sketchbook, drawing a fancy dress for one of the cardboard dolls in a book of cutouts (when she grew up, the relatives told her, she might be a costumer like Aunt Margaret, who had gone from assistant wardrobe mistress at the opera to fashionable hat designer). And afterward, when the others exclaimed jestingly that there was a Patti among them, a young Jenny Lind come to call, Isabelle, older sister of the future Mary Gay, said quite audibly, "More like a sick calf if you ask me."

"This child will scale the heights," Louis said at supper, toasting the birthday girl with ruby-red claret. His cheeks burned crimson as the wine. His brown eyes in the candlelight were bright as the cat's-eye ring on the little finger of the hand that held the glass. He'd promised to give Mary the ring someday, for it fascinated the child with its bar of imprisoned golden light that shifted restlessly across the bronze surface, the color of her eyes and his, their legacy, he said from her Russian grandmother, his mother.

"Louis!" Honora cautioned. "It is dangerous to encourage such fantasies. Permit the child her childhood."

"This girl is a voice," he insisted. His words, his eyes, the ring, the candles, the wine—hypnotist's tools, seducer's tools—held Mary enthralled. The others reminded him that no woman in the family had ever been more than a gifted amateur. Their hearts were too susceptible to be otherwise. They married young and bore children. Besides, Geylins didn't make good singers (Aunt Denise who sang wasn't, after all, a Geylin by birth), for they were too moody. Better suited to piano or strings. The Pecks also, said Honora, the gifted amateur who had married her piano teacher and sometimes found his family a rich diet. Her people too, said noble-browed Honora, the professor's daughter, were prone to melancholy and wild swings of temperament.

"There has to be a first," said Louis good-naturedly, a little hoarsely, as the guests began to take their leave.

"Go to bed . . ." Honora said, softly, insistently, her pale blue eyes fixed on her husband's face.

But Louis kept talking, for besides having the look of a fever, he also had had too much wine. He spoke of how they would train Mary and not make the mistakes of stupid people who let a girl sing through her teens; how she would play the piano but keep silent in adolescence while the voice was changing and the body maturing. . . . "And when she is sixteen or seventeen," he said with a definiteness that caught Mary's attention, "we will send her off to the dragon with the piano of gold, to Pauline Selva, for if there is a woman in America who understands the mystery of the female voice it is she, though she breathes fire like Fafner."

Everyone laughed as though he'd made a joke. But Mary, sitting silently now that supper was over, on the tapestry window seat behind the family Bechstein, knew it was nothing of the sort.

That was Mary Geylin's eleventh birthday. The best she'd

ever had and the best she ever would have, till Charlie Grace entered her life. As her twelfth, the first without Louis, would be the worst, until the one she skipped entirely.

The day after Mary turned eleven, Louis Geylin took to his bed with pleurisy, which in due course became pneumonia, as Honora had always feared and loudly prophesied would happen if he didn't take better care of himself. By the end of the second week he was dead.

And Mary, clutching his ring, watching with haunted dry eyes from the dark parlor the men carrying Louis' body to the big black car downstairs that waited by the door of their building, knew that it wasn't an ordinary cold he'd neglected this time, but her cold: her birthday cold. She didn't need her grieving mother to tell her that, to say, "Ah, if only he hadn't gone to the opera that afternoon, if only I hadn't let him"—she didn't need the scene over the ring to tell her how Honora felt, whom she thought was really to blame. Mary could read her mother's mind, and her own.

"Give me that," Honora said, when she returned from the funeral home and found Mary sitting on the window seat, holding the ring in her hand, putting it on, pulling it off her third finger, which one day would be big enough to hold the band securely. "I was looking everywhere for that ring. Where did you find it?" Honora's handsome classic face was pale and puffed, the freckles standing out like crayoned dots. Her blue eyes glittered strangely.

"It's mine. He wanted me to have it. He gave it to me."

"You are wrong. That is a gentleman's ring, Mary. Louis had no sons. You are not his son. He wanted to be buried with that ring. Now, please," holding out her hand. "Let us do what he wished." And then, as Mary made a fist around the ring and shook her head, Honora spoke harshly. "Haven't you done enough Mary? I want that ring. Are you going to give it to me?"

"No. You can't have it."

Honora had won, physically, though it wasn't easy to take anything away from Mary by force, for the child was fast and wiry and strong at eleven, with a tomboy's body below that solemn girlish face. But Honora was twice her size and more than twice her weight, with big powerful pianist's hands and arms. Finally the woman opened the child's hand, took the ring, and, breathing heavily, went into the kitchen to prepare dinner and weep some more.

"She shouldn't have done that," Isabelle said, who had been watching from the door of the bedroom. "I believe you."

Mary looked at her sister with big brown eyes that were blank from fury and grief, then nodded. And in time Mary came to believe her own story, that her father had given her the ring on the last day of his life, taken it off his finger and pressed it into her hand; risen like Lazarus from the dead and given it to her with his blessing; that it wasn't she who had taken the ring off his finger as he lay there, cold and lifeless, and put it in her pocket.

Isabelle and her mother never spoke of the matter again, as they never spoke again of Mary's eleventh birthday. Honora got a bad look on her face when anything reminded her, such as a certain kind of bright icy weather, or talk of the opera . . . such as Mary's singing.

Nor did Mary ever speak of the ring or that birthday again till the evening Charlie Grace gave her the ruby necklace and she said, "I know about stars. My father had a ring with a star," and told him about Louis' last gift and how her mother had taken it away and buried him with it; and how she had sworn nobody would ever remove anything from her by force again; and how she had also made a vow not to sing again because her wanting to sing, her love of singing, had somehow killed her father. "You are a strange young woman, Mary Grace, a remarkable young woman," Charlie Grace said. And there was wonder and perhaps a little fear in his eyes.

So when at her twelfth birthday party Aunt Denise had asked Mary for a song, Mary had refused. Just a simple little song, Denise had insisted, like "After the Ball," which the girl gave such a lilt to, why the great Rose Hart herself, who'd introduced the song at the Chicago World's Fair, didn't sing it more sweetly. "I don't feel like it," Mary said, her jaw tightening.

No one had taken Mary's refusal to perform seriously. Everyone else had taken a turn, the boys at the piano and violin, Boris on his cello, Denise singing a festive Handel air; Mary, they all knew, was too competitive to stay silent long. The relatives had pressed and finally ordered her, as if she wasn't the birthday girl, to "stop her nonsense." At that, Mary had said flatly, "I'm not going to sing." And when Honora said, "Oh, Mary," in that loving concerned way, as if you could just pass over things that you'd said, or done, or looks you'd given, just like that, forget them, the girl added, "I'll never sing again."

Nor did she mean to. Never intended to lift that beautiful clear youthful voice of hers seriously in song again. She would stick to her piano and follow in Louis' footsteps that way. For, besides guilt and superstition, she carried the devil's own pride and stubbornness within her, and already a clear sense of her own ability to sway others, whether to make them happy or to punish them. She'd sung for her father; he had believed in her while those others had laughed, and he was dead. The devil with it . . . and them.

"And what made you change your mind?" Charlie Grace would ask.

"Madame Selva . . . your friend," Mary answered, "and all those cows and canaries she had me playing for. Thumping the piano, the little accompanist, the studio Cinderella, day after day . . . I knew I was better than them." And again she almost believed her own story and would have gone on believing it, and Charlie with her, if he hadn't found one night a little pouch, with a medal, a pearl stickpin, a button, a lock of blue-black hair, and a blue-black scarab ring—the other ring in the past of Mary—which an angry, heartbroken young woman had refused to throw away.

CHAPTER 3

1916

At the very center of the noisy, pumping, thumping heart of Chicago, around the corner from the opera house, and a block south of Orchestra Hall, stood the Fine Arts Building, one of the grand old skyscrapers of Michigan Avenue (in 1884, the year it was erected, an amazing ten stories high). There, on the top floor, Pauline Selva had her studio.

Long before Mary Geylin auditioned for the job of her accompanist, on her way to or from her piano lessons with Maestro Feuerman, the ambitious young girl had seen the formidable lady in the elevator, swathed in furs, her head wrapped in velvet or satin, a small dynamic woman surrounded by an outer garment of heavy scent, musky and disturbingly different from the fresh lavender cologne Mary's mother wore. Always with the singing teacher would be some eager maiden or other, leaning close to hear a last word of advice, or bending under the weight of guilt at having performed poorly in her lesson. Cows, Mary would think of those maidens, and see herself in their place . . . forgetting for a moment.

To Mary, Pauline Selva did not look like a dragon or a witch or enchantress or any other fairy-tale creature, but precisely what she was, a woman rooted in the world. And what a world—Paris, Dresden, Vienna, St. Petersburg—the world of prima donnas and maestros, of tenors and dukes, of champagne suppers and twenty traveling trunks, of tantrums, tears, and the highest devotion to art. Here was no ordinary passenger in a Chicago elevator on her way to or from work, not even the usual professional musician or dedicated aesthete, but a former star, who was still an amazing artist. Once Mary had heard Madame Selva sing at a teachers' recital a Mahler song, an eerie lament in a minor key that evoked moonlight and cobblestones and the ghost of a dead lover, and the old woman's performance, the controlled pathos of her voice, had moved Mary to tears. Here was a personality who, if she wished, if she took a shine to you, as she had to a handful of fortunate young men and women since she had returned to Chicago to teach, might change your life. Even if you were just her accompanist, there to make money so you could follow Maestro Feuerman East, to the Curtis Institute where he'd just taken a position.

"There is no money to send you to Curtis," Honora told Mary the summer of 1916 when the clever girl, a year ahead of herself, graduated from high school. "Maestro Feuerman took you for nothing as a favor to friends; but even if you get a scholarship to the conservatory, there are too many expenses."

"I'll make the money," Mary said. "Madame Selva is looking for an accompanist for next fall."

"That will be interesting," Honora said, giving her a penetrating look. "For you to play for singers, day after day. It occurs to me, Mary—"

"Don't say it, Mother," Mary said. "Please do me the favor of not saying it."

But: "Tell me something, Miss Mary Geylin," said Madame

Selva, sitting in the high-backed chair that was her listening post while Mary sat at the amazing piano, which wasn't brown like theirs at home, or black like Maestro Feuerman's Steinway, but golden—scrolled and garlanded and painted—an instrument you might expect to see in a palace or bordello but scarcely in a working studio, even in the Fine Arts Building. "Are you very serious? Or are you too clever to be serious?" "I am very serious," said Mary Geylin, after a pause that indicated she was clever as well—clever enough to understand that in spite of her gold piano and certain photographs on the studio wall signed with loving and flowery inscriptions, so, too, was Madame Selva. That fancy piano had the hardest action and most sumptuous tone Mary had ever felt or heard.

"And tell me something else. Do you also sing?"

From the moment the girl in her saucer hat, with her crown of braids, and big brown eyes and sweet round face, walked in the studio door, the singing teacher was skeptical, as she told Mary later. Her credentials as a pianist were impeccable to be sure: the child of Louis Geylin; the pupil of Leon Feuerman, who'd sent a glowing letter of recommendation; experience accompanying her high school glee club, her endless musical relatives. And when she sat down at the piano, she squared off to the instrument like a real professional, straw skimmer removed, sleeves of her sailor dress pushed up. A Schubert lied, an aria from *Don Giovanni*, a florid eighteenth-century setting of a psalm: whatever the singing teacher gave her to play, Mary Geylin read the music easily, tempo steady, dynamics controlled as if she could hear the voice of the singer in her head. "A few false notes, but not many," said Selva, impressed. "I can spot nerves."

The child's gall was altogether superb, coming there at all given her age and the way she looked, and she had even asked about money before a fee had been suggested, in a calm stubborn way that reminded Pauline Selva of every pianist she had ever known.

"So you are going to be a great virtuoso someday. You play well. You are very musical," Madame Selva said when the trial was over. But even as Mary had smiled in answer, the shrewd old teacher was thinking this girl, so serious and stolid when she frowned in concentration, was, smiling, far too pretty to face a keyboard all her life; her smile displayed the beautiful white teeth and the generosity of the rosy mouth, called attention to the sparkle in those wide-spaced staring dark eyes and the delicious flare of the nostrils; in the smiling face of Mary Geylin, Madame Selva saw, all of a sudden, a Gilda or Zerlina, and the girl had the figure to match. Even a babyish sailor dress scarred with the lines of too many lettings-out could not disguise the rounded prettiness of Mary Geylin's body. Had she ever considered singing, Madame Selva asked, did she have a voice?

"No," said Mary flatly, "I do not sing," and she met the old woman's curious gaze straight on, without flinching, which was an act of considerable courage. For though Madame Selva's henna-red hair might be pulled back simply in a bun and the skirts of her black working dress lie heavy about her ankles, though her resonant speech might be as unaffectedly middle-western, for all the years in Europe, as Aunt Denise's, there was nothing easy about the woman's personality. She was as formidable close up as she had seemed as a stranger in an elevator.

"Interesting." Madame Selva returned Mary's look with a blue-gray gaze that made the girl feel very small indeed and yet magnified, every blemish exposed. "I've never known a girl as attractive as you and as musical who didn't think she could sing if she really wanted to."

"I don't want to. I don't like singing."

"If you don't like singing, why are you here? You'll be hearing it night and day."

"I need the money," said Mary Geylin, and her color rose.

And with that bit of cheek she got the job—along with a lecture on seriousness.

"I care about nothing else in the world but music," said Mary.

"Not even the election!"—teasing her a little, as if to say, it's all right, you know, I understand you, you and I are going to be friends. Madame Selva rose from the chair where she'd been sitting all the while, standing, hands on her hips, looking at Mary, who also stood now, polite, attentive.

"I've no interest in politics."

"Good. Look down there in Grant Park," pulling the girl to the window, pointing an accusing finger at what appeared to be a rally down below at the edge of the park, with a man on a flag-draped platform orating while people waved placards which, the old woman said acidly, could as easily read *If you want war vote for Wilson* as *"If you want war vote for Charles Evans Hughes."* "Donkeys all!" she said. "And those ones too," pointing to an obvious group of suffragettes who were picketing the rally, waving the banner of the Women's Peace Party. "I want none of that in my studio. No electioneering, no war talk, for I have students of every nationality. Your predecessor carried a soapbox, most unfortunately. And what about young men? Do you have time for them?" The singing teacher paused to give the girl another of those sharp looks. "There's a tenor who comes here for coaching in whom I take an interest. Gianni Amara. Watch him work, for he's a real artist in the making. But steer clear of him otherwise. I don't stand for nonsense, as that last girl could also tell you."

"Oh, I've no interest in young men either," Mary Geylin assured Madame Selva and, picking up her belongings, paused for a last look out the window, beyond the crowded green of the park to the lake beyond, shining under a blue September sky with one great freighter poised on the horizon; paused and sighed in a way that Madame Selva said later was scarcely the sigh of an unromantic girl.

And then: "I knew your father, Mary," the teacher said softly.

"You did?" The girl's heart gave a leap.

"Yes. Here, and in the old days in Paris. I'll tell you some pleasant stories about him one of these days. I'm happy to give his daughter a chance. Patience, my dear, and all things will come to you."

For a moment the older woman's gaze softened, not so much for Mary as for herself, some memory of herself at Mary's age.

Then she straightened herself up and, going to a shelf, picked up a stack of scores and handed them to the girl, saying, "You might familiarize yourself with these. I can't abide fumbling. In the studio, the singer reigns supreme."

When Gianni Amara arrived at the studio the first time, as if carried up from the avenue on a strong breeze off the lake, he had seemed such a tenor cliché Mary wished her sister had been there to do one of her wicked cartoons of him. There was the look in the mirror as he hung up his hat; the kisses for the teacher and the big bright smile for the new little girl at the piano that seemed to expose every white tooth in his big wide mouth; there was a self-satisfied story about the summer just past, on tour with the San Carlo Opera, concerning the Japanese soprano Miss Hizi Koyki, who had sung Butterfly to his Pinkerton, funny but more than a little risqué. Alas, now he was back to earth for the moment, singing the messenger in *Aida*, which would open the Chicago opera season, but later (he lost no time in telling Miss Geylin when Madame Selva was out of the room taking a telephone call) he'd been promised a crack at the Duke in *Rigoletto* and after that, with any luck, Alfredo or Rodolfo, and then she'd hear something.

His clothes were as brash as his manner: checked suit, azure tie with a pink pearl stickpin, shiny pointed shoes only slightly less red than his lips, and the carnation in his buttonhole. His face was more merry than handsome, with snapping brown eyes and a pirate's mustache, his curly black hair impossibly glossy; and though not yet stout and of a respectable height, he was well on his way to a blurred chin line and a strained middle button on his jacket and vest.

Yet once he stood in the bow of the golden piano and began warming up on the idiot syllables of vocalizing, he seemed less comical, for his voice rose easily as if he were conversing, and then not comical at all when he began hitting those shining top notes, one after another, right on pitch: A flat . . . A . . . B flat . . . B. . . . And his face, singing, took on dignity. His open mouth did not flap like a rooster's or look round and pink as a hippo's, but was masculine and forceful. As he went to work on his role she caught the cast of his profile—unlike his full face, serious business indeed—strong and sensual with a square thrusting brow and Roman nose, a romantic profile Mary didn't want to take her eyes off. She noted, too, that though his conversation might be frivolous, he gave as careful attention to a five-minute supporting role as he might have to a star aria.

Then, having satisfied the crusty lady sitting in the chair to the right of the piano (quiet now, though a moment earlier she had been interrupting, demonstrating, exhorting), having even delighted her with the polish of his messenger's delivery, the tenor suggested he might demonstrate his real prowess by singing "Celeste Aida." Now the full voice came out, strong, easy, and sweet: the most beautiful sound in the world, Mary thought, that of a true, young vibrant male voice raised in a glorious melody. There was breadth to his manner, a contagious goodwill; you believed him as Radames, the conquering hero felled by love. And when he let go his high B-flat, without forcing, straight on, it was like a bolt of lightning that went right to proud invincible Mary's heart.

Then it was over and they were back in the studio and Gianni Amara was a flashy young fellow with an ordinary South Side Chicago accent, putting on his hat, tucking his music under his arm, saying to Mary Geylin as she closed the piano, "You have a feeling for Verdi and a strong touch, like a man's," and to the teacher, "I believe you've found a treasure." Off he went then, leaving Mary Geylin flushed and absurdly shaken.

The next time she saw him, her heart gave an odd lurch. She was happy. She wanted to bring him a present, or get a rise out of him. After an afternoon's work on *Traviata*, as the tenor was going out the door, she said, "You have a feeling for Verdi, Gianni Amara, and a strong voice, like a man's." He turned back to give her a startled look, as if he didn't know whether to be annoyed or amused. Then he laughed, played on her the full brilliance of his big grin, and raised high his black eyebrows. "You also have a sense of humor, Miss Geylin," he said. "That's unusual for a piano player, man or woman."

[33]

"Don't be cute, Mary," Madame Selva warned her, after the door closed. "Stick to business. You're doing a good job here. Don't spoil it by being fresh."

"He's fresh," Mary said sweetly. "But I'm sorry. It won't happen again."

I have a crush, she thought. How funny. Crushes happen to other people, not me, not since I was thirteen and had a crush on cousin Walter Geylin, which was hardly the same. What an odd little secret business a crush is, so personal, so tender, so free and pleasant. For the other person doesn't know, doesn't feel. It's just there in you, when you look at him, or hear him speak, or in this case sing. Your feeling. Safe. Hopeless.

And that was all it was, really, till the day he got her to sing: a crush, less embarrassing than most because Mary Geylin was too disdainful to act on her feelings and behave in the silly manner of some of Madame Selva's students around the tenor, and the young man for all his grins and jokes had work, not flirtation, on his mind that fall. There were bad habits to erase, picked up on the road; an excessive fondness for vibrato and sobs, as if he were trying to prove that an American-born tenor, raised in Chicago's Little Italy, could sound more Italian than Caruso or Gigli. He had a diction problem also, too often sacrificing clarity of words for richness of tone, as if he'd forgotten, the teacher kept saying, "the first lesson learned here," that singing was poetry and music merged, a form of speech and communication, not just animal sounds, however glorious. But how seriously he went about correcting his imperfections, as if to make himself better were the most important thing in the whole world, for him, for Madame Selva, for the opera house, for mankind itself, and womankind, including little Mary Geylin.

"Don't you see he has no use for your nonsense," Mary wanted to say to Josephine Sanders, Clara Stoller, Amelia Ann Potter, known as the Rhinemaidens, big, blond, and chesty, and birdlike Luisa Pollini, the little coloratura, and all the others who went running after Amara, who brought him presents, wrist warmers, hatbands, cigars, even jars of chicken soup from home when he had a cold; who blushed and giggled in the corridors when he passed, who hinted for dinner invitations and haunted the cafés that were his cafés, and hung around backstage at the opera house calling themselves his claque, his pack, the Johnny vamps.

Ah well, she had no use for them anyhow, those cows and canaries who never said thank you, only blamed her—her tempo (precise), her phrasing (sensitive), her dynamics (as written)—for their mistakes. No compliments for her strong fingers or way with Verdi. A poor excuse for an artist you are, she'd think of Josephine Sanders or Luisa Pollini, no future Melba here, no new Tetrazzini there. For no matter what liquid sounds the teacher could elicit from her flock, with one or the other of her "little tricks," as she called them, and some days it was as if she'd opened a faucet, the way she could unclog a tight throat and cause a cow to fly with a melody like a skylark, or a canary to sound human, no matter how she gave of her woman's experience or her own powerful old voice, she'd never make them great because they weren't great people—so Mary Geylin in her pride and confidence judged, though she was absurdly wrong in one case. She had no pride, no confidence yet about other aspects of life, about her own attractiveness even, but about talent she was sure she knew; and knew Amara was of a different order, had a seed of greatness in him; and for a time was content to watch him work, learn from him, from behind the keyboard, thinking herself invisible.

Once, though, he winked at her, not in the middle of something jolly and wicked like "La Donna è Mobile" but while singing a tenor aria about death and God from the *Messiah*, which he was preparing for a Christmastime church performance, as if to tell her he saw through her, into her, knew exactly the effect he had on her, poor child. She would remember that wink.

Then one morning in late December, during the week between Christmas and New Year's when the studio was closed, Madame Selva telephoned Mary Geylin at home and asked her to come in specially to work with Gianni Amara. The bad weather had brought good fortune his way, in the last part of the opera season; the star scheduled to sing *La Bohème* was in the hospital, and Amara, the house tenor, who'd never had his crack at the Duke or Alfredo, who had sung messengers, heralds, servants, courtiers all of the fall, was finally going on the next night as Rodolfo.

When Mary saw the score on the studio piano, exactly the same as theirs at home, with a pale green cover and pretty lettering and medallion, the one she had put away forever in the piano bench, she felt strange and a little sad. But as they began to work, she was surprised at the confidence with which she could play that particular music for another to sing. The sadness passed and the strangeness changed into something else, an excited feeling that was like the feeling she used to get as a little girl when she wanted to sing something, amaze everyone, when she knew, if someone gave her the chance, she would show off.

"Ah, please, what is *wrong* with you today?" Mary thought an hour later when once again the singing teacher had interrupted the tenor and said, Let's try from the beginning, and Mary tinkled out wearily once more the opening of "Che Gelida Manina." Such a perfect thing when well sung—tenor's prize song—but not likely to win any prizes the way he was singing it today, in a tasteless manner that might have gone over in the Denver Cow Palace or the Des Moines Coliseum, she thought scornfully, but was not likely to please a discriminating Chicago audience, or a weary end-of-season critic. "I'd like to put a cold hand on you," was the message delivered by Mary Geylin's expressive eyes; too much holiday, that was his trouble, too much game and wine, too many late nights, she thought, with Josephine or Luisa: a flash of jealousy passed through her. Ah, she could cry for him that he was going to make a mess of his big opportunity. Even Madame Selva, who was generally more tactful with the young man than she was with her young ladies, was out of patience. "They'd pay you good money to do that in vaudeville, Signor Amara," she'd snapped a moment ago, and Mary had barely suppressed a snicker.

The young man was looking furious now, at both of them. "Is there something wrong, Miss Geylin?" he asked, interrupting himself this time, giving Mary a look with those merry eyes that was not charming, that was like a knife being flashed, and she could believe he'd been the toughest boy on his block, headed for the jailhouse till someone had listened to him sing in church one day.

She shook her head.

"You look in pain as if you were at the dentist? You find my singing a drill?"

"Stop it," said the teacher. "Listen to me, Gianni . . ." But the young man waved at her to be quiet.

"Why don't you try if you think it's so easy," he said to Mary Geylin. "You piano players are so damn smug. Such cowards, too, hiding behind the big instrument. Tinkle, tinkle, tinkle. If you had to open your mouth, really give out . . . Why don't you show me how you'd sing the scene. Sitting there like a smart little mouse with big cat eyes but no big smile for Amara today. Pauline has always told me one day you would sing, with that jaw, that chest. What's wrong? Are you afraid? Why don't you sing Mimi's aria?"

And something cut through Mary's pride and stubbornness, her childish vow, her desire to punish the family, something in this room stronger than any wars at home, something that cut through her foolishness and odd behavior, something simple, and real, real as anger or love or the desire to be seen and admired.

"All right," said Mary, "I will."

Softly, so softly you could scarcely hear, she began to sing the familiar words . . . "Mi Chiamano Mimì, ma il mio nome è Lucia . . ." but then less softly, gaining confidence, eyes fixed on the score; faking a little, but stubbornly continuing, warming up as she went along, carried along on the words, the story they told, and causing the young man's expression to change slowly from anger to surprised attention, from a frown to a crooked disbelieving smile. "Sing out now," he ordered, "give it your voice."

"You'll do better if you don't try to accompany yourself," Madame Selva said. Her voice and face were without expression but something about her was arrested, alert, as to excitement or danger, as she motioned Mary to stand at the bow of the piano while she herself sat down at the keyboard. "Don't you want to run along, Gianni? We'll start fresh in the morning."

"No, I'm going to stay if you don't mind."

So Mary would remember the three of them that day—herself the grave young innocent in a girlish sparrow-brown wool frock, her head crowned by braids, singing with a knowledge beyond her years; the old woman in black at the piano; and behind her, the vain and handsome tenor, in a fawn suit that fitted him so tightly he looked as if he'd been to the upholsterer—would remember their eyes, two sets, one blue-gray and anciently wise, one dark and warm, drawing the voice out of her, that was nothing like the little girl's voice Louis Geylin had heard long ago yet had the same peculiar effect on the listeners. (Though Gianni would eventually get cut out of the picture, and the moment would be reduced to the woman and the girl: "One day I sang for her. . . .")

As Madame Selva would say, there was something about the way she used her voice in that particular aria that was right. Hearing it, you felt relieved that something in this world could be so right. The tone wasn't huge, not yet, but sweet and distinctive; it wasn't the sort of voice that knocked you over, blew you out like a gust of strong wind a candle, but an insinuating voice that hooked into you, a shimmering voice that had a darker feeling about it than most such high, light sopranos. But volume was Pauline Selva's specialty; volume could be acquired; it was that pretty sound that mattered, that sheen, and the musical feeling that went with it, as if the girl, singing, had suddenly found her power of speech. Still, as she came to the end of the solo for the second time, the teacher would have called it a good audition, a promise of things to come, but scarcely a finished performance. But then the young man pointed to the score, indicating that they should go on, for he would like to sing the duet with her and finish the scene. They spoke the few lines of dialogue back and forth, staring at each other, the challenge in his eyes turned to something else, something kind and encouraging and respectful; and when their voices joined, the tenor holding back his volume

[38]

for the unpracticed girl, pacing himself to her, gold lining up beside silver, joyfully confessing love, it wasn't a promise or a trial but the finished performance of two people born to sing together.

When it was over, Madame Selva was silent for a moment. Then she said dryly that Miss Mary Geylin, who hated to sing, seemed to have found her voice, and that if Signor Gianni performed like that in the opera house tomorrow night, he'd make her a happy woman; but now she'd appreciate it if he'd be on his way and Mary would lock up, for she was very tired and would like the day to be over.

"Are you going to let me teach you, Mary?" Madame Selva asked after Gianni departed, quickly, as if embarrassed, once they'd stopped singing, saying only at the door, "You're good, Miss Mary Geylin, very good. . . . I wish it was you singing tomorrow night, not the screamer they've got."

"Am I going to have that pleasure," Madame Selva said, "and perhaps an explanation?"

"No explanation, please," Mary said meekly, "just the pleasure. And the hard work."

The old lady gave a little grunt, it was hard to tell whether of satisfaction or mockery. "We'll start right after the holidays, Saturday mornings," she said. And then, gathering her things up quickly now, "You needn't bother to come in tomorrow. I'll work alone with Mr. Amara. That will be better. I won't scold you for what happened today because sometimes in life something out of the ordinary is meant to happen. But let us be ordinary from now on and very sensible."

"And my job?"

"Well, of course you'll keep your job. How otherwise would you ever pay me?"

Then the teacher was gone, leaving Mary to lock up. As she went to turn out the piano lamp, she noticed on the carpet something shiny. Stooping to pick up what she thought was a coin, she saw it was a button off Amara's vest. She laughed. He had really exerted himself. Popping a vest button was scarcely a romantic thing for a young man to do. Still. For a moment she held the button in her hand and then quickly touched it with her lips, before putting it away in her purse.

"It's that tenor, isn't it?" Belle said that night in the darkness of their room, when Mary told her, not even sheepishly, just in a very matter-of-fact and businesslike manner, that she was going to take singing lessons from Madame Selva. "He got you to sing again, in spite of Daddy and everything. I'm glad. But don't tell Mom that part of it or she'll lock you in the house and throw the key away."

The next morning, Mary did something she had laughed at the cows for doing. Leaving home early, telling her mother she was going to spend some time looking at pictures in the Art Institute, she went instead to the Viennese coffeehouse near the opera where she knew Amara generally took his breakfast. She found him there at a table alone, behind a newspaper, like almost everyone else in the café hidden behind black headlines that had no reality that morning of New Year's Eve, 1916, in the noisy room, bright with tinsel and Christmas balls, and the laughter of young men. At a nearby table sat Josie and Amelia, the cows, buxom and pretty, first deep in conversation, then looking at the tenor with wide, moist, empty eyes, but he paid them no heed. "Well, Miss Geylin, I didn't know you came here too. Sit down," said Amara, motioning to a waitress to bring another cup and more coffee. "Funny you should come in. I was just thinking about you." The look he gave her was warm, rueful, even a little shy.

"I woke up thinking about you," she said, looking at him as she had never looked at a man before.

"That was strange yesterday. Is she going to teach you?"

"Yes."

"I'm glad. I have so much I'd like to ask you, but there isn't time, is there." And then, grinning at her, "You don't sing like a man." She had no answer, only a slightly foolish smile.

"You and I should go soon."

"I'm not playing for you this morning. It's you and her."

"Oh? That's too bad. She's probably worried now," looking at Mary, shaking his head. "She thinks I'm a terrible character around girls. I'll see you at the opera house tonight, won't I?"

"I can't. I'm going to the theater with my sister."

"Oh, sisters! Tell your sister you have something better to do."

"She's planned it for weeks. It's my birthday present." She wouldn't do that to Isabelle, who was a good friend these days, not even for Amara. "No more sitting around with the folks on New Year's Eve," Isabelle had said. "You're almost seventeen. We're going to take you to the theater and supper and Ralph is getting a friend." Ralph was Belle's beau, not one of the callow youths she brought home from the department store where she worked sketching ladies' dresses for advertisements, but "a real prospect," Honora said: Ralph Dillon, Esq., smart young lawyer met at a party, square-jawed, bright eyes, with a political bent, and North Shore connections, a family with a big house on the lake in Evanston.

"Well, too bad for you, and after all our hard work," the tenor said. "You'll miss something." She could have sworn he sounded disappointed.

"I'll come next time."

"There isn't a next time. I'm finished here after tonight. I go back to the San Carlo."

"Oh *no.*" Now she was the one to sound disappointed. "When will you come back?"

"In the spring. I sing at Ravinia next summer . . . maybe," looking at the paper.

"But *you* wouldn't go. . . ."

"You think singers don't go to war? I'm no slacker. You won't catch me singing for the generals."

He stood up, pulling her to her feet. The cows were leaving also, flouncing out just ahead of them without a word of greeting, not amused obviously by the tête-à-tête between the handsome tenor and the keyboard mouse.

"It's not fair," she said, "just when we were getting to know one another," her shyness gone, too late, looking at him in a way that made him tell her severely to stop.

"You're too young to look at a man like that. Especially this one." He took the hand she held out to him and, instead of shaking it, put it to his lips, a joking gesture. His mouth, under its bold mustache, was not a joke, though. It was warm and heavy, with bristles that tickled; where it had rested felt empty afterward. How would that mouth, she wondered, not singing, not talking but just a mouth, feel on hers? The thought caused a shiver to go through her. "Your heart's showing, little Mimi," he said, touching the vein at her temple. He ran his finger lightly down her soft white throat between the chin and the round, girlish fur collar of her coat. His stare, warm and curious, was not a joke either.

"Mary," she said, "call me Mary."

"Mary. Sweet child. What a woman you will be one day."

And that, so easily, could have been that.

Except for the war. People do funny things in wartime. But then the war is over, and what are you left with, what have you got. A few memories, a hangover, the horrors, a baby, wanted or unwanted, a flag with gold stars, a broken heart. . . . Hard feelings, Mary Geylin would say.

Through the winter of 1917, Mary Geylin fed on dreams of Johnny Amara, of him singing, of herself singing with him. His face rode the cloudy skies of her sleep like a bright moon (a moon with curly hair and merry brown eyes and a big bold nose and blinding smile). Every night, almost, was St. Agnes' Eve, when virgins fast and dream of feasting and love and the nuptial couch. His voice rang in her night ears, twined around her own. Singing, he kissed her or put sweet candies in her mouth. She dreamed of sweetmeats and kisses and singing as a man lost in the desert dreams of cool water, the sweets she'd forbidden herself because she was trying to lose her baby fat, the kisses he'd never given her, the singing of pretty songs Madame Selva forbade. It was scales and more scales, vocalizes, arpeggios, that was all the beginning singer could do, no words even, just *lah* and *leh* and *mah* and *moh*, idiot noises like the noises of a piano tuner. Which was what they were doing, the teacher said, tuning up the instrument that presently she would learn to play. But Mary knew even hard-hearted Madame Pauline was pleased at the way she was mastering the technique. And though she never received so much as a postcard from the young man, the teacher told her one day, "I had a letter from Salt Lake City from our little tenor. He asked after you, how you were coming along. Well, I wrote him."

It was almost easy to be patient that winter, waiting for the spring when Amara would return and the days would have strong color again; and possible, in Chicago, in the first months of 1917, no matter what the headlines shouted, to believe war wouldn't come. Still possible, that winter, in the isolationist Middle West, to believe that an uncertain coalition of Wobblies, populists, radicals, Quakers, labor leaders, old-time businessmen, the Women's Peace Party, and Chicago's own Jane Addams, not to mention its mayor, Big Bill Thompson, who looked to the German-American vote, would keep America out, especially when you came from a family who held themselves above politics, above the fray (except for Isabelle, who secretly thought war would be exciting and planned to nurse in France). Possible right up to the day of the great recruiting parade that on the last Saturday of March, just four days before the President made up his mind, passed down Michigan Avenue, great phalanxes of men in uniform marching to John Philip Sousa, the entire Loop a blaze of banners, of handsome stern-eyed Uncle Sams pointing a finger at *You* . . . while silken Stars and Stripes floated like bright clouds overhead. That morning, as they watched from the studio window, even the singing teacher couldn't keep war off the premises and Mary Geylin got so carried away she began singing with the brass band.

"Why are you so excited," the old woman said to the girl, "when all that music means is that young men will die?"

Then Mary remembered a painting hanging in the Art Institute of rearing horses and bodies in mud, of blood and staring eyes and screaming mouths, and stopped singing.

[43]

"What's your name? I don't know you, Madame Selva is not here," said Mary Geylin to a stranger in a high-necked uniform and shiny puttees, with cropped hair and a trimmed mustache.

"I don't know you either," he said. At the studio piano practicing, in a light yellow frock, her hair piled up on her head like a golden-brown brioche, with the score of *Don Giovanni* before her, singing "Batti, batti," Mary knew she had made quite a picture as he came in—all afternoon she'd waited there, posed thus, singing appropriate airs, waiting to be surprised, and surprise.

"Only four months late, that's all. I'll be back in the spring . . . I'll send you a postcard. . . ."

"There's a war on, or haven't you heard up here?"

"We've heard. Every Saturday we hear the parades down Michigan Avenue." She continued to sit at the piano, he stood against the door, cap in hand, neither of them moving, trying to catch up, to match these two strangers, an army private and a pretty girl, stock figures in a city gone to war, with the bygone familiars—a little piano mouse, a dashing tenor—in a singing teacher's studio. How had he looked before? She could barely remember. Flashy. For all his attempts at stylish dressing, like any number of other young dandies. Now, dressed like a half-million others, he was particular, unique, the olive-green uniform setting off his dark-haired, dark-eyed good looks in a way that made him brighter, though dark, than any blond boy could ever be. He didn't look like a singer in uniform; he looked like a soldier.

"How do you like the uniform?"

"It suits you. It makes you look younger. And thinner."

"I am thinner." He preened a little. "Ten pounds. You look older."

"I am older. Eight months older."

"Where's Madame Selva?"

"Gone for the day. She had an important meeting."

"That's too bad. I wanted to say good-bye." Still standing there, examining her and obviously puzzled by the way she simply sat there, waiting.

"She was sorry also. She said for you to call her at home tomorrow."

Her feelings hadn't changed. At the sight of him she knew they were stronger than ever, tender girlish feelings, grown over the months into something different. She didn't want to give him a present or get a rise out of him, now. She wanted to be touched and held, feel arms around her, a mouth on hers. But he felt nothing. She could see that. He was looking for Madame Selva.

"Well," she said lightly, "you can say good-bye to me instead," still not moving, playing idle notes on the piano.

"What's wrong, Mary?" he said, moving toward her now, leaning on the bow of the piano as she continued to play. "Why the freeze?"

"Why didn't you write? Why didn't you come back when you said you would?"

"That's too boring a story."

"It's been boring here without you."

"I don't believe that. You're looking too pretty. Why are you even prettier than when I left? Who are you so pretty for?"

"No one. You," making a glissando with the back of her finger.

"Why, little Mimi, if it was any other girl I'd swear she was flirting with me." But he wasn't telling her not to look at him that way now; he was staring right back at her, smiling. "What's happened to you in eight months?"

"Very little, outside of this room. I was maid of honor at my sister's wedding."

"And in this room?"

"I'm learning to sing."

"Are you going to sing something for me, little Mimi?" he asked and the teasing look in his eyes concentrated and hardened into something else, more than amusement and mild pleasure at the sight of her, more than simple friendliness; the way Private Amara stared at her that afternoon she would recognize later in her life for what it was: the first time a man had looked at her with real desire.

"I told you before, no Mimi. Mary. Mimi was a fool."

Closing the piano, she stood up and moved toward him and what could he do but take her in his arms and kiss her, since that was obviously what she wanted, and he was happy to oblige. He planned no more, he said later—a quick brush of the lips and then perhaps he'd take her dancing, for she looked dressed for a good-bye dance on a warm night in late summer, dressed up as if in hopes of just such an invitation. While she felt like showing him she wasn't such a child, such a beginner, that she didn't know how to kiss. And so she changed what was meant to be a sweet, quick, light piece of stage business; put her hands to the back of his cropped head and held him hard. And as his mouth fastened on hers in response, she felt sensations she'd not felt before, quite different from any vague stirrings she'd felt kissing a high school boy under the mistletoe, sensations hot and fast and specific as turning on the wrong tap. When they broke away from each other a sigh escaped her, not a schoolgirl's titter but a soft woman's sigh.

"So you are like that," he said.

"Like what?"

"Like that," kissing her more deeply, his mouth feeding hungrily off hers.

"You don't giggle, Mary," he said presently, something changed further in the way he looked at her, something pointed at her from the center of his soft brown eyes, hot and red like the afternoon sun baking the city outside, coloring the lake purple. "You don't giggle or blush like a schoolgirl."

Kissing her again, his hands moving over her light muslin dress, he made another discovery. "You don't wear corsets."

"I like to feel free."

"To hold you . . . is . . ."

"Is what?"

"Too dangerous."

They went tea-dancing, a safer way to hold each other, on the marble-floored ballroom of a hotel by the lake. She'd called Honora and lied to her, a real lie, not a child's hysterical fib, told her she was going with a gang from the studio to a good-bye party for a friend who was going overseas.

"Why are you so damn young?" he said as they held each other in a slow sad waltz about love and loss. "I'm not that young," she said, floating the words at him like the notes of a song, allowing something to come at him from her dark eyes, out of the depth of her fiercely stirring blood. Her dress was buttercup yellow, her shoes and stockings white, and the tiny seed pearls around her neck were those of a little girl, but the red rose she'd stuck in her hair telegraphed a different message, as did those eyes and the body pressed against his.

"Dear pal," he said presently as they cut across the dance floor in a lively one-step, "I believe I'm falling in love with you, what a joke."

"Love" was too poor a word to express what she felt, too much of a used-up family word. "You make me crazy," she said.

"Oh no," hiding his head in his hands, still dancing, mocking despair. "Not crazy."

Then feeling a recklessness she'd never known before, born of wine and music and a man's body hard against hers, "I want to be yours before you go," she whispered.

"You don't know what you're saying."

"Yes I do. Yes. . . ." She saw him dead, gone forever, dead like the men in the Art Institute picture, ground into the mud, or was it only that she had to pretend to see him dead, for that was an excuse to herself to cross a line so dangerous it was like passing through fire or slipping under ice, yet unbearably exciting.

"I'm bad," he said later, in a taxi, the street lamps passing in a blur, flashes of light, then dark, then light, then dark, as his hand moved under the airy skirt, past stockings and garters, under lacy knickers, over soft silky white thighs, toward the warm wet secret place only her own fingers had explored, "but then so are you, sweet girl, sweet wild girl waiting for this, waiting for stupid Amara to wake up; I should have guessed about you."

It was only a dozen blocks from where she lived, as it turned out—his place—a ten-minute walk all those autumn months, west and a little north in the old German section of town, a flat above a rathskeller owned by the widow of a violinist who rented out rooms to young artists because the sound of practicing made her less lonely. The place was still full of possessions that he'd never cleared out, his clothes and belongings strewn everywhere; an untidy young man, untidy as a girl despite six weeks in the army. The sight frightened Mary, as did the sight of the bed, with the barred iron head and foot, a very definite bed where he'd spent the night before, still unmade, with knotted pajamas of maroon silk part of the tangle. "We'd better get married," she said. "Strangers get married in wartime." "Dearest, we're not strangers and there's no time to get married. We'll be promised to each other." She'd tried to leave, reason returning, wildness receding, and Honora's face appearing before her. But now he wouldn't let her go. And her feelings for him and the sensations consuming her body were stronger than fear.

Afterward, he took care of her with a kindness that wouldn't let her brood, though he was furious because she'd deceived him. Having thought her a virginal schoolgirl for nine months and then for an afternoon and evening discovered her to be a sly strumpet, and having taken her like a strumpet, he had not been happy to discover that, though sly and wanton, she was also virginal. "You won't marry me now," she said sadly.

"Don't be foolish," and he took the ring he wore on his little finger, gold with a blue-black scarab, and put it on the fourth finger of her left hand, where it wobbled.

"You're mine. I love you. You belong to me now." Then he gave her his pearl stickpin, for what use would that be in the army, and his medal—his marksmanship medal—a joke.

She told him about the button. He laughed. Each snipped a lock of the other's hair.

"Husband," she called him, that night, and again the next afternoon, and Sunday morning, and again in the early part of Sunday evening . . . throughout the weekend, in which he saw nothing of Madame Selva or any other friend he had intended to wish good-bye to, and very little of his mother. As for her mother,

Mary found love provided the necessary courage to lie, again and again. "Sweet husband. Heart's darling. Dear lover husband."

And so she addressed him throughout the war, in gushing sentimental letters, the outpourings of a Mary Geylin she didn't know. Flowers had come the day after he left with an impassioned card and a promise to write every week. But it had been four of her letters to his one, which was the way she supposed it was with men, though Belle's Ralph wrote weekly, this correspondence proudly exposed, tied in packets with red ribbon, sometimes read aloud to the family (Mary's letters, mostly, were hidden from the sharp eyes of Belle and Honora). Yet it was Belle, with her gay packets and self-confidence and wedding ring, who was filled with foreboding because once a month her drunken mother-in-law, who lived in the suburbs and knitted endless pairs of unusable socks for the boys in the trenches, would telephone to say she'd had a dream Ralph was dead. While Mary, the guilt-ridden, who every time she looked at her mother's face in church was sure she'd be punished, was nonetheless equally sure her lover would return to her because a fortuneteller had read her palm and told her so; because after what had happened, he had no alternative.

CHAPTER 4

1918

Just the way her singing teacher waited for her that last Saturday morning in October, in the closing days of the war, was enough to tell Mary something terrible had happened. For Madame Selva wasn't sitting erect at her golden piano, exercising her gnarled fingers and powerful old voice in an aria or lied, but at the writing table, bringing with a trembling hand a cup of coffee to her lips, and the look on her face was grim. But the fighting was almost over; they were home free; surely.

"What is it?" Mary asked, her heart thumping in a sickening way, the motion rapid like the pong-pong-pong of distant batteries through woods that Amara had described to her in his last letter. She knelt beside Madame Selva, the picture of a quiet girl who had waited out the war, who had knitted and rolled bandages, studied and worked, but not entertained soldiers in canteens, not run around, for she was a vestal, worshiping at the altar of high art. So it had seemed to her family and so it seemed that day, as she knelt there, a shy and reserved maiden in training, wearing a gray sweater suit, her hair neatly plaited around her head: Pauline Selva's most devoted student. Mary Geylin, arrived just in time to support the shocked old lady in an hour of grief. That's what the puckered-up face, the knobby spotted outstretched hands said: not "Come to me for comfort," but "Come, comfort *me*, for he was my darling boy."

"Gianni Amara's mother just telephoned me," Madame Selva said, clutching at Mary, shaking her head in disbelief. "Our friend is dead."

Mary Geylin cried, *"No,"* feeling all the color and body heat drain out of her and her head very light as she asked the questions —How? Where?—and received only vague answers, for the old Italian woman Signora Amara had been hysterical, Madame Selva said, and scarcely understandable. *"È morto,"* she had kept saying over and over, *"Gianni è morto, mio figlio."* That was all. For how and when, they'd have to wait for the notice in the papers. But what did it matter, whether by sniper or shell, whether in the dark woods of Argonne or across a muddy, mired stretch of no-man's-land. Was it *true?* Yes. Was she sure? Yes. Why? Why him? Why now? Mary stood up, holding on to the table, feeling queer and dizzy, thinking she must leave, must get away from this room where he was everywhere, Amara of the golden voice and merry eyes and tender hands and body made by God to fit hers. Thinking, he shouldn't be dead and the old woman alive. Thinking, wildly, he couldn't be dead, for if he were, then she, Mary, had to be dead also like the poor Siamese twins.

Then, remembering that painting, the eyes, the mouth, the mud, she gave a second moaning *"No!"* and for the first time in her life fainted.

When she came to, Madame Selva was beside her on the carpeted floor, holding her, passing smelling salts under her nose, and looking at her with a pitying expression.

"Oh, Mary. I knew you were fond of him. . . ."

"Fond of him?" the girl murmured. "He was *everything* to me."

"Everything?"

"Yes. Everything," looking at the old woman with large staring eyes. "I adored him. He was . . . my . . . lover." She said the word slowly—"lover"—carefully, caressing it as one might a lifeless body. "We were going to be married after the war."

"Oh, my poor girl. My foolish girl. I might have guessed. But how would I? You're so young." Arms rocked her, hands smoothed her, a head was bent to hers. "My poor girl," she kept saying, over and over, till Mary, who did not accept pity easily, said, "I'll manage, of course. It isn't as if I'd had him so long. Not like you. Poor Madame Selva."

"Poor Miss Geylin, who wasn't interested in young men."

"Oh, don't. Don't be cruel. If I'd thought you'd be cruel I wouldn't have told you. Why did I tell you?"

"So as not to go crazy. Because you wanted to . . . because you had to."

Presently they left the building arm in arm and went to a quiet dining room in a hotel not frequented by people from the Fine Arts Building or the opera house and drank enough small glasses of sherry to numb the pain, and then some hot soup, and began making the sort of bitter, half-joking remarks people find comforting at such times. And Madame Selva said, "Everyone's life has a painful secret. A secret that's almost too much to bear. This will be yours." There was something in her voice that bothered Mary, other than pity, beyond compassion: a sternness that the girl found surprising in a woman who, though never married, had had her share of lovers. "I'm not ashamed," Mary said. "I have no regrets."

A few days after the Armistice, telling the girl in secret mourning it would be the best thing in the world for her, Pauline Selva arranged for Mary Geylin to sing at a great victory gala to be given in December for the benefit of returning veterans.

"I don't want to sing the national anthem at a victory gala," Mary said. "I don't want to be one more soprano in a flag. Victory. What has it brought me! I'd rather sing something at a wake,

[52]

something sad and mournful by one of those new composers, something that sounds like the wind shrieking."

"Don't be a melodramatic fool. You've been begging me to let you sing in public. All right. Here's your chance. Put something sad into 'The Star-Spangled Banner' if you want."

"Can't I sing something else? 'The Star-Spangled Banner is so boring. People won't even *hear* me. Couldn't I sing something thrilling at least, like 'The Marseillaise'?"

"Don't be a goose. Make something thrilling and blood-curdling of The Banner. You are an artist, a trouper."

"I'm not an artist. I'm not a trouper. I'm nothing."

"You'll be nothing, I promise, if you don't stop moping. Trouper! Your nature is the problem. I fear you have too romantic and silly a nature to be a great artist. Learn to handle your nature. Put it to work for you. You'll sing for him next month. You'll sing instead of him. There's a void to be filled. Grow up and fill it. No man can be that important in your life. The terrible irony is, because of this experience you'll sing better than before. This experience will add dimension to you. And the next time you'll be more careful of yourself."

"I want to die. I could die of the influenza. I wouldn't care."

"You won't die," Pauline Selva said, her face curiously hard, as if she had a reason to be angry.

At home Mary was so disagreeable to her mother and to Isabelle, whose Ralph would be returning in January, they told her the devil had taken possession of her. Though she looked like an angel, never prettier, and sang like one too, she behaved like a demon. And why? What was eating her *now?* But Mary said nothing of what was on her mind or in her heart, even when Belle questioned her with tact and kindness. Well, that was her right, to be private and keep silent. But it wasn't her right, Belle would tell her later, to be a bitch. "But that's what happens when you have troubles," Mary would say. "Oh, listen," Belle would retort, "there are mean drunks, too, and then there are kind, sloppy drunks. The same applies to people with troubles. It's whatever your nature is. You have a secretive nature. It isn't the troubles

[53]

you can't handle, a brave girl like you. It's the secrets. Watch out for secrets. They can pull down everything."

But when did Mary ever listen to Belle? When did Mary ever listen to anyone. "I'd watch out for the unvarnished truth," she would say to Belle. "That can be very boring."

Between the private advising of next of kin and the appearance of a name on the printed casualty list of dead, missing, and wounded in the newspaper there could be a gap of anywhere from two to six weeks. The notice about Gianni Amara appeared in December, just a week before the gala, after such a long lapse of time Mary Geylin had begun to feel a lunatic hope that he was alive after all, that there had been a mistaken identification or that his hysterical mother, who spoke and read no English, had got it wrong. Or Madame Selva had heard it wrong. Well, someone had got a lot wrong, she thought bitterly. For the name leaped out at Mary, one focused name in a blur of print, not from the column of the dead but from the list of men missing in action. And next to his name was another name—as there were names beside all the casualty names of mothers or wives or even an occasional father. "Sergeant Giancarlo Amara; next of kin, Mrs. Josephine Amara," with an address in Brooklyn, New York.

Husband. Dear husband. Heart's darling. Dear little husband.

"*You knew,*" Mary accused Madame Selva, shaking the paper at her.

"You mean about Josie? I had an idea. I hoped for your sake I was wrong. But what difference does it make. He's dead."

"But he's not dead. He's listed as missing in action. Why did you tell me he was dead?"

"His mother said *morto.* 'Missing in action' is presumed dead, is dead," the teacher said harshly. "My great-nephew was missing in action for months. He's under a white cross somewhere in France. Don't hope. Don't distract yourself from the life at hand with hope. Forget him."

"I plan to," Mary said flatly. "He's dead to me anyhow. But why didn't he tell me? Why did he lie? I thought he was good and kind. Why did he deceive me? Why did he take advantage of me? *He didn't give me a chance to change my mind.* Why was I such a little fool?" But there was more anger than complaint or grief in her low voice.

"Who knows, dearie, who knows." Madame Selva responded, giving the young woman a deliberately bland look as if the picture of Mary as a victim was not quite authentic, not something to dwell on. "He was in New York for a while before he went to France, Josie was in New York. Perhaps he got drunk one night. It could have happened afterward, after your time together. Or before. She certainly threw herself at him here, for two or three years. There may be some logical pathetic explanation. A secret marriage. A child. Perhaps indeed he meant to divorce her and marry you after giving a baby a name. Life! This is life that you wanted so passionately to partake of! The mystery is life, the utter frustration, the urge to go on. Better to have him gone than yourself."

"And I still love him. Right now, if he walked in that door . . ."

"He won't," Madame Selva said quietly, pretending to believe. "Realize he won't."

It was over, in an afternoon, the secret she'd hugged to herself for so long: in one day Mary Geylin, heroine of her own tragic romance, a passion grand enough to be in an opera, transformed into Mary Geylin butt of a banal joke—a *scherzo*, as Gianni would say, a peccadillo. She thought of the letters she had written him and blushed and grew cold at the way in those letters she had spoken for both of them. She thought of how infrequent his own letters had been. How cagey. Dead or not, she had begun to hate him. He took me by force, she told herself, he took my body and he stole my heart; no one will ever steal anything away from me again. She began to believe that. She had been only seventeen: in the eyes of the law, that was rape. At home, she threw out everything that had to do with him, his picture, his letters, an opera program, the newspaper review of his debut in *Bohème* that had called him full of promise, an audience winner, the slick, posed photograph of him hatted and bearded and scarfed to play Rodolfo. Yet when it came to the ring he'd given her, and the stickpin, and medal, and the popped vest button, and the bit of hair pressed in a locket . . . she couldn't. She put those in a little pouch at the bottom of her jewelry box to deal with later. For all her hatred and fury, she still loved him, and only when she sang or played the piano did some of the confusion of loving and hating him at the same time resolve itself, in the pure and separate domain of music, the making of which was a sport and a pastime and a conquering as exquisite as love. A wiping out.

"It blows your mind," her son, or was it her grandson, would say years later of an experience, a concept, a performance—a vulgarism she deplored, yet understood. And that, she would think, was what Charlie Grace heard at that gala victory concert, me blowing my mind. Me, singing for Gianni Amara, singing him out of my life and Charlie Grace in.

2

Now picture Mary as Charlie first saw her, standing to one side of the curtained stage of the largest, grandest, most opulently gilded, garlanded, cupided, chandeliered, rose-lit ballroom in all of Chicago; little Mary Geylin, a grave child-woman with a moon face and staring dark eyes, draped in a tricolor flag, her braids coiled and gleaming beneath a red, white, and blue cardboard miter, getting ready to open her pretty mouth and sing, *Oh* . . . *say* . . . *can* . . . *you* . . . *see* . . .

To Mr. Charles Grace, stuck in the second row of an audience of hundreds, the girl looked terrified. Restless and cross, with no possibility of escape, young Mr. Grace had put in a long enough afternoon—the Great Lakes Chorus intoning "The Hymn of Nations"; the local John McCormack pouring his heart into "Kathleen Mavourneen" and serenading with Christmas carols a troupe of road-company Ziegfeld girls posed as Santa's helpers; the Mayor of Chicago auctioning off such items as Tom Mix's spurs, a lock of Mark Twain's hair, and an Iron Cross taken from the body of a fallen German ace. Not even a burst of coloratura fireworks from Amelita Galli-Curci, sensation of the Chicago Opera, could redeem such twaddle, endured by the man from New York for the pleasure of seeing his sister make a fool of herself in the final tableau. Why should C. S. Grace, who knew a thing or two about talent, feel such concern for that pretty, ridiculously trumped-up young lady?

Then the curtains opened behind them on the "Living Tableau of Victory" with the most fashionable beauty in Chicago, Mrs. Clarence Wakeman Vail, the former Mathilda Grace of New York—his sister Tilly—posed on a golden pedestal as the Statue of Liberty.

It was a rare appearance, for she wasn't, Tilly insisted, some dim-witted young society matron who advertised Pond's or made charity bows to satisfy her vanity or interrupt her boredom. Only in honor of the cessation of hostilities and the safe return home from overseas of her brother and husband would she have consented to such a display. Her condescension was rewarded by polite applause and approving nods from the front rows where her friends sat, though from the rear, where the less-expensive seats were, came cheering and whistling. Indeed, under a play of rainbow spotlights, surrounded by an honor guard of soldiers, sailors, and marines, against a twinkling panoramic background representing the New York skyline, Tilly was a splendid sight, with her Greek goddess face, her costume and spiky tiara designed especially for the occasion by Brooks of Broadway, her magnificent bosom thrust forward, her exquisite white arm holding high the papier-mâché torch. Even bored Charlie, sitting between his brother-in-law, the banker who resembled a pugilist, and a small niece twittering beside him like a wound-up toy, had to take notice.

How could any mere singer, scared out of her wits as she obviously was, Charlie wondered, be anything but an anticlimax with Tilly there stage center. But then, as the orchestra struck up the introduction to the national anthem, the girl motioned, with an arm every bit as perfect as Mathilda's and a gesture every bit as queenly, for the audience to rise, bestowing upon the assemblage a burning look and faint smile that dared them and coaxed them at the same time. At that moment, as he told Mary later, Charlie Grace felt that prickle, that dowser's-wand twitch he got sometimes, and implicitly trusted, that told him what he was about to see and hear might be a real performance, the first of the afternoon.

From the opening bar the young singer held herself steady, true as struck crystal, along that leaping jagged impossible musical line; and delivered those words no one quite remembers as if they made perfect grammatical and poetic sense. Her warm direct soprano made people instantly think they knew where, and who, they were and what they felt—that's what Charlie Grace would tell her that day, and what people would always say about Mary, whether Mary Geylin, Mary Gay, or Mary Grace—that she delivered an urgent, personal message—or that she *was* an urgent personal message telling her audience how they must respond. So that afternoon in 1918, when she was just beginning, it was as if she were speaking to every one, saying, Listen to this music you've heard all your life, this anthem nobody can sing, about a strange night when men died and a torn flag kept flying, listen how stirring it is, how those wrong leaps, if you know how to take them, are right; listen how brave it is—brave like all those dead boys over there who fought through the nights—who died in the mud—and doesn't it give you gooseflesh? As her voice soared easily and freely past the place most singers, even trained ones, begin to scream, "The Star-Spangled Banner" seemed natural and seamless and thrilling "as 'The Marseillaise,'" he would tell her later, and she would smile as if he'd said just the right thing. And she didn't sing it as an opera singer might have, he noted, fancily or overpoweringly to make the chandeliers rattle, though she filled the room with the clear ring of her voice. She sang simply and slowly, a little under tempo, with an echo of melancholy to the summons that recalled just slightly a bugler playing taps.

Mary Geylin sang and Charlie Grace, the sophisticate, the bitter veteran, nearly a dead ace himself, the eastern boy slumming in the sticks, was touched: touched as he had never been before, and not just because the young woman stirred patriotic feelings he never knew he had. Exchanging a look with his brother-in-law, he saw fighting Clarrie Vail, too, was visibly moved, though little curly-haired Jeanie on the other side squirmed as any child would through "The Star-Spangled Banner," even when sung by a siren, even when your own mother was up there on stage, motionless as a living statue in the circus, while a hundred men in uniform shouldered arms and saluted.

"Now everybody," Mary Geylin called, "everybody join in," and in that huge room her voice still rose, golden and clear, above the raggedy rumble of "everybody" singing.

All these things Charlie Grace would tell her at lunch a few days later. Mary only knew she hadn't disgraced herself. She had indeed been terrified at that moment the man from New York had felt sorry for her; yet her nerve had returned as soon as she began to sing. "This is your chance," she'd told herself; "if you take it well they will know who you are and so will you"—and so will he, wherever he is, heaven, hell, purgatory, or, a vegetable, in an American Red Cross hospital, that no-good, rotten, sorely missed, horribly mourned love I'm singing for. She knew her voice had been under control, that all those many months of painstaking work in the studio had borne fruit: she could do what she pleased with that perfectly tuned instrument, with the song, with the crowd. But still she hadn't expected the roar . . . that hard rain of applause . . . those shouts in the front of the ballroom as well as the rear. Most certainly she hadn't expected the haughty Mrs. Clarence Wakeman Vail, daughter of the great Shakespearean actress Jean Archibald and Joseph Grace, the famed actor-manager, to climb off that pedestal and pull her stage center, saying, "It's for you, sweetie, it's all for you."

And bowing, bowing, smiling, opening her arms as though she had heard this glorious sound and seen those rapt faces all her life, Mary Geylin was free. And a prisoner forever. And so was Charlie Grace.

At the reception afterward in one of the foyers off the ballroom, Mary found her family: Honora, gravely handsome but too large in gray crushed velvet; Aunt Margaret, with the same thick auburn hair and stout figure, except more suitably dressed in black satin and pearls, as befitted Miss Margaret Peck, owner of the smartest hat shop on Michigan Avenue; sister Isabelle, pretty as the White Rock nymph, if the nymph had clothed her nakedness in peacock-blue moiré, so fine of bone and bright of coloring you wondered what Ralph Dillon, when he returned to a struggling law practice, would do with such a beauty. There was Uncle Boris, tall, broad-faced, and saturnine, with a permanent expression of disapproval, there even when he played joyful music on his cello, and Aunt Denise smiling seraphically as she did even when behind the high altar of the cathedral she sang of betrayal, death, and Crucifixion, and cousin Walter heading for Curtis Institute, and cousin Daniel, still in his lieutenant's uniform, just back from France. Mary's family. They would age, become an embarrassment or source of pride; another generation would be added, wives for the prodigy and the veteran, a veteran for the nymph, but that was the nucleus—backstage drivers, performance after performance, year after year—scolding, essential, inescapable. So the voices tuned up that day.

"Once you opened your mouth," said the proud mother, "nobody so much as looked at Mrs. Clarence Wakeman Vail." "Like a match to straw, niece," said Uncle Boris, but warily, as if mistrusting the fire of what he'd heard. "Though a little too much vibrato," said Aunt Denise, whose own "churchy" voice was true and sexless as a celeste. "Time to get out of Chicago, if you ask me," said Philadelphia-bound Walter, and Honora looked daggers: "When Chicago made her? What nonsense." Louis, someone said. Louis saw, Louis heard, Louis knew, and we all laughed. Would he not be proud, and everyone spoke of Louis till Miss Peck, trying to keep things light, which was difficult sometimes with the Geylins, turned the conversation to the lady Liberty on stage. "Wasn't Mrs. Vail gorgeous, though? She is a customer, you know. Though she couldn't hold a candle to our Isabelle here." "Oh, looks," said Belle scornfully, "who cares about them in this bunch. Looks are just something God gave you."

"So's a voice," said Mary, speaking for the first time. "Not something to get a swelled head about. That's what Papa used to say," testing herself, speaking his name lightly, but as she did she saw her mother and aunt exchange a look.

Then, having had her fill of the family, Mary went to join Madame Selva, a different being on such an occasion from her studio self, pliant and sociable, even flirtatious, and very smartly turned out in beige brocade and diamonds. Standing by her teacher, Mary Geylin began receiving compliments from strangers. On Pauline's cue she smiled and shook hands and even curtsied were the person grand enough. "That's Paul Nash, the agent, that's Clarence Vail, that's Hector Potter of the opera board," Madame Selva intoned. "That was Mrs. McCormick, yes, dear, that's Mazarelli, the great voice doctor here from New York, that's General Bell, that's Monsignor Kelly, that *was* the mayor, Mary, with Galli-Curci . . . that *was* Governor Lowden. . . ."

"And who is this?" Mary asked, pointing to a slight, narrow-faced man who was approaching them, sipping champagne punch, smoking a cigarette. She was struck by the bright blondness of his hair, unusual in a grown man, and the exceptionally smart cut of his dark blue suit.

"That's Charles Grace," Madame Selva said as if the name needed no further identification.

"Dear Madame Selva," the man said, taking the singing teacher's hand and kissing it, not quite seriously. "I never see you anymore now that you've buried yourself in this terrible city. You and my sister."

Charles Grace . . . well named, Mary thought, whoever he was, for he made her think of things pious and knightly and aristocratic, of a stone angel above the door of a church, or someone you might call Your Grace. He had a long carved face, pale deep-set eyes, a sharp beaked nose, and a thatch of straw-colored hair, thick and straight, that no amount of careful slicking would ever keep in place. Encased in that suave diplomat's suit, his body seemed trim, the body of a man perpetually in a hurry, on the move. She wouldn't have called him handsome exactly, not like— she suppressed the name—but in a row of seats, or a class picture, his face would have caught your attention. It had . . . authority.

"Charlie Grace! I heard you were here with Mathilda for the holidays," Madame Selva said. "A miracle you're even alive, I understand." Mary noticed now that there was decoration in the lapel of the man's suit, a tiny red rosette. She noticed, too, that in his presence the retired diva was fluttering like a girl with her first crush. "Wasn't Tilly divine? I always believed she should go on the stage. I told your mother that. No one listened, of course. 'Dear Pauline,' Jean said, 'I want my daughter to have a decent life.' "

The introductions were made, and as Madame Selva turned to speak to another friend, the man named Grace said, "Do you know who I am, Miss Geylin, other than the long-suffering older brother of the lady on the pedestal?"

"No, I don't," giving him one of those disarmingly direct looks of hers. With his dapper clothes and clipped voice he seemed an obvious self-satisfied easterner and looked too amused. That much she knew, no more.

He smiled, a wry smile bracketed with lines that was not without charm, though considerably older than the youthful sunny grin of the other (that was how she'd start to think of Amara: the other). It was hard to tell the age of Mr. Charles Grace, for he had the kind of fair-skinned face that sets early and doesn't change, but she would have guessed (correctly) that he was close to thirty-five. "I'm the producer." Producer? More like a banker or diplomat, she'd have said, but, "What do you think a producer is?" he'd ask. Now: "You might have seen a show of mine here, just before the war, called *Darling Girl* . . . a pleasant little piece."

The thump of her heart must be audible, she thought. That was the show she'd gone to with Belle and Ralph and a dull young man on the last night of 1916, instead of to the opera house to hear her love. How bitterly she'd regretted the choice. That miserable show. At least she could tell him she'd seen it.

"What did you think?"

"I liked the songs. The story was . . ." She hesitated.

"Delightfully preposterous. I can't even remember what it

was about myself. My new musical is going to have a much more interesting story. How would you like to audition for it?"

"How would I like to dance with the Prince of Wales?" she said after a moment's pause. It was like something out of that show, life imitating bad art.

"You might someday. I'm serious, Miss Geylin, you sing like a siren."

"Is that good, to sing like a siren?"

"I don't mean a fire siren. I mean one of those sirens on the rocks." There was a glint in the pale eyes now, sly as a schoolboy's. He wasn't so frosty as he'd first appeared. She had thought his eyes gray but on closer inspection saw they were green, a queer luminous green in which the pupils seemed oddly, intensely black. "Anyone who can sing 'The Star-Spangled Banner' and make me listen has to be good. I'm not especially in a victory mood. Not even in much of a mood for Christmas," and he put down his glass on the buffet to be refilled out of the big punch bowl, taking in passing an iced Santa Claus cookie and breaking it in two as if that took care of Christmas.

She shook her head when he asked her if she didn't want half herself. In another hour she'd be starved, but not yet. All the while he continued to scrutinize her. She'd taken off her tricolor draping and was aware that the contours of her figure were clearly visible in the white Grecian costume beneath that had been borrowed from the opera wardrobe. Yet there seemed no more lechery in the stare of Charles Grace than if he'd been examining a piece of porcelain or horseflesh.

"The show is going to star Rose Hart. Has anyone ever told you you look like Rose Hart? Do you know who Rose Hart is? Probably not, you're too young."

"Yes, I know. My parents never missed her when she came here on tour." Mary smiled, thinking of what her mother had said, that Rose Hart was the one popular entertainer Louis Geylin had enjoyed, "for your father was not above," Honora would say in a rare spirit of mischief, "appreciating svelte limbs, milky shoulders, golden hair, and a silvery voice that took more high C's in one evening than Nellie Melba in an entire season."

"That smile, Miss Geylin, would carry, along with the voice, to the last row of the balcony."

"Is that why you've been staring at me? Because I look like Rose Hart? My name, by the way, isn't *Ga*len. It's Gey*lin*, pronounced the French way."

"Ah well, we could fix the name. I'm staring because I'm thinking you'd be perfect . . ." From one of the reception-room doors Mrs. Vail, now wearing a floor-length black seal coat over her costume, her headdress replaced by a Russian-style fur hat, was summoning her brother. "Darn. Duty calls. I have to go. But I want to talk to you some more. Could you have lunch? The day after Christmas?" And seeing her hesitation, "I'm sure Pauline Selva will vouch for my respectability. She's an old family friend."

Honora wouldn't approve. But what Honora didn't know wouldn't hurt her; there were, after all, some things Honora didn't know. "I'd like that," said Mary.

"Yes, yes, I'm coming," Charles Grace called to the woman, who had fastened her furs and pulled her hat down to her brows and was standing with the imperious look of someone who was not used to waiting for the men in her life. "You might imagine her, from her bossy ways, to be my wife. Let's make it right here. That lovely main dining room. One o'clock. Don't forget now, I've a serious proposal to make to you." No smile, just a nod, a bright intent look, and then he was gone, and Honora was doing the summoning, motioning Mary with her own imperious gesture: Child, come on, time to go home.

"Who was that?" Honora demanded. "That gentleman who was monopolizing you so long?"

"A man named Grace, Mother. Charles Grace." Honora looked at her daughter in a way that told Mary her mother needed no further identification.

"You're very quiet tonight, Mary," Boris said at supper.

"Everyone else is very noisy," Mary answered, wondering if all families were as loud as hers, though for a time she had found their gatherings, after a concert or to celebrate a birthday or anni-

[64]

versary, good fun . . . not magical as when she was a child, before her father died, but warming at least. To eat the special food her mother and aunts made for such occasions, the rich breads and spicy nut-filled cakes, the smoked meats and rainbow vegetable salad perfumed with dill, the Christmas puddings served on the best china; to drink wine out of the ruby-red glasses with gold rims or tea out of cups you could see light through; to listen to the grown-ups' stories and be praised and pinched on the cheek for telling your own story well: all this had seemed to her one of life's bright spots. Once she had even pictured Gianni Amara at the table with her, eating the food and joining in the clamor. Now she felt more restless than she had when she was a miserable eleven years old, blaming this change on him who had betrayed her and was most probably dead, not thinking that a desire to change her element had been growing within her quite independently, a need to make her own noise, her own colors and smells and messes: hers.

"Tell Boris who you were talking to at the reception," Honora was saying now, then telling him herself, "Mr. Charles Grace, of New York and Broadway, that's who the pale gent was, Boris."

Around the table faces moved with a mixture of disdain and interest; the family showed off its knowledge; that must be the son of Joseph Grace, the great impresario, and the mother would have been Jean Archibald, whose Portia they had all thrilled to, of course, though the son looked to be more after the quick buck, and "What on earth would he be talking to you about?" Boris asked Mary, as if suddenly recollecting that she was the one who had met the gentleman, whose experience had unaccountably vaulted over everyone's.

"He liked my voice."

"Everyone liked your voice." Boris spoke dryly as if there was something he hadn't liked, something that had gone out of his jurisdiction. "I would have enjoyed meeting him if I'd known. They say he is the one young man on Broadway with taste. We would have had things to talk about."

[65]

"Most certainly." Aunt Denise smiled at her cosmopolitan husband, such a man of the world. "Pauline and Clement. They sang at his parents' house once."

"Of course . . . that's how Pauline knows the family."

"It was one of the great musical houses of New York."

So the conversation left Mary, supposed star of the evening, who made no move to keep the attention on herself and remained silent for the rest of supper while across the table Belle stared at her.

"What do you think he wants?" Belle asked later in the darkness of their small bedroom, always either too cold or too hot, as dark at noon as at twilight, piled with girls' effects, the piles occasionally toppling, the disorder inundating. "My, wouldn't it be great to be rich and have a lady's maid?"

"And your own room and bath. I think he's going to offer me a part in his new show."

"They'll never let you."

"Why would I want to?" said Mary haughtily. "But if I did, they couldn't stop me."

"That's certainly true. When did anyone stop you from anything? Remember when you were going to be the world's greatest pianist, and then the new Melba or Mary Garden again—"

"Shut up! Belle, don't talk about things you don't know about." The look she gave her sister, before bursting into tears, was one she tried not to give Belle, or anyone else, except in darkness, for it wasn't kind.

"Spoiled brat," Isabelle muttered under her breath, tired of being guardian angel to the family star, absorbed in her own problems now, waiting for Ralph to come home and rescue her from the strange limbo she'd been living in for a year and a half now, a married woman still under her mother's roof, and seeing the distance between herself and Mary—who though younger by three years was not under Honora's spell—widening.

"Ah, he's naughty, naughty to put silly ideas in your head," said Madame Selva, looking fierce as an old gypsy, her face sour under the perfectly coiffed auburn hair.

She had begun cross that Thursday morning and remained so, though Mary had had a splendid lesson, and all because first thing, when Aunt Margaret's shop opened, thinking she had plenty of time, Mary had gone to buy a hat with her Christmas money. It was the prettiest hat she'd ever owned, a brown velvet tricorne trimmed with beaver that set off her profile and matched her eyes and made a costume of her old brown tailored suit fit to lunch with Charles Grace at the Blackstone. She'd run all the way from the store to the Fine Arts Building gasping from the cold, but still she'd been late and nothing she'd done seemed to please the old woman. She'd sung a beautifully even scale and a perfect ladder of arpeggios, every note a pearl; she'd sung the sweetest Zerlina ever to charm a Don, and a noble Handel air. There was fire in her throat, freedom in her feeling, and the broad long line of which Madame Selva would sometimes say, "Now, that's what I call bel canto" . . . but not today.

"I'm never late. I know you came in specially"—though the studio was closed for the holidays, Madame had agreed to give Mary some extra lessons—"I'm sorry."

"Sudden change alarms me. Have some coffee."

"No, thank you. I'm going out to lunch."

From the thermos jug on the writing table Madame Selva poured herself a cup and from the bakery box took a heavily sugared cruller, which powdered her broad bosom as she ate. The smell of that coffee, so evocative of Amara, hurt, but not so much as a week ago. "Who are you lunching with, miss, that you bought a new hat and were late to your lesson?"

"Charles Grace."

"Charlie Grace? Why does he want to have lunch with you? I don't think it's proper for you to have lunch with him. Does your mother know you are having lunch with him? All right, it's none of my business, but it is. . . ."

Telling her why had launched the tirade. "A serious proposal, eh? *Serious*. He's nothing, this Charlie. Nothing like the man his father was. He'll never be anything but a *son*"—as if to be such a pitiful thing were to be some sort of public nuisance, like a drunk or panhandler. And waving away Mary's protests, "I don't know what he has in mind for you, but I do know something about what has happened to these . . . discoveries . . . of young Mr. Grace in the past. Ask him from me, if you please, whatever became of Frances Lark or Barbara La Ponte or May Bellow. What nonsense!" The old woman fixed on Mary eyes that were suddenly kind and extremely concerned. "You aren't having anything but a little fun, are you, my dear, after all the hard work we've put in together here?"

"Of course not." Looking at her watch, for she mustn't be late.

"Because I may have good news for you. I have an interesting lunch myself coming up after the weekend with Hector Potter. He may be considering sponsoring your studies abroad once things are back to normal. He wants to hear you sing."

It was what they'd discussed, so often, "studying abroad"— the doorway, the entrance, the final polish, the path to glory of so many American prima donnas . . . Eames . . . Farrar . . . Mary Garden . . . Louise Homer . . . Madame Selva herself.

"He said to me, after the concert, 'That is the first real voice I've heard in Chicago since the young Mary Garden,' and he is a cautious man, not given to casual enthusiasms."

Mary expressed excitement, but for some reason she didn't understand it was just that: expressing the excitement her teacher expected, not a spontaneous outburst. Nothing that would delay her, so much as a minute, from getting to her lunch on time. "*Attention*, Mary," Madame Selva said, in French, as she went out the door, meaning more than attention, meaning: Take care.

He was waiting for her at a window table in the main restaurant of the Blackstone Hotel, a bright haired, dark suited modern gentleman, drinking a cocktail, looking in the soft pearl gray luminosity of that vast and formal and unreal dining room very real and sharp: more perhaps than she could handle, for all her boldness, she thought as he stood up to greet her, but immediately, as they sat down, he put her at her ease by telling her he liked her hat; and she knew enough not to say, "That old thing," but to thank him and tell him she'd bought it that very morning, with some Christmas money, in honor of this lunch. At which he gave her a perfectly grand smile, as if to say, I like you, Miss Geylin, I like the way you handle yourself, I like your honesty, and she knew, no matter what happened, they were going to be friends. She had never had a man friend before. The idea made her feel grown-up and sophisticated.

"How was your day, yesterday?" he asked, signaling the captain to bring menus.

She shrugged and made a little moue. "All right. Nothing special. How was yours?"

"All right. Tell me why this was only an . . . all-right . . . Christmas, for a girl who had hundreds of people cheering Sunday afternoon?"

She hesitated. "If you tell me first," she said, for the expression on his face was so kind, the look in his green eyes so sympathetic, she had an inclination, right then, to tell him everything about herself, and if she had, right then, it might have been a different story between them. But he said, "I don't think I want to do that, darling," in a way that made her draw back instantly. "I was just making small talk, always a mistake," and turned their attention to the business of ordering, as if they'd blundered into a stage of relationship they were not nearly ready for.

She had never been in such a restaurant before, nor seen such a menu, with seafood and game and poultry and grillades, and too many grand desserts to choose from, St-Honoré, peach Melba, chocolate bavarian cream, baked Alaska—a menu that proclaimed more vividly than any number of victory galas or ringing bells or marching brass bands that the war was over and surfeit back upon the land. Yet she behaved immediately as if used to such luxury and saw approval in his eyes, along with amusement, when she turned, not to the headwaiter, but to him, her host, just as the etiquette book said, to give her order, asking if she could have potage mongole and filet mignon, puffed potatoes and creamed spinach, and yes, asparagus too. "I am starved," she said prettily, knowing instinctively that with this man she could have anything on the menu, or off, and not worry about the cost. But then she had not been one to choke on her first cigarette, either, or her first glass of champagne, or wonder where to put her nose in her first kiss. As false Amara had remarked, she did not giggle. Yet would laugh gloriously in bed one day with Charlie Grace: "a cool collected one," he'd say on their honeymoon, "who is not so cool after all."

Though if you'd suggested such a thing to her that day, she'd have laughed in a different way, for that was not how she saw Charlie Grace, then, not at all. She saw intelligence, not passion, in the eyes; mockery, not sensuality, in the mouth; capability, not tenderness, in the big bony hands. Foolish Mary.

"Excellent," he said, taking a sip of claret, then nodding to the wine steward to fill their glasses and clicking his to Mary's, "Let us make the most of such happiness before dryness descends on this puritan land. And now I want you to listen. . . ."

His proposal was such a simple one, yet so disconnected with any reality Mary Geylin had previously known, that she could only stare, at first, at the flat suggestion that she come to New York a month hence to try out for a small but important part in the operetta that was going to mark Rose Hart's Broadway comeback. "*The Divine Daisy* is its name," he said, though that might change, taking in the expression of slightly amused disdain on Mary's face; the part she'd be so perfect for was that of little Daisy, more fancily known as Marguerite, in other words Rose Hart's daughter. It was the role they were expecting to have the most difficulty casting, for reasons too obvious to mention to anyone acquainted with dear Rose.

"She can't be a mouse, this girl, for she is supposed to look and sound like Miss Hart," he said, "and she has one lovely song to sing that calls for a trained voice, yet she can't steal the star's thunder either, which is why we want someone young and unknown. I won't try to summarize the plot except to say it has to do with a down-and-out actress making a comeback, whose life has been shattered by the loss of her only child in a scandalous divorce . . . and tell you no more now, for I can see from the gleam already in your eye, Miss Geylin, that you're about to pronounce the word: banal." He seemed to talk without interruption, yet all the while without apparently chewing or swallowing he managed to drink and eat and drink some more, the coordination of the performance intriguing her. "But I promise you it's not going to be a banal show. The libretto—we call that a book—is by Robert Harmon Leeds, the music by Harry Dresser, the young composer whose songs you heard in *Darling Girl*. It's going to be the first literate operetta since Gilbert and Sullivan wrote their last, and all-American to boot. I can't guarantee anything, but if my associates . . . and Miss Hart . . . feel as I do, I can tell you we're famous for what we can do to launch a young performer. Now what do you have to say? Are you interested?"

Mary had been listening without interrupting, quietly eating, glancing from time to time out the window at Michigan Avenue, at the passing traffic, at the darkening air that threatened snow, and obeying a remembered injunction from her mother always to hear a person out. Now she gave him a mischievous smile. "Madame Selva said to ask you what ever happened to Frances Lark and May Bellow and Barbara somebody?"

He made a sound that was somewhere between a snort and a chuckle and gave her a shrewd look. "Tell Madame Selva that Barbara La Ponte is a big star in movies now. Frances Lark is married to a millionaire and has twins. May Bellow . . ." He shrugged. "I can make mistakes. You would not be a mistake." His stare was cool and definite and a little scary as if somehow, just by the power of those green eyes, he could hypnotize her into saying yes. "I want you to come to New York. You'd be a fool not to."

For a moment she ate in silence, but it was hard to swallow when her heart was beating so fast, as on the incline of the roller coaster or the moment before a kiss. The last time it had beaten so hard was for Gianni, for the two of them, for love. Now it was beating for herself alone, for something safer and surer than love. Except . . . "You see, I'm studying for a career in opera," she said. "I'm a long ways away from the stage."

"Yes, yes. I know. Pauline's prize pupil. I personally think you have exactly the voice and looks and"—the pause effective because until then he had spoken at such a clip—"and intimacy for the more popular musical theater. I admit I have a prejudice. But why not give it a try? How old are you?"

"Nineteen, in another two weeks."

"A respectable age. I congratulate you. But young enough so there would be plenty of time to go back to Verdi and Puccini if that's what you want."

She shook her head, smiling, as if it really wasn't a serious possibility.

"Meantime you'd be getting stage experience, making good money—we are known also for our salaries—and having a lot of fun."

"I don't have that kind of voice. I come from a family of serious musicians."

"What a pompous thing to say," said Charlie Grace, a glint in his green eyes that made Mary aware of a temper lurking somewhere beneath that suave exterior, sternly controlled. "Why don't you be quiet and eat before you say any more pompous things like that and let me talk for a while. I thought you were starving. Look at that plate. Cold creamed spinach, ugh!"

It would become one of their jokes later, not cold creamed spinach, that would be no joke, but "Let me talk awhile," for Charlie Grace's "awhile" could extend a lunch till four in the afternoon, a dinner till dawn. Except he hadn't expected it would be necessary to talk so much that day, tell her just how she'd affected him the other afternoon, and everyone else in the audience, over and over, and how she could, with the right handling, in his opinion become an overnight sensation, and how though he wouldn't tell her opera was dead, since Verdi and Puccini were his gods, he would venture to say that what they were doing with the Broadway musical comedy these days was awfully alive, and that Mr. Irving Berlin and Mr. Jerome Kern and Mr. Harry Dresser to his way of thinking were young gods, American gods or if she preferred, heroes. He had expected to have time to drop in that afternoon on Barbara La Ponte, who happened also to be at the Blackstone, some ten flights up, in town to promote her latest picture . . . not sit till four persuading Miss Mary Geylin that it might be worth her precious while to come to New York and at least see.

Was it going to be so hard, he wondered, after a proper lapse of time, of course, after the show was safely settled in for a good run, to get her into bed? He did not wonder, however, if it would be that hard to get her to marry him, for marriage was the last thing on his mind. Foolish Charlie.

"Why do I have only two scenes?" she inquired finally, in a way that made him laugh and also know he had her on the hook now, wriggling.

"Because you are twelve when your mother runs off with another man and your father tells you she's dead. And you don't see her again until you are twenty." Now, at last, he called for the check. "But what a scene when you do! Singing the same song, again, as a countermelody to something Rose is singing . . . oh, I tell you, it's the best musical theater since *Tosca*, and no one dies."

"I like that," Mary said. "I could play that. I could feel that." She and Honora had been separated for a long time, but lately they had been reunited, not in some dramatic moment, just over the days; she could put everything into such a scene.

"Of course, Rose could hate you," said Charlie, paying the check, wanting to secure matters.

"She won't," Mary said, giving him such a bright sweet smile, he told her long afterward, such a classy proud look, he wondered if she wasn't going to be more of a handful than he had imagined.

Outside, snow was falling, just like in the paperweight that stood on her desk at home. Had Mr. Grace from New York ever seen anything prettier, Mary Geylin demanded, as they turned onto Michigan Avenue, than this city of hers in the snow lighting up for night? He smiled at her as if to say, Nothing prettier, at least not with you in it. Mary would leave her city soon, and not

[73]

come back except to stop off herself at the Blackstone Hotel, between trains, Hollywood-bound, or to attend a family wedding or
funeral. . . . Honora would come to her . . . Belle would move
to New York. But all her life she'd dream of this avenue, a ribbon of splendor stretched between those old Chicago skyscrapers—
first skyline in the world—and the lake, and especially at this
changeover time of day, dusk. It was an hour that had always
thrilled her, with day people pouring out of offices and shops, hailing taxis or lining up for trolleys, while out of other cars, or on
foot, came the first of the evening people in search of pleasure in
the restaurants and theaters of the nighttime Loop. She had never
felt the potency of the city twilight more intensely. That was what
a new friend could do for you, she thought: hold out the possibility of life when you'd thought life finished.

Yet that was also the moment, as they walked through the
lightly falling snow up Michigan Avenue, that they saw the hearse
waiting at one of the big intersections for a policeman's signal to
turn. Clearly visible within were two small coffins. It was a sight
peculiar to that year and one you could happen upon almost any
time of day or night, white boxes that almost certainly held the
bodies of influenza victims, children. They had been lucky in their
family and immediate circle of friends; no one had died, though
Aunt Denise and Walter had both been very sick, early in the
fall. Still Mary shivered, death with her once more, after an absence of hours. She felt Charles Grace's grip tighten on her arm,
his step quicken.

"Life's scary sometimes, isn't it, Mr. Grace?" she said.

"Charlie, please. Life is terrifying, Mary—can I call you
Mary? And unbelievably cruel. But *so* interesting." From the way
he spoke and held her arm she sensed he might be thinking of
something as painful as she was, whatever it was that had made
1918 a rotten Christmas for him also. "The first anniversary
of my mother's death," he would say later. "I understand," she
would say, "it's terrible, that first anniversary." But that was
later, when they were exchanging bits and pieces of each other's
lives, carefully, always holding back something. Then, "Interesting, even beautiful," Charlie said to Mary, hailing a taxi. "And

[74]

that mixture of beauty and interest and danger is in your voice."

She thought he was going to get in with her, but instead he opened the taxi door and gave her some money, telling her it was his pleasure to treat her to the ride, as it would be the pleasure of the Grace office to pay travel expenses for her and a chaperone should she decide to come to New York. Through the cab window she gave him a big smile. "I'll come," she said, for as she told him later, once you've decided something, why play hard to get.

And so much for Barbara La Ponte, Charlie thought and, instead of returning to the Blackstone, went through the iron portals of Chicago's most venerable men's club in search of his brother-in-law and a farewell game of billiards.

"Madness!" said Pauline Selva. "At your age it would be madness. If you were older, then you could make a real choice. Because it would be a choice: once you go that road you might as well forget about anything more serious. If you are even tempted by such a proposal you have no business in this studio." The teacher looked at her prize student with sudden malice. How ugly she was, some days, Mary thought. "And what has it been all about for you? Was it only a young man who caused you to see yourself as a great artist?"

"No! You know that's not true."

"And now that another young man thinks he's discovered you are a music hall act, a cheap vaudeville turn—"

"He's not a young man to me, that way. And what he suggests is not cheap."

"Enough of a young man so you went out before lunching with him to buy a new hat. He may not be your sort . . . yet . . . but I assure you, you are his. I saw the way he was looking at you. I assure you also that when bonnie Charlie makes up his mind to get a girl, he gets her. He is not unattractive to women."

Even as Madame said the words, Mary felt a frisson and knew that if a fortnight ago it had been the truth, now she lied to say he meant nothing to her that way; the bold black handwriting on the card with the flowers for her birthday—out-of-season daffodils and tulips bringing sunshine into a dark apartment—had meant something, and the message: "A respectable age indeed! Best wishes, Charlie Grace." And his voice on the telephone about arrangements, passed to her by a secretary, cool, dry, yet curiously personal, even through the static of long distance, had caused her heart to bound.

"You must say no, and think no more about it." Now the singing teacher looked not so much ugly as old. Her age had always been a mystery and one she delighted in, but she had to be seventy and looked it this day. "Don't break my heart, child. Why did you sing for Mr. Potter if you planned to go to New York? He does want to be your sponsor. We've been talking about teachers. What would you think of Jean de Reszke? Are you listening? Yes, the beautiful Jean, that wonderful man there on my wall! He's opening a school in Nice. Think of it. Orange blossoms and palm trees and blue water and hard work—the sort of work you're up to—and the sort of teacher to place you in one of the European houses, Monte Carlo, most probably for a season, then Brussels . . . then Paris . . . Marguerite for your debut, I'd think. . . ." The more she talked, the fainter her voice seemed to Mary, receding further and further, shrinking, dwindling, as Mary thought of another sort of Marguerite, a daisy. . . . "But you have to be patient," Madame Selva was saying. "You can't go off on excursions. If you don't go through the training like an athlete, two or three years more at least, you'll have no chance at anything big. You'll ruin your voice for anything except a music hall turn."

But I'm not patient anymore, Mary thought. Impatience, that was another of Gianni Amara's gifts to her. Anger and impapatience.

". . . And that's why I'm so disgusted with young Mr. Grace. He was brought up among singers. He knows all that."

Mary could have said, "I'll think about it," and walked out of the studio and never come back, but she wasn't a bolter. So she said what she'd been thinking: "In two or three years I could be dead."

"Melodrama. Cheap melodrama."

"That's how I feel. What he suggests sounds worthwhile. Not cheap. The song he sent me is not cheap. It's beautiful. Young-sounding. Romantic. I want to try." And then: "I believe in fate. Fate decided to kill Gianni Amara. Let fate decide. If I get the part I'll know one thing, and if I don't I'll know another."

Madame Selva didn't make any one of a number of pronouncements the young woman might have expected. She only said, "Those Grace men." She stopped, smiled, a peculiar smile, for it wasn't thin or nasty but rather young and sad, incongruous in the wrinkled face, to have that heavy turned-down mouth lift itself in such a girlish smile. "Those Grace men can be charming and persuasive when they want something and then they can . . ." and the teacher, still with that odd dreamy smile on her face, used an amazingly vulgar expression, so vulgar Mary thought perhaps she'd misunderstood.

"You heard me," Pauline Selva said, looking tough and old again. "Who knows. Maybe I should close up shop. I am too old to take another disappointment. Maybe I should go back to Paris where the winters are not quite so severe and the food is much better and the young people might still listen to the advice of Pauline Selva. Let me hear from you—or no, don't bother. I have a feeling I'll hear about young Mary Geylin whether I want to or not," then waved her good-bye with no more ado.

Honora simply shrugged. "You have that look on your face, Mary," she said. "You'll do what you want."

She didn't mention Louis—forgotten Louis. She didn't bring up years of sacrifice and hopes or ask, Why? For Honora didn't seem to think, really, when they came down to it, that she, the mother, knew enough to tell this daughter what to do. Mary, when her time as parent came, would always think she knew enough and better. But Honora didn't think that, perhaps because she sensed she'd lost control of this daughter long ago; that Mary was someone special, outside of ordinary jurisdiction.

"Now, Mother," Mary said, "they'll pay for both of us to come to New York. How about it? Even if things don't work out, you and I could have some fun."

"I don't think right away," Honora said a little stiffly. "I want to help Belle get settled in her new place. If things work out for you, then we'll see. I'll come along after a while. You can stay with your cousin Sonia. She's always begging for me to send you. I'll write her tonight. That's better."

"Sonia! She lives a million miles from Times Square and she smells of cats. When she came to visit all the way out here she smelled of them. And she has coffee breath. She shakes, she drinks so much coffee. I'd rather stay at one of those nice places where girls in the theater board."

"No, dear," Honora said firmly, for there were some things she could be stubborn about herself. "I want you to stay with Sonia, for she'll keep an eye on you." The look mother gave daughter was not naïve. "You need an eye kept on you, Mary," she said gravely, in a way that made Mary flush. "And don't be unkind. Someday you also might smell and shake and live a million miles from nowhere. You just don't know. Besides, she doesn't live a million miles from Times Square, only about eighty city blocks."

"Cousin Sonia . . ." Charles Grace would say ruefully. "What else could a man do about a girl who lived with her cousin Sonia but propose honorable marriage?"

Cousin Sonia, who played harp with the Philharmonic, who along with her cats and her coffee nerves had a sense of humor and an air of absolute respectability, Miss Sonia Geylin was Honora's parting gift to her daughter.

CHAPTER 5

1919

In classic fashion, then, a young and talented and slightly damaged girl named Mary Geylin boarded the train for New York, wearing her new Christmas hat, her old raglan coat, and a pretty sashed dress borrowed from her sister; carrying her father's Gladstone bag of worn black leather and a stylish calfskin hatbox, parting gift from Aunt Margaret Peck, the only one of the family to say with true enthusiasm, Good luck, child!—though the whole group in a last-minute show of solidarity was on hand at the La Salle Street Station to wave good-bye. There was also a packed lunch from Honora in a painted tin box that Mary would keep her makeup in for years to come. The rest of her things would follow, Honora said, if . . .

She went off thus, proud, scared, determined there would be no "if" about the matter, and without knowing the final fate of Gianni Amara. There had been no further notice in the newspaper. Madame Selva had received no answer to a letter she'd sent Josie Sanders, Mrs. Josephine Amara. But something had moved on with Mary Geylin. She didn't telephone or look up Josie when she arrived in New York, although she had promised herself grimly that she intended to do so. From the morning she presented herself at the stage door of the Grace Theater for her audition till the opening night in Boston eight weeks later, she had one thing on her mind: not to fail.

Never in her life, having made up her mind to do or get something, had Mary Geylin failed, at least not when the matter was in her hands; Gianni Amara in the end had not been in her hands, or so she could tell herself. Yet she might well have failed that winter morning; felt curiously humbled as she approached the stage piano, suddenly aware of just who was out there in the second row of the Grace Theater beyond the doused footlights, so visible and audible—a Medusa trio to turn the bravest girl to stone. There was a cool nod from Mr. Grace, as if he and she had never before met; a pleasant automatic smile from the rumpled, high-browed Mr. Robert Harmon Leeds, different from the avuncular smiles Mary had received from the train conductor and the porter in the station, different from the taxi driver's leer; and a hard appraising look from the aging beauty who sat between them. There was the one Mary knew instantly she had to please—Miss Rose Hart, that witch, who said at first, "I don't see it, Charlie, I don't see it at all!" as if Mary weren't present hearing every word or as though they were talking about another party entirely.

"Well, perhaps a bit," Miss Hart said presently, softening a little, "she is exceedingly pretty," and the flush that had come into the young singer's cheeks had made the comment even more justified. Then the great star had called to the man at the piano, sharply, as if he were some gum-chewing rehearsal pianist instead of Mr. Harry Dresser himself, to transpose up a bit if he would, for the girl's voice was high. "And could we take it slower," Mary Geylin begged the black-haired, olive-complexioned young man at the piano, who wasn't that much older than she and might remember when he'd been a scared kid himself. "Just a little slower," she said softly, for she hadn't practiced the song at quite such a clip. "That's the way it goes, Mary," the light, ironic voice of Charles Grace called; "Mr. Dresser likes to have his music sung the way he wrote it."

"But yes, a little slower," interrupted Miss Hart, "and you dear, Miss, this time not so heavy, *un poco più giocosamente* . . ." as if she expected the untried girl not to know what she was talking about. But Mary had done as she suggested with no hint of petulance. A smile from Mr. Dresser had helped, and another remark from Mr. Grace: "You've got a trained voice, Mary. Try to sing, now, as if you'd never had a lesson, as if you were talking."

And whether it was that she had done better—as it seemed to her she had—that, taking things a little slower, a little higher, a little more lightly and cheerfully, her voice had soared, followed the leaps of the song called "You" easily as a saxophone might— or simply that she had responded to the great star's remarks with none of the offense they deserved—finally Rose Hart had turned to Charles Grace and said wearily, "You're right, she is the best of the lot. At least she doesn't make me want to throw up." And it was Charlie Grace's turn to smile. Then: "Report for the first run-through next Monday," he said gravely, handing Mary a slip with an address on it. "Miss Hart thinks you may do. And see that you are on time." There were no congratulations. No invitations to lunch. No pleasantries. Just Monday at ten.

And yet for a moment Mary was utterly happy. This triumph, this sweet plucking of a prize was better than love, she said to herself, walking up Broadway in the bright noontime sun, remembering how brilliant, how magical and unreal the scene had been the night before, when cousin Sonia had walked her around Times Square . . . the flashing rainbow signs, the throngs of merrymakers, the people in evening dress stepping out of taxis and limousines, gathering under those glowing marquees with the charged names: John Drew . . . John Barrymore . . . Laurette Taylor . . . Maxine Elliot . . . George M. Cohan. . . . Nothing could have prepared her for that fairyland blur of color and movement, as nothing had prepared her for the tawdriness of the theater district by day, the dirt, the swirling litter of ticket stubs and torn programs, the seedy eateries, the panhandlers and drunks interrupting the progress of ordinary citizens hurrying to and from their places of work. Yet last night Mary had not been happy. She had been a tourist, gaping like the rest, and hating it. Now . . . "To you, you": she hummed the song that would become her theme (it had sent her, if no one else yet, out of the theater humming), heading uptown, too excited to climb back on the trolley, too curious about this strange new city where in late January the sun shone and the air was thawed out; where on an island running up the center of the avenue people sat on benches, bundled up in coats to be sure, but still sitting—in January!—feeding the pigeons, reading the newspapers (in Chicago they would long since have turned to ice).

On and on she walked, the new girl in town, the air and light a magnet pulling her along the undistinguished thoroughfare that was Broadway above the theater district but that nonetheless had an atmosphere about it, that peculiar New York sense of all those others, thousands of others new to the city who had stepped along such a backside thoroughfare, as Mary Geylin was stepping along now on a crest of hope; who had bought, as she did, an apple off a stand, and smiled at a policeman and carefully placed a coin in the hurdy-gurdy man's cup and told a stranger how good it was on such a day to be alive. She understood quite well there was another side of the city, slightly to the east, breathtaking and beautiful, as beautiful in its own way as Michigan Avenue or Lake Shore Drive, yet feeling that very first day what she would always feel about New York: that it wasn't any view, any vista of green park or sparkling river, or majestic skyline or a million twinkling lights, that was the key to her adopted city, but only to be in motion in it, on a fine day.

So she kept walking, striding along, around Columbus Circle, and slightly to the left, following Broadway, another few blocks, and then a few more, past shops and wedding-cake apartment houses of gray-white stone, past fruit stands, bookstores, haberdasheries, and movie houses, the mood not even broken when thirty blocks above Times Square she spotted the statue of a bearded man in a cutaway and, pointing to it across the avenue, asked a lady on a bench, "Who is that?" "That's Giuseppe Verdi.

You know, the opera fellow." "I know," Mary said, "I know very well." But nothing could faze her that day. And before she knew it, without ever getting on the trolley, the excited girl found she had covered the eighty or so blocks between Times Square and Morningside Heights, found herself back at cousin Sonia's, crying, "I did it, I did it," twirling the small trembling lady around and around, right off her feet, waltzing her caretaker through the cheerful, sentimental, candy-pink flat that smelled of cats and coffee yet now was home, cradle of good fortune. And it was as if the making it home on foot, the penetration of the city, was almost as much of an accomplishment as getting the part.

Then, having landed the part, there was the all-absorbing matter of keeping it. Of not being fired. Of not allowing the possibility even to occur to Miss Hart or the gentlemen when certain problems became evident, during rehearsals, that one obvious solution would be to eliminate the daughter entirely. There was no time except in troubling, sometimes cruelly specific, dreams for Mary Geylin to think of her old life. There was no time even to think of a new life that way, a temporary new life. "Thank you," she said to Harry Dresser when the young composer asked her to have dinner with him. "But I'm not going out with anyone right now. Maybe later." He didn't ask again. "I figured," he said, "you were reserved for somebody else."

The old life was dead, the new life a question mark, on ice, and after that out-of-town opening the susceptible young Miss Geylin was Charles Grace's Mary Gay, and Mary Geylin was no more. "It's young, it's snappy, it's not so far from your own name, it's how I see you," he'd said. "I like it, Mr. Grace," she'd replied. "I won't give you a fight."

She was Miss Mary Gay, born of the head of Charles Grace, self-invented, self-perpetuating, who sneaked in on the world in Act I, Scene 2, of *The Divine Daisy* in Boston's Colonial Theater, and by the end of the evening had stolen quite a bit of Rose Hart's triumphant night for herself. But not till the end, which was, after all, the way she and Mr. Grace had planned it.

"Modestly charming, that's how I want you in the first scene," he had said, "a lovable twelve-year-old." And that was how he had her in her first scene, and what people said of her in her first scene: "Charming! What a charming child!" Sitting at an old-fashioned upright parlor piano in braids and a pinafore, practicing "Happy Birthday to You" for the mother called Daisy who would come home too late, with her big dark eyes and round rosy cheeks, she was a Renoir: *jeune fille au piano* . . . doing a childish bit in a high, silvery mock-child's voice. "Happy birthday to you, Happy birthday to you. . . . Happy Birthday, dear, dear Momma"—a little flourish there around the "Momma" —"Happy birthday to . . ." And then the pause, before the last "you," as the orchestra came in softly and the girl at the piano took off on the words "To you . . . you," in a deceptively simple melody such as a musical child, fooling around on the piano, might improvise, and simple improvised words around "you" and "me" . . . "you for me . . . no me without you . . ." twirling around on her stool at the finish and giving the audience the kind of sweet girlish half-smile, tremulous and eager, "last seen around these parts," one of the critics would note, "on the face of Miss Lillian Gish before she left the east for Hollywood."

At the end of her first-act scene, when the angry father, Mr. Hugh Carlton, leading baritone of the day, burst in, shooing the child away, ordering her to pack, the spattering of applause for sweet little Miss Gay playing sweet little Daisy junior was lost in the crowd's noisy greeting of the popular Mr. Carlton, and when a moment later Rose Hart made her well-prepared-for entrance, calling, "Daisy, Daisy darling, where are you?" there was pandemonium. And the play went on. No one much went up the aisle in the first-act intermission raving about Mary Gay, or whistling her song, though there were a few, so the spies would report, to ask who the child was, the delightful little girl.

Not till the end of the second act, as Daisy grown-up, in mauve tulle and silver slippers, under a stage moon, in a stage garden, did Mary Gay take off with a childish ditty in rather the same manner as she had taken off with "The Star-Spangled

Banner," did she play on the audience the full force of that brilliant smile—a smile that no longer recalled anyone else's, that was hers, hers alone, commanding them to listen, ride along with her as she soared with the word "You . . . you," higher and higher in a ragtime cadenza, singing now not for a mother but for a young man, a bridegroom-to-be, as the long-lost mother stands on the sidelines listening, waiting to be recognized. Pure hokum, pure gold, the critic of the Boston *Globe* would call the scene. "No me without you," sang Mary Gay in that high, haunting voice unlike any other, "no stars, no air, no blue, no sweet dreams, for me, without you . . ." and the audience went wild, and there wasn't a man out there who didn't want to protect her and make love to her at the same time, including Mr. Charles Grace.

So Mary had the experience of stopping a show cold. Miss Hart had to wait before moving stage center, joining the girl in the duet that would provoke the biggest ovation of all; had to let the little girl sing her one-verse song all over again from the beginning, and add a dainty flourish or two, for this, the third time round, as if for a flash she were singing a syncopated "Caro Nome."

And delivering that song, which would be her first hit, the girl did not think, as she had only a few months back, singing "The Star-Spangled Banner," of a treacherous lover. She thought of those she owed her life to . . . of her mother . . . her father . . . her teacher . . . and above all of him, the blond and dapper showman out there at the back of the orchestra, listening, though while singing she had fastened her gaze, as he had told her to do, at a place just below the balcony . . . and fancied that it was from the balcony first, even before the orchestra, that the shouts had come, the swell of applause. "If you hear it from the balcony," he had told her, "you can tell the orchestra to go to hell."

That was Boston. After the New York opening, the only man in her life would be Mr. Grace, though it would be a while before she'd get around to telling him. Opening night at the Grace Theater confirmed the out-of-town murmurings about a new girl, a lovely new girl who just killed you, that girl, who broke your heart without stealing anyone else's thunder. It was Rose Hart's show all the way, a love affair between theatergoers and a great performer returned home. But between young Mary Gay and the audience had occurred a different kind of love: love at first sight, bright and shining.

In every notice, too, shone a small glowing mention of Charles Grace's latest discovery. *The captivating Miss Gay . . . the beguiling, the charming, the exquisite*—those were the words the critics chose—*the heartbreakingly young and innocent with the face of a wild flower and the voice of an angel Miss Mary Gay.* "She has tones in her silvery voice to charm the heart out of you," wrote one world-weary gentleman, "and the joy and abandon of youth, this well-named Miss Gay, and yet an entrancing modesty as if knowing that the distance between herself, a beginner, and a great star like Rose Hart is as yet immeasurable. As yet."

It was a welcome to put everything else out of Miss Gay's mind except what happened on that stage eight times a week and the man responsible, who said one night toward the end of May, alone with his discovery in his office under the eaves of the Grace Theater, "You are magic, my sweet, and so clever," for he knew his Mary already: an immodest girl who had followed his instructions to the letter. . . . "Be good this time but not so good that Rose will have you fired, at least not till we open, and the next time I'll make you a star."

Then he took her small round chin in his hand and, holding it, leaned over and kissed her lightly. "That's for being such a good girl," he said, then kissed her again, less lightly. She closed her eyes. His mouth on hers was new and sweet. Kissing a girl, Charles Grace was not such a cold fish after all. When he released her, she looked at him differently and he at her. How funny to feel this way about Charles Grace. How funny to see in his pale green eyes, not the dark brown eyes of the other, that pinpoint of desire, though as he held her Mr. Grace continued to talk of business.

"I've told Rose, by the way," he said, "that she can't have you for the road. I've just bought the rights to a charming Viennese operetta that's never been done here. The old story of an innocent country girl who comes to the big city, only we'll make it little old New York instead of imperial Vienna, and a tenderloin tout instead of a wicked baron who approaches the girl. The opening song should suit you. It's called 'I Never Talk to Strangers.' I'd like you for that girl," still holding her, lightly tracing the line of her cheek, her eyebrows, the rim of her ear. "But maybe you have other ideas. Maybe you want to go back to your studies. Go abroad as you planned. I told you I wouldn't try to hold you."

"I don't want to go abroad. I'm right where I am. Your Broadway suits me," trying not to think of the letter in her bureau drawer, forwarded from home with a Paris return address. But something about her voice and eyes, the voice a trifle too vehement, the eyes a trifle blank, caused Charlie Grace to ask again, "Are you sure? Sure I did the right thing to steal you?"

"You didn't steal me. Nobody steals me. I came because I wanted to."

He gave her a last kiss, this one on the tip of her adorable nose, and would not kiss her again until after another opening night, the opening night of *The Girl from Out of Town,* the following autumn, at which point he kissed her a great deal—as one of the critics noted, "It was surely the sweetest naughtiest mouth in New York, and out of it came silver candy, pearls, diamonds posing as notes"—kissed her and murmured extravagant words of love and praise in an effort to calm her down, he said, because that same critic, having praised her lips, her eyes, her smile, and her ravishing way with a song, had said she wasn't yet much of an actress or comedienne. "Next time we'll make you a comedienne," he said, and just to make certain there would be a next time, asked her to marry him.

But he knew, he said, that first time he held her in his arms, way back in May. Knew the jig was up, from the way she was staring—staring past him at something on his desk—at the photograph between the stand of telephones and the big inkwell, the one of his sister Mathilda holding a baby in lacy christening clothes. Following Mary's eyes, Charlie Grace began to laugh.

"What's funny?" asked Mary.

"Possibilities," he said, "unanticipated. Except."

Except, he would tell her later, and thereby annoy her considerably, except for what his sister, the lovely Mathilda, had said in Chicago over the Christmas holidays of 1918. "That girl," Tilly said to her brother, "that singing wonder. You want her for your stage, you say, and in your bed, you don't have to say, but where I bet you'll have her in the end, sweetie, is in a big silver frame on your desk with your ring on her finger and your baby in her arms and the family jewels around her neck. I can tell a good girl when I see her, and a stubborn one to boot."

And it was Tilly who staged the wedding, between hit show number two and hit show number three, staged it—with a certain amount of interference and help from the stiff-necked Mrs. Honora Geylin—at St. Thomas Church with all the aplomb and panache of a triumphant Charles Grace second-act finale. And after the curtain fell: all was well in the bridal suite of the Plaza Hotel; and in the flower-laden royal cabin of the S.S. *Petrarch*, which sailed the next morning for Naples. Alone in a stateroom, naked, they liked each other.

Only: "Who?" Charlie Grace asked his bride on the third or fourth night out, when he'd had too many cocktails followed by too much champagne. His voice was cold and dangerous as it could get when he drank, though never before had he spoken in that voice to her. "Who was it, Mary Geylin?" The use of her old name made her shiver.

"No one you know," she answered fliply, and then when she felt his hand too hard around her wrist, "A soldier in the war," she said quietly, understanding this was not the time, with this particular man, for flipness, though he himself had answered certain questions she had posed with considerable flipness and finally told her it was none of her damn business. "Something wretched," she said. "Brutal. Not love. He forced me. Don't make me talk about it."

"I don't want to talk about it. Terrible things happen in wartime. Only what happened to the fellow?"

She hesitated. *Please,* she had written after the third letter came from Paris, from the one who was meant to be dead, saying that at least he deserved an answer, some sort of word, yes or no. *Please don't bother me anymore,* and enclosed the newspaper announcement of her engagement to Charles Grace. *You are dead, and so is Mary Geylin.*

"He was killed," she answered, setting her own trap.

"Good," said Charlie Grace. "I'll never mention the subject again."

And then came *American Beauty.*

One more warm-up exercise for Mary, a chic little review called *Three-Ring Circus,* and then the show which would tell Mr. and Mrs. Grace whether or not she was going to make the leap from being good, even very good, from being all those wonderful adjectives: magical, enchanting, beguiling, from being full of promise, poised for flight, to being—after all the words had spent their fire and showered back to earth—a star, a simple fact.

It was a question of finding the right character, that was all, Charlie said, and he found her in the *Saturday Evening Post,* in a story called "Anna," which he gave to Messrs. Dresser and Leeds to fashion into a script and a score; a character his Mary could slip into as easily as her lovely hand into a small suede glove; a character he personally had fallen in love with. Anna. Anna Bellini, the spirited anarchist's daughter, fresh off the boat from Italy, who after setbacks and challenges is reborn Miss Annie Bell, all-American beauty, aspiring songstress, who sings her way into America's heart and the heart of the man who discovers her, though nearly loses both—adopted country and fiancé—for the love of reform politics.

Such a strong character, such a *good story,* Charlie would insist, which was what he always said about his latest show, and always would say, understanding even as he said it that, what would matter (and always would matter) most was "the Mary," that was how one of the critics would put it. The sweet and sassy Mary, of the golden looks and silvery voice and newly-acquired sense of humor, singing her way through the magical Dresser and Leeds score that everyone recognized right then and there was something special. There might be more important songs to come later from the same gifted team, and more important shows; but there surely could never be a score quite like that of *American Beauty*, so fresh, so inventive, with such a rush of melody; as there would never be a Mary quite like that Mary, so fresh, so inventive, so effortless, as if she had yards and yards of voice to spare and years and years of life ahead of her to sing, to act, to capture hearts.

So the scenes built that opening night, in the early spring of 1922, and the songs kept coming, one after the other. Mary alias Anna, in a straw hat and shawl on a boat deck, practicing her English, spinning a carousel waltz around the word "gold"—and "Catch the Gold Ring" was born. Anna in her mother's wedding dress, brightened with a red ribbon, at an audition, switching from a naughty soubrette's air nobody wanted (though bands that spring would play ad nauseam "Mimi the Midinette") to rag-time, to prove she could sing "american" and "The Radical Rag," a full-throated, ribald number was zestfully hurled at the audience. Anna, now Annie, in a shimmering evening gown, the toast of New York, setting the trap for the impresario, the unobtainable man—Mr. Hugh Carlton, who else—in his own rooftop music hall, introducing "He Doesn't Even See Me" (the season's romantic fox-trot), forcing the reluctant hero finally to serenade her in return in his rich booming baritone—and up, up to the rafters went the title song, "American Beauty." And still to come, in that same first act, the quartet: Mary, Hugh, and the comic duo, her father the anarchist, his sister the suffragette, the ones who were going to get the heroine into trouble in the second act, making such grand harmony, such foot-tapping, finger-snapping razzle-dazzle of "Red, White, and Blue Girl" that it took three encores before the first-act curtain was allowed to fall. "They stop the show with every damn number," someone was heard to complain in the intermission. "At this rate we'll be here till dawn."

Nor was the second act a let-down, with its angry citizens and police, its mayor and governor and President of the United States, its Annie Bell march, its picketers' tango, its Fourth of July riot, finally calmed by the girl who began the mayhem in the first place. And when Mary Gay, alone on the stage with Hugh Carlton, sang a reprise of her opening song, about the gold ring, asking if the one you caught for yourself and the one some man put on your third finger were one and the same, the laughing, cheering people out front shouted back the answer: they were, for an American Beauty and they were Mary Gay.

But for Mary herself the moment, the glorious moment, would not be when she heard those cheers, that thunderous applause, and knew everyone in the theater was on his feet, except for the men on the aisle hurrying out to meet their deadlines. Nor would it be when she read what those gentlemen had written, the words telling her that she was more than good now, more than very good, even more than magical, enchanting, exquisite, captivating. No longer full of promise or poised for flight, for she'd fulfilled the promise and flown to stardom.

The moment this time would be after the last bow, when the curtain had gone up and down, up and down for nearly fifteen minutes; when the flowers had been handed up and everyone had come on stage, all the pale unpainted ones in white tie and tails, the director, the orchestra leader, the costumer, the composer and lyricist, everyone except for the man who refused to come onstage, who never took a bow, the blond eminence behind the scenes, now standing in the wings; when finally the curtain was down for the last time, and then and only then Mr. Charles Grace stepped onstage and in the very spot where a half hour earlier his wife and Hugh Carlton had kissed, passionately, with utter conviction, took Mary in his arms. Looked at her hard, telling her with his look, his green eyes, that this was what he had imagined the first time he laid eyes on her and heard her sing.

Then he kissed her urgently, firmly, coolly, for everyone to see and note, if they felt so inclined, the difference between simulated passion and the real thing.

And Mary the new star received the kiss like everything else that evening with sweetness and humility as though it were her due.

That night she didn't think even fleetingly of Gianni Amara, or wish, as she had, in spite of herself, on certain previous opening nights, that he might be there out front to witness her triumph. He was absent, totally, blissfully absent from her mind. Not till days later did she note this curious and most welcome turn of events and congratulate herself: finally, finally.

CHAPTER 6

1925

So to the famous ruby, which was Mary's present from Charlie upon the birth of their first child, a son.

"I have something for you, Mrs. Grace," Charlie Grace said to his wife the night she came home from the hospital.

"More presents! You've already given me too much. He's my present, the cub—how can anything be so tiny?"—giving little Louis, tawny red-faced baby soon to be nicknamed Lion, back to Nanny, settling languidly into her pillows, wondering at the strangeness after all this time of there being a baby in the nursery above. Better than four years since their wedding, since she had come into this house as a shy young bride, calling it too big, too grand, too much in every way for a girl of twenty, though not paying attention as long as he ran it, handled the servants, and let her live there as in a hotel, for she had work to do, other matters on her mind. Four and a half years and several shows later, the house had shrunk, or she had grown. Jean Archibald's house was now home to Mary Gay, her imprint was on it everywhere, her books and music and woman's things, her photographs, the modern art and furniture she and Charlie had bought together, the jewels . . . and more precious than anything, those huge framed posters in the study, those stepping-stones to stardom in gaudy paints: *Charles Grace Presents Hugh Carlton in "The Girl from Out of Town" with Mary Gay and Eileen Collier . . . Charles Grace Presents Rose Hart, Hugh Carlton, and Mary Gay in "Three-Ring Circus": a revue . . . Charles Grace Presents Mary Gay and Hugh Carlton in "American Beauty." . . . Charles Grace Presents Miss Mary Gay in "Glitter Girl."* She was her own star now, bright as Venus, everything Charles Grace had hoped for, everything she had promised. All New York and then all of the country sang the songs she introduced. Women copied her looks, her clothes. Families flocked to her shows, for they were clean shows, quality shows, dazzling to the eye and ear, sparkling with beautiful girls and saucy jokes, yet innocent. Hard men, calling themselves critics, wrote her mash notes, proclaiming dancing in the streets, sunshine at midnight, moonlight at noon, carriages drawn by gentlemen in top hats and all manner of unnatural phenomena, at the siren call of her voice—honey and ice, some said of that voice, silver with a blue lining—at the glow of her smile, so wise yet so unspoiled—at her way of making the sort of modest, modern fairy tale that was a Charles Grace musical seem real, witty, truthful, and just a little—oh, so charmingly—offbeat. The world's riches were hers. And now she had a son.

"Sometimes I get scared," she said, accepting the large square package wrapped in slick white jeweler's paper. "It's not good to have so much, to be so spoiled—even if you've worked like hell for it." Her husband grinned at her, knowing it was her meat and drink and impetus, to have so much, to be so spoiled, to work like hell . . . and then looked ridiculously solemn, for all the world, she said, as if he were presenting her with the crown jewels. She'd received many such packages since she'd come to New York, grown well accustomed to the look of a Cartier or Tiffany box. This package, though, even before she'd torn the paper off, she knew was different.

Opening the antique velvet case, she stared.

She had heard mention of the Grace ruby from time to time, since her marriage, from her sister-in-law, from Rose Hart. "Jean in that ruby and a black velvet gown with that carrot hair," said Rose. "One of the sights you don't forget. No painter would dare." "That ruby . . . brrrrr," said Mathilda, and shivered, whether from distaste or titillation was hard to tell. Mary had known, vaguely, that one day the important necklace might be hers. Somehow she had pictured a clear stone, the color of claret or a drop of blood from a pricked finger. She had recalled the time when, as a child in Chicago, she had seen Jean Archibald as Portia, the frail figure of the great actress swallowed up in lawyer's robes, her red hair covered by a curly gray wig, yet all fire; remembered the way, little girl that she was, she had thrilled to the commanding voice: "Tarry a little; there is something else. This bond doth give thee here *no jot of blood.* . . ." Just so, like blood, had Mary imagined her late mother-in-law's ruby. But this jewel was neither blood-red nor clear, was of a milky color, not crimson, not mauve, but somewhere in between, and imprisoned within was a luminous shifting star that made her heart beat uncontrollably and a shadow pass across her eyes.

"Doesn't it please you?" he asked quizzically, a little disappointed. "Are you like my sister, Tilly, who once told Mother the stone looked like an all-day sucker, which is why perhaps it came to me?"

Mary shook her head and her eyes dimmed. Why did it have to be a star, she thought, to make her so terribly sad, to catch at her heart in a way she'd forgotten and make her remember the star in her father's ring and how she had imagined, as a child, that if she cracked open the gem, liquid light would spill out, the secret substance of life itself. " 'Beautiful' is too poor a word," she said finally, sitting up straight to let him clasp the necklace around her neck. She held up the mirror he gave her so she could admire herself, her beauty, different from what it had been at nineteen, a woman's beauty now, composed of enormous dark eyes, a pale flower face, wavy shining light-brown hair, still, as her husband commanded, uncropped (she was six months away from that escapade of the hair)—old-fashioned hair pinned and piled and wrapped, though not quite so winsomely as that of America's other uncropped sweetheart, Miss Mary Pickford. Neither vamp nor flapper nor childlike innocent was Mary Gay, but a classical enchantress, without date. The necklace suited her, turned her from nymph to duchess. Mary Grace. "The only grace," as one admirer called her. "Such graces do not come in threes." Yet.

"What are you thinking about?" Charlie said presently. "You have that look. We're in our fifth year of marriage, yet when you get that look I feel I don't know you at all."

"I was thinking it's strange about stars," she said, sipping the glass of champagne he'd poured for her, thinking perhaps if she said something the ghost would vanish. "My father had a ring with a star. How real that star seems, yet it's only a stone cutter's trick. Unreal, my daddy used to say to annoy my mother, as the star of Bethlehem."

"I would have enjoyed your father, I think," said her husband, smiling. "Tell me about him." And when she was suddenly silent, as if cornered, "You never care to talk of the old days but now that we have a son named Louis Geylin you will have to. Indeed, now that we have a son named Louis Geylin," he said, looking at her more closely, "you will perhaps stop making one excuse after another not to visit the city where your people come from, where every other American who can afford it goes—except Mrs. Grace."

"Ah, don't bring up Paris again," she said, "Paris is Pauline Selva and the life that wasn't. Paris would only confuse me. I will not be confused!"

And so, to distract him from the subject of Paris, as they drank a bedtime glass of champagne and heard faintly from the floor above the baby cries of their son, she told him about her father's cat's-eye ring, his last gift to her, and how her mother had taken it away. Then she told him about her vow never to sing again.

"You are a strange young woman, Mary Grace," said Charlie, "a remarkable young woman. What made you change your mind?"

She told him about the cows then. "Remember," she said, "one Saturday matinee, ages ago, right after *The Girl from Out of Town* opened, in my dressing room. A big blonde named Josephine Amara, with a little boy. Scarcely room for her and me in that tiny dressing room. That was one of the cows." Why? Why had she said that, she wondered, even as she said it. What perversity caused her to say that? The star in the stone, she supposed, the talk of the old days.

But then what perversity had caused her to keep, in the secret compartment of her old jewelry box, the chamois pouch with the little trinkets, not to dispose of it, even after Josie's visit, and the letters postmarked Paris that had preceded the visit, even in her new happiness of marriage to Mr. Grace? Even after *American Beauty*?

Or was it precisely because of *American Beauty* and those mysterious long stemmed red roses that had arrived on her twenty-third birthday, along with all the other floral tributes for Broadway's brightest new star, not from Charlie, not from anyone else she knew, but from some secret admirer with a card signed in the florist's handwriting just that . . . "an admirer." And then they had arrived again, those same flowers, on her birthday last year, and again this January . . . those magnificent roses that nobody she knew admitted to having sent, that Charlie said must be from some poor crazy lovesick millionaire, final testimony that she had arrived. But she had this suspicion, this flickering ridiculous notion, about those flowers, about Gianni Amara and those flowers that she couldn't quite shake, no more than those memories: the train of memories set off by the ruby.

Charlie was smiling now, yet looking puzzled. "But you gave it up for me, your father's prophecy. He hardly imagined you in a Broadway musical called *The Divine Daisy*, or even *American Beauty*."

"Girls have betrayed their fathers before for love."

"Love? Was that it? I thought it was impatience."

"Love," lying back in his arms, letting him untie the ribbons of her creamy lace peignoir, fingering the jewel. "I hope it doesn't have a curse, this famous ruby," she said, smiling up at him.

"No curse," he said, untying the last ribbon, kissing her gently as if she were a tender madonna instead of his fierce lover of former days. "Only a condition."

He was going to make a joke; she could tell from the twinkle in those frosty eyes.

"What is that?"

"The woman who accepts it must love and be faithful to the giver till she dies."

"Oh? Really? Is that so?"—responding with a teasing look.

"Before my mother, who did not test its powers," he continued blandly, "the jewel belonged to a beautiful and temperamental leading lady of the Comédie Française whose royal lover killed her in a fit of jealousy. Originally it belonged to a Persian caliph, so the story goes, who got rid of a half dozen of his favorite wives, thanks to the stone's magical properties."

"Stop, stop," she said, feigning amusement; and then, all of a sudden, something broke through the making of dialogue, the repartee. "Don't speak of death," she cried, "only of life! Our life!"—trying once again to push aside the knowledge that the other was not dead after all but alive and well, and singing in Paris. "I am so happy! Completely, perfectly happy!"

"You lie," her husband said quietly, surprising her as occasionally he did. "You will never be perfectly happy. If you could be, if I thought I could make you perfectly happy, I probably would never have married you."

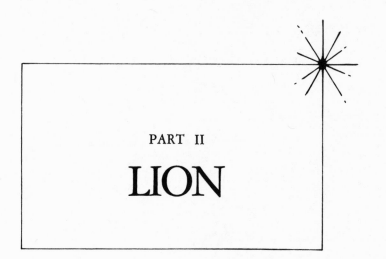

PART II

LION

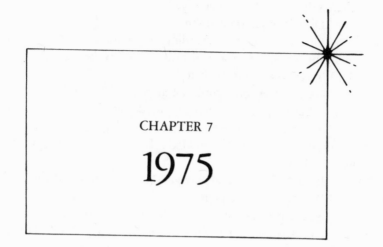

CHAPTER 7

1975

"I decided to go with that car to get Mother after all," Louis Geylin Grace, known as Lion, said to his wife, Serena, who was seated on the side of their bed sticking a gold rose—final flourish—on the package for Mary. "It's downstairs now."

"There! That does it!" said Serena, admiring her handiwork. Then she stood up to give herself a last glance in the long mirror, thinking she looked terrific in the red, green, and gold caftan Mary had given her for Christmas. His mother would be complimented to see it worn, but after the party Lion would have to tell Serena she looked a fright. The material was like the wrapping paper on Mary's present and the colors not flattering to his wife, especially not in January, when her rich olive skin turned sallow. The cut was wrong as well, doing nothing for her full-busted, slim-waisted figure, and the heavily embroidered neckline caught her curling brown hair. He sometimes wondered if there wasn't a resourceful malice at work, that every year his mother gave his wife a garment that Serena thought glamorous but that was just a little off. "She'll like that," he could hear Mary say to the salesgirl. "That's her taste."

"Do I look all right, Lion?"

"Fine, fine," he said, standing before his own dresser mirror, giving his smooth hair a final brush. "Positively regal. Stop fussing. It's better without the belt."

" 'Regal' is a code word, not always for 'becoming.' The hell with it. But why are you going? I need you here."

"The maid's sick. She's all alone. She may need help with her dress or that damn necklace. Listen, she's probably more nervous than you are."

"Poor Mary. I'm not nervous. No word from April?"

"Would I have kept it a secret?"

"Such a prima donna, April. Without having earned the right to be one. At least your mother is the real thing. One has to have a certain respect for the real thing. But your sister . . ."

"Serena!" His look was a red light to stop her. He could feel the old hot family anger and loyalty welling up in him. "Don't talk like that. You're not attractive when you try to be tough."

"Sorry. Just trying to make things ordinary. Like we were any family."

"We aren't any family," he said. "What family is . . . *any family?*"

He was done now, perfect from glossy gray-blond head to shiny black shoes; tie straight, studs and cuff links flashing green fire, shirt snowy, waistcoat firm; broad, pale, intelligent, slightly feral face, accented by dark brows and near-green eyes, a strong nose, and a slit of a mouth, framed by that thick wavy hair that as the years went by allowed him still to be called "Lion" without appearing utterly ridiculous. He looked like neither of his parents, though as a boy he had seemed a small copy of his father and with a hat on was said to resemble his paternal grandfather as a young man. All in all his image pleased him: New Yorker in a dinner jacket. A classic look that hadn't changed much, except for the width of the tuxedo lapels, since 1925, the year of his birth. Yet it was 1975, half a century later. A quick half century, too quick, or not quick enough.

"Why is it, Miss Watkins," he said to Serena as he opened the bedroom door, preparing to leave, "that whenever we do something for my family your temper gets so foul?" He knew he was being unfair. His became just as foul; in his own way, he was just as nervous, when it was a question of her parents and brothers. But he was upset about the party, or at least certain aspects of it, while Serena was simply annoyed and discommoded, after nearly twenty years of being a Grace, still claiming herself an outsider, ill at ease with the famous, the friends of Mary Gay. Shy—that was the word she fell back on. So shy. "Is there anything before I go?"

"To do?" Her exquisite face mocked him, the face he'd once compared to Garbo's in *Ninotchka*; he'd been paying for the compliment ever since. "Everything's done. You could look in on Emma and Marjorie and tell them they look terrific—if they're dressed, that is. If not, tell them to get a move on. What shall I do about the seating? No April, and the last-minute surprise, God help us all, Mr. Max Brandel, but it's still not an even number."

"I'll take care of that."

"Lion?"

"*What?*"

"After we get through tonight we have to talk."

"I look forward to it . . . *pretty.*" She was still, after twenty years of marriage and nearly thirty years of friendship, very pretty, even in that damn sack of wrapping paper.

"Seriously. I feel peculiarly in need . . ." She paused.

"Of what? Two weeks in the sun? I explained."

"No. Just. Peculiarly in need."

"Oh well, you'll get over that," he said. His conscience was clear. It had been clear for five years. Anything before that was ancient history, beyond the statute of limitations, in the trash with the old tax records. As for Serena, it would not have occurred to him that anything could disturb her conscience at all.

He knocked on Emma's door. On the central panel was a snarling lioness, warning intruders off, and a lot of little stickers.

"Fifteen minutes till curtain time, Miss Grace," he called, a joke she'd long outgrown.

"Go away," came the muffled scream. "Don't come in. I'm naked. Stark."

"You'd better hurry up. Your mother needs you. I'm going to get Grandma." He could imagine what lay behind the door, the unspeakable mess of teenage indecision: by now she would have tried on every dress, every pair of shoes and tights, and the floor would be strewn with the discards. There was something to be said, at times, for an old-fashioned household in which the mother of the family marched in and said, This is what you're going to wear, and this, and this, and that's that.

Next he knocked on Marjorie's door, pristine except for a single French sign. *Défense d'entrer.* "Hold it, Pops, hold it," he heard. Then, amazingly, this door opened slightly, revealing his older daughter dressed in three towels: rainbow towel sarong, orange towel cape, scarlet towel turban. Behind her the room was relatively tidy, the gaudy poster-shop chamber of a college freshman home only for weekends and vacations, emerging from the slum years, though he could imagine the condition of the bathroom. "For Christsake, kiddo," he said, "why did you wash your hair *now?*"

"I used the wrong shampoo before."

"Well, get it dry fast. Or is the dryer broken?"

"Nope. Relax, Pops, everything's cool." The face under the turban was pink and saucy, with glowing golden brown eyes and the arched black brows that were a family trademark.

"Your mother's not cool. She's been dressed for ages and she's jumpy as hell."

"Marie Antoinette was dressed in plenty of time for the guillotine."

"None of that now. It's going to be a wonderful evening."

Up went the eyebrows, up, mockingly, curved, the crescent mouth. How he adored, yet could spank, this comical seductive girl draped in a doorway who was said to be the spitting image of young Mary Gay, and could sing as well. What gave with Marjorie anyhow, these days, he wondered. She was entirely too comical and sassy and seductive, slipping away from him before his eyes.

"Anyone heard from Aunt April?" she asked.

"No. And your mother's having stage fright. Wake, Jennifer, the Lump . . . Grandma . . . Aunt Isabelle and old Sasha . . . Verna Michaels . . . and Harry Dresser and the Jacobses . . . and all those cousins. Whew! Is the masterwork wrapped?" Another matter to make him perspire and give Serena stage fright. The girls' by now notorious scrapbooks, labor of many months— *This Is Your Life, Mary*—every important year covered except the one that their father had suggested they take out: 1933. Three oversized albums, embossed in gold, the contents stolen from trunks and boxes and filing cabinets and purloined out of a news magazine morgue. It was the job Mary had been saying for years she wished someone would do—not since the twenties had she had proper scrapbooks—yet now that it was done, would she be pleased? Was he pleased?

"Of course it's wrapped. You want to see?"

"No. I want you to get dressed. I hope she likes it."

"She *will!* Don't worry. It was better when we were poor, wasn't it, Pops? And still rushing around the kitchen when the doorbell rang. There was no time for stage fright then."

"Who was ever poor?" Louis Geylin Grace said loftily, pushing his firstborn back in her room, forgetting days that had no reality for him, didn't count, when he wasn't Louis Grace, personage, author of three successful novels, only difficult old Lion, son of Mary Gay, you know, and Charlie Grace—remember?— grandson of Jean Archibald and Joseph Grace, trailing a pedigree and a decent war record, not much else.

On the way down, the elevator stopped on seven, letting in Judith Sturgis dressed for an important evening, dark and delicious in a fur-trimmed hooded velvet cloak that reminded him of the sort of thing Mary wore when he was a child. Judith smiled. He smiled. "I understand you have an occasion in the family," she said. "Will you congratulate your mother for me."

He nodded. "I'm going uptown," he said abruptly. "Can I

give you a lift, Mrs. Sturgis?"—speaking in a lightly significant echoing tone, as if quoting something said long ago.

"Why thank you, Mr. Grace," as if also quoting a distant conversation. "That would be delightful." She paused. "Except I'm going in the other direction from you, Lion. *Thank God.*"

"Good night, J.D.S.," he called.

Leaving her standing in the lobby while the doorman whistled for a taxi, getting into his waiting car, Lion Grace felt a brief pang. Once, to be in the same building as Judith would have been so . . . convenient. Hell, would have been heaven. She must have been thinking that also, for the irony of her glance was almost insupportable to him.

As he approached his mother's house, a dozen blocks north up Park, a block and a half west, he felt the old uneasiness. This part of the city had changed less than most since his boyhood, kept its proportions except for that red-brick monster at the corner of Eighty-ninth and Madison.

"Remember the future," Judith had said on one of their walks, though not the one when they'd run into his mother. "The futurama. The world of tomorrow. Whatever happened to tomorrow? It's here and it's banal."

"That's a good title for the novel," he'd said, and *Remember the Future* had done well, changing much about his life, including Judith Sturgis, the need for a Judith Sturgis.

The side streets, especially his mother's, were frozen in another time. He could be six, with Nanny Bross, riding home from a birthday party, waiting to be tattled on. . . . "Oh, when I tell Mummy how you behaved, oh, when I tell your dad, he won't laugh this time, mister smarty-pants, I promise." Or ten, walking the route himself, wondering what would greet him when he walked in the door, what he'd done now. Or sixteen, just before Pearl Harbor, riding with a girl in a taxi, bringing a girl home to dinner and wondering if Mary and April were going to kidnap her with charm or take one of their swift unpredictable female dislikes to a stranger . . . wondering what the house might have been like . . . if. Lion loved his mother and that house that had for so many years been his home, too much so, old friends like Judith said, but he did not approach Mary with comfort; approaching her, thought always of the crack, the fissure, the black stroke through his childhood and her life: 1933.

Every landmark was a jolt: the church before they turned the corner; the trees, bare crooks this time of year; old Mrs. Prince's house, the ice palace, which was now an embassy; the apartment where Judith, Judith Dresser then, had lived; the butcher, Nanny's friend, who sneaked gum to him as a little boy; Bradley's Florist— since 1890—where he'd ordered his first gardenia corsage. Finally came their house, so close to Fifth Avenue you could see the park from the bay windows—the Grace house—like the florist, dated 1890 and still standing.

"I may be a few minutes," he said to the chauffeur, pulling out his keys (every time Mary changed the lock she sent him a new set, as she still sent over a Christmas stocking), keys making him think of April, who always lost hers, damn April anyhow, for being such a mess, though let Serena say that and he'd smack her.

He didn't slam the front door but shut it quietly, as he always did, knowing how his mother hated slammed doors unless she happened to be doing the slamming herself. Anyhow, it was his habit to move quietly, left over from the war when his life depended on knowing how to creep, to stalk the enemy silently.

Inside, before going upstairs to find Mary, he went into the kitchen to say hello to Ninon, forgetting Ninon was in the hospital. Still, it was an unbreakable routine, to look in the kitchen first, see what was up, get a whiff and a taste of what was cooking on the big old black range, hear the backstairs news and the weather report on the mood of the lady of the house upstairs. The kitchen was bare, spotless, stark white as an operating room, except for the stove and the flowered oilcloth on the servants' dining table. A cook's kitchen, a place where Serena, who did all their cooking herself, wouldn't be caught dead; she called it "the morgue." Yet that bright and hideous oilcloth, purple, pink, and yellow, do you know who chooses that, he'd say to Serena, and refreshes it every year: Mother, because it reminds her of the oilcloth in her own mother's kitchen back in Chicago years ago and because at two in the morning when she can't sleep, it's not Ninon's kitchen but her kitchen where she makes nocturnal feasts and sits communing with those pink and purple tulips.

Bare, spotless, white, silent, odorless, was the empty kitchen . . . except. Simultaneously, Lion noticed the florist's box—"Since 1890"—unopened on the floor, smelled a faint acrid sweetness that was not his mother's perfume, and heard the scratching and the muffled cries coming from behind the closet door. Instantly the classic New Yorker in his chesterfield and white silk scarf, stepped out of an old Peter Arno cartoon or a Philip Barry play, dropped that cloak and pose and turned into another Lion Grace, his every sense alert to the certainty something was wrong. He didn't, as another man might, free the cat. Nor did he storm upstairs, three steps at a time, calling, "Mother."

He went up quietly, quickly, till he reached the last few steps before the third-floor landing—the red-walled landing with the old master drawings, school of Tiepolo, Dürer, Rembrandt, which didn't like sun—when he moved even more cautiously, knowing the peculiar properties of that staircase, the giveaway step. He stared at the closed door of his mother's bedroom that should have been open, was always open at this hour when she was alone in the house.

Then he heard the voices—his mother's and the other's— sounds and words so unexpected that for a moment he wondered, as he had wondered long ago, standing in that same haunted place, if he might not be dreaming. And he did something he hadn't done since he was a child: put his ear to the door to hear more exactly what was being said; trying to decide what the smart thing to do would be, the course of action that would be least dangerous to the woman within who was being threatened by an intruder as if by a husband, or lover, a man in some way involved in trickery, betrayal, his or her own.

CHAPTER 8

1933

He was a little boy, not quite eight, standing on the mysterious third-floor landing with the red damask walls and priceless drawings that were there because they didn't like the sun and everywhere else, except on the landings, the house was brilliantly sunny, the brightest, sunniest house in all of New York City, the little boy liked to boast, even on a rainy day. Those drawings, lit by clever hidden spotlights so they seemed to glow from within, frightened him and intrigued him at the same time: the very old woman; the laughing toothless man; the armored knight slaying a dragon; the burgher in furs who looked so heavy and threatening; the fighting lions; the trumpeting angel called "Fame"; the landscape that never ended. They piqued his imagination and peopled his dreams, and years later when he was a man he would put them in a story in a way that would be upsetting to the women in his life, his mother, his wife, his sister, even his young daughters, because in the story there were no women, only men; all the women in the story had disappeared or died.

"Why don't the drawings like the sun?" the boy asked from time to time.

"Because they are very old," answered his father, who was proud of those drawings and brought visitors up to see them as if they were something rare and marvelous. "Because the sun would fade them."

To the child's clear naked eyes, though, the drawings were already faded, barely discernible. They matched his father, he thought, who was a man finely etched, yet faded, with his gray-blond hair and wintry-green eyes and thin fair skin tracked with fine wrinkles, a man of line and little color except for the spots of red that stained his cheekbones when he became angry. Subtle like his father, the wonderful Charlie Grace, the wizard of Broadway, were the drawings on the third-floor landing, and far less obviously marvelous than the paintings in the living room below that were his mother's pride, that overwhelmed you (like Miss Mary Gay herself) with their rainbow charm, whether of water lilies or rooftops or rosy young girls dressing their hair. People weren't polite or thoughtful in their comments about the paintings in the living room (no more than about Mary herself). They didn't say of Mary's paintings, as they did of Charlie's drawings (and sometimes of Charlie himself), that they "grew on you"; they simply said, "Ah!"

Only he, Lion, could appreciate the nature and secrets of the drawings on the landing; the way they talked to him when he sat on the tapestry bench, impatient in his best clothes, waiting for his parents, who were taking him to some delightful place; the way the people in the drawings sometimes took on shapes other than their own, or left their delicate golden frames and floated up the third turning of the stairs to his floor, into his room, and into his dreams.

It was a dream of one of the drawings that had wakened him that night, or so he thought; a dream of the man in furs with the hard eyes coming after him, speaking to him in an evil voice. He was going to see his parents as recently they had asked him to do. "Don't bother Nanny anymore if you have a nightmare, Lion," his mother had said. "Come to us."

But now he stood frozen—a small fair-haired boy in peppermint-striped pajamas, wandered by accident into the nighttime region of the gods—as through the thick, high mahogany door he heard voices. The voices of his parents quarreling; the god and goddess quarreling and shouting like ordinary mortals; like the people across the garden his mother called dreadful; like the people he sometimes heard in warm weather, going east of Third Avenue with Nanny on an errand, the ones Nanny called no better than animals; the god and goddess, master and mistress of the most envied house in New York, were carrying on like the cook and the butler who had to be let go, though valued, because they fought so dreadfully when off duty, she screaming like a fishwife, he bellowing like a bull.

Nightly and two matinees a week—every night but this one, Sunday—his mother *was* a goddess, or almost a goddess, on the stage of his father's theater. She was playing Helen of Troy, the most beautiful woman on earth, which was only fitting since she was the most beautiful woman in New York City, with a voice that melted all mortals, even the critics, even the butcher and the policeman at the corner and most especially the little boy Lion, though he pretended embarrassment when the butcher called, "Nothing but the best for America's goddess," as he hacked away at a piece of prime beef; or the policeman said, "I went to see your mother in *That Belle, Helen*, the voice it melts me like the sun melts that dirty ice over there"—which was more or less what the little boy had read a while ago in his father's *Times*, or was it the *Tribune*. "Miss Gay could sing for me in a palace or a hovel, a Hooverville shanty or an Arctic igloo," the man in the newspaper had written, "which would cease to be Arctic forthwith. She is all out beautiful and vocally on fire, an old-fashioned gleaming-voiced alternative for jazz-drugged New Yorkers."

It was 1933, midwinter, and hard times had the city by the throat. (It wasn't everyone, the boy was told, when he picked at his food, who was lucky enough to have roast beef for Sunday dinner, and he was not given his usual laugh when he volunteered a preference, if the truth were told, for chipped beef, creamed on toast, like Nanny made on Cook's day off.) The best Broadway shows reflected those times: were skeptical, and of the moment, torn off the front page of today's newspaper (though promising a rainbow around the corner), except for the new operetta at the Grace. And even at the Grace there was unusually sophisticated fare. Mary the Gay, Mary the Good, Charlie Grace's wife and prima donna, after a two years' absence and a so-so Hollywood fling, just before Christmas had flashed back into view in an opulent revival of *La Belle Hélène*, called *That Belle, Helen*, causing the critics to turn cartwheels over their favorite golden girl, and all of New York to sing an eighty-year-old Offenbach score with witty new English words and a song about Venus that was not translated but left in the original naughty French: *"Dis-moi, Vénus, quel plaisir trouves-tu, à faire ainsi cascader, cascader la vertu."*

The little boy didn't know what the words meant, but he sang and whistled the triplets—*"cascader, cascader la vertu"*: they danced around his head like the sound of his mother's voice. He understood the policeman and the butcher, though, hearing them speak, he shuffled and ducked and pulled at Nanny's hand.

Only a while ago he, too, had been to see his mother, Mary Gay, onstage. On this very spot where he was standing now, in such alarm, he had stood a week ago Saturday in a fever of excitement, too excited even to fuss about putting on his hated velvet suit, calling to his father through the door to hurry up, the car was there, they'd be late.

Only a few Saturdays ago he had sat beside his father in the stage box of the Grace Theater and known bliss.

Bliss was a woman in a spotlight with a spill of golden-brown curls, white powdered skin and glittering dark eyes, opening her mouth from which dripped tones like honey, like pearls, like diamond dew. Bliss was a smile directed straight at him. It was his earliest memory, even more poignant than the smell of her perfume or the touch of her skin, his mother's voice lulling him to sleep with a mournful old song—singing of poor Malbrough going off to war or Pierrot's friend begging by moonlight to be let in the door—such sad songs always, but always followed by that bright broad smile and a wink, a Mary Gay *clin d'oeil*, as if to reassure her baby boy that there was a comedy to the sadness: she and he shared this secret.

But he didn't, like another performer's child he had heard about, howl to see her thus exposed on stage; howl because he had to share her, and their secret, with a thousand others in the audience, not to mention a handsome leading man onstage who turned his sweet French tenor around her rich soprano in an amorous duet of dreams and kisses. Nor did he wriggle and complain like his sister, April, who was removed in the intermission by his aunt and did not return. He sat motionless, like a proper little gentleman. But then so had the naughty boy always sat, he was told, when watching his mother onstage, as if hypnotized; two years ago when he was not quite six, and a year before that when he was four, April's age now, though he would not remember the earlier times, only this one.

And at the end of the performance his father gave him a rose and whispered to him to throw it at his mother when she took her curtain calls. He made a perfect throw, did the round-faced child in the blue velvet suit, for he had perfect aim. The rose fell at his mother's feet and she blew him kisses while people in the audience looked up to stare. "I think you'll be something with the ladies when you grow up, fellow," his father said. And afterward, backstage, his mother called him her knight, her rose cavalier, and her speaking voice was warm and honeyed also.

But now she was shrill as Moira the cook, her voice grittier and colder than gutter ice, saying, "Fool! Take your hands off me! It is nothing you've found out about Paris, Mr. Detective, nothing! How dare you!"

And the man god, his courtly father. "That dad of yours, Mr. Charles Grace," said the doctor come to look at Lion's throat, listen to his chest, and examine the telltale red spots behind his ears—"that man knows more than anyone alive how to bring beauty to his stage and pleasure to people, and when you grow up, young man, I bet you do the same and make a million dollars in the bargain." "That dad of yours, the only man in the world who can work under pressure and never raise his voice or lose his delightful sense of humor," said blond Loretta the secretary, who stopped off to see Lion recovering from the red spots and write a page of shorthand for him, letting him pretend he was his father dictating a letter. The penciled chicken tracks fascinated the child, as did Loretta's red nails, so long they curved over. "Even in these times a good man. That man is imperturbable."

Other Daddies in the winter of 1933, Lion knew from his school friends and from overhearing the nurses gossip in the park, were being impossible. Terrible things were happening in other houses: a daddy telling a mother there was no more money—a daddy suddenly dead—a daddy disappeared off the face of the earth—a daddy run off with another lady—but not in his house. A hit had come to his house, thanks to the imperturbable man and the siren lady who had taken a trip to Paris, France, to see some sick old woman, some old teacher of hers who was dying, and returned with a crazy idea about what she wanted to do next; and the imperturbable man had said, thoughtfully, "Maybe that is not such a dumb idea, Mary, for you . . . Helen of Troy . . . maybe that's the change you need." *Imperturbable*. Lion like the word, it made a picture. He said it over and over, imperturbable, imperturbable, imperturbable, till his tongue got twisted.

But tonight his father wasn't giving pleasure, wasn't imperturbable. His father was dealing out pain. "Lies," his quiet-voiced father was bellowing, like Herbert, the recently departed butler. "Lies! Lies! Lies! Here a lie, catch! And another, catch!"

And his mother was shouting right back.

Why were they shouting so, the little boy wondered, when they loved each other, adored each other?

That the man and the woman adored each other was a well-known fact, at home and abroad, and that they adored the little boy, Lion, and the little girl, April. At home in their big cheerful house with its gleaming bay windows and stately decor, the glamorous Graces were a family, a colorful loving family, with jokes and passwords, ceremonies and games. It was a rosy, golden atmosphere in which the little boy lived, he would remember afterward, except for when he was sick, in swollen misery, or confined to his room for a lie, or a bit of pilfering, or for nearly killing himself climbing out of his parents' window onto the tree in the garden, or nearly killing his baby sister playing horsie. A warm, orderly nursery life it was, with such an abundance of toys and storybooks, of jolly furnishings and comforts, that it was perhaps ordained that in command should be a nagging Nanny in white to disturb his peace along with the whining of the cry-baby April and the ceaseless yapping of Bonnie, the cocker spaniel. "Otherwise," he would say in later years, giving that lopsided smile that so annoyed his wife, "it was possible I might have been considered spoiled."

For they weren't, the young Graces, prisoners of the nursery even, poor little rich kids, tyrannized by servants, who never saw their parents. The upstairs, backstairs routine was broken daily by exciting visits into the region of the god and goddess; into their bedroom with the oversized bed that had a coverlet like a silver lake; into his father's study–dressing room with all the books and his mother's music room with the old Steinway piano and the high-backed tapestry chairs; into the downstairs living room with the beautiful paintings and the velvet sofas big as admirals' barges and the formal paneled library; and all the way down to the dining room off the garden, newly modernized, all white and mirrored like a room from the snow queen's palace. There were excursions, too, with the god and goddess into the great world beyond, not Nanny's world of boring errands or school or Central Park but a dazzling city that embraced white-tabled restaurants, concert halls and theaters, darkened movie palaces like Chinese temples, and the great noisy blue-aired arena where the circus came every spring and the ice hockey players in the winter and the horses in the autumn.

And in the summer there was the green shuttered cottage by the Sound, just a field away from the bigger green shuttered house by the sail-dotted blue water where Aunt Isabelle and Uncle Ralph lived, and the cousins, which was his second home, his link with ordinary family life; his own peculiar definition of ordinary, that is, which didn't mean not rich or not special or not rising above the terrible times, only not famous: not Mary Gay and Charles Grace.

At home or abroad he was Mary and Charlie's droll little boy who made them laugh, had his own magical ability: to get himself out of scrapes by making the grown-ups laugh. As his mother could move people to tears with her voice; as his father could cause everything to turn to gold, make people do his bidding, and animals and machines as well; as his little sister could cause strangers to stare and gush over her unusual pink-cheeked smoky-eyed blonde beauty; so Lion could make the grown-ups laugh. He was funny.

The nightmares didn't fit in, nor certain things that happened in school, the fibs and pranks and petty thefts. But still he always had an answer. He could hang by his knees from a perilous railing on an ocean liner steaming into New York Harbor; reward his father for taking him on the most exciting adventure of his young life, on the Coast Guard cutter to meet his mother's incoming boat from Europe, by nearly getting himself killed, for instance. And when his parents were shaking him for taking such a chance, he could say, "I just wanted to see the Statue of Liberty upside down," and they would stop and laugh, the idea seemed so droll to them. "The Statue of Liberty upside down looks like Aunt Tilly," he had said, and they had forgotten their anger in their delight at his comment.

But they were not laughing that night.

"Lies, lies," his father was shouting as the little boy stood frozen outside the door. "How beautiful you look in your necklace as you stand there and lie. Little lies. Big lies. Lies to me. Lies to yourself. It's the lies even more than the fellow. The fellow is nothing, I agree."

Now his mother, who had been shouting also only a moment ago, was crying. He could hear the sobs.

"Why didn't you leave? Why didn't you run away? Helen of Troy, is it? Paris can have you. I'm through, Miss Geylin, Miss Mary Geylin. And without me—*where would you be? What would you be?*"

And then his father came out of the bedroom, throwing the door open and storming past the boy in a blind fury, an anger so intense he didn't see his own son drawn back in the shadows. A floor below, the library door slammed.

But his mother saw him when she came to call her husband back. His mother was wearing the Chinese wrapper Aunt Belle had brought her from Hong Kong, black, with the red and silver dragon, changed out of her evening clothes, though his father was still in his dress suit. They had been to a fancy party, all dressed up when hours earlier they had come to say good night, his mother in a low-cut dress of violet satin and her ruby necklace and a velvet cloak, her gilded curling hair held back by diamond combs. "Where are you going?" the boy had asked them. "To dine with a duke," his father had replied. "A royal duke of France has fallen in love with America's Mary Gay." Though in her Chinese wrapper, with her hair tumbling about her shoulders, she was still wearing the necklace. She stood there, starting to shout something down the stairs, her hand at her throat, touching the stone of the necklace, and caught herself as she saw the little boy, tossing her head, stifling her sobs, and giving her son a faint smile.

"You've had a bad dream, haven't you?" she said and put her arms around him, bending toward him. As she bent, the necklace swung, catching the light, the star seeming to burst out of it. "Your father is upset about business. You mustn't mind. Come in. I'll give you a candy and we'll talk awhile till you forget that nasty nightmare."

And Lion went in with her—into the sanctuary, the serene silvery-gray bedroom punctuated with splashes of pink, the pink of fresh bouquets, of the needlepoint rug made by his grandmother, of the portrait over the mantel of his mother, April, and himself—into the place that made him happy, like the enclosed garden in the country, that was earthly heaven—and saw on the carpet of his parent's usually spotless bedchamber, as if someone had thrown them there in distress or temper, the treasures. The little objects that a month or so earlier his mother had told him he should never have retrieved from where he found them in the trash—the scarab ring, the pearl stickpin, the funny old button, the medal in the shape of a star, the glass locket with the curl of hair, and the soft pouch that had held them.

When she had found the boy playing with the trinkets that

afternoon, she had said, "Those are old things I wanted to get rid of."

"But they are nice," Lion had said. "That's a nice pin and a good ring and a pretty locket. What is the medal? Why did you want to throw them away?" And then, when she was silent, "Did they belong to my granddady? Your Daddy?"

She had looked at him in a way that made him think he had guessed correctly.

"Maybe you're right," she had said with an odd expression in her large dark eyes. "You are a funny little fellow, Lion. Your odd little ways someday are going to get you into trouble. Get us all into trouble." And then he'd heard his father's voice saying, "What's up, Mary? What's he got into this time?" "Nothing," his mother had said quickly, putting the trinkets in her pocket. "He was only playing."

Now, seeing the direction the boy was looking, his mother leaned over and began picking the objects up, along with some scattered letters and what looked like a theater or opera program. "Now, Lion," she said, "there is no reason to hide them or throw them away. I can keep them forever and it won't make any difference."

Once again she began to weep. He asked for a candy. She gave him several, rose-colored pastilles like pretty jewels that melted on the tongue, and told him the story of the old painted tin she kept them in, along with other dressing table odds and ends. But even as she told the cheerful story of the girl with the lunch box on the New York-bound train, making him forget about his nasty dream, she could not seem to stop her weeping. He asked if she was crying about Paris, though uncertain which Paris he meant: Paris, France, where she had lingered too long the previous winter or the handsome sweet-voiced Paris who loved Helen. "I told you, it was about business," she said in a way that made him sure she was fibbing. Now something occurred to him, a thought too terrible to leave unspoken, though she was giving him his glass of ice water and saying she would take him back to his own room.

"Is it me?" he asked in a small voice. "Something I did. The little fellow who lies and gets people into trouble?"

"*You?* You think grown-ups would be so angry over a little boy like you? You think you are that important?" She might almost laugh. But no. It is too hard. "He's angry at me, you ninny, but tomorrow it will be finished or the day after for sure. Come on, now."

On the red-walled landing, hand in his, she hesitated for a moment, looking down to the next floor; then pulled him up the stairs.

That was 1933, in late January or early February. By the middle of March his father, Charles Grace, was dead. Nineteen thirty-three: the year he'd cut out of the scrapbook, though some of the sweetest family pictures ever taken of him and April, of him and his mother, April and his father, the four of them together, came from the beginning of that year. But his mother hated those photographs, posed for in the drawing room one winter afternoon as a birthday surprise for his grandmother Geylin. They were too cruel, Mary said. Too cruel a reminder of the golden days, of how happy they had been, how blessed. And Lion hated them for another reason. They were lies—his mother, his father, himself, pretending to be happy—though he didn't say that. He only said they made him too sad.

For what Lion remembered of that winter of 1933 was his father angry. As angry most of the time as he had been the night of the quarrel. Angry on the stairs, passing the children with the briefest hello. Angry in the entrance hall as he put on his hat and coat. Angry on the telephone, talking to his office. Angry in the pantry, giving an order to the new butler. Angry at the breakfast table, not making jokes with Nanny over some bit of news in the morning paper, though not necessarily shouting; very quiet in the morning, with a gleam in his eye, as he lit into Lion for some infraction of the rules that in another season might have made him smile. Also angry at the opera house, at a Saturday matinee in the family box, though it was one of his favorites, *Tosca*, and Lion's first opera, a long-promised treat. Angry at the Central Park boat pond, sailing Lion's Christmas schooner. Angry even at the wheel of his roadster, driving Lion to the boatyard in Connecticut, to see how the winter work on their real-life sailing boat was coming along, though the father had told the son more than once that a man should never drive when drunk or angry. On the way back into New York, that afternoon when Lion had started asking questions about next summer, his father had swerved too suddenly, taking a curve badly, blaming the conversation, and saying he was in no mood for questions about tomorrow when today was such a headache.

"Headache? Why?" the little boy asked.

"Business," his father replied. But still when Lion asked when his father was going to teach him to drive, Charlie brightened. "The summer you are twelve," he said, smiling.

So there were cracks in the anger, in that six-week period, as there were cracks in the ice that country afternoon. His father wasn't angry the day of his eighth birthday, March 1, when more pictures had been taken. Nor had he been angry late that same night when Lion had stood on the red-walled landing and heard through the bedroom door laughter instead of quarreling; his parents talking quietly and then both of them laughing about something to do with his birthday party, in a way that made him return upstairs without knocking, not wanting to interrupt that precious laughter. Instead he woke up Nanny about his birthday night stomachache.

But a few nights after that he had heard the bad voices again, and bad laughter, laughter that wasn't warm, and strange riddle talk that made no sense about his mother's necklace—the ruby necklace—that was her most valued possession. "My price is above rubies, oh yes," his mother was saying, half laughing, half crying, "far above rubies." And "Witch" he heard his father shout before he ran back upstairs once again without knocking, or was it something worse his father was calling his mother, one of those words Nanny had made him taste soap over.

Yes, anger was what the boy remembered, enough of it concentrated, fixed in his mind, unleavened by his mother who during those weeks was simply not around much, except behind the bedroom door, so that when the accident happened—when his mother told him the terrible news about his father—Lion blurted out the unforgivable words: "He has been so angry all winter. I knew something bad would happen. I knew it!"

And his mother, deathly pale, already in black flashed him a terrible look, a wicked look, almost as if she hated him, though a moment earlier, telling him the news, her pale face had been suffused with love, love breaking through the dark sorrowful eyes, love in the light touch of fingers on his face, love and wonder at the miracle of him, the beloved boy, the fact of him, still there alive, who would have to take care of her now, grow up fast so he could take his father's place.

It was a Monday afternoon, the second week of March. Though the woman had received the phone call from the police at dawn, the boy knew nothing till the end of the day when once again he found himself standing on the red-walled landing, preparing to knock on his parents' door, told by Nanny his mother wanted to see him.

He was in his pajamas and wrapper and slippers, his hair slicked down like a little man's, fresh and clean from his evening bath. He and April had spent the day at Nanny's day-off house instead of going to school, an unexpected surprise. He had got himself so delightfully dirty digging in Nanny's backyard that Nanny thought she would never get him clean when he got home; but then Nanny hadn't paid much attention to him out there in her muddy yard; she wasn't feeling well, she said, and kept blowing her nose and wiping her eyes, as if she had hay fever, though it wasn't summer. He would tell his mother about Nanny's March fever to amuse her at her dressing table, while Ninon was working on her hair for the night's performance, pinning up her golden-brown hair in fancy Helen of Troy ringlets.

But standing outside the thick high mahogany door, Lion hesitated. The sounds coming from behind the door were not the expected five o'clock sounds of Ninon and his mother chatting in

French, twittering French like birds in the yard. The sounds were of his mother crying, crying in a way that was different from the crying that had gone on all winter; scary crying, like someone in pain. Lion ran back upstairs to Nanny, who took him down again and knocked firmly. To his surprise it was his Aunt Belle who opened the door.

"Come here, Lion," his mother said, opening her arms. She was faded like the drawings on the landing, without color. The boy had never seen her without makeup or her own brilliant natural coloring. She was wearing black. He had never seen her in black except black velvet. Even her stockings were black. She spoke carefully, as if she were reciting memorized lines, dealing out the words, one by one.

"You know your Daddy was driving in from the country last night, Lion."

He nodded. He knew his father was coming in from the country. He had been disappointed on Saturday morning because he had wanted to go with his father and his father had said no, not this time, he wanted to be alone.

"There was an accident. He wasn't paying attention. The road was slippery. He has been so tired lately, so much on his mind." One by one she dealt the words out. "They took him to the hospital." The little boy knew. He still hoped. But he knew. He could see his father at the wheel of his roadster, in his tweed cap and driving gloves, taking a curve badly, swearing.

"He went to sleep in the hospital and he didn't wake up. He is dead, Lion."

Though he had heard the word now, though he knew, he didn't believe her.

"Of course not," she said. "Of course you don't believe. I remember. My mother said to me, his body is dead." She repeated the words, looking at the boy with those loving sorrowful eyes. "His body is dead. But *he* isn't dead."

"He is in heaven," Lion said, though only that day, at lunch, he had made April cry, telling her there was no heaven up there, up there was sky and planets and stars and space, empty space. *Heaven comes in handy* would be one of his sayings later.

"That's right. The angel came and took him to heaven. He is happy there." Lion had heard Nanny say that theirs was a godless house, but he knew his mother believed in angels. His guardian angel. The angel that brought April. In his mind an angel looked like Aunt Isabelle with wings. He could see the angel holding in her arms his transparent father. But he could see something else: his father's face in the car . . . his father's face on the landing . . . his father's face, on and off all winter, and he cried out those words about his father being angry, angry all winter. "So angry," he cried. "A man who is so angry should not drive a car."

And his mother looked at him with those horrified eyes and began to scream. "No! No! Don't say that! Never say that again! Everything was perfect . . . perfect . . . fourteen perfect years," she cried after him as his aunt hurried him out of the room saying, "Come away, Lion, come away."

And Lion didn't need his aunt to tell him he must never say such a thing again, about his father being angry, that it was an awful thing to say to his mother at this moment; and that he had better get that imagination of his under control. He didn't need the look on his mother's face when she came into his room the next morning to tell him about arrangements: that his grandmother was coming from Chicago to stay for a while; and that April was going with Nanny to the country but she had decided that he, the only boy, though young, should be at his father's funeral. The mask of her face, the cool smoothness of her voice told him something had changed between them, and there was nothing he could do to take back what he had said. He couldn't even tell her he was sorry. He could only try to be simple. Already at eight he knew that much: that the only hope with a creature as mysterious and unpredictable as his mother was to be straight and open yourself. And so "My poor Daddy," he said, that was all, letting the fact overwhelm him, letting the tears come, hot gushing tears, feeling her arms close around him, knowing she was crying too; not understanding any bit of what had happened, only that they were crying together. But after a while his mother stopped crying and released him, saying in that smooth cold voice

[123]

that filled him with anxiety, "I must be a wicked woman for God to punish me this way. Yet I have made people happy, thousands and thousands of them."

"Oh no," the little boy said as she moved toward the door, widening his eyes, begging with his eyes. "You are good. *You are good."*

And he never spoke of the matter again, until the spring he was eighteen years old and about to go to war and suddenly reckless and brave after too much farewell champagne said to his mother, "Now that I am grown-up, would you tell me what the trouble was? I know there was trouble. Was there somebody else, Mother? You were so beautiful and he was so gray and tired. Was that what he was angry about?"

"Gray and tired!" she said. "Your father was the most attractive man who ever lived. There was nobody else. But he was jealous. He was always jealous of my leading men, if you must know. I almost retired because of it. He told me once his father had been the same way, and it was a fact that Jean Archibald never kissed anyone onstage. So stupid, when he spoiled you for all other men, that Charlie Grace. And when he was jealous he drank. He was drunk the night of the accident. Not just angry. Blind drunk."

"He was jealous of Paris," Lion said, incredulous. "Jealous of a singer?"

And this time she was silent, only looked at him in that old way he remembered from his childhood, as if he had guessed correctly, though she wasn't going to say one way or the other.

"And you blamed yourself. I knew you blamed yourself for something."

"So you did, you clever boy," she said, "so you did," and there was an edge to her voice and an irony in her glance, and she did not give him the big bright smile she usually did when speaking of his cleverness, but suddenly became serious. "And you will have to be clever, cleverer than ever, my brave son, in this terrible war." Then the next week he was gone with his mother's blessing; standing on the red landing, receiving his mother's final desperate kiss, still not sure she had told him the whole story; guessing but not sure. No more sure than he had been at eight years old, when he heard his mother talking to the important men the day after his father's funeral, only sure of what he, Lion, had to do.

"I can't," Mary Gay said to the gentlemen gathered in the upstairs study in a grouping that was as familiar to Lion as the arrangement of furniture, except for the missing person, the sharp-faced man with gray-blond hair who would have been sitting behind the desk, feet up, hands clasped, listening, waiting for everyone to finish before he said, "Okay, but this is the way it's going to be, and don't ever say 'I can't,' Mary, because of course you can."

"I cannot go back on that stage," she said, "and sing that silly woman, sing of love and dreams and moonlight and Venus. Helen at the Grace . . . no one expects it," she was saying to George Jacobs, partner of Charlie Grace and Lion's godfather, and to Harry Dresser and Bobby Leeds, his closest friends, who had written his wife's greatest successes, including the adaptation of Helen. "The understudy, I hear, is good."

"Very good. So good in fact—"

"But I don't care. I saw that writeup. If you thought to goad me, dear friends, well, that is another Mary, I'm afraid. I'm happy if the girl is a new Cinderella. Talented girls need their breaks, indeed they do, even if it is somebody else's disaster . . . death. . . ."

The boy, who had come to say good night to his mother, stood listening for a moment, crumpling in his bathrobe pocket the article torn out of the afternoon paper that Ninon had pressed upon him, saying, "When you say good night, show her this, about this young demoiselle who has stepped so easily in her shoes, see if she likes that, not to be irreplaceable." Then, politely, he knocked, though the door wasn't closed.

"Come in, darling," his mother said. "You know everyone." She was pale, composed and formal, in the same high-necked black silk dress she had worn to the funeral. "But say good night quickly, for we are having a business discussion."

The boy looked at her reproachfully. He was disappointed in her, this wan and spiritless lady in black speaking so generously of an understudy who had caused one of the Broadway critics to proclaim the birth of a new star. She was not his mother. And she would never sing again. He knew now. He wasn't sure at the funeral yesterday. Her silence in church while everyone else sang his father's favorite hymn was understandable—who would have expected her to sing—though Lion had seen her poor throat working as if she was actually trying, because they were making such a botch of that beautiful Bach chorale and she would have liked to show them for Charlie's sake how the thing should properly be sung. There were many reasons why Mary Gay for once in her life would have remained silent, including the certainty that someone, Aunt Tilly Vail no doubt, would have made the crack: "You could have bet she wouldn't miss an opportunity to perform, not even at her own husband's funeral." But that was yesterday. Today was different. What might have been wisdom yesterday was folly today. So he was sure.

"What's the matter?" Mary said, holding out her arms so her son could give her a good-night hug. "What's wrong, my funny boy? I mean, everything is wrong, but what is specially wrong?"

"You will never sing again," he said, standing where he was, not wanting to go into her arms.

"Did you hear us talking? It is better not to listen outside doors since you always get things wrong or miss the important point. Remember that. Listening at doors, peeking through keyholes . . . it is better to hear and see nothing. I'll sing again. Only not Helen. No more Helen, that's all."

"But Helen is what is now," said George Jacobs. "And we're afraid, Mary, if you don't go back on . . . what will you do? Go crazy."

"I'm there already. Besides, nothing would come out. I actually tried, yesterday, in church. I could scarcely breathe, let alone sing."

"She'll never sing again," the boy repeated. "I know."

"What do you know, kid?" said Harry Dresser.

"He knows nothing," Mary said; "say good night, there's a good boy, and run along."

"Of course your mother will sing again," said Dresser, motioning Mary to be quiet. "Your mother is Mary Gay."

"She knows." The boy looked at his mother, who could read his mind. "She knows what I am thinking. I am thinking of a story."

He was thinking of a story Mary told him many months ago, to pacify him when she announced she was going to Paris to see her teacher and might indeed miss his seventh birthday, but even if it meant missing that all-important occasion it was necessary for her to make her peace with the old lady before she died. It was a story the boy understood, like a fairy tale, a story of blame and pride and guilt and forgiveness: the queer little girl who blamed herself and her love of singing for her father's death and swore never to sing again; the old teacher in the studio with the golden piano, half witch, half fairy godmother, who cleverly tricked the girl at the keyboard to cast off the spell she had put on herself; the magic first lessons that broke the spell and the endless work, night and day, that came after, until the prince from New York stole the prize pupil out from under the singing teacher's nose. Yet the story had scared him a little, telling him things about his mother's nature that troubled him.

"I am not eleven years old," Mary said now, reading his mind as he knew she would, though that of course was precisely the problem. His mother was a child, forever eleven, who had told him once that at eleven she was as old as she would ever be—herself—formed—though that was not true of everyone at eleven, just certain special people, she had added.

And then, as if she saw she had fallen into a trap, "There is, besides, no connection," she said, her eyes blazing with anger, blazing as they had not when she heard of the understudy delightful enough to become Miss Gay's replacement.

Now the boy felt hot under her gaze; somehow in front of these men he had given away a secret, something private between them. He knew what no one else knew, because he had overheard a quarrel, that once again guilt and pride and penance were in-

[127]

volved; he didn't know why, or how, only that he was sure she intended to do damage to herself. But stubbornly he said, "Remember when my father made me go back in the ocean, and get back on the horse."

"Ah, don't tell me such clichés, at eight years old, and your father made me get on another airplane after we'd made an emergency landing. I know all that."

She stopped under the boy's steady gaze, a green gaze that reminded everybody too sharply of Charlie.

And then, "Do you hate Mary Gay?" the boy said though he was not sure whether this was something he had imagined or something he had actually heard her say, during the course of the past year, behind the bedroom door . . . *I hate Mary Gay . . . I hate Mary Gay!* And his father had said, *Keep it a secret, please.* "And if I did?" she said, returning her son's gaze, not as if he reminded her of Charlie Grace, but as if for an instant he *was* Charlie Grace.

"I would be very sad," the boy said, "for I love her."

And George Jacobs looked at Lion and thought, the boy is going to do it, by God he is going to do it, and would tell Lion this the day the two of them met at the matinee of *Helen.* "You did it," said George Jacobs. "What none of us had been able to accomplish you did. You are a clever little fellow, I hope not too clever for your own good."

His father was dead. His mother was singing a song about Venus. An audience was on its feet cheering. He was cheering. What could he make of it? Why was he there? "To learn something," his mother would say, "to understand what it was you made me do."

In the matinee audience, people had forgotten, those who knew or who cared, that this was a woman who less than a fortnight ago had tragically lost the husband she adored. If any of them had clapped at her first entrance out of sentiment, cheered for gallantry and tradition and a show going on, now they were applauding a performance, giving thanks for the gift, pure and simple and unmediated, they were receiving from the small vital woman onstage, with gilded curls and exaggerated eyes, who was making such ravishing sounds it didn't seem possible even Mary Gay was singing. It was an angel there singing, a siren, a creature not quite mortal, making people forget their troubles, and hers. The eyes were dead, if you looked at them closely, but the voice was alive: "A voice can rise above dead eyes," his aunt would say to Lion. "Once before in her life I saw this happen. . . . She was singing 'The Star-Spangled Banner.' . . ." "That was the day she met my father. . . ." "So it was," his mother's sister would say, "so it was."

And the boy too received the gift; he too had forgotten. For the first time since the terrible morning when his mother told him his father was dead, the child's spirits lifted. He was detached from himself, floating—floating like a soul in an angel's arms; detached even from his special relationship to the woman in the smoky spotlight, yet drowning in it. It wasn't bliss, simple bliss as it had been before, but something more adult, more perilous.

He didn't really understand what was going on in that stage boudoir—Helen of Troy's Grecian bedchamber turned into a naughty French farce boudoir—as the handsome Paris sneaked in, and the mischievous Helen pretended she was dreaming; nor later, in the second-act finale, when the waltz came up—the great sweeping waltz everybody knew, from string music in a restaurant, and hummed leaving the theater—did he know what the woman with the gilded curls, in the dress like a nightgown, was singing about: that she was commanding Paris, the vile seducer, to flee . . . though he would be back in the last act, the tricky fellow, to carry her off for good. The dialogue came and went too fast, the jokes were above the little boy's head, though the poor deceived Menelaus made him laugh, just to look at the comedian's face. Lion only knew he was being beckoned by a siren, pulled toward the woman at the center of the stage, who was his mother, who was a bewitched and magical creature named Mary Gay. He, her son, was one with all the others.

"Did you learn something that afternoon?" she would ask him later.

"I learned something," he would say, "that I couldn't use."
Except to help her.

And he would help again, two years later in the spring of
1935 when after two seasons at home his mother was being urged
by George Jacobs to go back to work, to star in a musical about
the early life of her old friend and mentor Rose Hart. Finishing
off the run of *Helen* was one thing, an act of desperation and
bravura, Mary said. Embarking on a brand-new project without
Charlie Grace was something else. Lion understood. "She is
scared," said the schoolboy, growing up fast, looking solemnly at
his godfather. "She is scared without Daddy." "Scared," said
Mary. "I am not scared of anything. I want to be home for a while
longer, that's all, and be a mother. I like being a mother, God
knows I've earned the privilege."
The boy shook his head. "What a terrible thing," he said,
his face very straight but something in his eyes dancing a bit—
"Just like Charlie," his mother would say, "I thought he'd in-
habited the cat but perhaps it's you, his own son"—"What a terrible thing," Lion said. "She is scared to go back to work and we
are scared she will not go back to work." And then, most confi-
dentially to his godfather, who had gray hair, black brows, a red
face, and a twinkle, "She has been *awful* at home not working.
She has not been our mother. If she doesn't go back to work my
sister and I are going to run away." He made a gesture: a knap-
sack over his shoulder; a cap over his eyes; a hop onto the freight
train; Jackie Cooper and Shirley Temple.
"Lion, Lion," his mother said, "Get out of here," and he
knew he would catch it later, but he also knew he had given her
a little push . . . helped. And even if he caught it from her
there would be a reward from his godfather: an afternoon at the
ball game, a lunch at his godfather's club, a new radio . . . something like that. For if one form of terribleness was exchanged for
another, still the terribleness of Mary getting ready for a show
was healthier than the terribleness of her staying idle.
It was a different sort of helping out, he would say later, than
might be expected of most boys with a widowed mother, giving

Serena one of those smiles. It wasn't going off on Saturdays and Sundays or after school, making money selling newspapers or delivering telegrams; or doing the heavy chores, too rough for a woman, that the father would have done; or preparing to quit school at fourteen to go out and make his way in the world. It was simply from time to time handling her. That was all. Making her laugh, or making her furious. Keeping things cool for her or making them a little hot for her. Sitting on April, who wasn't so tactful, wasn't so easy in the role of handling the unusual woman who was their mother. Ignoring, pacifying, humoring for the cause: to get Miss Mary Gay up on that stage and keep her up on that stage, "and in the process, incidentally," he would say, "saving ourselves from a fate worse than death: the stepfather."

For as Mary always said, from the day she put off her mourning and went back to work, there was no time for love, no time for men, even if she'd found a man to compare to Charlie Grace. "You are the man in my life," she said to her clever son. But Serena, as always, with that faintly superior arched brow and that little secret smile, would tell him he was foolish. "A stepfather would have been the best thing in the world for you," she said. "And the only thing that saved you from a fate worse than death, sweetheart, in my opinion, was a war, a very big war, an extremely wasteful way to save a young man's soul."

"A war and you," said the little boy grown-up, who was only a little boy, after all, when the crack went through his life, leaving his father and his childhood on the far side.

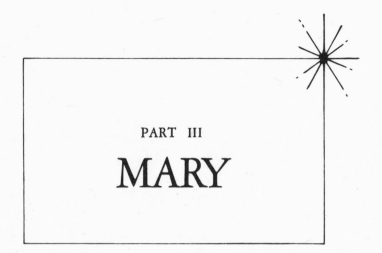

PART III

MARY

CHAPTER 9

1975

Although the thief had her undivided and hypnotized attention, Mary knew the moment Lion had come into the house. She knew and the robber did not, which gave her only a momentary advantage.

She knew, not from a slammed car door out in the street, nor from any clear sound within the house itself, such as a bell or a door closing or ordinary footsteps that might have alerted the intruder. She knew with a woman's ear, the ears of a wife and mother and mistress of an establishment. She recognized the change in tone of her house when someone was coming quietly up the stairs, late at night or too early in the morning, trying to escape notice.

She hoped she was wrong, but she knew. No one else except herself and Ninon had a key. It had to be Lion, the idiot, tiptoeing up the stairs as he had done so often in his teens, over a Christmas or spring holiday; stealing up to surprise her on her birthday. Why, he could frighten an old lady to death, doing that, especially an old lady with a skittish heart, she thought sharply, annoyance for a second causing her to forget her predicament, that she was bound in a chair and a thief who already had half a million dollars' worth of jewels in his pocket was now trying to take her necklace.

Lion! Come after all to escort her to the party as she'd originally expected and wanted him to. But that was a day ago, when she'd expressed displeasure at the news that, rather than fetching her in person, he was sending a car; that he couldn't be spared at home just before the party. She had been disappointed a day ago and scornful of the pure Serena, such a perfect wife and hostess, yet so nervous before a party she couldn't release her husband for the twenty minutes or so it would take him to fetch his mother on the night of her seventy-fifth birthday. But this morning, when mother and son had talked, she'd been pleasant as could be.

Oh, Lion, you idiot, she thought, really frightened, go away, vanish: this is my battle. You'll only get hurt or get us both killed.

"Take your hands off me," she had said only a moment ago to the robber, and twisted and turned. "Take the rest and go. You have the most valuable. This is not so valuable, you fool, though valuable to me. And too easy to trace. It is an object of sentiment. It was given to me by my husband when our son was born."

"Really, Miss Gay," said the robber, "really," beginning to laugh, as if he knew there was a flaw in the sentiment, a trick, like the ruby's star. "No kidding." She had struggled against his touch a moment ago: he had hurt her and said, "If you don't keep still, I'll choke you."

But now she shrugged and became quiet, realizing he could work away as long as he pleased but he'd never get that clasp undone; and that whatever happened she must not protest too loudly, for then the boy would surely come in, if indeed that was him out there; otherwise he might know enough to wait: might guess that waiting was the best chance.

And in the quiet she remembered how she had gasped once before in her life when the man who had given her the jewel in the first place had pulled it tight against her neck instead of undoing the clasp as she had asked him to do and started in on her again, saying, "I could choke you, Mary, for lies, so many lies . . . lies . . . lies."

How many times had he been at her, in those six weeks before the accident, that terrible Charlie she didn't recognize, who wouldn't listen, wouldn't give her a chance, wouldn't believe her even when she was telling the truth. So many times she'd lost count, since the night of the trinkets and Monsieur le Duc; over and over the same song: *Daddy's little trinkets, eh? . . . dead was he, the soldier boy who raped you, or alive and well and singing in Paris? . . . "All Paris is in love with your wife!" . . . "Ah yes, Monsieur le Duc, all New York is in love with my wife!" . . . "But your wife while in Paris was always at the opera house, hardly ever available, one hardly saw her! Your wife, I think, fell in love with a certain tenor, my wife also is crazy about that fellow, he has all the women eating out of his hand, as you say" . . . It is a joke, Mr. Grace, the duke tells me, it is a joke. And what about all those other handsome little fellows you swear have meant no more to you than upper servants . . . Mr. Hugh Carlton . . . Mr. Lanny Roberts . . . and Monsieur Paul Malette, our delightful Paris . . . ?*

And then in an access of rage she had broken the clasp and, with trembling fingers, made that gesture she had regretted for the rest of her life more devastating than any in a long life of inadvertently loaded gestures—had broken the clasp and taken the great crimson stone swaying from its ladder of diamonds, the object she prized more than any since a cat's-eye ring long ago— yes, more than that other ring with the blue-black scarab—and flung it at the man she loved the most—yes, more than the man alive and well and singing like a god in Paris—crying, "I never liked it in the first place, your precious ruby, I don't want it anymore. Take it. Take it and be damned. I have never been unfaithful to you. Never." And although no one who had heard could have doubted what she said, her husband wasn't listening, was staring at the stone lying at his feet; was picking it up.

And thus in that single violent motion she had sealed the

fate of Charlie Grace, or so she would always believe. That was what she had done, somehow invoked the ruby's curse, and she had known this the minute she saw his face, even paler and more furious than it had been six weeks earlier. He had turned and left the room, the necklace in his hand. She had known it then, and not when the policeman in uniform had held the jewel in his meaty fist, saying, "It was on the seat beside him in the car. We figured it was valuable, you should have it." And she had cried out again, only this time it was a soundless cry, the mouth open and no sound coming out.

The gunman was cursing now; hurting her again, though she was motionless.

"You'll never get it," the lady said to the thief. "There's something wrong with the clasp. I have the devil's own time undoing it myself. Once I had to call the jeweler, get him out of bed to come and release me." She spoke firmly, with confidence, in a way that would be a signal through the door: I'm all right. I'm handling this. Stay where you are. For there was no mistake. Someone was on the landing. She could feel the imperceptible movement, the creak of the place that always betrayed the creeper no matter how silently he or she crept, whether it was a husband, a son, or a daughter, or a woman friend staying the night with her, up to no good . . . or a man who was her lover who was no good.

"Then you open it," said the thief, with a swift gesture untying her hands. "Try hard, old lady, because if I don't get it, I expect I'll kill you. Out of pique, you know. I figure you have about three minutes, Miss Gay," said the thief who no longer looked like the local florist's assistant, or a tenor she'd once known costumed to play Rodolfo, but like the criminal he certainly was.

CHAPTER 10

1935

I dreamt that I dwelt in marble halls, with vassals and serfs at my side . . . sang Charlie Grace's Mary Gay in a strawberry-blond wig and a jet-trimmed lavender gown, and the opening-night audience sent out beams of love, she could feel them, long before she heard the cheers, the roar of approval, the hard rain of applause. High and free the angel voice soared and then sank, warm and velvety along the swooping three-quarter lines of Rose Hart's theme song. "The loveliest lady of them all," one of the critics would begin his mash note to Miss Mary Gay, "with the loveliest voice. . . ." Lady Mary, back in town, playing to an audience of a thousand and within that thousand an audience of just three: two children in a stage box and a man from abroad, a tenor on tour, in New York for a concert, seated in the rear of the orchestra, who might or might not appreciate the delicate irony of that particular song.

I had riches too great to count . . . could boast of a high ancestral name . . . but I also dreamt, which pleased me most,

that you lov'd me still the same . . . sang Lady Mary in Act I,
Scene 4, of *Rose*, warmed up, smiling, enjoying herself hugely,
singing better than she had out of town . . . better, could it be,
for that man in the rear of the orchestra? Surely not!˙And yet
something was in the air that night, an excitement, a building up
to the cheers, the huzzas. Something in her reaching them. And
once again she knew the thrill of holding the crowd, and the
golden moment, in her hands, the point of contact that at the song's
end would explode like love.

 . . . *That you lov'd me, you loved me still the same.*

 Because the voice was there, unblemished, faithful instrument. She could sing—sing rings around anyone on Broadway.
Angry, broken-hearted, a devil loose inside . . . it didn't matter.
The voice came out honey and roses. And the face was there, the
sweetheart face and the incandescent smile, the package of charm
that had once come from the heart and now came from the brain.

 And those children were there in the stage box with their
aunt and uncle and grandmother, golden-haired April in rose
velvet and lace, not yet eight but poised as a twelve-year-old, and
clever Lion, out of velvet, wearing a smart blue Eton suit, a ten-
year-old princeling who threw a rose unprompted, when his
mother took her curtain call, a perfect red rose bought with his
own allowance. "No more wriggling from Miss April," Belle
would say later. "Miss April was transfixed as her brother, though
for different reasons, I suspect; he's in love with Miss Mary Gay;
she's down there on that stage."

 What did it matter, Mary thought, hugging the children
afterward in her dressing room, letting them in before the mob,
if she was difficult sometimes, lost her temper and burst into tears,
so the boy looked furious and sulked and the little girl stamped
her feet and had her own fit of tears. What did it matter if Mary
hid from them for days on end, turning them over to the nurse
and the servants and scarcely speaking, when they could have tonight, share tonight, and in the wake of tonight's triumph, a whole
series of good days, good times, to make up for the bad days, the
days when she was so tense and unapproachable. They under-

stood. They were theater children, after all—on both sides—
Graces, Geylins . . . Gays. Those shining faces, those looks, the
message of those eyes—you were wonderful—you are wonderful
—that was what made life worth living, though Lion seemed embarrassed when she called him her Rose Cavalier and she understood he was growing up.

And April. What about April? Who unnoticed in the confusion slipped behind the screen where a moment earlier Mary
had changed out of her costume into the hand-painted silk
peignoir she wore to receive visitors. And then, just as Mary exclaimed, "Where's that April?," the child emerged in the plumed
hat of the last scene, striking an attitude with the jeweled cane,
not singing the reprise of "Marble Halls" (already at seven
people joked about her inability to carry a tune), but in high
melodious speech perfectly imitating the last spoken lines of the
play, her mother's voice delivering the envoi: "Thank you, thank
you, dear friends," the little girl cried, "God bless you, may the
night be yours!" in so utterly bewitching and accurate a manner
that Aunt Belle and Uncle Ralph and Grandmother roared.
"Well, Mary, who knows," said Belle, recalling a certain birthday
dinner long ago. "This child, I prophesy, will scale the heights."
"Over my dead body," said Mary in a low firm voice that could
reach and convince the heavens, though she smiled and applauded
and removed the things gently from the little girl, saying, "Minx,
what a minx to make fun of your mother."

This is me, thought Mary, telling the children good night,
sending them home with her mother who had come to New York
for the opening, as she had come to every opening, but was not
a burden; "rather the contrary," her daughter said of the stalwart
Honora. "Mother is one of those people who improves with age."
And then, finally, Mary let in the mob, the first-nighters, who
told her before she read the first review that she had a hit on her
hands, that she was wonderful, just as the children and her mother
and sister and brother-in-law had told her, though the first review
that began so well ended in annoying her, she couldn't have said
quite why, except it made her sound, well, "like an institution,"
she would say a few afternoons later to the first-nighter who had

not come backstage, the man at the rear of the orchestra. "At thirty-five do I want to be 'magic for all ages'? This year's 'birthday party queen'? Perdurable! Is that what I've become? Well, well." The man had also ended in annoying her. He had said she was lovely—so lovely she had brought tears to his eyes—but those were the only tears he was going to shed from now on: no more for what might have been, such as he had shed after seeing the movie of *American Beauty*. "That movie," she said, "don't speak of that movie. You should have seen the show. I thought . . . somehow . . ."

"I wish I had. That husband of yours," said her friend from the past, "he knew what he was doing when he stole you away from Pauline; the Grace Theater is where you belong; Mary Gay *is* you. I didn't know that before."

And the line would form at the box office; and those Saturday and holiday matinees pull in a new generation of fans, little girls in party dresses who would remember her after the war; schoolboys in their first long pants who would make Mary Gay, during the war, a love object, an institution of a different sort. And in the pages of a highbrow magazine would appear an appreciation, midstream, by a writer who amused himself from time to time by elevating a popular entertainer to the rank of "artist" —a serious attempt to define what nobody had ever quite defined, the peculiar quality of Mary Gay's voice and personality that made her one of the originals, a star who stood alone. "Our last golden girl," the writer called her: the last of the old-time voices, of the Broadway prima donnas who had stepped into the new times. The fair one, the clear one, the angelic one who could do anything with that haunting silvery voice of hers except sing dirty, sing low and mean, which, the author seemed to imply in his lordly way, was what really great art was all about, the mean, the low, the dirty.

At thirty-five, without Charlie but cloaked in his aura, trailing the reputation they had made together in the twenties, his memory part of her picture, Mary had survived, and even increased that reputation Charles Grace had so expertly won for her.

As for the man in the background, the old friend who had survived with her, his luck had taken as good a turn as hers. The same month, December 1935, that Mary Gay came back to town in *Rose,* Gianni Amara made his New York concert debut at Town Hall in a beautiful and classy program that drew a small house but caused the music critic of the *Times* to wonder why such a splendid artist had been overlooked by the Met and prompted a second sold-out booking farther uptown. That was how, finally, and more or less appropriately, he had come back into her life, the old lover, the idée fixe, the man who had done her wrong yet always shadowed her wonderful marriage. Mr. Giancarlo Amara, not seen in eighteen years face to face, only onstage through opera glasses; Gianni Amara, last heard from sixteen summers ago when he tried, too late, to win her back by mail and his answer, finally, had been a few curt words and a newspaper notice of her betrothal.

"Marvelous," she had said when he called. "Come to the opening and come by for a drink on Sunday. I have to go to a boring party that night, but come around six and we can talk."

2

How nervous, how stupidly excited Mary was when she heard the doorbell that evening and the sound of Ninon's voice telling the visitor to go upstairs to the drawing room, Madame was expecting him. What was she up to, she wondered, all of a sudden, not to have said, it's too late, it's all too long ago. Well, at least she wasn't seated at the piano, but standing in front of the fireplace mirror, her evening bag on the mantel, fussing with her hair, which did not please her, wondering why, for that matter, she was going to so much trouble for a Sunday night gala, a tribute to a great lady of the theater who was no friend of hers, rather the contrary. Why she hadn't refused the benefit as well?

But how foolish the trembling, the anticipation, the dramatics; what a storm over nothing. Why, he was just an agreeable middle-aged man who entered the living room quickly, excited as a boy to see her, this suave, portly, dark-browed cleanshaven fellow with the receding hairline and the well-cut dark suit that camouflaged his girth. The swaggering fellow she had watched with such fascination, night after night at the opera in Paris, spring of 1932, and almost fallen back in love with, had been a humbug: a fake, that youthful stage Amara, wigged and mustached and costumed to play Rodolfo and Don José, Pinkerton and Turiddu and the gallant Cavaradossi. The real-life Amara of the middle thirties, in his own early forties, looked like a prosperous businessman or civil servant, a *petit bourgeois père de famille.* And yet, standing in the doorway of her drawing room, staring at her posed by the mantel, he did not seem to realize he was not the old Gianni, the wicked heartbreaker of 1917; for he had the same sort of crooked disbelieving smile on his face as the day he first heard her sing, or the day he kissed her. But hadn't he seen her just a few nights ago onstage? What a phony, she thought.

To see her onstage had been less startling, he would say later. Onstage she had been a performer, timeless, apart; onstage she had been Mary Gay as Rose Hart, an uncanny impersonation, a brilliant double exposure. To see her thus at home was the real shock, the double exposure that hurt: Mary Geylin as Mrs. Grace, the beautiful widow and society matron, the heroic mother of two. Yet her face matched the voice now—the old voice of Mary Geylin, the voice of Mimi—was haunted and heart-shaped, with a dark aspect to it spilled over from the dark eyes, though the hair was very bright. And the body sheathed in a clinging evening dress of silver cloth was a sultry woman's body, more of a woman's body, even, than it had been onstage, in hourglass gowns or spangled corsets and flesh-colored tights. As for the necklace, the famous ruby, that most certainly was a woman's jewel . . . a very rich woman's jewel. But what the man could see, still, around that soft white neck was a string of tiny seed pearls, and "Oh, listen," he said from the doorway, "you don't fool me. I know it's you, Mary. I'm in the right house."

And to her utter astonishment, as his hands clasped hers and the warm brown eyes, never quite forgotten, scrutinized her face, she knew it was him, though she said, "I don't know, I just don't know what to think."

Overweight, hair receded and slicked down, chin line blurred, he was not that changed when he smiled. A charming fellow still, an emotional fellow—could she have imagined wetness in those warm brown eyes, the easy tears of a sentimentalist? —an inquisitive fellow, looking around her drawing room in an unselfconscious manner, letting his eyes rest for a moment on the golden piano that Mary had bought from Pauline Selva's estate; an older friend, the piano, even than she. Then it was back to staring at his long-lost love, no longer the young girl, the child he had seduced. Relieved, that's what his look told her, he was so relieved and delighted with what he saw—and what he had heard onstage—and clearly oblivious to the mixed emotions he himself was stirring in the woman before him; for how could Gianni Amara disappoint anyone! Once in his presence, how could anyone fail to be charmed!

Meantime, Mary was trying to understand how it was possible that Charlie Grace should be dead while this fellow, who was meant to be dead in 1918, was still alive—very much alive— and in her house.

Now he was telling Ninon yes, he would like a drink, a whiskey and soda, bestowing on Ninon the friendliest look as if he knew Ninon would be on his side, instantly in his corner; and Mary was saying she would also have a drink, one for the road, something with lemon and gin, though already she was beginning to wonder if there was going to be any road that night, outside the confines of her own house. It was so quiet and inviting at home, this frosty Sunday evening, with everyone gone to Long Island to get the country house ready for Christmas, the children, her mother, Nanny, and all the servants, except for Ninon and the woman who came weekdays to help with the cleaning. And her visitor was standing in the bow of the piano—the reference too obvious surely, too tasteless—saying a pity she had to rush off to this fancy party because they could have had a good reunion, he and she, at the piano, looking at her now as if something still existed between them—she being she and he being he—certain old ties, never broken; as if, after five minutes in her company, he was remembering, eyes brightening at the memory, *everything*; as if, dear God, there was something romantic about this meeting. Well, he could stand there, striking a handsome pose as if about to burst into "Celeste Aida," though fat and middle-aged, but she would sit on the sofa that faced the piano because to her fury her knees were shaking, and how, with shaking knees, could she convincingly convey to him the information that what was romantic to her at this moment—and the only romantic possibility —was the new show at the Grace that Mr. Amara was now paying her such pretty compliments for; was having an audience on its feet cheering for Mary Gay, for the widow Grace and the man who made her a star and then deserted her, not for eighteen years, but forever.

But what was he saying now, the annoying fellow, the revenant, now that Ninon had come with the drinks and gone out again, and he had taken a seat on the sofa, not right beside her, but too close for her not to feel a flicker, a definite registering of his male presence.

"Here I am telling you what I thought of you, my dear," he was saying, "while you . . . *you!* Seven times in the opera house, or was it eight," he was saying, "and never once came back to say hello to an old friend. Did you think you were invisible?"

"Yes," she said sharply, too surprised and annoyed to answer cleverly. "I suppose Pauline told you. What a busybody. Dying, less than three months to live, but up to her old tricks."

"Were you that disappointed?"

"Not in the least. I was . . . enchanted."

"Go hear him sing at least," the wasted old woman in the red wig had said to the visitor from New York who had once been her prize pupil. "He is marvelous, our little tenor, everything he promised, a true artist, but you are a great star. He can't touch you."

"So you have forgiven me," said Mary to Pauline Selva.

"What has the teacher of Mary Gay to forgive? Who knows if Mary Geylin would have been such a star. The whole world loves the voice of Mary Gay. Even I love the voice of Mary Gay. And the whole world knows once again the name of Pauline Selva, thanks to Mary Gay. It was not necessary, my dear, to thank me in quite so many interviews. I knew how you felt."

"Dear friend, dear friend . . ."

"No tears now, Mary. I've had a splendid life." And then the old woman had closed in: "It was not necessary, even, to come. But since you have come to Paris, after all this time, go hear him, Mary. Accept the fact that you did not make the trip only for me."

That had been romantic indeed, watching Gianni Amara night after night, thinking herself anonymous, Madame X in beige, in a stall seat, dead center, opera glasses trained on the handsome tenor who didn't know she was there, or so she imagined, trained on the sopranos he sang with who might have been her, watching him, drinking him in, surfeiting herself on him and her own lost hopes so that never again would he come into her dreams or poison her thoughts . . . betraying her husband as truly as if she had crept back into the golden-voiced cad's rumpled bed. More truly, because as she listened and watched she had regretted, bitterly regretted, everything the second man, her second lover, her husband, father of her children, had given her, beautiful ungrateful witch that she was. Witch or the fisherman's wife, and if it had not all been taken from her a year later it had in any case been turned from gold to dross.

"Tell me what you thought of the *Bohème*," asked Gianni Amara, bringing her back to her living room, the present. "Our piece, yours and mine?" Still he stared at her in that exasperating manner as if in another moment all would be forgiven and they would fall into each other's arms.

"I thought it good. And the *Tosca*. And the *Carmen*. He's forty years old, I thought, and sings like a youth, with a boy's open throat. Still hitting those high notes like a ball player. But most of all I enjoyed your Pinkerton, the cad in uniform."

"*Vieni, vieni,*" he'd sung in the love duet to the helpless pinioned Butterfly with the chalk-white face and dark staring eyes made up to look slanted, and the woman in disguise, in the single stall seat, had remembered too sharply little Mary Geylin, dark-eyed, helpless, pinned in the embrace of a dark-haired soldier boy whispering *Come, love, come*, and wondered how it would have been if those other letters, those last letters, the ones he had sent after the war, that were not cagey, that were the outpourings of a trapped and remorseful young man, painfully candid, had come before she had decided to marry Charlie Grace. Then she'd switched the opera glasses around to the wrong end, to infinitely distance the stage, as well as the past, and resolved not to see him. Lost her nerve or came to her senses, what did it matter. If in fact she had gone backstage, and seen this pleasant middle-aged man staring at her so peculiarly now, everything might have been different. The *funniest thing happened, I can tell you now*, she might have said to Charlie Grace instead of shrieking, *Nothing, you have found out nothing*, and weeping and carrying on because in her heart she was guilty.

"You make a wonderful cad," said Mary in her silver dress to the visitor, giving a faint smile, too curious now not to ask whether during the course of the year 1922, sometime during the run of *American Beauty*, he had not perchance come to the Grace Theater, though never backstage to see an old friend.

"Me? Not come backstage, or let you know I was there?" That was not his way, he could assure her, not his way at all.

"Those flowers on my birthday," she continued with the same faint smile, "all these years." But he didn't seem to know what she was talking about.

And then, cutting through the banter, closing the distance between them, he posed the question, the only one that mattered: "Why couldn't you forgive me?"

It seemed an impossible question, best answered by silence. He had after all stayed married to Josie the cow and fathered two more children by her that were surely not little mistakes he had to give a name to. Besides, he guessed the answer without hearing it, that she had long since forgiven him, that being Mary Geylin she had never deep down blamed him, only herself. She started to rise, but he took her hand now and pulled her back.

"Oh, Mary, Mary, sit down. It is you, isn't it," smiling at her, shaking his head. "Why didn't I tell you the truth right off, is that it? I tried to tell you. It was like trying to tell something to Niagara Falls, to tell something to that girl. I gave up. I thought. Who knows what I thought, certainly not that I was going to be reported dead," he said wryly. And then: "I loved that girl a lot. I've always wanted to tell her that."

"I loved that young man a lot. I guess I did tell him that but he didn't believe me. He just thought it was Niagara Falls." Staring at him now, hands on her lap, thinking this was the moment, right now, to put down her drink, stand up, gather her things, and say in the friendliest voice imaginable, "Well, it's been nice, old friend, really nice to see you." Instead, not moving, in a low voice full of pain and anger, "The trouble was, before you were such a son of a bitch," she said, "you were very kind. You helped me. You held out a hand. But then you had to pull me to you . . . give me the Amara whirl . . . and make your getaway . . . *a real son of a bitch*."

And that was the moment he could have stood up, because nobody called Gianni Amara a son of a bitch, not even a woman he had once been in love with, and thanked her for the drink and taken his leave. But instead he laughed: laughed right in her face. The pleasantly sentimental middle-aged man had vanished and in his place was the young Gianni Amara, at once furious and amused. "You always did have a sense of humor, Mary," he said. "If it hadn't been me, it would have been some other fellow that summer or for certain the next winter. I've never known a girl who wanted it so badly or enjoyed it so much when she got it."

And instead of slapping his face, she said softly, eyes holding his, "No. No other fellow. Only you."

For a moment they sat there silently, staring, reading each other's thoughts and feelings, considering what might have been. Then she went into his arms and that was that. Eighteen years it was since last she'd felt those arms around her, but nothing much had changed. Mysteriously, inexplicably, she wanted him, only

[149]

him, no other fellow, just this one who made her body catch fire instantly, simply by putting his mouth on hers, as if she were seventeen, without preliminaries.

"But what about your party?" he asked.

"I was going to behave very badly at that party. This is a better way to misbehave."

There was one moment when she hesitated. Standing in front of her dressing table, she had let him help her undress, unbutton the buttons, unhook the hooks; she had watched in the mirror the silver dress fall and the lace brassiere; watched as his hands moved over her breasts that were no longer the ripe young breasts of Mary Geylin, but it didn't seem to matter to him that the breasts of Mary Grace were perhaps past their prime, no more than his waistline mattered to her. Those were their bodies now. So. If anything, the drive toward each other was even more implacable, more compelling, than at seventeen and twenty-five. Only when it came to the necklace, something in Mary resisted. "No," she said, bringing her own fingers to the clasp as he tried to unfasten it, distressed all of a sudden at the sight of the bed, one side turned down for the night, the large lonely widow's bed. "What *am* I doing?" she said, unfastening the necklace, holding it in her hand for a moment, staring at the ruby.

"Exactly what you want," said the tenor, "as you have always done," and taking the necklace out of her hand, putting it gently down on her dressing table, he tightened his hold on her.

"So this is what you . . . call . . . misbehaving," the man said presently in the darkness.

"No . . . it's what . . . you . . . call . . ." and the woman laughed and spoke a word she had never spoken before, though she had known the word since the summer of 1917 when he had taught it to her. But never had she herself used such a word before, or allowed a man, since this one, to use it in her bed, not until tonight when she said it again and again, liking the feel of it, the rhythm of it, and the way hearing it on her lips shocked the man who had taught it to her in the first place; shocked him, then roused him and brought him toward her even more fiercely.

"And what do you call this?" he said afterward, when she had turned on the bedside lamp and they were looking at each other and touching each other's faces. He was ready to call it love, he said, true love, right then and there. But she only continued to stare and smile and touch his face. Then she asked him to go downstairs and get wine and something to eat from the icebox, anything he found would be fine, and to bring a tray back upstairs, for she was famished, yet didn't dare to move beyond the confines of the bedroom, out onto the landing, downstairs, through her house. And that perhaps was her way of calling it love, to let him bring them sustenance—light her forbidden cigarette—fondle her and catch his hands in her disordered hair, saying, "Beautiful, beautiful, such beautiful hair"—and to keep him with her for the night instead of sending him away to his hotel as discretion and caution might have dictated.

Nor in the morning, when she found him sleeping there beside her in Charlie's place, did she wake him and tell him to get out. When he stirred, opened an eye, grinned at her, and said, "If your family and public could see you now, Miss Gay," she kissed him and pulled him once more toward her.

And when, a few days later, he sailed for home, she wept, afraid she would never see him again, that the promises of Gianni Amara to return meant nothing.

On the other hand, when he did return to New York in the spring of 1936, exactly as promised, and told her he had asked his wife for a divorce so they could be married, she wasn't sure at all. Even before the children came home that Sunday afternoon in May and the bad week began, Mary wasn't sure, didn't want to talk, not yet, didn't want to think about all the problems, about Lion and April, about money and two separate careers, about Paris and New York, and how it all might be worked out for a lifetime, not just a weekend, this precious weekend when once again she had arranged for an empty house, turned the Grace house into a secret hideaway for lovers.

But Sunday afternoon in the garden they were beginning to talk, just a little, over a late lunch. It was a good garden to talk in, sheltered, secluded, cut off from traffic and street noises, with high walls and trees, tall trees that caught the afternoon sun, and a magnolia and a dogwood that dropped curling white petals; and under the trees grew ivy, and along the far wall, in a place that caught the most sun, flowers bloomed: tulips, daffodils, iris. In this peaceful springtime garden, the man said, lingering over coffee, there was no sense of New York. Even the coffee tasted of Paris. Living in New York might not be so bad after all. He had never wanted to come back to the States. Only a serious offer from the Metropolitan might have tempted him, but the Metropolitan had never made what his agent considered a serious offer. Now things were different. His concert tour had been a success. Another was planned for next autumn. Half the year in Paris . . . half the year in New York. There were problems, of course. But love would find a way. Would it not? No? Yes? He took her fingers, one by one; looked at her quizzically, a man in love trying to act suave.

And then, unexpectedly early, she heard the doorbell, the commotion in the front hall, the sound of the children's voices. "We'll talk at dinner," she said hurriedly, in a way that told him she wanted him to leave, that she wasn't ready yet to mix her two lives. "I wonder why they are home so early."

To her surprise it wasn't April who flung open the french doors and bounded into the garden, announcing her return, curious to see who the guest was, but Lion. Lion who shook hands with the stranger, and stared, posing a question with his eyes: Who is this? The young master of the house registering a male presence, though men came and went in his mother's house as casually as women—coaches, teachers, professional friends, colleagues, journalists, or the pleasant aristocratic gentlemen who escorted Mary Gay to parties, the ones the children called "the gray suitors" and ignored. How did the boy sense instantly this man was different—

or did he sense his difference? Or was it simply her own guilt, Mary wondered, to see meaning in that extra little stare, not quite friendly, and in the way Lion cut across the visitor who had asked the boy a polite question about his weekend, to tell his mother something important: that April had not been feeling well, not since yesterday morning, and had a temperature, and Aunt Belle thought they should get a doctor. And the fact that her son had neglected to kiss her: that registered also.

That was the start of the bad week, the message called out across a stranger in the garden; and Lion's reaction to the stranger would be forgotten until long after the bad week was over, when Mary would remember an interchange after the visitor had left.

"Who was that man?" Lion asked, something about this tone of voice causing Mary to stiffen.

"His name is Gianni Amara."

"Who is he?"

"The opera singer. From Paris. An old acquaintance of mine. He is on his way to some singing engagements in the Middle West. I knew him when I was a girl. Why?"

"I just wondered. I never heard of him. Or did I?" He had a look: something was troubling him. And then, "Was he bothering you?" Lion asked.

"Bothering me? What do you mean?"

The boy shrugged. "I just thought. You know. He might be somebody not so nice who was bothering you."

"Why would you think that?"

Another shrug. "Because you looked upset."

"Oh, stop studying me," Mary said, lashing out at her son as she rarely did, feeling cold, not quite understanding why the boy was making her feel that cold. But then she didn't really understand why, when she telephoned Gianni Amara to tell him she couldn't meet him for dinner after all, that the little girl was very sick and she was waiting for the doctor, why when her lover suggested he return to her house to keep her company, she lashed out at him as well. "I hate company when I'm worried," she said. He hoped she would be less worried in a few weeks when he returned to New York. It was hard when you were worried

about one of the children to think about your own life. "Hold the thought for the little girl," was all she said as she hung up.

Please, Mary prayed, passing the nurse in starched white on the stairs, the young one with a cap who wasn't Nanny, the special nurse the doctor had ordered, *please let it be all right.*

Please don't do this to me again, she prayed, holding April's hot hand, listening to her heavy breathing, feeling her shiver, *please.*

Please, she prayed in the too bright hospital waiting room, smoking one cigarette after another, *make her get well, if she gets well, I promise . . . I swear. . . . Please.*

Fight, April, fight, she cried, soundlessly, in the darkness of her own bedroom, after the doctor had ordered her home, knowing that this was the crisis, that crisis she remembered from long ago, when she had prayed and cried soundlessly, a little girl just a bit older than April, and nobody had heard her cries and prayers, but this time, somebody heard, somebody acted, and at six in the morning the doctor called with good news, such good news. And she understood quite clearly what she had promised, what she had sworn.

And all the while, onstage, throughout that week, every night but Sunday, and Wednesday and Saturday afternoons, in a strawberry-blond wig and a big plumed hat, striking an attitude with a jeweled cane, Mary had sung a love song to her audience, thinking of no man, only of her little girl, wondering how this terrible wrenching feeling had come upon her, this mother love that tore you apart—sneaked up on you year after year till it tore you apart.

"It's been the most terrible two weeks, the worst of my life, barring two or three," Mary said to her lover across a restaurant table, playing with her food, the too rich cheese and pasta supper dish she had thought she had an appetite for.

"I understand," said Gianni Amara, who was having no trouble finishing his plate and was now helping with hers. "It wipes out everything when one of the children is sick. But she's fine now, you've had a happy ending, so you can stop thinking about that and . . . Mary? Look at me, Mary! Think about something else now." The black eyebrows were raised, posing a question; the brown eyes were serious for once, without merriment.

"I have thought, thought a lot. Thinking makes a person sensible."

"Yes?" Misunderstanding deliberately, smiling now, hand for a moment close over hers.

"And it's not sensible, darling, it just is not sensible," motioning for the waiter to clear her plate, saying it was delicious, perfectly cooked, only she wasn't hungry, taking a sip of wine, hoping she could get the thing said right, lightly, so he wouldn't be difficult, wouldn't make her cry. "New York. Paris. Two careers, two completely separate lives. Five children."

"Children. Children go along if they have to. You'd be surprised."

"My boy will not go along easily. My little girl . . . it would be love at first sight, the minute she laid eyes on you, if I know my little girl. But Lion. He's a funny fellow. He senses things he has no business sensing, puts stories together that should be way above his head but aren't. To the boy you and I would always be messy."

"The boy? Or you, Mary?" said Amara, finished with his food now, lighting a big cigar, looking at her over the flame of the match, dropping the match on his plate. "Children forget and go on about their business. And someday they have their own grown-up lives and then they begin to understand about things like love and quarrels and death, the things that matter, that you and I sing about. I have children also. A funny fellow. A girl. And a big boy eighteen, with problems. Forget the children. Forget even my wife. It's me. Do I matter to you, and how much?"

"A lot," she said. But. Only. Only not enough to marry, was that it, he demanded, or something else? Could it be money, did she lose a lot of money if she remarried? Yes, as a matter of fact she did, she said, but that wasn't important, she could make her own money. Or could it be someone else? No one else, she said. Yes, someone else, someone sensible.

"Who? Who would be sensible, Mrs. Grace?" asked Gianni Amara when he understood. The expression on his face was an old one, from way back, the one that made her think of the tough boys on the block, of a knife being pulled.

She didn't bother to make up a story that would annoy him. "No one. I'll never marry again. I'll never let myself love again. Be with a man I like, yes, an old friend, if I please. When it can be arranged discreetly. But love . . . my love brings bad luck."

"You are a strange woman," Amara said, looking at her through puffs of smoke as Charlie Grace used to look at her sometimes—such an unexpected reversal—to see in the warm expressive brown eyes of the other that green look of skepticism, even, a little, of fear. "Too complicated for me."

"I know that," she said with a flash of old honesty. "I lost my chance of being simple when you"—giving him a bright smile —"*died.*"

"Long before that, I think. Yet we could be happy. I could make you happy in a way that husband of yours could not."

"No one is happy."

"I am happy," said the tenor, motioning for the waiter to bring the check.

Looking at him, she thought: You are. How odd. If only it was catching. "But it doesn't have to be good-bye," she said, a little frantic now. "There's no reason for it to be good-bye."

"I don't know about that, my dear. A transatlantic arrangement . . . that would not be sensible, to my mind."

And then, even more frantic, breaking her own resolution not to tell him about the bad week, to play the game well, "Listen," she said, "you don't understand. You don't understand about my luck. I was so scared. Truly scared. She could have died. Eight years old. My baby could have died. I knew she shouldn't have gone away for the weekend. She looked poorly on Friday. The nurse said something, even. I said, 'Oh, Nanny, you fuss too much. It's bad for the children to fuss over them so much!' But all I was thinking about was how I wanted to be alone with you and have the house to myself. I am bad luck, Johnny. You say 'complicated.' But I sometimes think they are one and the same. Mary Gay, the birthday party queen, as bad luck as some torch singer, some poor woman singing the blues."

And though there was ample evidence of Mary Gay's witchery in his past and might be more to come in his future, Gianni Amara laughed and kissed her, saying he would be back soon, very soon, and take his chances, however bad the luck of those who loved Lady Mary and were loved in return.

But it wasn't soon at all. The next time they saw each other was eight years later; and the place was not New York, a quiet house arranged for lovers, but Paris, a just-liberated Paris, still sick and reeling from the war. And the meeting place was a hospital where Gianni Amara lay, thin and gray, in a narrow bed and Mary Gay, in a rumpled tailored suit with a USO armband, bent down to kiss his white hair and say softly, "Really, Johnny, really, aren't you old for this? But then you always did say you wouldn't spend a war singing for generals."

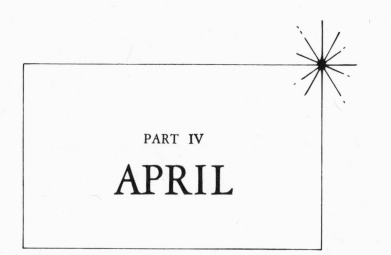

PART IV

APRIL

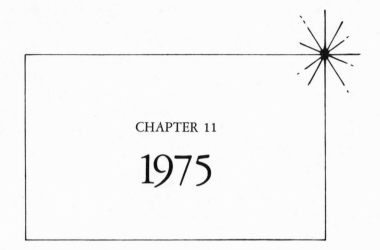

CHAPTER 11

1975

As alone in the world, that night, as she pictured Mary to be, though twenty-eight years younger and not without family part of the year, hating everyone, fighting everyone, in misery and disgrace and a state of utter indecision, April Potter sat at her bedroom dressing table trying to make up her mind: to go or not to go.

"If you could call it that," her mother would say, of the bedroom, of the dressing table, of any room or piece of furniture, for that matter, in April's apartment. But it wasn't simply a case of the pot calling the kettle black, as Aunt Isabelle would say. Mary was disorderly, to be sure, and a worse hoarder and accumulator than April. Mary would never have grand throwouts as her daughter did, hurtful throwouts in which a decade's worth of letters would go, precious mementos, photographs, postcards, and clippings, all *out*—as heedlessly tossed aside as the bits of foreign change and the broken beads and single earrings. But there was a certain arrangement to Mary's chaos. Things had a place to which, once a week or anyhow once a month, they were restored by Ninon or Mary herself. Whereas April lived in the sort of mess where nothing had its place or boundaries and everything overflowed: desk papers onto vanity, makeup onto kitchen counter; the piano top a bookcase, the bookcase a gallery, and so forth. The excuse had always been "the girls" or "that Billy" or a husband in a hurry, insufficient domestic help, or April's own preference for working at home. But even with the children gone, except on holidays, and the husband permanently departed and April for the moment unemployed, her habitation swarmed with debris in a way unknown to the lady in the great house across the park.

Still, surveying the scene, an outsider would see a remarkable similarity between the surfaces of Mary's sideboard and April's old-fashioned dresser, something she had bought at an auction of the furnishings of a fashionable hotel, at which she sat on an old piano stool getting ready . . . just in case.

"I doubt it," she'd said to Lion that morning. "And you and Serena wouldn't want me, the way I'm feeling right now." But she might, at the last minute, change her mind, for she did enjoy, like Mary, a dramatic gesture. When there was no present drama in your life sometimes you had to invent it.

There was also an eerie echo of that other bedroom, just across the park, in the way April was now holding the oblong case that held her ruby, sapphire, and diamond bracelet, flexible as a ribbon, as a tricolor band on a Fourth of July hat, such as young Mary Gay had worn in *American Beauty*; then toying with the bracelet, which had been Charlie Grace's present to his wife when she, the wished-for, prayed-for daughter, had been born one rainy April afternoon; April Grace, conceived on the Lido, born during a New York shower, on whose wall hung, framed, the original sheet music of every "April" song ever written— including "Haunted April" with her mother's face in a blue heart —all autographed by the songwriters. Of course, when Lion was born, Charlie had given Mary the ruby, a somewhat more important souvenir. But no matter. The bracelet now was April's, Mary's wedding present to her, though Mary would have gone out and bought something brand-new, even more razzle-dazzle and expensive, she loved the marriage so much, of April Grace to John Wakeman Potter. Nobody had ever been promised or given the ruby, though. Nobody even knew the disposition of the necklace in Mary's will, a closely guarded secret. April suspected her mother had left it to a museum. Serena the witch said it would be buried with her. Lion made no comment except to say that their mother, though a sentimental woman, was also practical and would do the right thing.

Like Mary, April was tied to the symbolism and sentiment of objects that defied time; and like Mary, she herself was one of those time-defying subjects, her reflection in the mirror a trick and a mockery . . . "A joke in poor taste," she said aloud, unconsciously, unwillingly aping Mary's manner of speech even, feeling her eyes sting. Damn, not when she'd done the job with the eyeliner three times before she'd got it right, clear and unsmudged, for unlike her famous mother she wasn't handy with her fingers.

A very poor joke, that she was forty-six years old, well into middle age, yet should still on certain days look like a young woman. The eyes were the key to it, nearly green, vulnerable, thickly lashed, finely drawn, and infinitely expressive. Too expressive, Wake Potter always said, too big for the small heart-shaped face, giving off too penetrating a light. Eyes that early in life had given April the illusion that like Scarlett O'Hara—like Vivien Leigh playing Scarlett O'Hara—she could charm her way in, or out, of any door, any heart, any situation she desired. Only she was a blonde—a green-eyed blonde, once very fair, now tawny, never brassy. Class. A classy blonde, rarest American type, that sleazy flattering man—reminder of the old days—had said at lunch, and looking not a day over thirty-five, and had not understood why April had said loudly, "You think that's *good?*" For the daughter of Mary Gay and Charles Grace no longer wanted to look different on the outside from the way she felt inside; inside, recently, she had felt quite clearly and definitely the more than a quarter of a century that lay between herself now and the self that had married Wake, the self that had walked away from Max Brandel, from a whole other life. Twenty-eight years was vertiginous; what must Mary be feeling, fifty-five years away from the girl who married Charlie Grace?

And then there was the muck of in between. That, even, was twenty years away. Ten years away.

But she'd promised herself not to care, anymore, what Mary was feeling. Too much of her life already had been spent wondering and worrying about what Mary was feeling, what Mary was thinking, what Mary was thinking about her, April, every time her life took a new turn, leaped off on yet another fine fresh start, as it might be about to do now.

"April's is the kind of life," Lion once said, with that insufferable accuracy of his, "in which one thing never leads to another." Five years of modeling for a fashion magazine, one job with a photographer, one book of photography, one part in a television soap opera, one political campaign, one bit part in a movie, one scouting job for a movie producer, one chairmanship of a cultural board. April Potter, talent at large, once called pretty *and* smart *and* gifted, temporarily indisposed, still trying on different slippers to see if only one would fit and make her the true child of Mary and Charlie, the true child of 1928: worthy.

Maybe the answer would be to do what Wake Potter had recommended a long time ago, get rid of the bureau and all vanity, get rid of the piano and Charlie's scrapbooks, get rid of the bed that had once been in his bachelor apartment, get rid of the portraits and all the hauntings; but how to get rid of the rhythm of Charlie's speech, the dry wit forever caught in the memoirs of others, and the music of Mary's voice, of the fun they had and the way they loved; the tragic ending: the legend. "Your problem," said Wake Potter, the pompous pontificator—right as usual— right as Serena—"is different from Lion's; it's not that you want to be another Charlie Grace or another Mary Gay, but that you want to be, are determined to be, a story, a front-page story, a headline, no matter who gets hurt in the process."

Well, she wouldn't be a story this night, and that was that.

So April put the bracelet back in its box, sweet glittering thing, supple as chain mail, and as useless and out of date, but still fun to play with, roll up and down, as once with her Scarlett green eyes she'd thought she could play with men's hearts, but it hadn't worked out that way; not when the heart you tried to play with was the heart of Max Brandel. She was the one who'd been played with. Next she took off the dinner dress, slinky flame-colored jersey cut on the bias and low-necked, the dress meant to put Serena to shame, leaving it a puddle on the floor; and rewrapping herself in a dark blue terry-cloth robe she'd been wearing all day, she went into the kitchen, made herself a drink, and turned on the oven—"Not to put my head in, folks," she muttered to herself, "but to heat up the stew from last night's dinner."

Then in the living room, she turned on the evening news: Walter Cronkite, with whom she'd been through so much, assassinations, marches, elections, spring huggermugger, to hell and back, not to mention the moon—Walter who'd talked to her and soothed her through the worst days—Walter who should be running for mayor of New York, President of the United States, instead of the fools who were, Big Daddy Walter—she blew him a kiss, watched and listened for a while, then took up the morning paper to see what the other Big Daddy, dean of Washington correspondents, had to say for himself. Under the morning paper was yesterday's *Post,* but she hadn't faced that: not yet. "Wonderful," people had been saying on the phone all day, "it's a wonderful piece." But that was too difficult to deal with, that it was a wonderful piece; besides, Mary always did know how to give an interview.

It was toward the end of the news, in such rapid succession it seemed simultaneous, that the telephone rang, the house phone rang, and then her front doorbell. The phone was a collect call, long-distance from Mary Beth. The house phone was to tell her a lady was on the way up; at the door was the lady: Aunt Isabelle. Not seen or spoken to for longer than April cared to think about, though always remembered at Christmas. The angel of the Lord herself come to call: appointment in Samara. For if Aunt Isabelle was at her door, what on earth was going to keep April safe from the party? Good old Aunt Belle, in sables and sensible galoshes and a lace mantilla over her high blue hair, leading with the nose, looking not like an avenging angel, but the American version of every gorgeous ravaged old English actress you'd ever seen play a madwoman or grandmother. A double chin kept Aunt Isabelle from the flawless geriatric beauty of Gladys Cooper or Diana Cooper, but she was handsome, distinguished, rich-looking, a dowager of the old school as she had been a proxy mother of the old school, "more grand," Mary used to say, "than if she'd been born to a Gold Coast Mamma and Papa in a lakefront castle." And full of spirit to come here, to be standing as if she expected something wonderful to happen.

"Greetings," April said to the woman who had once been her conscience and sanity, on whom she'd turned, finally, when she couldn't stand the sound of Aunt Isabelle's voice, even if that voice happened to be speaking the truth, especially if it happened to be delivering what Aunt Isabelle called "a few home truths." "I've got Mary Beth on the phone. I'll be there in a sec."

"I'll wait." Not removing her outer clothes, Aunt Isabelle settled down in front of Walter Cronkite, who was saying good night, making a face, looking as if she'd like to spit in Walter's eye for the way he dared to speak to her. Then, picking up the remote-control box, she clicked off the set and waited.

"Mommy?"

"Hi, can I call you back," April said to the distant daughter she missed too much, yet knew was fine, doing just fine at her job in her father's city, better off there than here. "Someone's just walked in the door."

"To take you to the party? Great! That's all I wanted to know. If you were going." Mary Beth had a way of jumping to wrong conclusions that was not always an accident.

"No, dear. I'm not up to it. In this family, if you're not up to something, well, you don't do it. You should know that by now."

"Oh, Mommy, couldn't you? If you could go and turn it around?"

"I can't."

"Dad's going."

"I don't believe you."

"He is. Dad, Jenny, and the Lump are all going. It's turned into a circus. Nobody will even see you."

"This could be the night Serena loses her cool—at last. We had a good Christmas, Beth. Let's not push the luck."

"Yes, we did. I miss you, Mommy."

"I miss you." One of the things no one quite understood, given what a bad girl April was, was what nice children she had, and how those children cared about her. "But listen, sweets, Aunt Belle is here, that's who walked in the door. I'll call you back."

"Don't. I'm going out. Mommy. Take care. Mommy . . . you know what Dad would say?"

"I know: what a bunch of twerps. Me the worst."

Aunt Isabelle, whatever you might think of her, was not a twerp. And she had a way of making everything seem instantly natural. Four years since April had seen her, yet there was no awkwardness. You could love her or hate her, be bored by her or amused, or made so nervous you babbled, but the one-to-one view had the ease of total familiarity.

"Oh, April," she said now in the harsh musical voice that she had painstakingly acquired years ago when she and Uncle Ralph first moved to New York. Oh, April: three syllables that could make April freeze or feel good about herself, depending on the intonation. "Oh, *April*, I want to talk to you. . . . Oh! April! That is beautiful. . . . Oh, April *dear*, would you *mind*. . . . Oh, April, you are a fool . . . you are a wonderful girl . . . you please me, you disgust me, you bore me. Tonight, unbelievably, it was: "Oh, April, please."

"Who sent up the reserves? Lion?"

"No one. It was my idea." By now embarrassment should have overcome both of them, just thinking of the last time, yet there was no embarrassment, only the performance that was Aunt Isabelle's way of dealing with life; she and Mary, were, after all, sisters.

"No dice," said April, using an old expression of Aunt Isabelle's for: nothing doing, no way, forget it. Once Aunt Isabelle had been an electric force, the reserve and law because, when you'd been little, you'd loved and admired her and thought her the prettiest lady you'd ever seen; you'd imitated her speech and mannerisms, been fascinated by the life she and Uncle Ralph and the Dillon cousins led. The holidays and seasonal moves from town to country, country to town, dependable as the moon; the things they "always" did, as opposed to Mary, who lived a life in which there was nothing you "always" did . . . how reassuring it had been to April. And when during the war she had gone to live with Aunt Belle, so her mother could go overseas and do her bit, how she enjoyed the normality and routine and went along with it, though never quite fitting, for you couldn't ever really fit when you were Mary's kid, trailing the legend, evoking the memories. Still, it was cosy. Until . . .

Until April, and Lion to some extent, had understood how fully Aunt Isabelle had to win, not just at cards or games or in an argument, but in all ways, and that she was after all as poor a loser as Mary. Yet she had at least taught you the games. Yet: April's problem, not Belle's, not Mary's, not Wake's, not Serena's, not even Lion's much anymore. April always saw the "yet" and "on the other hand." April was not arbitrary. So even now she was going to have to see Aunt Belle's position, the simple plain gallantry of her having come, at her age, as well as the loftiness of it. Nonetheless.

"The answer is no, Aunt Belle."

"Isn't it a little childish," Belle said quite mildly. "Finally, isn't that what it comes down to. Shall I tell you something," pulling out a high trump. "Wake's going."

"Thank you for telling me what I already knew. That's his choice. I suppose he's going to protect Jenny."

Aunt Belle made another one of her faces, worse than at Walter Cronkite, but said nothing. The face strengthened April's resolve. Just one of those faces, from anyone, a single remark about the way she, April, led her life and how her children led theirs, and she'd walk out.

"Oh, April. . . ." It was the other voice now. "Your mother is unhappy and doesn't understand what went wrong."

"The years went wrong, Aunt Belle, too many years."

"Soon it will be too late. She'll be dead. This is an occasion, after all."

"What are you trying to tell me? Soon?" April felt a terrible thumping at her throat.

"I don't mean literally. I don't mean your mother is sick. As far as I know, she's healthy as she's been all her life. I mean it's soon for all of us, at our age."

"I sent flowers, Aunt Belle. I went around at Christmas. I don't see *anybody*. I don't go to *anybody's* birthday. I'm a black cloud and I'm tired of pretending, putting on an act."

"I don't see it's improved your life. Making breaks. Lashing out at everyone. Giving in to yourself. You're not free. You're still a victim. You don't look very happy."

"I'm not. But I'm alive and out of the cage. I swore something, after Wake left. I swore I would never sit captive again."

And then, "Aren't you curious?" Aunt Belle said. "You were always the most curious little girl. Just like your mother. Aren't you tired of being sick? Come on, put on that snappy dress, brush your hair, I see you set it and very pretty it is too."

"You're so practical." April took a sip of her drink and moved uneasily in the chair where she was sitting, as far as possible from Aunt Belle without being unnecessarily rude. "So regular. That's why I could take things better from you than Mother. You don't understand how queer the rest of us are."

"Practical, yes. Regular? What is regular? You think our childhood was regular? You think the distance from where your uncle Ralph and I started to where we landed is regular? The gold ring, April. Like that song your mother sang in *American Beauty*. Two gold rings in one family. And to do it together, your uncle and me, and stay together. And then have him die like that. And still marry again at seventy? *Regular?*"

"That was terrific! That was the liveliest thing that's happened in this family since Lion wrote his first book."

"There's a new life around the corner for you too, April."

It was at that moment that the phone rang again.

"You'd better go, Aunt Belle. It's almost eight. You'll be late. I have a present you can take for me. And you can tell everyone I have the flu—oh, let it ring," glaring at the telephone, white like everything else in April's living room except for the red and brown Indian rug, the new decor, her latest most unfortunate attempt at a fresh start.

"Ah, no," Aunt Isabelle said. "You must answer your phone, dear. Really you must. It could be one of the children. I'll wait."

"Yes. Yes. This is her speaking. This is me. Oh. You." She pressed the receiver close to her ear so Aunt Belle couldn't instantly identify the caller, whose voice, though not loud, was penetrating and unmistakable. He was calling, this unmistakable person said, to confirm the information that she was *not* coming to the party. Various calls had come throughout the day designed to make her change her mind. This refreshing call from her ex-husband was to make sure that she did not change her mind, for it could be, under the circumstances, awkward, and he, the caller, would of course bow out.

"Don't worry," she said, laughing. "Please don't worry about that. Dear God, what an extraordinary evening. Good to talk to you," said April, still laughing as she placed the receiver back. "A bore," she said to Aunt Belle. "Even more of a bore than your niece."

And then a change came over April that Aunt Belle would say brought her back nearly thirty years, to the days when April lived with her; when a phone call or letter or something in her school or private life would cause April to take action; to cast off adolescent lethargy or despondency, emerge from a black cloud, or brown study, or blue mood; something that would not necessarily bring peace to her guardian but that would mean the girl had decided after all to live, to give life, or someone, or something, another chance; the mournful voices on the Victrola singing of love and death would be switched off; the shower turned on; the body would move from the bed and a flicker of mischief would come into the lackluster green eyes.

So now: "Supposing," April said to Belle, "supposing not for Mother's feelings necessarily, or my pleasure, or even family solidarity, or even for you, darling, but supposing I *used* the evening?"

"Exactly," said Belle. "That's all I've been saying. All."

CHAPTER 12

1945

When Mary Gay came home from overseas in the autumn of 1945, April was at the airport to meet her, and a prettier, more touching reunion of mother and daughter was never yet witnessed by a crowd of fans or recorded by Fox Movietone News. You couldn't fake that kind of joy.

Yet riding out to the airport on a dark and rainy October morning, excused for the day from school to meet her famous parent, April Grace was nervous. She hadn't seen Mary in nearly a year. Better than two years, if you counted the entire stay with the cousins broken only by flying visits from Mary between this theater of war and that. To link the woman in the news pictures —Mary Gay in a sun helmet, flashing her notable smile from the wheel of a Jeep; Mary Gay in a sequined sheath, cradling a mike on an open stage encircled by ten thousand GIs; Mary Gay in boots and fatigues with a four-star general on an atoll—to connect such a wartime heroine, coming home from a final stint in the Pacific—with your own darling peacetime mother—there was an awesome task, part of the puzzlement and privilege of being such a daughter.

There had been letters, of course. But letters had always been a poor bridge between Mary and April, and long before wartime. Mary had a block about writing letters, Aunt Isabelle said wryly, and April was bad also, so bad about writing, though Isabelle herself for all the war years was never without her pad of tissue-thin blue airmail paper and her fountain pen, scribbling, scribbling to her loved ones overseas, with a penmanship that was art—scribbling to her sister, Mary, and her nephew, Lion, to her sons, Ralph and Kenny, to her goddaughter, Caroline James, in the Red Cross, to Geylin cousins April had never met—keeping the mail she received in return in a special trunk, Belle's magical treasure chest. And it was a fact, someone would note, that those who had corresponded during the war with Isabelle Dillon returned, each and every one of them, alive and reasonably well. "No matter, you are talkers, you and your mother," Isabelle said to April. "All eyes and hands and voices. A day's talk and the strangeness will vanish, you'll see. Besides, look at yourself in the mirror, if you're nervous. Your mother will never nag again."

Nightly lectures, however, on her weight, her skin, her posture, her fingernails, were not the daughter's worry. No one knew better than April that between sixteen and seventeen, for her, the promised miracle had occurred. Promised, that is, if you did all those *things*—wore your retainer and put Noxzema on your face, drank Ovaltine at night and Postum in the morning while giving up chocolate and avoiding Mr. Coffee Nerves—if you used Ipana toothpaste, Lavoris, and Mum and bathed with Palmolive and rinsed your hair in lemon and beer, or, if you wanted to color it, the purest mixture of peroxide and vinegar, if you ate raw beef and carrots and drank water eight times a day and stopped biting your nails, if you did all these things and many more, the miracle would happen.

And indeed because she'd worn it faithfully, the retainer was gone from her teeth; because she'd had willpower, her nails were long and polished; because she'd taken pains, her hair shone and her skin was clear as a Pond's bride. Underweight, not fat, had been the adolescent problem of April Grace, but the tonics had been drunk, the sharp edges rounded. She had bosoms now, round apples like the Flemish Madonna in the Metropolitan Museum; and carried herself proudly—Grace, April, triumph of Miss Garson's posture class. No longer was she an angular tomboy who fought against her looks, but a glistening blonde who had let those looks take over.

She had liquefied her walk and the expression in her near-green eyes, which people from a distance thought dark brown because her lashes were so sooty. The green was a surprise, the man she loved and his friends all said; so strong, that green. She even enjoyed shopping now, felt deliciously feminine in the new fall costume she was wearing that morning under a dramatic rain cape: a dark green dressmaker suit trimmed with velvet, high-heeled alligator pumps of the sort she'd sworn never to break her neck in, gold at her wrists and in her ears, a beret tilted on her bright curling hair. She'd been wearing the suit on the day the columnist spotted her with Aunt Isabelle and Lucy at the Colony restaurant and later reported that lunching with one of this year's loveliest debutantes, Miss Lucy Dillon, was a young lady slated for glamour-girl stardom the following year, Miss April Archibald Grace, daughter of, granddaughter of, etc. The next day, the Stork Club press agent had called about an eighteenth birthday party.

"Glamour girl of the year indeed!" snorted Isabelle. "Think of poor Brenda Frazier, poor Cobina Wright, poor Oona O'Neill. We have been so careful."

"I agree. Publicity should be earned," said April, daughter of, granddaughter of, in a way that caused Aunt Isabelle to give her niece one of those looks: Oh, April, what are you up to now?

Oh, Aunt Belle, who just wants a nice young man for me, wouldn't you be surprised, April thought now, sitting back in the limousine, pretending herself a young star of the theater, smoking a cigarette in the affected way of someone who has just been given permission to smoke, pretending that in the car with her was her co-star, Tony Marcus, and her director, Max Brandel, the three of them on their way to a party, wondering if her mother would be on her side, if what she was up to, which would so horrify Aunt Isabelle, would be agreeable to Mary Gay. Out the window the sky looked black and rain fell heavily against the panes, obscuring the ugliness of the drive to the airport. April tried not to think of the bouncing plane up there, or the other kinds of bad weather, the bad weather of Mary's bad days, the storm of Mary's opposition that was so much worse than the bad weather of Aunt Isabelle's bad days because it was such an unbearable contrast to Mary's good-weather days, which were magical, heavenly in a way unknown to the older sister.

Then, miraculously, the long drive was over, and the anxious waiting at the gate. The plane materialized out of the rain, landed, taxied, and came to a stop. Mary came down the ramp, instantly recognizable in slacks and a polo coat and slouch hat, waving to the crowd that had all of a sudden gathered and swelled at the sight of her, shouting back greetings to a man who called, "Hi, Mary, I saw you in Africa," and to another who called, "Hi, Mary, I saw you in Liverpool," and another, "Hi, Mary, I saw you on Guam," smiling a big red-lipped smile for the photographers, then pushing them away, saying, "Buzz off, boys, I want to see my kid," running, running toward April, dropping her pocketbook as she threw her arms around the girl and held her hard, laughing, crying, examining the wonder of her, for it had been a long ten months.

"Oh, April darling," she cried, "you've grown up! You've turned into a beauty."

"Let's have a picture of you and your beautiful daughter," a photographer shouted. Mother and daughter smiled, twin smiles, bright and full-lipped, then again, then just once more, before pushing aside the waving arms of the autograph hounds and escaping into the waiting limousine. And April basked in the glory and pride of that moment. Not jealous, as people said later she must have been, as Wake would insist she'd been all of her life and why not admit it; she was the one, after all, who had given Mary permission to go overseas in the first place. Simply happy, she was, overflowing with relief because this tired, glamorous, enchanting woman she adored, who adored her, was home for good.

For two weeks as they settled back into their house with Ninon and a new cook and butler unpacking, rearranging, putting objects back in place, clearing away the last traces of the wartime tenants, April put off telling Mary what was really on her mind, though there seemed to be nothing they couldn't say to each other. For a fortnight they talked as long-lost lovers might, incessantly, passionately, obsessively, trying to catch up on each other's lives—on April's adolescence, on Mary's war. They talked as they dressed and undressed, wandering in and out of each other's bedroom; they talked over supper trays in the library and on weekends as they ran around town with a decorator, looking at materials and carpeting and all manner of sparkling goods to give the old house a newer postwar look.

They talked of Lion; hotheaded Lion who had refused to go to college under the V-12 program, though he'd been accepted at his father's Princeton; who wanted to get into action fast, and had enlisted in the army the week he graduated from prep school. They recalled the terrible scene Mary had made at the idea that her son would be a GI, a wretched private slogging through mud, though Lion had bet her a hundred dollars (and won his bet) that he'd earn himself a commission in the field; and then the way, by pure coincidence—of course!—a few months later Mary had asked April how she would feel about her mother going overseas for the USO. And Lion had written: "How many mothers do you know who would arrange like that to follow their boy to the fighting front?"

Laughing, but with suspicious moisture in their big beautiful eyes, mother and daughter waxed sentimental over the missing man of the family, and talked of the precious Thanksgiving that Lieutenant Grace and his mother, Mary Gay, had managed to spend together in the South of France. And April said, Yes, Lion had written the drollest account of that holiday, and had Aunt Isabella told Mary yet her thought: that Lion's wartime letters were good enough to be published. To which Mary responded,

"No. What an awful idea, those letters belong to us, they are private, and please let's not distract Lion who has one thing to do when he gets home—go to college," saying this in a way that made April certain it was better to put off a little longer disclosing her own plans.

So they talked of danger and close calls: of the air raids Mary had come through in Palermo and London, of the times she had sung ten miles from the front under an umbrella of Spitfires, to muddy unshaven men just pulled out of foxholes, of flying in a formation of B-17's with a fighter escort and through storms in a Piper Cub that seemed flimsy as an orange crate, of ditching in the Azores. But equally they talked of April's emergency appendectomy; of her terrible flight through a storm with Uncle Ralph from New York to Washington; of the red-flag day when, disregarding her own safety, she had pulled her friend, Serena Watkins, out of the surf at East Hampton and mother and daughter clutched each other and said, "Stop! I don't want to hear, I couldn't have borne it, if anything ever happened."

They exchanged. They talked of heartbreak in hospitals, Mary's battlefront hospitals where she had sung bright songs of hope to men without hope, but also the home-front hospitals where April had served as a nurse's aide. They talked of where they had been the day Roosevelt died. They were friends, equals. Mary told her Eisenhower story, her Patton story, her Churchill, Nimitz, Monty, and Ernie Pyle stories, and April listened enthralled but no more so, it seemed, than Mary, who laughed so wickedly when April told her junior miss tales of Gordon the ensign who always blew into town with money, of Peter the flier, the one all the girls had crushes on, and Murray the Exeter heel, and "What about love?" asked Mary, the new Mary who was her daughter's friend. "Who'd you love, darling?" And April admitted she was not sweet seventeen, that she'd been kissed by lovely freckled Peter and had her heart bruised by witty Murray, that louse, holding back carefully the name she couldn't talk about, not yet, not till the right moment. Mary responded so cosily to all this talk of love, so unlike Aunt Isabelle and Mrs. Watkins, who pursed their lips and spoke of reputation and self-control, that April dared ask her mother about herself, for there had been rumors, items in the gossip columns.

"Such as *what?*" Mary asked, too sharply, in a way that made April wish she had kept quiet. "Who? Go on, *who?*" There was something angry in the mother's eyes, wary, ready to pounce. "*Where?*"

"In some Broadway column. No name. Just big brass. A stupid joke about big brass."

"Big brass?" Whatever it was that had caused Mary to give such an awful look, the moment had passed. "Is there a general in my life?" Mary responded, once again cosy and amused. "Or a famous correspondent? There is no one, darling, no one who can compare, you know that. No man will ever touch me, beyond a surface sort of thing. Nothing's changed that way," she said, her voice hardening. "When I see these widows of exceptional men, my age or a little older, making fools of themselves, marrying some young and pretty fellow who might have been fit to polish their husbands' shoes or trophies, it revolts me."

But it was twelve, nearly thirteen years, April thought. A dozen years and a war—wasn't that enough time to mourn, the girl wondered. Her mother had wasted the last of her young womanhood already; lost her chance for a romantic liaison, thought the daughter, looking at her middle-aged mother with the pitying eyes of seventeen; but she could still do something classy and sensible. Such thoughts April kept to herself, though, sensing too much pain and danger in the subject. She said only, "It could be an old and ugly fellow of great importance and unusual charm." But Mary had become unreasonably angry anyhow and said, "What could a baby like you understand of love or importance." And once again April decided to put off, just a little longer, sharing her own real news with this mother who was Mary Gay, the widow of Charles Grace.

But finally one evening about two weeks after Mary's return, when mother and daughter were sitting together in the opulent bedroom that was the center of Mary's private being, and the room no decorator had been allowed to change, except to provide a fresh version of the same silvery-gray materials that had been there when her husband was alive; finally when the mother brought up with some definiteness the subject April kept changing —of where she was going to college—the girl said quietly, "You see, Mother, about college—I'm not really thinking in terms of college at all."

"Oh?" A pause. Then another *"Oh?"*

What an idiot she was, April thought, to be made uneasy by a simple pause, a cool look, a faintly raised eyebrow, the inflection of one tiny word: *oh*. The girl didn't rush into the pause, though, as she might have once, but waited, as the man she was in love with had told her to do, in his most recent lecture about poise and the handling of others.

"You want to be a butterfly, eh, like your cousin Lucy?" Mary said, lighting a cigarette—a sure sign something was making her anxious—offering one to April. "Come out and go to Katie Gibbs, I suppose. But your cousin Lucy is a dunce."

"No, I don't want to be a butterfly and come out and go to Katie Gibbs, though there's nothing wrong with being a secretary and cousin Lucy is not a dunce," said April all in one rush. And then, looking her mother straight in the eye, the way Max told her to do, "Can't you guess? You of all people?"

"No, April, I can't guess. You'll have to tell me," said the mother quietly, all attention.

"Dramatic school? Summer stock?" Mary said presently, in a way that told April she had not been so stupid, after all, allowing them a couple of carefree weeks. "I didn't know you were an actress. Last thing I knew, you were screaming at me as I left for the theater one night that for a million dollars you wouldn't be an actress, or singer, or any sort of performer."

"People change, Mother. Remember I wrote you I was in a play."

"Tell me again, darling," her voice softening, her manner all at once becoming reasonable, almost cajoling. "Tell me everything."

The story amused the mother as the daughter told it. How one day, nearly a year earlier, Mrs. Stark, the school drama teacher—that's Genevieve Fawn, the actress, Mother, she knows you—had come upon April Grace in the corridor loudly and mournfully describing to her friend Serena Watkins how her heart had been broken over the Christmas holidays. "April, my dear," said Mrs. Stark, fixing a big freckled hand to April's shoulder, widening those liquid brown eyes that in her newly hung Sardi's cartoon were all you saw, "why is it you are not in my dramatics club? Why are you not trying out for *Twelfth Night?*" "Because I can't act," said April. "How ridiculous! No girl with such a fine and carrying voice as yours tells me she can't act, especially not a girl named April Archibald Grace," said Mrs. Stark. "You *are* my Orsino. Come to tryouts tomorrow." It wasn't exactly the talent scout tapping the sweater girl at Schwab's drugstore, April said, but flattering nonetheless to be fingered thus by Mrs. Stark, who herself had just landed a brilliant part in a new Broadway play. And she happened to love *Twelfth Night.*

"Me too," said Mary amiably. " 'If music be the food of love' . . . truer words never were spoken. That is amusing. Jean Archibald's granddaughter playing Orsino. She was a famous Olivia, you know. Poor Jenny Fawn, still teaching in a girls' school."

"Not poor anymore, Mother. Don't you know? She's in *Kingdom of the Blind*—the lead"—her heart beating fast now, just saying the name of the play, his play.

"Oh, *that!*"—making a face, as she had been making many faces since her return, over the current offerings on Broadway, a Broadway Mary said she did not recognize. "Tell me more about you."

"I was good, Mother. I didn't know what it was like before to be . . . your daughter. Then I was the lead in the spring musical."

"Musical! Now that's too much. I know you can't sing."

"Neither could Walter Huston. We did *Knickerbocker Holiday,* and I played Peter Stuyvesant. You should have seen me with my peg leg. You should have heard me sing 'September Song.' "

"I would have liked to hear that. 'September Song' was one

of my big numbers overseas, you know. The boys loved my Kurt Weill—'September Song,' 'Speak Low,' 'My Ship.' " Humming a phrase softly, looking into space. Then, "But you should play a girl."

"I am this year." *I couldn't believe,* said Max Brandel, director of *Kingdom,* when he came backstage, *that a seventeen-year-old playing an old fellow could touch me so. But next year you must be a girl. . . . My Mercutio, next year,* said Genevieve Fawn. *Nonsense, your Juliet,* he'd said, staring at April as a weary jaded man can sometimes stare at a girl and be mesmerized by freshness, innocence, potential.

"Well," said Mary. Again a faraway look. A troubled look. "Juliet, eh? So you've got the bug. Oh dear, April, I don't *know."*

"Please don't close your mind. Don't listen to Aunt Isabelle."

"Belle! What does she know. But seventeen." A shadow crossed her mother's face. "How young it is, how desperately young. When I was seventeen, I wanted to sing Juliet."

"Juliet was desperately young. Wait till February. You'll see."

And then "February?" said Mary Gay to her daughter April Archibald Grace, "I can't possibly wait for February," sitting up on her bed where she'd been lolling against the pillows, in a nightgown and bed jacket, getting ready a while ago for sleep, now wide awake, sitting up straight, cross-legged, out of the covers, her ancient pose when she was studying a script or score. "Let's hear you now."

Terror. "Oh, not now. . . ."

"Yes! Now!"

In front of the bedroom fireplace while Mary watched from the bed, April stood absolutely still for a moment, her eyes closed, disintegrating, dissolving, chopping to bits inside of herself the person of April Grace, terrified at the idea of reciting for her mother yet wanting to show her something, allowing the body of April Grace like a clear vessel to be filled with the liquid essence of Juliet, trapped, trembling, yet brave, demanding love. "Use April to play Juliet," Max had said the day she'd gone to his flat for tea. "But don't confuse them." And then, "Pretend your girl friend is a boy you like," he said. "That's what you'd do if it was some actor you didn't give two cents for. Pretend," he said slyly, "Serena Watkins is that handsome Tony Marcus all you girls have crushes on." "I don't have a crush on Tony Marcus," April said. And then, making a joke of it, "You know perfectly well who I've got a crush on and have had a crush on since I was thirteen years old and went home with Ruthie Stark for supper and there was this *man,* this young genius, living in the Starks' spare room, who'd just come to New York and who talked to thirteen-year-olds as if they were interesting. . . ." "Oh, I see," he'd said. "A year younger even than Juliet." But he hadn't laughed at her.

Thinking of Max now, who was curing her of being scared, opening her eyes, she began her favorite speech, the one she already knew by heart, beginning *Gallop apace, you fiery-footed steeds* . . . "Speak out, April," her mother urged. "Don't be afraid, and not so fast." Mary didn't speak again until the girl came to the great crescendo of the speech, when "Give me my Romeo," she cried, "and when he shall die, Take him and cut him out in little stars, And he will make the face of heaven so fine, That all the world will be in love with night." At that moment April knew she had touched Mary. "Ah, yes . . . yes," her mother murmured and unusual tears sprang into her eyes.

"Very nice! You have passion, April," Mary said when the recitation finished, looking at her daughter with those glittering dark eyes that didn't widen like Genevieve Fawn's when she stared but narrowed, rather; glinted; and April's heart gave a leap for what other appreciation was so hard to get but when you had it so precious. No other, she would have said a year ago; one other, she might say now. "Yes. I think. Crude, of course, and un-governed, but indeed," said Mary Gay, every inch her professional self now, as if appraising some stranger at an audition. "I'll be extremely curious to see your finished performance. There's no reason not to get those college applications in as a safety measure. But yes, I will talk to Miss Fawn about alternatives. You have a

[181]

good voice, and a face that moves well. You might have talent."
Her eyes moving now to the wall of photographs, to the central
picture of Charles Grace, in top hat and tails, on his way into
the Grace Theater, her expression cryptic and sad.

In the end, that was the only thing that interested her, April
thought. Talent. Her own or anyone else's. And him, the man on
the wall, what he might think, what he might say.

"But dramatic school," she went on. "How do we know
which one. Your father never gave two cents for dramatic schools.
He used to say . . . ," smiling, yawning, as if sleepy yet relaxed.
"Well, never mind what he used to say, it wasn't polite."

Oh, Mother, she thought. Twelve years. Twelve years. Wake
up, before it's too late. Look around, won't you? Smile like that
and speak of someone living. I know now, what it's about, such
smiles, such feelings.

"Good night, darling," said Mary, holding her arms wide
now, giving April a tender hug, then taking her face in her two
hands. "Such a lovely face," she said, "such a Juliet face, such
a moonstruck, starry-eyed face."

So had Max then taken her face in his hands, and looked
in her eyes before kissing her, making a mockery with their eyes
and mouths of all previous looks and kisses the girl had known.

"I'm not saying no, darling child," said Mary.

If only she had left it there, April would think later. Not
pressed her luck. But April was foolish; April was impatient;
April was seventeen. And so, pausing at the bedroom door for
one last good night, she said, "Will you come with me next
Sunday, Mother. The Starks—Miss Fawn and her husband are
having a party. They'd like us both to come. They have such
interesting people always."

"*Always?*" Mary said, following the word with one of her
timed pauses. April felt a prickle at the back of her neck, the old
prickle that told her, too late, she had made a mistake. "Have you
been often to Miss Fawn's parties?" Mary inquired. "I didn't
realize that." The voice was sleek, silky, measured. "I didn't know
you were going to grown-up parties. Well, I'd be delighted,"
Mary said with great definiteness. "Delighted to go with you."

"Brown people," Mary would later call the group assembled in Genevieve Fawn's apartment that first Sunday of November 1945. Clever, nervous, not quite top-drawer, she would dismiss them all, "fawn-colored"—except for the young director named Max Brandel, and the young actor of impudent handsomeness named Anthony Marcus. Them she would call black, black retrievers stalking the brown birds. And that studio–living room; so like an aviary, didn't April think, Mary would say, with all that foliage and the gilded balcony like a perch and the chirpings and flutterings of so many minor actresses, though at the time, "Charming, darling," Mary Gay said, giving her daughter and the assembled company a smile so dazzling that her cheeks were grooved with dimples. "Now introduce me, darling, take me around to meet all your charming new friends."

In a simple black velvet suit, pearls at her throat mingling with a fichu of lace, pearls in her ears, a tiny black velvet skull cap on her burnished helmet of hair, Mary Gay was Broadway royalty come to call on the peasants as she went around to this one and that, so gracious, so apt. Foolish, impatient April, to think for a moment she and Mary were equals, to believe she, seventeen-year-old April, could "bring" Mary Gay to a party. Ridiculous April to seek approval for her interesting new friends like an eager puppy and to think Mary wouldn't single out the one who was more than a friend and recognize him immediately.

"This is my mother, this is Ormand Grey" (that movie, Mother). "*Of course,* you were that divine psychopath killer." . . . "my mother, Kevin Stark" (Miss Fawn's husband, Mother). "Of course, how proud you must be of Jenny but you, you did it all." . . . "This is my mother, Brian Orchester" (that story, Mother). "Of course, divine, in the last *Bazaar,* though a bit over my head." . . . "These are the Goldmans, Lucille and Kenneth, and Karen Draper, Chloe Jenkins, John Vasarov, Gloriana Bellehaven" (Dame Gloriana, Mother, from London). "Of course, darling, darling, how wonderful to see you in New York, I still remember that *Winter's Tale.*" . . . "This is Robert Melancon" (you've heard). "Of course." . . . "Skip Hubbard (you've read). "Of course." . . . "Professor Schwartz-Niessen, Dr. Wildman, Mademoiselle Lefèbre . . . and this is Verna Michaels, Mother" (author of *Kingdom*, Mother) "and Tony Marcus" (the juvenile lead in *Kingdom*, Mother, ah yes, Mother!) "and Clifford Banks" (of the Downtown Players, Mother, don't look as if you'd like to arrest him!).

For at that moment, to April's amusement, even Mary had to stop the cocktail party spiel, step off the moving platform of her progress through the room as she shook hands with the strikingly handsome young actors, the dark one and the sandy-haired one, who spoke to April as if she was part of their circle, telling Miss Gay how much they looked forward to performing someday with her daughter, to the summer theater, to the prospect of April. The slick dark male beauty of a Tony Marcus did not, for some reason, especially excite April, nor the statue goldenness of a Clifford Banks, but her mother, the girl had always suspected, had a secret weakness for the vain Latin type, or the Greek god, though would die rather than admit it; was staring now, though her tone of voice was brisk and motherly.

"Summer," said Mary, "is sometime off," in a way that made April wish she had briefed Cliff and Tony to go easy on Mother, who hadn't quite caught up with the new April.

"Play with you two," April said. "That will be the day. Press your shirts and make your coffee would be more like it."

"Oh, Max will see you jump the line," said Cliff. "We wouldn't let Max do that to April."

"Ruthie, maybe, or Chloe . . ." Tony gave April a big grin, the one that made the matinee matrons sigh, though April thought it rather an empty grin, for the eyes stayed cool, and he could switch it off, as he proceeded to do when speaking to Mary, with grave politeness. "But more important," he said, "when are we going to have the pleasure of seeing you on the boards again, Miss Gay?"

"I don't know my plans. Only to spend time, a lot of time with my daughter," said Mary, giving that daughter a look that conveyed a clear message to tone it down. And then, turning to

Verna Michaels, "So marvelous," Mary said, "that someone has finally written for Genevieve Fawn the play she deserves. Who is that, by the way, now with Jenny? That wicked-looking fellow over there?"

"That's Max Brandel," said Verna Michaels.

"Ah *hah*," said Mary, once again freezing in that disconcerting way of hers. "That's the fellow who directed your play, isn't it? The newest wonderboy. Well!" Mary looked at April, who was still chatting with the young actors. "And has the summer theater."

"That's right," said Verna Michaels, and then, as if she didn't realize yet she was a peasant being addressed by royalty, "Say, Miss Gay, I didn't write that play for Genevieve Fawn," she said belligerently. "I wrote it for myself at the suggestion of my psychiatrist. If you think I wrote it for Jenny you can't possibly have understood the play."

Oh, but she hadn't been yet, Mary said. She couldn't concentrate on anything serious yet, just being back from overseas, her eyes for a moment sweeping Max Brandel, Tony Marcus, Clifford Banks, Robert Melancon, John Vasarov, the entire room with another look April could read clearly—where were you boys in the past three years—and wanted to tell her, Max Brandel was 4F because he'd had rheumatic fever as a child—had a funny heartbeat—and did his bit in New York and Washington; John Vasarov was a refugee; Clifford Banks was only just eighteen, though he seemed much older; Robert Melancon had been overseas, longer than Mary, with *This Is the Army*; Anthony Marcus had been in the air force and had only half a leg, though you'd never know it from the way he handled himself. "How romantic," Mary would say acidly when April did tell her. Now the great star was explaining to Verna Michaels how she had a thing about . . . couldn't even say the word, it was so odious to her, and thus hated to identify in a play or a novel with a character that you knew in the end . . . for this reason had never been able to read *Anna Karenina* or *Madame Bovary*, but soon, soon, she would be there, third row center. How nervous she is, April thought, all of a sudden.

"Ah, if you have a thing about suicide, we will scare the wits out of you," said Verna, who resembled, so Mary would say later, speaking of difficult subjects, Virginia Woolf, if Virginia had had small eyes and a square jaw and had not been beautiful.

"I'll look forward to that," said Mary, turning her back now on the disagreeable Miss Michaels to take a good look at Max Brandel. He was pale and tired that day and not looking his best, April thought, in a black turtleneck and baggy corduroy suit, but even so he stood out in the room more brightly than anyone. Talking to Miss Fawn, catching the hands of his disheveled auburn haired star (like one of those red brown ruffled hens, Mary would say later, dear Jenny bird), holding her hands as if to say affectionately, Take it easy, it's your day off, he was as usual directing.

"So that is Mr. Brandel," said Mary speculatively. "I'd imagined someone older. I must see that play. And other plays. Things have changed too quickly in three years. Introduce me, please, April, to your Mr. Brandel."

"But how could you know, how *could* you manage her?" Wake Potter would say years later when April began to undress for him more than her body, to uncloak her miserable inner self and reveal April for the poor creature she knew she was. "That strong captivating woman who decided on the spot, without warning, how she was going to react, and you a baby just beginning to stop crawling. Why, she was the most glamorous woman in America then, and bewitching. Everyone was smitten. I was smitten. That charming vagueness, that artist's absentmindedness, that lovely laugh—that smile—then zappo, wham, the shiv. But how would you know she'd seen through you so fast—you, so proud of your acting—and get on the phone to Aunt Mathilda and say, 'You must have us for Christmas, you are dying to have us, aren't you, darling, I want April to have a change of scene, if you take my meaning.' And if you had known, what then? Would you have behaved any differently? Would you take us back, you and me? Would you take back the kids? Say, Mrs. Potter, you could have stuck to your guns, you know, if you were all that dedicated. You didn't have to be swayed."

"You were very swaying then," April said, "and I was very young."

"Max Brandel. My mother, Mary Gay—Mrs. Grace," unwittingly making of this particular introduction a ceremony. Mary stared. Max grinned, used to being stared at. Max Brandel, the blue-eyed Jew: looked like no one April had ever seen. There should have been big brown eyes to finish off the handsome, high-browed, swarthy Semitic face. Instead there were blue eyes, sharp and narrow, which now focused on Mary, mother of April.

"What a lovely mother and daughter," he said. "The resemblance is striking."

"Is it? I always thought April looked like a Grace. Would you take us for sisters, Mr. Brandel?" she asked mischievously.

"No, Miss Gay," giving her a level look. "I wouldn't take you for sisters, although I can see how someone who was less of an admirer of you both might make that mistake." And then, immediately, cutting off another mocking remark from the older woman, "Say, have you seen this kid of yours act, Miss Gay? It's something. Of course she had a good director. It's amazing what Jenny Fawn can do with a group of schoolgirls."

Not: Say, Miss Gay, I'll never forget you in *Lady on the Rocks*, or: Say, Mary, I saw you in Naples, but: Say, Miss Gay, have you seen your kid act? That was Max for you: no tact. But, "Tact," he would scoff later, "your mother is not a lady to be handled with tact, she's the sort to see right through tact." "All these professional kids," he added. "Ruthie Stark. Karen Draper. Tony Marcus, who's in *Kingdom*. Clifford Banks. Your April is one of them. Well, there might be a reason for that," giving a little for the mother, a small salute. "She doesn't come from a family of wooden Indians exactly. I hope you are going to encourage her to join us next summer."

"Go away, April," Mary said. "And you come with me, Mr. Brandel, while I get myself a drink, and tell me exactly how good my daughter is—how good all these kids are—and about that theater of yours."

She was on the warpath, April thought, wishing, too late, she had never brought her, wondering what had ever possessed her to think that the minute Mary laid eyes on Max Brandel she would not know what was going on in her daughter's mind and heart, know exactly whom it was April loved. Still, joining some of her friends—Ruthie Stark, Tony Marcus, Serena Watkins, who had a crush on Tony, and Clifford Banks, who was bright and good-looking but a question mark, said by catty people to be AC/DC—April tried to behave flirtatiously with party gaiety, throw up a smoke screen and ignore a foolish stab of jealousy at the sight of her mother talking so intently to Max. Chatting with her friends, the girl became aware that Tony, pretending to be engrossed in the conversation, also had his eye on Mary and Brandel. "And to think that is the all American beauty," April heard him say to Serena, "the one we pinned up above our bunks and were in love with, that tired, good-looking, middle-aged mother."

"An all American beauty," Serena said. "How funny. Mary Gay? Mrs. Grace? The prettiest voice in the world, I agree, and so elegant to look at but hardly a soldier boy's delight."

"Oh, yes," said Tony the veteran. "You should have heard her, seen her like I did, cradling a mike on a stage in Palermo, in some abandoned old theater. I'll never forget it. She'd sung everything, songs from the nineties and the twenties, show tunes, popular ballads, even an aria or two, always with this amazing tenderness. Well, who am I to tell April how her mother sings," bringing the daughter into the conversation, and April nodded and smiled. "And when finally she'd finished, she said in this hoarse voice, 'I can't sing anymore. I've run out of voice. I hope I've been able to bring you the spirit of your sweethearts and wives and mothers.' And then down the aisle came this great tall fellow covered with mud, wearing a whole arsenal, no more than thirty minutes out of action. He walked up on stage . . . have you all heard this?"

"No," they chorused, Serena, Ruthie, Clifford, and April,

who was trying not to watch Mary and Max; trying to react as a loving daughter should to one more story. "Go on, go on—"

"He walked up onstage and took hold of the mike. 'I'd like to say something,' he said to Miss Gay. 'You don't look like any-body's sweetheart or wife, or God knows like anyone's mother.' Then he lifted her chin and kissed her on the forehead and said, 'You look like Mary Gay, a sight for sore eyes, our all-American beauty,' and turned around and marched out of the theater. He'd said what we all felt. And then suddenly her voice came back and she managed to sing one more song. There was a roar—you wouldn't have believed that roar."

"I believe it," April said. "You think she's had it, and then there she is, all the way back." Why had she brought her? This room had been hers, April's; now it was hers, Mary's.

"You and she are pals, I can see that," Ruthie said. "You are just crazy about her." She wasn't being ironic.

"Oh yes," April said.

"Your mother is impressive," Max said sometime later, find-ing April alone in the small study off the living room, alone with the books and the remains of other people's lap suppers, a tall girl in her first black afternoon dress, made suitably young by a turquoise collar.

"Isn't she?" said April, sulking, feeling out of sorts with the party.

"But nervous. Terribly nervous. Everything she's accom-plished—it takes its toll. I may have done some good for you, though she didn't give me too much chance. And people kept interrupting. Dramatic school: probably yes. The summer theater: probably not. She says she is thinking of taking you to California. Perhaps the three of us could lunch sometime."

April was smiling again. He wasn't kidnapped but rather cool. He spoke of Mary not as a glamorous colleague—he was, after all, in age nearly thirty, halfway to Mary's generation—but as a mother to be won over.

"How is it with you at home?" he asked now, bluntly. "Will she help you in what you want to do or will she make obstacles?

Often people like your mother, who've come a great distance in the world themselves, who've taken many risks, can't bear to see their children taking the same risks."

"I can't tell. I'm scared." She looked at him. I'm scared to be pulled back and down; scared by compromises like this dress I'm wearing, grown-up black but with a Peter Pan turquoise collar; scared I won't be April anymore. By a look she wanted to convey her fears, and he said, narrowing his eyes a little, "If you're scared, darling, you'll never make it," and lightly ran his hand over her bright hair, giving the curls a tug.

"Hey, you two," said Tony Marcus, joining them. April smiled at him, liking the way he called them "you two."

Then April saw Mary. "There you are," her mother said, staring at the threesome in a way that made the daughter even more uneasy. "Don't you think, love? You have school tomorrow."

School! Need she?

In the taxi going home Mary was unusually silent, saying only that in the old days when, to please the public, theater people changed their names it made for prettier names. Not till she had closed the front door and locked up for the night did Mary say what she was so obviously thinking: "I'm not crazy about those people for you, April."

"Why? They're wonderful for me."

"Much too old. Not a group for a young girl like yourself," said Mary as she walked upstairs, turning off lights as she went. "Stick with Peter the flier and Murray the louse if you ask me," smiling, trying to keep it casual. "Stick with your kind, with Lucy and her friends and little Serena Watkins," preparing to say good night, but April followed Mary into her bedroom.

"My kind? You think?"

"I *know*. I'm awfully tired, dear, and you have homework."

"No! Don't send me away, don't say things like that and then, good night, dear, go do your homework," holding on to the memory of Max Brandel's words . . . if you're scared you'll never, never, never . . . "It's not been that happy living with the cousins. That was my war effort, to live with Aunt Belle and

[190]

Uncle Ralph and Lucy, so you could make millions of soldiers happy singing 'September Song.' But it didn't work as well as I pretended."

"But you did such a good job of pretending, why spoil it now?" Mary said on the edge of anger, not liking, April supposed, the remark about 'September Song.'

"Your daughter doesn't fit in your sister's world," April went on stubbornly. "Not really. Would you want her to? Subscription dances. Club life. East Hampton. It doesn't quite work for the daughter of Mary Gay and Charles Grace. Those people tonight, they make me feel alive. Myself. They want me."

"You—do they want you, my dear—or your father's name?"

"Me. That's the world that works for *me*."

"Then I feel sorry for you, April," Mary said, taking off her velvet jacket and skirt and her creamy blouse with the lace jabot, carefully hanging them up, putting her dainty suede pumps in the shoe bag; she had learned to be tidy during the war years as April had learned to be tidy at Aunt Belle's, and neither one of them had entirely returned to the old habits. So soft and alluring was Mary now, in her pale slip and silk stockings, softer and more alluring than any woman of forty-five had a right to be, in the light negligee she put over the slip as she sat at her dressing table to remove her makeup. But there was nothing soft or alluring about her voice as she spun her image of brown people, brown bird people never quite reaching the top.

"Talent," she said, wiping off the cream with swift strokes, "along with the talent you have to have the drive," patting the astringent vigorously with a piece of cotton, then starting on the night cream, sticky and yellow, working on the famous face, which was a piece of equipment, like the voice, to be preserved, her burnished bangs tucked up under a pink hairnet so you saw the frown lines for a moment, the marks of time that had made the bangs a good idea. Now her appearance was as hard and antiseptic as her words and her dark eyes were implacable. "Do you have the drive? You have to have the desperation, the furies at your back, hell as well as heaven in your dreams. You have to be crazy out of your mind to try for the leap. Are you desperate? Are you

[191]

crazy?" Then turning around and looking at her, not in the reflection of the dressing table but directly, unmediated: "Do I *want* you to be desperate and crazy?"

"A week ago you did. Right in this room," said April, so readily falling into a trap, giving the wrong answer, the poor April answer when the right answer, the Mary Gay answer, the Mary Geylin answer, would have been, "It's not what you want that is important, it is what I want. Help me to do what I want."

"That's true. I did see something. Oh, darling, I saw so much," Medusa dissolving once more into the lovely mother siren, without claws or scales, only not quite. "And I'll see you on the stage in a few months and know something more. But I also saw something tonight that frightened me. I was reminded by a miserable gallant woman like Gloriana Bellehaven of the road down. Even by poor Jenny Fawn, so nervous, so high-strung, who had to wait till forty-five—my age—for her first starring role."

"She's happy," April said. "She doesn't know she's poor," thinking, You're not being candid. Someone else frightened you in that room you aren't mentioning. I saw that look. Max Brandel frightened you. He reminded you of something. *Seventeen is so young.* Seventeen. What happened to you at seventeen, April wondered, or were you ever seventeen, could you have ever been seventeen. And what happened to you overseas that you aren't talking about anymore than I'm talking about Max, only what is happening to me is good, and what happened to you couldn't have been good or you wouldn't be the way you are, so hard, so bitter.

Outside her mother's door, on the red damask landing, April stood for a few minutes looking at the drawings. It was an ancient reflex, from childhood, to pause there, coming out of her mother's room after a difficult discussion or a scolding, wanting to go back and get in another word, wanting to kick someone, hating her mother, hating herself, embarrassed to go upstairs to her own room and face herself. Ugly old things, she thought of the drawings that were her mother's most treasured possessions, after her jewels, because she and Charlie had bought them together, each one having a significance, a private meaning. Why would two people who were as happy as her young mother and her young father, as blessed by the gods, have been attracted to such queer and menacing scenes, such grotesque figures? They were romantic to her, the father she barely remembered except as a shining figure, holding her on his shoulders, his blond hair in her little fingers, or tossing her up in the air like a doll; the mother who was everything to her; but their natures eluded her; which meant her nature eluded her, for if she didn't know or understand them, how could she know or understand herself?

Mary didn't do anything so obvious as to forbid April to go to any more of Genevieve Fawn's Sundays or go off of a Saturday with Ruthie Stark visiting friends in the Village. Nor did she do anything so obvious as make fun of *Kingdom*, only saying, after she'd been to see the play, "That is a rather cruel play and makes me feel funny about the people who put it on." She simply provided irresistible alternatives: theater tickets, opera tickets, country visits to old theatrical friends of Charlie Grace's who were dazzling to April, who were not brown birds; dinner and dancing in town at the Rainbow Room with other old friends who happened to be welcoming home attractive uniformed sons. The Sunday evening April had plans to go with Ruthie and Tony and Max Brandel to a workshop production of *The Sea Gull* was the Sunday evening Mary invited her daughter to a gala dinner at the Waldorf in honor of one of the great returning generals, and what girl was going to turn down such an occasion and a new ballgown for an evening of Chekhov? And then Mary sprang Christmas in Chicago: fascinating Aunt Mathilda, who insisted they come, that such a visit was years overdue; a houseful of new cousins; parties, gaiety. An adventure. A small adventure, perhaps, compared to some, but April hadn't been to Chicago since she was five years old. April did not protest.

So it was well after the holiday plans had been set that April came home from school one afternoon to an unfriendly Mary, who said coldly, "That actor Tony Marcus called you. He's giving a birthday party this Sunday for Max Brandel and wanted to invite you. But remember you and I have a date Sunday with the Jacobses."

"They only asked me along with you to be polite. All they want is to talk to you about a new show. I want to go to this party."

"The answer is no, April," Mary said after a pause.

"What do you mean?"

"If you don't want to go to the Jacobses I can't force you. But I mean, no, you can't go to an unchaperoned party in a man's apartment."

"There will be chaperones. Miss Fawn and Kevin Stark will be there. And the Goldmans."

"The answer is still no. There's no point in discussing it." And then, "I was hoping it wouldn't come up. But, April. These are not young men I consider suitable for you. Max Brandel. Tony Marcus. That other one, Cliff. Or anyone else, for that matter, I met at Jenny Fawn's, including that writer fellow, Hubbard, the one who looks like a prizefighter. Bad news, and out. I forbid you to have a date with any one of them."

Forbid? Could she?

"They're my friends, Mother."

"Friends! An attractive girl like you could get into trouble with such fellows so fast it would make your head spin. Very sleazy fellows. Not even all fellows from what I hear. People would begin to talk. You don't know, people are dreadful. Oh, I know, my darling, I know how you feel. When I was seventeen I had no fear and no use for what people thought, but then there wasn't much temptation, I was a vestal virgin worshiping at the altar of high art," trying to put lightness in her voice, in that annoying way, as if to say they were sisters at heart. "As you, darling, if you want to get anywhere in the theater, must be a worshiper."

It was April's turn to pause and give her mother a long stare. Then: "What happened to you at seventeen," April said, "that you're so frightened for me. *What happened?*"

"Nothing, my dear," Mary said finally, "not a thing except I learned how to sing."

[194]

"Because you were never seventeen," April said, her voice as flat and tight as Mary's. "Young! You were never young." Her amazing mother, who looked most days no more than a slightly tired thirty, suddenly was a hag to her that day, like the old woman on the wall of the red landing, in an unbecoming turban that hid all of her hair except the harsh bangs and made her skin sallow. Her amazing mother was no different after all from Aunt Belle or Mrs. Watkins or any of the mothers who ran their daughters' lives from a rule book; who didn't remember that young is not only headstrong and hot-blooded but smart about itself, and knows its own time; and even if not so smart, needs to make its own mistakes and thereby learn and grow. "You were born old, hard."

Mary sighed. "Maybe I was. Maybe that's the difference between you and me."

"I can't come, Tony."

"Why not?"

"I just can't," keeping her eye on the pillow Mary had embroidered for her long ago. *Never Complain, Never Explain*— Mary wisdom. "But I'll send a funny telegram. Miss me! Tell Max to miss me!"

"Call Mr. Brandel," said the message on the hall table, in Ninon's handwriting. It was a sign to her, the fact that Ninon had taken this message rather than her mother; a command to be bold.

"Max? It's me. April."

"April! I've missed you. Why haven't you been at Jenny's? Why didn't you come to my party? Why haven't you been by with Ruthie to see me? Why haven't you been by after your piano lessons? I figured we'd meet over the holidays, but Jenny says you're going away. So I called to see if we couldn't have that lunch I promised you before you leave. How about Sunday?"

"Fine," said April.

"What's the matter, April, why are you nervous? Do I make

you nervous? Does this place make you nervous? Eat your lunch. If you don't like omelettes why didn't you say? Drink your wine! We aren't having fun the way we have other times. Why do you keep looking to see who's come into the restaurant. Why are you acting like a criminal?"

"Because I lied. I hate to lie. Because my mother forbade me to go out with you. She thinks I'm skating with a friend." He was so exciting to her, so vivid, despite his greenish night-owl winter pallor, his circles and buried eyes. His voice went through her, an actor's voice, deep and resonant—an affected voice, her mother had said, so foolishly, for the voice was almost the exact masculine counterpart of Mary's own voice. Was this "it," she wondered, the transporting "it" they talked about, the mystery: love.

"Well. A real-life Juliet. Good God! All for me. But then enjoy your escapade, darling. Why be scared? I'll protect you."

"She's scary. She's been scary ever since she met you that day at Jenny Fawn's. She is terrified of you. Terrified you're going to seduce me—or use me—use her precious name." Not that I'd mind, giving you my body, or name, or anything you wanted, she thought, but . . .

"No wicked thoughts now, April," he said, reading her mind, one of his charms, the way he could do that. "So your mother won't let you go out with me, eh?" He laughed. "She must be jealous. Tell your mother for me to go—" He paused, reflected, censored; the woman was, after all, the girl's mother. "To go jump in the lake, Lake Michigan, since you'll be in Chicago."

She smiled. He smiled. Foolish smiles over an omelette and a glass of white wine, across a checked tablecloth, in a sunny window. For a while then it was all right. His face. His big nose, like a disguise-kit nose. His beautiful mouth. She would have liked to feel that nose nudge the palm of her hand, had an impulse to touch his face, his lips. Instead she smoked cigarette after cigarette. He didn't know she loved him. He didn't know how much it meant to lie to her mother, to be so scared that someone might walk into the restaurant and see her and tell Mary. She

couldn't help it: she adored Mary. To fight her made April unhappy, as if deep down she always suspected Mary might be right.
To go through all that for just a friendly lunch, no more, wasn't
worth it, and so, shyly, she said, "I love you. You're the first
person I've ever loved. I have to tell you that. I don't expect you
to love me back, but I wanted you to know."

He didn't laugh at her. He treated what she said seriously.
"You're so pretty," he said. "Such a golden girl. The real thing,
not movie make-believe. Who knows, one of these days. It
wouldn't be so tough to love you. But I have a girl already,
April."

She stared at him. How could he have a girl? Had he forgotten, so soon, the day he had kissed her, begun to make love to
her, and then, remembering who she was, and how old, who he
was and how old, hustled her furiously out of his place as if it was
her fault for tempting him; but then being so nice a few days
later, in a safe public tearoom, telling her things about herself
that had made her happy, made her strong for Mary's return.
How could he have forgotten? How could he, a man, be as
treacherous, as big a baby as Murray Lewis, Murray the louse?

"You mean serious? You mean you're going to marry?"

"Serious. But not going to marry, I don't believe. Not something happy, April. A long involvement, though."

"You mean you have a mistress."

"Sweet. You are so sweet. So young. But someday you'll be
grown-up. And someday, when you're grown-up"—he looked at
her hard—"you and I could be something, I think, Miss Grace.
So don't get in the habit of letting your mother run your life. It's
all right at seventeen, still. She might even have a few right ideas
for seventeen. But at twenty-five, humiliating. At twenty-five a
mother should only be fun, or there in a jam. And you for her.
Remember, the most important thing now is what you're going to
do on that school stage in February. From that we'll know something—really know something—about the future."

"She'd agree with you there."

"So. She has a few right ideas. Use her that way. Use Mary
Gay. And take courage. You were brave to come here today. Next

[197]

time, do better than that. Be brave and enjoy yourself at the same time."

She left with his voice in her ears, his face in her mind's eye, the brush of his lips on her mouth. A light kiss, different from the one he'd given her earlier, that merely marked a place in a barely begun book. She'd get rid of that mistress who was something unhappy; she was, after all, April Grace, born to make an unusual and dramatic life. A man like Max Brandel was her destiny, her kind, not some "nice young man" as Aunt Belle would say. "I'll bring back a bottle of Lake Michigan water for *you* to jump in," said April, and left the young director more piqued than he wanted to admit.

But what she came back with was Wake Potter's ring on the third finger of her left hand, a canary diamond big and yellow as a headlamp.

3

They met, April Archibald Grace and John Wakeman Potter, gilded youths, star-blessed pair who with those bucks, those names, should have been happy forever, at a dance at the Blackstone Hotel. In the same grand ballroom where twenty-seven years earlier Mr. Charles Grace of New York heard Miss Mary Geylin sing "The Star-Spangled Banner," and fell in love on the spot, there did Lieutenant Potter sweep off her feet Miss Grace of New York. Only not on his stage and then in his bed did Wake Potter desire Miss Grace, but only in his bed and on no man's stage, and would make that clear, right from the start, quoting his grandfather Hector, who had once wanted to make an opera star of that same sweet Mary Geylin. "He who marries an actress," said Wake in the words of his granddad, a great old boy, "must stuff her mouth with dollar bills or be stone-deaf."

"Cut!" said the young man in the marine dress blues with two loops of gold braid on his left shoulder. That was about all he said, too, just "Cut," then "Hiya, beautiful," giving the new girl in town a big fresh grin and a hard stare, which she returned with a happier expression than had been visible on her lovely face heretofore; she liked the look of him, whoever he was, with his white-blond hair and ruddy complexion, his blunt boyish features and hazel eyes that had seen hell somewhere and now appeared to be recognizing heaven: her. The look of him almost made her forget how furious she was, how unwillingly she had embarked on this Chicago holiday. No one had ever stared at her that way, at first sight, nor held her instantly so close, though the orchestra was playing a bouncy medley—"Let It Snow," "The Trolley Song," "Zip-a-dee-do-dah"—and everyone else around them was singing and being lively, dancing up a storm. But he only wanted to hold her, and dance half-time and not talk, for she was the blonde he'd been dreaming about for three long years, he'd say later when they played "White Christmas"; she was his white Christmas, in an off-the-shoulder holly-red dress, with a gold clip in her long glistening hair, just a little sulky and dégagé, with an expression that said: "Show me."

"What's your name?" she asked.

"Do you care, gorgeous?"

"No, actually," she said, caring only that he called her gorgeous and beautiful, not automatically like some guys, but as if it was a fact, definite.

"So don't make conversation, let's just dance." He held her naturally, gratefully, as if he were thirsty and she were something cool to drink, or hungry and she were something good to eat, or tired and she were a freshly made turned-down bed.

Then a navy uniform cut in, and after that a white tie with glasses, but then the marine was back and they played the game some more, no names, no talk, just two people acting out the fantasy everyone has at some time or other in life, of seeing a stranger on a bus or walking down the street or in a railroad station and thinking, That's for me, that animal is for me. Cut . . . cut . . . cut, beautiful . . . cut . . . cut . . . cut, gorgeous. . . . Every third cut it was him, except in the rumba set, for he didn't rumba; "Me doing a rumba," he said, "is like a donkey doing dressage."

"Hey, beautiful," he'd say. "Hey, stranger," she'd say, though they weren't such strangers after six or seven dances.

Not until the long last dance, when the lights were blue, and all the others, even the regulars of the evening, the navy uniform, the white tie with glasses, had returned themselves to their original dates and her own original date, drunken and negligent, had long since been dispatched by her cousins who were giving the party, not till "After the Ball" time, "Three O'clock in the Morning" time, "White Christmas" and "Goodnight, Sweetheart" time did he say, "I'm Wake Potter, by the way." And she said, "I'm April Grace from New York."

"I know you're April Grace from New York. Your mother asked me to look after you and cheer you up."

"Oh."

"Some heavy duty, looking after you."

"Oh," she said again. "I've made an ass of myself. You're not nice."

"No, you haven't. Yes, I am."

"Why didn't you say?"

"Because." And then he told her about how she was his blonde, *the* blonde, the one he'd dreamed of while others dreamed of home, and if he'd said, it would have, it wouldn't have, didn't she see—grinning at her, beaming at her, then narrowing his eyes and looking at her that other way, raising his eyebrows a little and . . .

"Yes," she said. "I get you. Stranger."

For a long time she could come back to that; beautiful . . . stranger . . . remember that night and think, even after five, seven years of marriage, if I keep being beautiful and he keeps being stranger, we'll be okay, for the way you start is the way you are.

"He's the nicest boy that ever lived, with the greatest family," said April's cousin Debbie the next morning, getting into bed with the visitor to gossip about the night before, as a maid brought breakfast and lit a fire in the bedroom grate.

There were fires everywhere in the Vails' apartment, though in the downstairs rooms the flames were almost invisible for the blinding sunlight that poured through frost-edged casement windows; everywhere was brightness and softness. The furniture was mostly velvet, soft to the touch; the floors and tables were polished like mirrors; the rugs were like the Persian flying carpets in a picture book, the Christmas tree encrusted with so many ornaments you could scarcely see the green. And from every window was the blue view, the marvelous sparkling vista her mother had told her about as a child, of a lake limitless as a sea, rimmed with great towers that caught the sun in a way unknown to New York. April would dream about that brilliant Christmas apartment for years afterward; would cry when her stay there finished, though when she'd arrived she'd been barely civil.

"Who?" April asked, feigning innocence. "Who's the nicest?"

"Who indeed," Debbie teased. "Though terribly shy. I can see he's made you forget a bit about N.Y.C." Deborah Vail had thick red hair and the Grace beaked nose and light eyes; bright hair, cool face, and the warmest manner April had ever encountered in an older girl, warmer even than cousin Lucy. Twenty-one, a senior at Vassar, her Chicago cousin treated April as if they were equals. Debbie was cupid, Santa Claus, Sts. Christopher and Jude, part of April's Christmas dream, and years later, when April began behaving so peculiarly, Debbie, moved to Santa Monica, was the one who remembered Chicago, remembered the beginning and said to April, run away to California, "Don't be a fool, there never were two people crazier about each other, never anyone else for him or you."

"I didn't think he was shy," April said. "I thought he was sexy." Just speaking of him brought on a body recollection of how sexy it had been dancing with Wake Potter, such a precise memory she could feel herself blushing.

"Oh yes indeed," said Debbie her new friend, giving her a long look. "If he is, he is. If he gets to you, he gets to you. Don't

I know. He was the first boy who ever kissed me, on the float once up at the lake. I was fourteen and I thought I'd been raped. He called, by the way, hinting around, so I invited him to lunch."

He was in civilian clothes that noon. Better to go to a ball in a sharp-fitting dress uniform, his friends had told him, than an old set of tails that didn't fit. But college tweeds were fine for a morning-after lunch. Even in colorless civvies, April thought, all it took to bring back the night before was one big grin, one muddy stare. Out of his uniform, he still appealed; feelings stuck. For the hour exactly it took to eat lunch he made conversation with April's mother, who happened to be Mary Gay, and the Vails, good conversation, the girl from New York noted, not too brusque, not too obsequious, cheerful, with a touch of seriousness when the talk turned to war stories as all talk inevitably did that Christmas of 1945. Then he took April for a walk, making it clear that was why he'd come and it wasn't any old after-lunch walk but their special walk. "That's the nicest, most attractive boy I've ever seen," Mary whispered to April in the hall as the girl was putting on her new beaver coat, the one that Mary had given her the night before they left New York, saying she'd need it in Chicago. April smiled at her mother's naïveté. That boy's intentions, if she knew her boy's intentions, were the opposite of nice. He was the one—not careful, protective Max, the man of the world, or Tony Marcus, whose taste ran to nutty glamour girls— an attractive young lady could get into trouble with so fast it would make her head spin. Naïve Mary. "Naïve, hell," said Wake later, when he was beginning to undress for his wife more than his body, to uncloak his disagreeable inner self. "She saw a Pot- ter, beautiful, don't kid yourself. Even if you're the famous Miss Mary Gay, Mrs. Charles Grace of New York, if once long ago you were little Mary Geylin of Chicago whose daddy was a piano teacher, you're impressed with a Potter, believe me." But that was later, that garbage. Then she only knew the way she felt when he put his hands on her shoulders in the elevator going down: like a poor frog in biology lab. Bzzzzzzzzzzzzzzzzzz.

"Hold on," he said, as they hit the brilliant freezing street, "some days you can get blown right off this corner. They put a rope along the hotel for people to hold on to. Other days it's the most beautiful spot in Chicago, like now, when there's a lull," holding her arm tightly as they crossed over to the esplanade that ran between the shore drive and the jagged frozen beach, sparkling with ice mounds, giving off fire like mica, though the lake wasn't frozen but a burnished blue sheet. "You never know ahead of time which it's going to be. Or picture this in the summer with the sunbathers and umbrellas and sailboats out there. It could be the Mediterranean. But even in summer if a big wind comes up it's not pleasant. I used to think about this corner during the war, hitting some of those beautiful treacherous beaches."

She'd think about that corner a lot, also, would the daughter of Mary, married to Wake, as the years went on, wondering how it was, when he talked of Mary sometimes, of her impossible changes of mood, that he didn't see he was talking of himself.

And then, in a frozen white and blue landscape, Wake Potter kissed April Grace, the veteran and the schoolgirl in a beaver coat, stock figures in a city returning to peace; gave her the hard hungry kiss of someone who hasn't held or kissed a girl in a long time. She might have turned to stone from the cold air and not noticed it. She thought of what her cousin Debbie had said and smiled. Another kiss wiped out the smile. "I like you, Miss Grace," he said presently. "You're for me." He looked at her inquiringly.

"You think so?" she answered, saying what she wanted with her eyes, with her gloved hand tightly holding his.

"Are you anyone's property?" he asked.

"Property? What a funny way of putting it. But no, nobody's property."

"Except Mother's?"

"Nobody's," she said loudly.

"Good. I like a girl who gives herself away."

"My daddy and I used to walk there," Mary would say. "How queer, that was my spot. How strange that you should love my city, how strange that you should fall in love there. And with such a nice boy." It got to be monotonous, that nice-boy bit, but

[203]

even her mother's approval couldn't change anything. It was easier to have Mary's approval. Even the presence, at every turn, of the ghost of little Mary Geylin, of Louis Geylin, the ghosts of Christmases long past, the ghosts of young Mary and young Charlie, and something else, the missing piece in the puzzle, couldn't make her feelings for Wake seem anything but unique, hers, newly invented. Even more than on the school stage, or at Miss Fawn's, or with Max Brandel, she felt her own person. April. Born to be Wake's person. This was "it," the mystery: the agreeable mystery, that is, as opposed to others not so agreeable, such as death, or God, which made her head ache. She forgave Mary. Mary was wonderful. Mary was just a silly mother like all the other mothers. She would have handled Mary when they returned to New York, she knew that now, except there wasn't anything to handle. Mary loved Wake, who loved April, who loved him back.

Even the incident with old Mr. Hector Potter, the day Wake took her to lunch at his parents' farm, didn't annoy April or intrigue her as it might have once. Nothing could annoy her, everything pleased her. She liked the parents and their farm in the rolling country to the northwest of the city. They weren't at all what she had expected, Mr. and Mrs. Freddy Potter, not elegant and worldly like Aunt Mathilda and Uncle Clarrie or the Lake Shore Drive Potters, Mr. and Mrs. Laurence Potter, the uncle and aunt who put up Wake in town. They were rough handsome country people with red faces and pepper and salt hair and a western air about them. They wore jeans and tweeds and took care of their horses, their dogs, cows, and barnyard animals, and scarcely let you know, except for the size of the house they called a farm, and the tended beauty of the grounds, that they were nonetheless Potters, more than comfortably off.

And they loved, just *loved,* they said, young people. Young people were the breath of life. So the talk, until the intrusion of old Mr. Hector Potter, had been first of country matters, a million miles from Lake Shore Drive or Fifth Avenue, State Street or Broadway, and then of April, who came to them representing the kids of 1945. They'd already heard from Wake, who'd been to the wars, but they wanted to know from April, who'd stayed home, how that was, and what she thought of everything—she'd never been so flattered—what music she listened to, what books she read, what people her age in New York thought about Truman, Hiroshima, the Russians, love and marriage. Then old grandpa, who had been silent till that moment at the table, like a child with a nurse beside him, frail with trembling hands though he was neat and his eyes were bright and his mustaches lively, then Hector, the great old boy, spoke up in a surprisingly firm voice, saying loudly, "Enough of this talk about the young people, what do young people know, what did they ever know! I want to tell you a story, Miss April Grace, of years ago."

She understood presently why everyone else had been talking across Grandpa, not letting him get into the stream of conversation. Once started, he had the floor, like the Ancient Mariner or that filibustering senator from the South he resembled; could not be stopped.

"About this time of year it was," he said, "and the war was just over, our war, and I was not so old as I am now, still in my prime. And a friend of mine, a retired opera star who taught singing, asked me to hear one of her pupils sing at a victory gala. 'If you like her, Hector,' my friend said, 'and I think you will, I want to talk to you about her. She has no money and she must go to Europe to complete her studies. She could be the new Garden, the new Melba! Ah . . . I see you know, Miss April Grace, now you are looking more interested, my dear. A small world, is it not. No one told you? Your mother never mentioned, in her rememberings, a Mr. Hector Potter?"

"Now, Grandpa, don't get excited," said Edith Potter. "It's not—"

"It's excellent for me, let me die excited, not bored, bored! Just to remember that girl! I went to the gala," he continued, "a dreadful affair, but my old friend the singing teacher kept saying, 'Wait, please wait.' Then this child, not exactly pretty, not nearly so pretty as you, my dear, but something more than pretty, came out at the end and sang 'The Star-Spangled Banner,' that was all, while all heck broke loose on the stage, your aunt Tilly Vail up there pretending to be the Statue of Liberty. Meantime this glorious voice went on, up, higher and higher. I heard in my imagination the greatest arias in the world coming out of that young lady's mouth. Excited! That was excited!"

Would he drop dead, right there at the table, April wondered, remembering Mary? That would be fitting. But no, he coughed a little, took a sip of water, and, shaking off the assisting hands of Miss Minna Groot, Grootie the nurse, continued his tale. "And it was all arranged. I met the girl. She had a calm exterior such as you associate with singers, but underneath, such passion, such fires; she had known early sorrow, you could tell. She had had a struggle . . . not all easy . . . poor but proud. We talked about money and about when she might leave. Jean de Reszke, the great tenor de Reszke, was to be her teacher. And then, before it could all be arranged and the final details settled, though after she had sung for me, in private"—he paused for a moment and sighed— "after a day of happiness she was gone—kidnapped, my dear April Grace, gone to New York. 'Why?' I said to the singing teacher. 'Why?' Well, you know the answer, young lady, to that. But I still wondered, *why?* Even when I saw her later on Broadway, and who would ever take back the marvelous Miss Mary Gay, I still thought of that young Mary Geylin, and what she might have been. Great artist. Great star. There is a difference, you know, though I am not certain which is better." He paused, finally coming to rest. "You must give her my best," he said, ready now to make his farewells, leave the table, and take his old man's nap, his Sunday lunch having been an unusually satisfactory one.

"Perhaps she'd drive out to see you," April suggested.

"Oh no. Don't suggest that. I'm not very well, you understand. Just give her my best. Tell her she has a lovely daughter." And then, as Miss Groot helped him into his wheelchair, "Are *you* musical, April Grace, do you have a voice?"

"Not like Mother. I can't really carry a tune," said April, remembering another April, the old man's story making her remember the April she had left behind in New York. "But I might be an actress," she said innocently, as if she and Wake hadn't had that talk the night before.

"Sure, sure," said Hector Potter's grandson. "And I'll wait at the stage door. Right, April?"

"Hector Potter," said Mary vaguely. "More darn people once you get to be who you are have stories. I don't remember. I don't remember at all."

"I didn't know you were that serious, Mother, about opera."

"I wasn't, I wasn't, I didn't have the right voice, oh, enough for the best light opera, but not for grand opera, not the power for a great opera house, to soar over a full orchestra." She was talking rapidly, the way she did when something was making her nervous or unhappy. For a long time April had had a feeling, vague and unclear, that there might have been someone before her father. Something odd, unhappy, that her mother wouldn't talk about. Was there more, perhaps, to Mr. Potter's story than he had told or her mother was willing to remember? In his prime —his early fifties, it would have been in 1918—Mr. Hector Potter had been an attractive man, judging from a photograph, with a gleam in his eye and a slightly raffish tilt to his top hat. But "Hector Potter," Mary said. "Hector Potter? No. No . . . it rings no bell."

"How sad," April said. "Poor old man. He remembered you so well."

It wasn't the first time she had had the experience of someone remembering a long and elaborate story concerning Mary that her mother denied had ever happened. Yet this was a story of 1918. Eighteen next to seventeen. What happened to you at seventeen? Such a glimpse into the past of her secretive mother once would have intrigued her, set her on a course of inquiry; Miss A. Grace, detective. No longer. She wasn't interested.

Only what went on late at night on the Vails' sofa or on the Laurence Potters' sofa was interesting to April. What went on late at night on one or the other of those sofas after the household had retired made everything else incidental, including Mary, especially Mary, including even Max Brandel, back in New York, and the life April had thought she wanted a few months earlier. There was only one thing she wanted now, night after night, and forever after, Wake Potter making love to her, him in her, the simple physical act, and during the day a tweedy figure taking her around his city—or any city—showing her the world; speaking in monosyllables and then all of a sudden coming out with a surprising fact, a story that made her think he wasn't so dumb after all; or just sitting across a table from her, drinking, putting food in his mouth, wiping crumbs away, giving her a big smile with his clean wiped mouth. But it was night, night that was their friend.

She thought of Juliet. The lines were more than music now: were real. . . . *Spread thy close curtain, love-performing night, That runaway eyes may wink, and Romeo Leap to these arms, untalk'd of and unseen. Lovers can see to do their amorous rites By their own beauties. . . .*

Her mother had her costume specially made at Brooks and followed for the pearl-embroidered headdress an old photograph of Jean Archibald. Luminous as an old silver daguerreotype was April Grace that February afternoon, yet bold and canny and stubborn as Juliet was, and crazy in a very modern way, the way of February 1946. She was a girl bursting with talent, people said. Nobody laughed, not even the seventh graders, at the spectacle of two girls making love. Serena Watkins, the Romeo, was dark and brooding, with a husky expressive voice, her notable breasts flattened in a bandeau. In black velvet doublet and hose, she made almost too convincing a Romeo. That was something later Lion Grace would not live down easily, nor let Serena live down: that the girl who finally captured his heart had played Romeo to his kid sister's Juliet. Still, Serena was nothing in comparison to April. Serena was intelligent, clear, strong. April— quivering, intense, stretched white—was magic.

Yet she walked away from it.

She walked away from Genevieve Fawn and all her teacher's plans for her, telling Miss Fawn that since Wake planned to finish Harvard and then go to business school, she would attend Radcliffe and perhaps could get involved with some drama group in Cambridge.

"Radcliffe girls don't do theater," said Miss Fawn, too disappointed to be mannerly. "Especially not Radcliffe girls married to Harvard veterans. They play house and have babies."

She walked away from Max Brandel, who came backstage with Tony Marcus. "Lovely," Tony said. "Lovely Juliet. Not too sweet. If you think about it, Juliet only caused trouble."

"Oh, I don't agree," April said. "Romeo was one of those idiots who couldn't time things right."

"Someday you and I could play it right," Tony said. "A real Romeo and Juliet. How about it, Max? Directing Marcus and Grace in *Romeo and Juliet?*" But Max said nothing, only gave her a somber look. She couldn't even hear all of what Tony was saying, as if he assumed that when she graduated from school she'd be joining them at the theater in Stockbridge, for Max's look. Not till Tony turned to Serena to compliment her on her Romeo did Max say, simply, "After such a performance, you must be tired."

"Not tired, but empty," April said, a troubled look on her face, something tearing at her for the first time since she'd met Wake Potter, something encroaching: the look in Max Brandel's blue eyes, the fierceness of his dark hypnotist's face.

"But it fills up again," he said. His eyes kept searching hers, asking questions, but not getting any answers. "What's happened to you, April?" he asked.

"Two weeks from Sunday my engagement is going to be announced," she said quietly. "In June I'm going to be married. Think of it. The class bride."

He only said, "Why?"

And she answered, "That's the way it happened."

"Cut," said Wake Potter, coming up with Mary and Aunt Isabelle and Lion, just back from Germany, three stages behind Wake in readjustment. Pale, thin, silent, and muffled. Lion was ill at ease in his civilian clothes, his New York skin; so thin in the face, so cropped, he almost didn't look like Lion anymore though he had earned his nickname, along with his commission and his medals, no question. No more bratty younger-sister jokes about that. Still, though finally a lion, he was not a gentleman, that returned brother of hers, not gracious or thoughtful or even terribly funny anymore, his very stance proclaiming he'd been dragged there. The cocky boy who'd walked out the door in June of 1943, saying to his mother and sister, "No whimpers, no bangs," was no more. In his place was a hard-faced, exhausted man who had walked into their house a week ago and gone straight to bed, not arising for thirty-six hours; an impatient man who looked at April in love and Mary the mother as if they were phantoms.

And now he was giving Max Brandel one of those dour looks, staring at Max—as was Wake Potter—in a way that April would have found insufferable if she hadn't been so crazy about Wake and so puzzled by Lion, so secretly concerned. Max, she saw through the eyes of her lover and brother, was a little odd. His clothes were sharp, his appearance an uneasy mixture of intelligence and flamboyance, his masculinity alien from that of Wake Potter and Lion Grace.

Making the introductions, April saw natural enemies. Yet Wake and Max were polite and spoke about her in front of her in a jesting manner while Mary looked on smiling. Sulky Lion made no attempt, after a gruff "Howdy," to join in the conversation. Instead he stared past the family group at something more interesting: the girl in the black doublet, who had taken off her mustache and shaken out her abundant hair and was now smoking a cigarette and talking to Tony Marcus. "Who's the Romeo?" asked Lion. "With the great stems?"

"Her name is Serena Watkins," said April. "She's more than a pair of legs, Lion. She's smart. Very smart."

"And the guy with her?"

"Anthony Marcus. A terrific young actor."

Her brother frowned. She understood. Tony, seen through Lion's eyes, was alien also: handsome in the way that used to be called patent-leather.

"A veteran, just like you, Lion, with a Purple Heart."

"An operator, I'd say." And Lion moved toward Serena and Tony, and that was the end of Tony, April would say many years later to Serena when they were not only friends but sisters-in-law. "More or less," Serena would say, in that cryptic manner that made you wonder if her life wasn't more complicated than she let on. The little vignette of Lion's dismissal, first of Max Brandel and then of Tony Marcus, seemed to amuse Mary, as if she hadn't registered the way Lion had dismissed her, Mary, his own mother, only a few nights ago. On Mary's face these days was a permanent look of quiet satisfaction as if she'd won some sort of match. But even that didn't matter. April didn't care if Mary thought she had won; didn't care if Max thought April had lost. Her feelings for Wake Potter were too strong.

So, changed out of her costume into the red plaid dress and beaver coat she'd worn throughout her Chicago holiday, April walked away from Juliet and all she represented, from April as Juliet, who was someone else's heroine . . . from that April.

There was just one curious moment when April looked back and everything seemed wrong to her and she thought, *I'm in a trap, in a glittering cage:* the moment when, at the bridal dinner, at April's request, Mary sang.

Until that moment the night had been April's. The mother of the bride had kept herself lowkeyed, quite deliberately, was Mrs. Charles Grace, a charming New York lady with a barely nodding acquaintance with Broadway's Mary Gay. Even the famous ruby wasn't shown off as it might have been in the old days in the scoop of a sensational décolletage, displaying the *belle poitrine* of Miss Gay. The jewel nestled undramatically in draped chiffon, twilight-gray, the sort of dress that cost a fortune at Mainbocher for the assurance of fading into the background. Long graceful sleeves camouflaged the lovely arms; many layers of skirt ensured there would be no sinuous clinging to the shapely legs; the golden-brown hair was strictly coiffed and tucked behind the ears, the makeup quiet. Mary seemed far less of a personality, indeed, than the rough-hewn Freddy Potters, givers of the bridal dinner, who off their farm, in a private dining room of the St. Regis Hotel, dressed and talked like swells, seemed to know everyone and have been everywhere though insisting they were simple country folks, visitors from the plains. The great star seemed, that night, less of a personality, even, than her own mother, in purple brocade and garnets, an unusual grandmother of the bride, who was no sweet old lady but a working musician still, handsome, forceful, with powerful pianist's arms and a deep voice, deep as a man's.

It wasn't till the period of toasts that the murmuring began around the room, the question—Will she sing?—reaching April by way of the man on her right, the junior Freddy Potter, Wake's older brother and best man. "I don't know if she'll sing," said April. "She doesn't generally at a party just . . . get up and sing. I suppose she will if she wants to."

"Of course she wants to," said Wake on her other side, looking at his future mother-in-law, seated between his father and Clarence Vail, many places down the interminable table. "Can't you see she's run out of conversation and is going out of her mind?"

"But you have to ask her, dear," said Grandmother Honora from the other side of Wake. "That's what she's been waiting for."

April's feelings were mixed. Part of her wanted, desperately, for her mother to sing; wanted all those Potters and Vails and Wakemans to be reminded of just exactly who and what that charming, slightly eager woman was. Six years, after all, had passed since Mary's last Broadway show, and who in the room had heard her overseas, besides Lion and Wake and the West Point Wakeman, Major General Donald Wakeman, who had told the story about the wartime Mary that had started the murmuring around the table. At the same time, another part of the daughter longed for the mother to stay in her place, in the background. But "Of course," April said to Wake, rising, going to Mary, who looked up at her daughter and smiled. "Are you happy?" Mary asked fiercely. "Are you happy, my darling?"

"The happiest girl in the world . . . almost," said April. "I will be the happiest girl in the world if you'll sing for us."

The room hushed. The woman in twilight-gray stood by the piano, hand on her breast in classic fashion, giving the company a faint smile. "My daughter has asked me to sing," she said almost shyly. "How can I say no? One song, for April, it's her song. . . .

She is going to sing "September Song," damn, thought tomorrow's bride, which was our song, mine and Max's, damn, and will make me think of him and the letter he wrote me in answer to the letter I wrote him. *Damn, damn, damn.* But no. Mary was only going to sing "April in Paris," a mild embarrassment, a remembered embarrassment from when she was a child and her mother's singing of the April songs was a form of joke, a source of teasing.

Only it might as well have been "September Song," April would think, for the way she felt. Sitting there at that long festive table, listening as everyone else in that room was listening, spellbound, to the haunting silvery voice spinning out the lines of the lovely song; listening as an audience of a thousand in the Grace Theater might listen, or ten thousand men sitting on a hillside somewhere in Italy, looking down on a makeshift platform where a small woman in clinging chiffon with golden bangs and smoky eyes made them think of home; listening to a bit of magic named Mary Gay who happened to be her mother, April felt a stab of pain, unexpected and terrible. The face of Max Brandel, stern, disappointed, horribly dear, was in front of her eyes; his voice in her ears, speaking the harsh words of his letter . . . words like *fool* and *waste* and *fickle* and *not steadfast, not your mother's daughter.* "I wish you luck," he had ended, "but what you are going to do makes me very sad." No manners, that Max. No gentility. Proving what she already knew, that he was no gentleman, never had been, never would be, no matter how great his success and his fame, and that was the reason she cared, because, gentleman or no, he told the truth and cared about things worth caring about, unlike all these people who only cared that Wake was a Potter and that her mother was a great star, not even understanding how great that was, how miraculous, not realizing what they were hearing. And for one very bad moment, April remembered that other April, the April who one fine day might herself have been a piece of magic on a stage, transfixing an audience; understood in that clear and freezing moment the possibility of what might have been—might not have been, too, but was worth the gamble, the try—a whole other life.

At that moment, as her mother sent those perfect notes at her, those jewels, those little balls of light, those exact and seductive phrases, no more than a trifle, just one little song, but listening to that perfect trifle, remembering the evening she had recited for Mary and Mary had said *yes . . . yes . . .* remembering Max . . . she wanted to bolt and almost felt she had the courage to bolt, throw everything over, less than twenty-four hours before she would speak the binding words.

Then the moment was over, something to be exchanged with other brides on a Bermuda beach, telling of their moment of panic, whatever it was, whatever brought it on, when they wanted to run, an amusing vignette. As people clapped and called for an encore, not too energetically, understanding that when Mary Gay had said one song, she meant one song, April embraced her mother with a dignity that was new to her and gave her a light kiss that was a thank-you and a farewell. Then she went back to being herself, April, bride of Wake, leader of the pack, center of the merry group, young individual talking about the possibility, after the formal dinner was finished, of going on to a nightclub, defying the rules, staying up, the night before her wedding, the last night of being Miss Grace, till dawn. But it had been an emotional few minutes, more complicated than anyone might have guessed other than her sullen brother, well on his way to total inebriation, who was bestowing on Serena Watkins his most cynical lopsided smile. "Screwed up? Who's all screwed up? Who *isn't* all screwed up?" he was saying. "And who cares, as long as you get to *be* somebody?"

Good luck, Serena, she thought.

And the course of April's life seemed to be settled, until the night some six years later when Mrs. John Wakeman Potter, loveliest of wives and young mothers, would see her own devoted mother, Mary Gay, in the company of the director Max Brandel, who had so brilliantly brought the fading musical star back to professional prominence, getting out of Miss Mary Gay the finest performance of her life. And as the family, and all of New York, celebrated, something would come apart in the carefully constructed person of April Grace Potter—though people who loved her might not realize it for years.

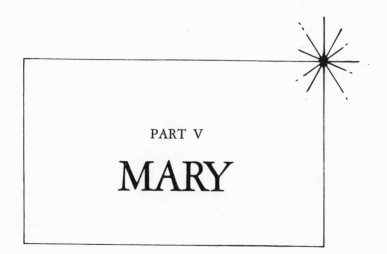

PART V

MARY

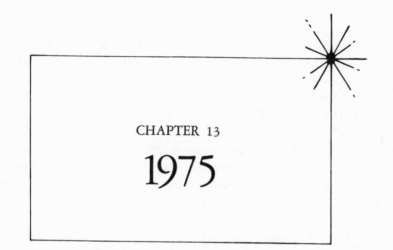

CHAPTER 13

1975

In the great house just a step away from the park, where the famous woman had lived for fifty-five years; in the mother's house on the other side of town from the impossible daughter and just a few blocks north of the apartment of the plausible son and touchy daughter-in-law where the first party guests would soon be arriving; in the haunted bedroom whose appointments—should the lady not survive—would be difficult to dispose of, for who in the family would want that bed, that dressing table, that Empire chaise longue, that velvet slipper chair covered with cat hairs; in the lavish, the too appropriate, the cleverly, painstakingly contrived set that was the Grace house, the action was nearly played out.

"Hurry up, old lady," the robber said, *"presto, presto."*

He was in front of her now, the gun poised, the mirrored eyes fixed on her, waiting.

Slowly she raised her arms, stiff and marked from having been bound, and felt for the clasp.

"What if I can't get it either," she said softly.

The man smiled, that maddening smile. "Two minutes, Miss Gay," he said, "till curtain time." Would the punk dare? Her heart beat with alarming speed. He moved the gun. Even though she was certain that Lion now stood on the landing, beyond the closed door, even knowing that the only course of action—if she could get the damn thing open, that was—was to give it up, she sat there frozen, something in her resisting, refusing to order those fingers to do their work.

Just so, at another period of her life, she had sat on the stage of the Grace Theater, the other Grace house, in a Victorian stage bedroom, in a stage velvet chair, at the climax of a musical play.

"As if bound, that's the way I want you to sit, Mary," Max Brandel had said, "bound, handcuffed, totally helpless. Before you even open your mouth. And when you do begin to sing, softly, as only you can, that soft singing they can hear in the last row of the balcony, I want you absolutely still. The only things I want to see move are your mouth and your eyes and your breathing and, oh, yes, you could tighten those fingers if you want. Do you see?"

"I see," she said.

"And you stay motionless until the moment you hear that shot offstage. But even then, you don't stop singing, you only stand and begin to crescendo, as only you can crescendo, right up to the high C—and you hold that high C until you bring the house down around your head."

So had spoken, very quietly, a director bringing back to life a fallen star who was putting herself on the line, preparing a last display, to the world at large and the family that believed her finished, of just exactly who, and what, the woman called Mary Gay was.

Such a woman, fighting for her own survival, can be deaf and blind to all but her own needs.

Max, she thought . . . in those stripped thirty seconds . . . waiting for rescue . . . or death . . . or the ultimate horror . . . Max, who only an hour ago on the phone had provoked her into saying yes, all things being equal, on this absurd night she was, yes, reasonably content. Only bored, Max, a little bored, and he had said, "I could fix that, darling, if you'd let me. I could fix that, Miss Gay."

CHAPTER 14

1951-1953

Until that spring night in 1952 when Max Brandel said, so casually and cruelly, "Well, it is difficult about April, but April is not the issue," Mary had not known about them.

In that crowded living room of Genevieve Fawn's, so noisy, so busy, back in the autumn of 1945, Mary Gay saw a threat to her daughter, but it was not Mr. Max Brandel. Not to a seventeen-year-old would that fellow, however brilliant, appeal. No more than Mary Geylin, at seventeen, might have been attracted to Leon Feuerman, the crooked-faced genius of a piano teacher she had planned to follow east to the Curtis Institute. It was that young actor Mary the mother spotted, that handsome Tony Marcus—so like the young Gianni Amara—with his black curls and dark eyes and classic features, his flashy attire and romantic story . . . that was the one, she guessed, though it might just as well have been the soiled Greek god named Banks, or the smooth-faced refugee fellow, Vasarov, with the accent and haunted golden eyes, or the sexy fox-faced singer named Melancon or the ex-marine sergeant, calling himself novelist, named Hubbard. She hated them all, those boy Romeos, sniffing around her daughter, who were ruining her theater, her New York. But April didn't know they were sleazy. April had a crush. A crush she had not cared to tell her mother about, though she had not stopped talking since Mary's return: such a gush of fake confidence, such a stream of red herrings. The sickness came back to the older woman too sharply, the symptoms, the fibs, the sudden lack of candor, the giveaway looks and gestures. There were even cows, Mary thought bitterly, the 1940s versions, hanging around the young actors, that hot-eyed Ruthie Stark in her tight-fitting cashmere sweater, and the ones with big hips in jerseys called Karen and Chloe. Cows for a temperamental girl like April to scorn and compete with and put out of the running; cows to make an unsuitable boy gleam like a treasure; seem more desirable than he actually was.

How bitter she had been that autumn of 1945, how blind to everything but her own pain, though no one knew. Even she hadn't known how bitter, she would think afterward, till she saw April in that room, saw her own young self in that room, and then saw herself in a dark tailored suit and USO arm band in that hospital in Paris, just a year earlier, and throughout the following winter and spring, whenever she could manage a few days between this frontline show and that, spend a few stolen days in the chilly, badly damaged, but blissfully deserted Paris apartment of Gianni Amara. The pictures were too sharp, too painful: of that wartime Mary, the one the boys didn't know about, nursing her lover back to health; seeing him put on weight and a bit of color come back into his face, though not into his permanently white hair; seeing him get stronger, though also seeing him come to terms with the fact that he would never sing again; helping him with that; telling him he must teach, that he would make a wonderful teacher, she knew, she remembered from the studio the things she had learned from him. Stolen days so happy, so curious, she couldn't bear now to think of them; to think of how they had ended, in early summer, just before she left for the Pacific, when she had said to him the words she thought she would never hear herself say: "I love you. I have always loved you. I love you with all my heart. Nothing else matters to me now. Nothing else ever mattered except the children . . . and Charlie. That was all nonsense eight years ago, nonsense. I want to be your wife, Gianni, whenever it can be arranged."

And he had responded with the unbelievable statement that it was too late. He loved her also, with all his heart; but it was too late to talk about marriage. Josephine and the youngest boy, the baby, quite old now, nearly fourteen, were returning to Paris, now that the war was over; Josie had been a good wife to him all those years, and very patient, very understanding eight years ago, and a wonderful mother to the children; too good a wife for him to walk out on now. And it was his turn to say to her, "But it's not good-bye, Mary, you know it isn't good-bye."

But she hadn't laughed and said she'd be back soon, very soon. She had said she never wanted to see him again.

"Why didn't you stay dead, Johnny," those were her parting words. "It would have been simpler."

Bitter. It was more than bitterness she felt. It was a hardness, a pride, a determination to spare her daughter from making the same mistake; she had gone wild, seeing April with that Mr. Anthony Marcus. Something about the way that handsome merry boy had smiled and pushed a hand through his thick black curls had gone through her, making her wild, making her remember, still, in spite of herself, the other, the one who had run out on her, long ago, and just last year . . . or so she chose to think of it.

Afterward she would admit, "I was a bit crazy that fall. Blind that fall."

But even sane and clear-eyed, Mary could not have imagined a girl looking twice at Mr. Max Brandel, the pale Svengali with the five-o'clock shadow. She, Mary, looked at him twice only because he was so annoying to her, such a cocksure fellow, putting ideas into April's head—blowing up a pretty gift into a major talent—and all for the sake of publicity, obviously, for the attention Miss April Archibald Grace could attract as a member of his company. A troublemaker, if Mary ever saw one, was Max Brandel, a manipulator of people whose hash she would soon settle.

I hope you will encourage April to join us next summer, indeed. *A remarkable girl, a serious girl, a talented girl,* indeed, Mr. Brandel. Very serious, very protected, is it, the summer situation with Mr. and Mrs. Goldman providing loving care for the apprentices, indeed, indeed, and the likes of Anthony Marcus and Clifford Banks and John Vasarov and Robert Melancon hanging around. Fat chance.

Thus: "It is not a question of encouraging, Mr. Brandel, it's a question of *allowing,*" Mary had said to him as they stood at the buffet in Genevieve Fawn's apartment, having a friendly drink. "We are an old-fashioned family, very European *au fond.* Will I *allow* April to join you? I know something about serious young people and talent and summer theaters." Upon the director she bestowed her famous smile now, like a spotlight, and made her brown eyes merry. "I imagine April and I will spend the summer together, somewhere. My own plans are not settled, but they could involve a stay in Hollywood." His impertinent answer was almost as provoking as the sight of April making a beeline for the young actor Marcus the minute her back was turned.

A few nights later, Mary went with her sister Isabelle to *Kingdom*—the gloomy masterpiece that was the most talked-about play of the year—and confirmed her feelings. The work repulsed her, though she recognized that Ruby Hollister, the minister's wife with a past, was quite a role for a middle-aged actress. Genevieve Fawn had been directed—overdirected—to a white heat; there was near-hysterical tension in the proceedings, the Brandel touch no doubt, that Miss Gay and her sister, Mrs. Dillon, found de trop. But as Ruby's illegitimate son the handsome Tony Marcus was magnetic and powerful, with a sullen seductive voice that went through you. "That's the one," Mary said to her sister. "I'm not sure," said Belle. "But why take chances?"

So Mary disposed of Genevieve Fawn and her circle, of Mr.

Brandel, the star maker, and Tony Marcus, the handsome stud, and all the other flashy dangerous fellows, as an intelligent and watchful mother can do, as a superstitious woman who believed in patterns and fate must do. Just the sound of the actor's voice on the telephone, asking for April, was enough to make her determined. And the child was hiding something, there was no question about that. As the caretaker of a nubile, impressionable girl, Mary felt absurdly close to her own mother these days. On the phone to Southern California (where the older generations of Geylins had retired a few years back, left Chicago all in a band, it seemed, in search of sun and easier living), in her weekly call to Honora, Mary said that autumn, "I understand now, I see now what it is to be the mother of a daughter."

Going about her business, then, the postwar business of Mary Gay, Mrs. Grace, the mother, was satisfied because in interfering with April's plans she had accidentally put in the child's way a treasure, the best young man in the world, who could give April a safe life, a good life, a normal life, one that would make her happy—for the girl wasn't up to the other life, a life such as Mary Gay's, not by a mile.

That April had not only admired the young director but been in love with him, on the brink of an involvement that might have been serious and lasting, would have seemed outlandish to her mother. Inconceivable. In love! If she was so much in love, what was it all about with Wake Potter? Never had a girl cooperated so readily in her own manipulation, Mary would say with some justice. But if she had seen the situation straight instead of crookedly, would she have behaved any differently? Would she not have disposed of Mr. Brandel in the same way as she thought she was disposing of Mr. Marcus, marched him out of her daughter's life?

Of course she would. She knew a bad character when she saw one, a man dangerous to women.

She would not, however, she didn't believe, have gone after that part in *Lady Ruby*, knowing it was Max Brandel's production. And most certainly she would not have let herself fall in love with the man.

"But of course you would, dearest Mary," said Brandel. "Don't you know yourself by now—a performer and a liar?"

"And a mother," Mary said. "That's what you didn't know—so smart, so *thick*. . . ."

"But even as a mother you continue to perform and lie."

By the spring of 1951 those people of 1945—that Mary at the peak of her fame; that April, shy, eager, with foolish stars in her eyes; that up-and-coming Max Brandel—no longer existed, and the dashing Tony Marcus, Brandel's best friend, so promising, so exciting a performer, had been killed at the wheel of his brand-new sports car, a Maserati paid for out of the earnings of his first starring role.

There was only waning Mary, her last Broadway show a fiasco, fled from Hollywood in despair with two miserable bit parts to her credit, cameo roles not exquisite; poor Mary, a lady supposedly in graceful, gradual, intentional retirement, but bored, miserable, hungering to get back onstage with a hit.

While Max Brandel, on the other hand, had risen fast, become one of the two or three most important directors on Broadway, known for what he did with women, especially difficult women of a certain age. And April was a publicized beauty, a face, a neck, a haughty expression beloved of photographers and top-notch couturiers. Mary didn't even remember that phase, the year April had thought she was an actress. April was the chic Mrs. Wake Potter, mother of Jennifer, Mary Elizabeth, and baby Billy Potter; she was also April Potter, high-fashion model, who looked back on the old days of April Grace—so she told everybody—with amusement and a faint shudder if at all.

In the spring of 1951, when Mary Gay read in a Broadway gossip column that her old friend George Jacobs was planning a musical version of *The Kingdom of the Blind*, to be called *Lady Ruby*, she had only one person on her mind: herself.

"Mary Gay? As my Ruby?" Verna Michaels said to her dinner companions. "Why not Jeanette MacDonald or Irene Dunne? Why not have Shirley Temple play Anne Frank or Mary Martin Medea?"

"I like that last idea, like it a lot," said Max Brandel. Verna was not amused.

They were a group of four—Verna Michaels, Max Brandel, George Jacobs, Harry Dresser—big theatrical names in the early fifties—gathered in one of those doggedly authentic French cafés way west of Broadway that Verna liked, though Max said the food had got greasy since the war and the scolding ways of the *patronne* too tiresome. But it was quiet, off the track for people they knew, perfect for this conversation, much of which was later recalled to Mary Gay by Mr. Brandel when it served his purpose.

"She's interested," said George Jacobs, who had been Charlie Grace's partner, the man who had kept Mary going after her husband's death and had to be listened to. "I'm given to understand that she might audition. Though naturally one does not speak of Mary Gay . . . auditioning."

"*Petitioning* would be more like it after that last disaster," said Verna. "A charity case. You don't see it, surely, Max?"

"I want to look into the possibility," said Max Brandel, the quietest but most powerful member of the quartet. "I met the lady once or twice right after the war when she was full of herself and her glory. The nightingale of the trenches. I didn't care for her much, or the way she manipulated her daughter, a sweet kid who wanted to go on the stage. But it's an interesting idea. She probably still has enough of a voice, and the part is not unconnected with her own life, what I know about it. I've always wondered what she would be like, playing a real woman, a bitch, instead of all those happy fairy-tale ladies."

"Ah, but she told me once," said Verna, "she has a *thing* about suicide."

"Perhaps no longer," said Max. "Perhaps during the course of some dark nights, at her age, she has understood or at least had intimations, a distant lightning flash, of such a possibility."

"Besides we haven't settled that yet, have we, darling," said George Jacobs. "The ending."

And then, before Verna could start screaming again that nothing would persuade her to change the ending, you might as well change the ending of *Romeo and Juliet* or *Oedipus Rex*, and never mind the movie of *Pygmalion*, Harry Dresser, a great survivor himself, who had known Mary longer than anyone in New York, asked if Verna had by any chance seen that show of his, just before the war, called *Lady on the Rocks*, which had starred Mary Gay as an exiled Balkan queen in love with a Soviet spy. No, thank God, if he would forgive her, she hadn't, said Verna. Well, then perhaps, continued Harry, she might have heard Mary Gay on a record, singing a song called "Haunted April." No, said Verna again, and furthermore she didn't believe Mary Gay could have sung that song.

"She sang it first and best, Verna. Long before it was picked up by the jazz musicians and the torch singers," said pint-sized, silver-haired Harry Dresser, Mr. Broadway, who was putting his own reputation on the line with this show, to try something so different in his sixtieth year. "First and best. Sang it in a whisper and shivered the pants off you. And long before that, before you were ever born, darling, did the same in *American Beauty* with 'He Doesn't Even See Me . . .' "

What Verna said then, about Mary Gay shivering the pants off you, Max Brandel would not repeat, though in the same Ninth Avenue bistro, when it became their place, his and Mary's, he would tell his star enough of the conversation to make her fighting-mad and determined, after a disappointing run-through, to show her real stuff.

It was quite literally the first time she'd auditioned—Mary Gay auditioning!—since the winter of 1919 when she'd stood by the piano on the bare stage of the Grace Theater in a softly sashed blue dress and sung the song of little Daisy—"You." Thirty-two years. Time spun. Time retracted and expanded and blew into nothingness like the universe and Proust did not have the key to it, nor Eliot either, those authors she'd struggled with one summer, seeking to improve herself, so she could talk intelligently to her brilliant young son who wanted to be a writer.

Now it was a somber-faced latter-day Harry Dresser at the piano, improvising dissonant chords that were not the chords or rhythms of the young and happy Harry Dresser, or even of his prewar self, the Harry of "Haunted April." And it was a middle-aged Mary, in couturier-constructed black taffeta, standing alone on a stage that was not the Grace or the Belasco or any of the great old proscenium theaters in which she'd once played, but an arena, a newly built circle, a pocket-sized Greenwich Village coliseum in which she was the gladiator fighting for her life (though they would, in the end, come into New York at the Grace). The thick dark-blond hair of Mary at fifty-one gleamed youthfully still, did not have the texture of dyed hair, but the face it framed was drawn, going at the edges. A little blurred was that clear chin line when she wasn't smiling; the chiffon scarf at her throat was more than an affectation now, was a tool, like the bangs: camouflage. And the dress had been made to order to disguise the spreading hips and call attention to the still-magnificent arms and legs, the dainty feet, and those small and perfect hands that were as essential to a Mary Gay rendition of a song as her face.

"Ready, Mary," said Harry Dresser as he had said long ago, playing a few bars of introduction. But Harry Dresser's eyes in 1919, like his songs, had a twinkle. The eyes of Harry Dresser in 1951 gleamed brilliantly like his music but had no twinkle. He is as nervous as I am, Mary thought. How funny.

Until that moment, way back then, she hadn't been nervous, as until that moment, now, she wasn't nervous. All of a sudden, as she had realized then where she was and who was out front listening, so she realized it now; realized the full indignity of now, though she herself was the one who had suggested coming like this to the theater, as if she were some unknown, to see how she felt, onstage, singing this music. But she hadn't quite pictured how uncomfortable, how angry it would make her; nor fully realized the fact that once again, out front, between two important men, sat a middle-aged woman, waiting to be shown, skeptical and impatient as Rose Hart: Miss Verna Michaels, who had recently been quoted in the press as wanting for this part no musical comedy star whatever, but an internationally famed prima donna—"a real singer."

Where was that straw-haired Charlie Grace to give her courage with these barracudas as he'd given her courage that far-off day, calling from the darkness, "You've got a trained voice, Mary. Try to sing now as if you'd never had a lesson, as if you were talking." Oh, she had soared that day, finally, and been so careful with the old bitch. . . . She'll do . . . she doesn't make me want to throw up at least . . . poor Rose. "Monday at ten," Charlie Grace had said, and that had been the beginning.

So now it was Mary Gay, the age Rose Hart had been that day, but not so well off as Rose, not so esteemed, nearly out of the running; middle-aged Mary who stopped the piano, saying, "Please . . . hold it a minute." For she couldn't get with the rhythm of Harry's playing, catch his new idiom, not exactly jazz, not pop Puccini, not Weill or Copland or Menotti, yet with something of all, and somewhere in the mixture a hillbilly violin, a harmonium, a zither. On her piano at home she had played and sung this fierce music so it sounded like 1938 still, melodic and orderly, giving it a shape as "Haunted April" had had a shape. "You've been hearing it wrong, or reading it wrong," said Harry Dresser. "It isn't *pretty*, Mary." And there was no one to speak for her from the darkness except, "Don't try to sing so well, Miss Gay," Max Brandel called. "Listen to him play. I know you have an ear. Listen now with your gut."

For some time Mary listened to this new Harry Dresser of the 1950s whose lyricist was not the urbane Bobby Leeds but a brash boy from Harvard named Jerry Bass, nearly unknown, a protégé of Verna's. Then she gave a nod of understanding and began to follow her old friend in this new raggedy mode that matched the prosody of Jerry Bass. Now she let something come into her mind and gut and memory from long ago, from a time before she had ever come to the Grace Theater; she remembered a brokenhearted girl saying to a stern teacher, *I'd rather sing something at a wake, something sad and mournful by one of those new composers, something that sounds like the wind shrieking* . . . and another memory of a widow saying to a group of concerned men, *How can I go back on that stage and sing of love and a new moon, sing that silly Helen, when I want to sing of a blood moon, of madness; if I had the voice I'd sing* Wozzeck, *tonight.* . . .

[231]

So finally she had such a song, a strange and sinister waltz that was like the wind shrieking, yet sensuous. *I'm in trouble, out of my depth, out of my head because once I was young and wild! help me, forgive me*: that was what the waltz said that Harry Dresser had written for Verna Michaels' Ruby . . . trapped Ruby, the wife of the crusading minister, trapped in her own lies.

"This is your chance," Mary said to herself, as she had said before in her life. "Take it, for God's sake, take it."

Now she let her voice soar in a different way, feeling the jagged line that was distant from the melodists, from Puccini and Schubert and Johann Strauss—and the young Harry Dresser—yet had its own beauty once you understood it, that was passionate, profligate, surprising, and folklike, rough as a mountain ballad, calling for a voice to be used in a way every coach she had ever worked with had warned Mary Gay not to use hers, if she wanted to hold on to its silver sheen, its amazing freshness. But what good was the silver sheen doing her now? Her last performance had been compared to Billie Burke's as Glinda of Oz . . . unfavorably.

And the man at the piano nodded. He didn't smile and wink as he had long ago, for it wasn't smiling, winking music, but he stared at her in a different way than he had before, and, looking to the people out front, asked her to do another number she hadn't prepared. She listened for a moment to his playing; studied the music; began to sing again, a rowdy number this time, harshly gay, in the tempo of a square dance.

"I like it," Max Brandel said quietly when she'd finished. "I like what you do a lot, Miss Gay."

Verna Michaels looked at him exasperated, yet accepting. "We won't do better," she said flatly. "I see that. How odd."

And then Verna turned to Mary, conceding something, offering something, making the first move toward friendship, that friendship destined to endure which would be one of the more curious by-products of the making of *Ruby*: Mary Gay and Verna Michaels, buddies. "You see," said Verna, "I couldn't imagine that silvery voice, that beautiful voice, the voice of 'Haunted

April," the voice I heard years ago in *Rose*, working with this music."

"I wasn't sure either," said Mary, "till today. I agree. It is odd." She gave a faint smile; she nodded, with a touch of hauteur, but it wasn't the old hauteur—royalty addressing the peasants— it was something more simple and direct: dignity, pride in having held her own.

"Not odd," said Harry Dresser, remembering the beginning. "If you've known Mary as long as I have."

"I'll have my agent call you tomorrow morning," said Mary Gay, all business now, to Max Brandel as he walked her to her waiting limousine. But her eyes were sparkling. Sparkling as the mica in the pavement, as the midtown spires that gleamed in the distance, a backdrop to the low Village skyline; sparkling as the air on this gorgeous New York afternoon.

Only a day ago a middle-aged woman named Mary Gay had thought back to herself at the age of nineteen preparing for her first audition and wondered bitterly how thirty-two years could be so short. She had wondered how it was possible that this adopted city of hers, so exciting to her once, so electric, so clear, had become so boring and confusing, so unrecognizable. Only twelve hours ago, at four in the morning, a fifty-one-year-old woman awake with a racing pulse had lain in bed, listening to the sirens, to the sound of a plane overhead, to throbbing music from across the garden, the sound of thumping, a young people's party, and waited for a heart attack, though the doctor insisted it was nerves; only twelve hours ago she had thought of death. Now the years were gone; death was once again something that happened to someone else. Years, what did they matter? She had a job to do, in this merciless, marvelous city that was hers again. She was happy.

"Thank you," she said to Max Brandel. What did it matter if as a man he was vaguely repulsive to her in his corduroy suit and turtleneck, with his tangled black hair and shadowed jaw. He had had a hunch about her. She had justified his hunch. "On

some days," she said, "don't you adore New York?" All days,"
he said. "Ah no! . . . don't tell me . . . is it possible you are
a real New Yorker?" "No Miss Gay. A middle westerner like
yourself." The smile she gave him as they stood for a moment
on the bright afternoon street in front of her waiting car was
bewitching and young; dimples formed in her cheeks. A ridiculous smile for a woman of fifty-one, he'd tell her. The look he
gave her was interested and equal, a curious look, she'd tell him
later, for a man of thirty-four to give a woman of fifty-one. Those
blue eyes: she hadn't noticed them before. Rather intriguing, those
narrow, bright blue eyes.

But no flicker. No little frisson. No sudden attack of hind-
sight concerning the crush, the oh so secret, oh so visible crush
of April. Nothing picked up from the look he gave her when he
asked, "How is April? Be sure to give her my best."

"April! April is in London right now, the lucky girl," she
said. "A real beauty. Perhaps you've seen her photograph in
Vogue or the *Bazaar* and not recognized her. And a mother, with
two beautiful little girls and a brand-new baby boy. Divinely
happy."

If April wasn't happy, who in the world ever would be, her
mother would think. Living in a beautiful flat just a block from
Kensington Gardens, while the gruff and attractive Wake Potter,
so shrewd about business, set up British offices for his New York
firm. Money to spend on herself and the children. An amusing
circle of friends. Every door open to her. And a profession that
worked well with being a wife and mother, a glamour girl on the
move. "All London is in love with your exquisite daughter," a
friend had written. There was no reason in the world, writing
April about the show, to feel self-conscious. Still Mary did the
letter six times over, to get the right tone, to mention Max Brandel
and Verna Michaels and Robert Melancon, the child's old ac-
quaintances, casually, almost as if they were peripheral to the
venture, focusing on herself and Harry Dresser, the two old friends
and colleagues, and the music, the strangeness of Dresser writing
and Mary Gay singing such a role as Ruby.

[234]

April wrote back—eventually—with equal care and casualness, congratulating her mother, wishing her luck and saying, yes, it was a coincidence that Mary should be working with these people, then adding, quite gratuitously it seemed to the parent, that it was also so *funny*, looking back on it, the way her mother saw wolves everywhere that fall in New York when the real wolf was Lieutenant hot-pants Potter in Chicago; life was very amusing.

Mary might have caught something from the tone of that letter, a warning for the future. Mary the mother, that is. But Mary the mother was on leave that year; grateful, simply, that April was temporarily abroad; and that Lion had emerged from his bohemian year, taken a job at a news magazine, dropped that seductive but unsavory lady poet, and gone back to squiring around town the mouse Serena, a more sensible way, in his mother's opinion, of killing time till the right girl came along. Mary that year wanted to live and work as if she had no children, no grandchildren, no life other than the man Max Brandel; no responsibilities other than that show and the preparation of a performance.

She would hate him. She would fight him every inch of the way. She would come to fear him for those blue looks, a repertory of looks, and that quiet voice—a word here, a word there, no yelling or public chewing-out of even the lowliest players, just a look, a frown, a suggestion that it might be better this way; and an occasional very bright, very warm, and slightly crooked smile.

The day Miss Mary Gay threatened to walk out it was only for a look, a frown, a voiced question, an intensifying light in his blue eyes: had he been mistaken? Could she do it after all? Could she break down Lady Mary, break the mold, forget her manners, play a tough, grasping woman, someone not nice? The day the ingenue walked out, not to return, had been for a look, a frown. The day he fired the costume designer, it had been for the costume designer's response to his "no"—a simple Brandel "no." On the other hand, the day Verna Michaels agreed to work with the famous play doctor instead of walking out, it was for one of those hypnotic "noes" also.

"No," he would say quietly to his star. "No."

She had never heard such a soft and terrifying word.

"Yes," he would say, and the "yes" would terrify her even more. "Yes, you can do it, you know," he would say, "you know what this is all about. Loss. Guilt. Sudden death. The grip of the past. Or if you don't, imagine!" "You've always wanted to act— really act," he would say. "Now's your chance. Or are you scared?"

And then, precious as sun in a March sky of scudding clouds, the bright crooked smile: That's it! That's it!

She would fall for all his tricks, abuse herself, make herself naked under the cruel spotlight of his glance. It would take them a year and untold ups and downs to get from that first audition to a New York opening night, trials Mary would later record in a tone of atrocious false gaiety in her memoirs. And Max Brandel would get from Mary Gay the performance of her lifetime, the one she had been born to give. Mary Gay as Ruby Hollister, magnificent, magnified, the voice stretched for drama, the preservatives taken off, the white gloves taken off, the fairy-tale lady playing a tigress, a fierce maternal creature, going down fighting, sacrificing everything for her husband's rise in the world, then sacrificing him for her child. He would also make Robert Melancon a greater star than he already was and yank young Carrie Coleman of the big round eyes and flashing feet out of the chorus and allow her to become the new Broadway baby (*good . . . not too good, Carrie . . . watch Miss Gay . . . careful*), give baby-faced Larry Rosen, in the old Tony Marcus role, his start, and seventy-year-old Gloriana Bellehaven, in a small character part, a reason to go on living. He would help Harry Dresser, Jerry Bass, and Verna Michaels win their Pulitzer Prize. And together, all of them, they would have a show that, as one pompous reviewer put it, would add yet another and more exciting dimension to an American musical theater already revitalized by the great hits of the forties.

Only Mary, the real-life mother, the real-life woman, would turn this triumph into an ugly business. Why?

One night in the early spring of 1952, very near home and that Broadway opening, when they knew finally they had a show, in a murky out-of-town grillroom in the basement of an out-of-town hotel, in an out-of-town city, Max Brandel would approach his star in a different way, pose a different question with those piercing blue eyes, as if he were doing her a favor, doing the old girl a favor, giving her the treat she'd been waiting for, the reward every woman waited for.

"Ruby is me," she said that Saturday night, the shouts and cheers they'd finally received that night still ringing in her ears, the standing ovation because finally the last ten minutes—the great and impossible scene—was right.

"I know. Don't you think I know," he said, in a way that gave her a curious feeling as if he knew, or thought he knew, more than he was saying. He put a finger to his lips. She could scarcely remember how once she thought him unattractive, with his dark looks—almost pretty, almost ugly—his crooked smile, how she had found the blue eyes menacing. Now his was the face she loved, as his fingers, touching her cheek, and his eyes holding hers, posed a familiar question. "It's up to you, lady," he said.

"Don't do me any favors," she said, laughing at him, not quite believing what had happened to her over the course of a long year, that at an improbable age she had fallen in love again. "I don't need any favors. Not quite yet. God, I disliked you the first time I ever saw you."

"Well, naturally. It was mutual." For a moment, though his hand didn't leave her cheek, there was a flicker as if he was going to say something she might not like, then thought better of it, or thought it not important.

"What? What were you going to say?"

"Nothing. Nothing to do with us, I believe."

"I agree," she said, though wasn't quite sure what she was agreeing to.

The word was *yes*, repeated several times, whispered, spoken, voluptuous, terrifying: yes . . . yes . . . ah, yes . . . that's it . . . yes. . . .

"It's crazy," she said later in the darkness of her hotel bedroom, a seamy room that had a transient air about it, waking up to what had happened and with whom; the very thing she had sworn would never happen to her, to fall in love; to be happy again that way; to allow herself to love a man who made love to her; to care enough to speak afterward. Only she wouldn't let him turn on the light. "I always swore. And above all, not a younger man. Young enough, almost, to be my son."

"But don't you know it's always crazy between a man and a woman," said he who had broken down the Lady Mary, onstage and now in bed. "No matter how ordinary it seems. And between parents and children also. Crazy."

It was every night after that, enough nights so that to give him up would be terrible. Shyly, a trifle embarrassed, they talked of marriage. He had a child, he said, a thirteen-year-old son by an early mistake, a college marriage to a co-ed, a fellow drama major at the University of Chicago, dissolved soon after the boy was born. Beautiful, brilliant, miserable girl—like Mary, a dark-eyed blonde. For a long time he hadn't seen his son. The mother had returned with the baby to her native Los Angeles. There had been great bitterness, though in recent years since Betty's remarriage he and the kid had had some good holidays together. A regular westerner, his son. A fine boy. He wasn't looking for children. He was looking for a new life on that stage; the thrill when finally the thing was right, alive, so you could hold it in your hand. Otherwise he frankly wasn't looking, hadn't been looking. She was an accident, but having happened . . .

Exactly her sentiments, Mary said.

They were sealed, pledged. Only.

"What happened?" Mary would say to Max on the telephone. "What is going on? Where is my daughter? You talked to her last."

And Max on the other end of the telephone would say lazily —he was, after all, a man on top of the world that morning— "God, Mary, I don't know. April's always been a sensitive girl, full of secrets. She should talk to someone, really talk some of it out."

"What secrets?" Mary asked. "Talk out *what?*"

"All the things that are bothering her, I suppose," Max said, sounding rather bored. "You and me, I suppose."

And the cold in her stomach began to spread, even as he was talking so lazily, so calmly, spread to her throat so her voice came out a whisper, a breath of ice: "You and me . . . *Why you and me . . . why?*"

2

It wasn't April Mary wondered about the night of the New York opening, but Lion. How Lion was going to react to his mother in such a role; and eventually, how Lion was going to react to his mother in such a relationship. *Fifteen minutes, Miss Gay . . . five minutes, Miss Gay . . . overture, Miss Gay. . . .* In the wings, by herself, waiting for the overture to do its work, Mary could imagine her son out front, stirring uneasily as the orchestra went into the waltz, the theme song, the mood song, but not a lilting old-time waltz such as he might remember from his boyhood, from the days when Mary Gay, his mother, was the birthday party queen, the singing sweetheart of Broadway. This was a dissonant raucous waltz, Strauss gone to the devil, Richard, not Johann. . . . Harry Dresser gone to the devil and come out the other side. It struck a pose, that waltz, that raggedy and furious overture, announcing the evening ahead as something different. But it was only a fleeting thought of Lion that came to the star, standing in the wings: little Lion in velvet, or in an Eton suit, throwing a red rose. Then she touched her good-luck medal and moved onto the stage to take her place among the chorus—first of a series of surprises, that she would be there, hidden, one of the crowd, unprepared for, unspotlighted, as the curtain rose. She had paid her dues to Lion long ago.

Of the others, the women in her life—her daughter, her

sister, her mother—she thought not at all, though when it was all over she would be interested to hear what her mother had to say, for this was the sort of role Honora had wanted her to try for years, only she had to stay glamorous . . . glamorous for her fans, glamorous for her family, the other members of the family who liked her as she was, the eternally familiar Lady Mary.

And "Puzzled indeed was my group," Honora would say later; at seventy-eight she was letting the sharpness come out, "expressed in coughing and exchanged glances during the overture and the first scene; Mr. Wake Potter's detachable eyebrow hit the ceiling; Louis the lion was stirring most uneasily, as was my dear grandson-in-law. Miss Serena was quiet, of course, the perfect lady, but startled; your sister, Belle, put on that brave smile, you know the one, and left it there; April, who can tell about April," her grandmother would say. "All around us you could see people were puzzled, not sure what to think of this new music, this new Mary Gay, but I liked it right off," Honora would say, "and preened myself a bit, thinking I was special." Thinking so through the first scene—a bonneted Mary embedded in a church congregation, invisible, though the star, until her voice rose a little above the others in a hymn—silent, though the star, as Robert Melancon sang his sermon—and the second scene—Mary in a quiet evening duet with Melancon on the church steps—and the opening of the third scene, in which Mary, alone at her kitchen table, a barefaced middle-aged woman in a bun and a dark dress, opened the morning mail, singing a ditty about the mail of the minister's wife in a soft, faintly amused voice: till she came to the letter that caused her to freeze and then grow wild in song, wild with thought of the past brought on by a lethal letter.

And thinking herself all this while alone in her excitement, as the song came to an end, the mother of the star, the majestic gray-haired lady in purple moiré clapped vigorously, conspicuously, thinking to start a movement, telling the stupid people around her this was wonderful, only to find her own clapping, her mother's cheers, drowned in a huge buffeting rain of applause and cheers and shouts of bravo from all around her, from the very ones who had exchanged looks and coughed during the overture, for it was a voice, the voice of Mary, not instruments, that strange music was made for, a voice that would make those off-center songs easy as speech.

"Everyone discovered you in that first big aria, the letter song, thinking themselves unique," Honora would tell her daughter. And so from then on the evening would proceed.

Mary only knew she was giving as she had never given before in her life; was telling the world what her family had perhaps suspected and the men in her life had always known: I am not Mary the gay, the good, the golden one—I am Mary a fierce woman who has known greed, lust, envy, pride, anger, all the deadliest sins save sloth—I am a little crazy—I am a character. She knew out of town that finally they had reached the place Max wanted. But out of town was not New York. She frankly hadn't expected the roar, the pandemonium that came at the end. Most of all she hadn't expected the look on Max Brandel's face. After the curtain had gone up and down, up and down, after the standing ovation for the stars, and the many bows for the villain, the ingenue, and the new juvenile lead, for the character actors, the fine old troupers, for the swift dancers and chorus of town maidens; after the composer had taken his bow and the author hers and an enormous bouquet of yellow roses from her children had been presented to Mary, finally to cries of "Director, director" the man who had returned Miss Gay to her public in an impossible role and won the gamble came onstage. He looked pale and slight in the bright spotlights, next to his costumed painted players, but dominated the stage and was smiling, giving her, his star, a quick bright crooked smile and then a great public embrace . . . and then the look that went beyond desire, that was simpler than love, a look of unadorned affection, of comradeship, of respect untinged with even the faintest fear. Her chance for something right. Honest.

And was it that look April found unbearable, Mary would wonder. Had the child imagined herself on a stage, someday, receiving such a look from a director or co-star . . . but that would have been a fantasy, unfounded envy, and April was not envious; one of the nicest things about her, so the family had noticed ever since she was a little girl, was her lack of enviousness, her generosity.

"Such a wonderful family," a stranger said, coming up to Miss Gay in Sardi's afterward, "there must be a picture." And someone did take a picture of the group gathered around the star's opening-night table, a picture that would not, however, be reproduced in the photographic section of her memoirs, to her editor's disappointment; "we all look too ghastly in that picture," she would say, though in fact it was an unusually good picture of its kind, and such a jolly lineup: the star herself, radiant in a satin *robe de style* and the famous Grace ruby, and her gypsy-faced director, unexpectedly suave in a tuxedo instead of his usual black turtleneck . . . the star's mother, such a great old character, so queenly, so erect, though going on seventy-nine . . . and the star's sister and sister-in-law, the slightly over-the-hill beauties, who both knew how to smile for the camera, and the star's suave brothers-in-law, the one who ran things in Chicago, the one who ran things in New York, who knew how not to smile for the camera. There were the star's cousins, the Geylin brothers, Walter the violinist, Danny the pianist, and their well-dressed European wives, and the star's ancient aunt and uncle, ninety if a day (never let it be said Mary was not loyal) . . . and of course the children, April and her smiling blond husband, and Lion and the solemn pretty girl he sometimes dated, who was not a *girl*, Mary had been heard to say, just a friend, you know . . . like one of the family.

Mary's family. Backstage drivers—performance after performance, year after year, scolding, essential, inescapable.

As for the director's family, a mother and married sister who lived in Cleveland, and a teenage son in school in Colorado, they sent telegrams. "Telegrams," said Max, "have a point."

All Sardi's stood up to applaud the entrance of Mary Gay on the arm of Max Brandel. Then, "There, Mr. Brandel," commanded Honora, who had placed herself in charge of the seating.

[242]

"Next to April, and Mary between you and Lion. There! Now everyone has someone."

"How nice," Mary said to her son, taking her place. "I haven't seen you in weeks."

"How nice," she heard Max say to her daughter, "I haven't seen you in years."

Mary talked to Lion and beyond Lion to Serena and Honora. Max talked to April and no one beyond, his back half turned to Mary, though from time to time he held a lighter for her cigarette, whenever she took one from the gleaming case—gold with a small ruby initial—that was the director's opening-night present to his star. Without ever looking at her he seemed to know when she wanted a light. Mary was concentrating on Lion, listening hard to Lion, though it was difficult sometimes to follow what he was saying, he pursued a subject so doggedly; listening equally hard to her mother, trying to interpret Honora's words concerning the show and the man who had made it possible, and discern what her mother was really thinking, and on which side, when the family began lining up, her mother would be.

But Mary couldn't help at a certain moment hearing April's voice, so clear, so steady, though the voice of Max beside her was a murmur.

"Ah yes," said April, "that is indeed my photograph, my face, you see plastered all over *Harper's Bazaar*, but it was always the face, I think, the bones, the hair, that fooled people into thinking I could act. What a joy, the world of the face! Ten to four, fifty dollars an hour, nights your own." In a red and gold sari, her hair crisp in the new short European style, a fashionable tossed salad of frosted blond curls, her white powdered arms and shoulders perfect, her neck interminable, April was dazzling, Wake Potter's captive beauty who, if Wake kept on as he was, might one day run an embassy.

"Wonderful, wonderful," the exquisite young woman was saying to the man who had befriended her for a season when she had been stagestruck. "And I've got three wonderful children, two little girls and a boy, and that's what matters." And then again, "It was Wake or the theater, and I chose Wake." But

[243]

finally, just before George Jacobs came to their table with the first notice, the special-delivery love letter to Miss Mary Gay from the most respected of Broadway critics, she heard April say, "But I wouldn't have imagined *this*. It's a bit rich, *this*."

Mary reached for the notice. Then she said to Max, "You read it, please, I can't."

"I think I'll read it aloud," Max said presently.

Mary was looking down, staring at her hands as he read . . . words about Verna Michaels and Harry Dresser, about Robert Melancon and Carrie Coleman and himself, the magician Brandel, words leading up to the phrases that would bring hot stupid tears to her eyes. "Better than all of them put together is Miss Mary Gay. Miss Gay of the golden hair and amber eyes, the angelic voice and siren smile, has let it be known for the first time in her long and inordinately successful career that she can act, as well as sing and make us laugh, and shed a tear or two. Now we know, Miss Gay. Now we know for sure what we could have guessed if we'd been as bright as you." Max read, and the tears blinded her, for the words he read, for the sudden sharp thought of Charlie Grace, the wish, though it was nearly twenty years now, that he might be alive and listening with her. And so she didn't see the expression on April's face that might have prepared her for the odd comment her daughter made when Max had finished reading, for the tight little voice of April on the warpath cutting through the happy exclamations of the other members of the party.

"Brown people, was it, Mother," April said. "It looks like the brown people have dealt you a pack of glory."

"Brown people?" said Max, giving a crooked smile.

"Yes! That's what she called all of you—and worse—isn't that right, Mother, life is so ironic, so funny."

Mary smiled brightly, determined to take her daughter's response as a bit of misplaced kidding. "Well, darling, I'd hate to think of what he called me. Life is funny, I agree, full of wonderful ironies."

"Behave, Miss April," Max said, softly, but not so softly Mary didn't hear.

"Behave, Miss April," Max repeated in answer to a whispered remark, *"that's the way it happens."* The look he exchanged with April made Mary uneasy, as if there was something she didn't know, hadn't caught, she who prided herself on knowing and catching everything.

And then Max stood up to toast Mary—his star, his lady, his love—and to make the announcement that caused such a commotion around the table, such excitement and surprise and ill-concealed consternation, that nobody noticed April leaving, or worried for quite some time, having noticed her absence, that she had not returned.

3

The phone call from Wake Potter interrupted one of the more delightful mornings of Mary's life: a morning of flowers and telegrams, of telephone calls, including two from overseas, and more incredible notices, the critics of the afternoon papers making it a unanimous yes—yes for *Ruby*, yes for Mary, yes for Max, who had had too much champagne last night and—speaking of yes, her yes to him—had certainly spilled the beans, but she had had to forgive him, half crying, half laughing, even thank him for spilling the beans like that, with all the family assembled, just blurting it out, he who never blurted . . . *Mary has done me the honor* . . . *Mary and I* . . . for who knew if she would ever have had the courage. It was almost too much excitement, she had thought that morning, before Wake's call, lying back in bed against her pillows, touching on wood because it wasn't wise, she knew, for her to dare to be happy; when she dared to be happy the green-eyed gods looked down and frowned . . . and said . . . *No!*

So there came, around noon, that call from a furious and anxious Wake, saying he'd been trying to get through all morning to tell Mary that April had disappeared.

They had quarreled, Wake said, about her leaving the party like that, and then about a lot of things, and he had said a lot of things for which he was sorry. Meantime she'd left a note saying she was going away for a few days to cool off and not to try to find her. She was sure he and Dolores between them could manage the kids for a few days; Dolores could stick them in front of the TV while cooking; if not, why not call her mother?

"What the hell did that guy say to her?" Wake shouted on the phone.

"I'm not deaf, Wake. Guy? What guy?"

"I'm talking about Mr. Max Brandel," said Wake in a quieter voice that was even more displeasing to his mother-in-law than his shout. "The brilliant Mr. Brandel, your husband-to-be, April's stepfather-to-be, who was talking, talking to her, all through supper, reminiscing about the old days, I suppose. What the hell did he say to my wife?"

"I don't know. I was busy with Lion and my mother. Watch it, Wake."

"Putting ideas in her head. April's scatterbrain enough. She could flip without a strong hand. You don't know where she is?"

"April didn't used to be scatterbrain, Wake," Mary said, feeling a sudden intense dislike for the wonderful Wake, the beloved son-in-law. "I haven't any idea. People walk out sometimes, when they can't stand it anymore. Even I walked out once, on my wonderful Charlie. I came back. She'll be back. Sometimes she does things, I've noticed that over the years, in unconscious imitation. Did you call Lion?"

"Lion went out of town on some assignment."

"Then try little Serena Watkins. She and April are very close. She knows how April's mind works."

"I've called Serena. Not a clue."

"Well, try Lucy Dillion then, and if she can't help, I'd check the airlines."

"What airlines? North, East, South, or West? Aren't you worried about your daughter?"

"No," Mary said firmly, though her stomach was churning and the back of her neck prickling. "I'm really not. I've worried too much in my life. Maybe it's that strong hand of yours, Wake, that's made her go a little crazy. I'd watch that strong hand when she comes back. . . ." And then, breaking a little, "But please—call me the minute you hear something. Call me one way or the other before I leave for the theater."

Her hand was shaking as she hung up; shaking as she dialed Max's number, which was busy.

April only went to Florida that time.

"The next time it will be farther," she said when she flew home five days later with a tan and lots of shells for the children. It was Lion, it turned out, who knew where she had been in case of emergency.

"I am upset also," Lion said when Mary asked him why he hadn't relieved all their minds. "I don't go around making scenes, that's all."

"About what?"

"What do you think, Mother? It was worth it, almost, to see the expression on Aunt Tilly's face, but not quite. . . . You might have given us a little warning. . . . *I want to propose a toast to Mary . . . my star . . . and future wife.* Oh boy."

"You were very polite," Mary said, "and Max was very drunk. He can't drink. Thank you for being so polite. But there's nothing to make a scene about. Poor Max. He was premature, I'm afraid, in his announcement, and most unwise—thinking to trap me. Nobody traps me, Lion, nobody. Not even you."

"You and me—why you and me—*why?*" she said to Max in the darkness of her bedroom the first night of April's disappearance. And when he was silent, "I suppose she's embarrassed, like Lion. I've always been so discreet, so careful. It's been easy enough. Nothing has touched me since Charlie died." The lie came unexpectedly. She had not meant to lie to Max, had not needed to lie to him for he had never asked her any questions that demanded a lie. But now, in the darkness, she persisted . . . Oh, the body from time to time. But never me. I suppose they are both embarrassed. I should be also. Seventeen years. You were born the year I was seventeen. That was quite a year, when I was seventeen. I used to laugh at middle-aged women with young husbands. One laughs till it happens." And when he was still silent, "And then I suppose there is some genuine distress at the idea, after all these years, that I will no longer be Mrs. Grace . . . and there must have been a big fight with Wake— was that it—you and I caused Wake Potter finally to show his true colors—it's taken me a while to get on to him. . . ." Talking, talking in the darkness, trying to talk her way out of the silence, till finally Max spoke, though he had been as singularly silent this night as he had been singularly talkative the night before.

"Oh, Mary, really. The star's children embarrassed. Forget the son-in-law, forget the son. You've spent too much of your life, and his, worrying about Lion. Let's look at the one who matters. April. It is difficult about April, but April is not the issue. I know, by the way, where she is. She's fine. Leave her alone. And let the husband stew a bit. He deserves to."

"You know? How?"

"I made it my business to find out. It wasn't very hard. I know how April's mind works." And then he began to talk about April, the dear April, the old April of 1945 who, alas, no longer existed.

What he was saying now made no sense to her. April was transparent as glass and couldn't lie to save her life. April had no wiles, no cunning. April was angry at Mary about that young man, what was his name, she couldn't even remember, blamed her mother still about that handsome intriguing young actor, about the career that might have been. And now, of course, he was dead—tragic—but would April's going to that summer theater have saved her would-be lover's life?

"Young man?" said Max. "Lover? I was the would-be lover."

"I assumed you knew," he said presently. Mary was the one who had remained silent now, feeling the hotness spread, the tingling in her extremities, the rapid pulse, a whole host of disagreeable symptoms connected with those occasional times in her life when she had to admit to being wrong about something.

Had to accept that she, Mary, infallible Mary, had made a gaffe. In this case a rather large gaffe, one she could not assimilate, that was about to bring on a terrible rage.

"Assumed I knew?" Now she opened her eyes and switched on the bedside lamp and stared at Max. *"Knew what?"*

"That we were very close, April and I. I'd known her from the time she was thirteen years old, after all, and her feelings for me weren't exactly a secret, though she thought herself invisible. The dear girl. What a handful she might have been. Oh, you got her out in time, darling, and very intelligently too. April told me, one day when she was brave enough to have lunch with me after you'd forbidden her. 'My mother is terrified of you,' she said. *'Terrified.'* But into what? What sort of life did you get her into, the poor child? What sort of life did I set her up for?"

"A very fine life," Mary said, out of bed now, on the chaise longue in a wrapper, smoking a cigarette, speaking slowly, trying to keep her voice steady. "But I didn't know. I thought it was your friend Marcus she was crazy about. Him, or that other one, the gilded youth with the dirty fingernails, but he turned out to like boys, so it had to be Marcus."

"Why? Why would you have thought that?"

"He was so attractive. So handsome. So dangerous. *You* . . . it never entered my mind. Never. No wonder she's angry at me. You must have thought me such a bitch."

"Way beyond that, Mary. Way beyond."

And then the black cloud broke.

"You and April . . . my daughter . . . taking my daughter's leavings. . . ."

Instead of taking offense he laughed, as men had laughed at her before when she said something too insulting. But the laughter wasn't getting through, not that night.

When she began screaming and throwing things at him, telling him to get out, he said, "I believe you're mistaking me for someone else."

"I am," she cried. "I am. Now tell me where my daughter is."

"Somewhere safe," he answered as he left the room. "Perfectly safe."

"You're a fool, Mary," Max Brandel said a few weeks later, in Mary's drawing room, the last time they met for any reason other than business. "Your daughter would not be that kind of fool. Not these days," said Max. "You and I could be happy."

She had heard those words before, she thought, but saw no reason to tell him; she had told him too much as it was.

"April is not an issue."

"You're repeating yourself."

"If you and I were happy, you could let those children go. Both of them. Give them a chance. Have you heard that before? I bet you have not, mother Mary. They've got their lives, you've got yours. Don't throw yours away. I'm down on my knees, begging. I have such plans, plans for when you won't sing anymore, plans for you to be on that stage till the day you die."

"Oh, listen," she said, "you can still put me on a stage. You can always put me on a stage, for that has nothing to do with my children. If you ask me back on your stage, Mr. Brandel, I'll come. Five years from now. Ten years from now. Twenty years from now, if we're both still alive. That's our story, after all . . . our real story."

As for the other story, the one that was Mary's secret: "So where are you going for your well-earned holiday?" said Lion Grace to his mother in the early summer of 1953 when he heard that for the month of July the title role of *Ruby*—in its second year and still doing stand-up business—would be taken over by Karen Draper while Mary Gay took a vacation.

"Paris," said Mary, smiling at Lion, smiling at the mouse Serena who was along for lunch that day, her on-again off-again presence in the young man's life a matter his mother had long ago given up explaining, to herself, or anyone else in the family, only that it seemed to coincide with the ending of some unfortunate love affair, another Lion debacle, so Mary was always rather glad to see the girl, though impatient with her shyness, her heavy way with a conversation, and the dreary way she dressed and did her hair, like a little ballerina, though with attention she could be quite striking. How striking she had been the day Lion met her, at the school play, in a black velvet doublet, shaking out her hair that was pulled back now in a tight bun, giving her the look, with those sloe eyes and that sharp nose, of a cartoon mouse.

"Paris? In July?" the mouse said now in her soft, breathy finishing-school voice. "Won't that be dreadfully hot? I thought everyone left Paris in July."

"No, that's August, dear. Paris is rather lovely in July," said Mary. "The bores have departed and the worst of the tourists haven't yet arrived."

"Paris!" said Lion, giving her a rather peculiar look, but she wasn't having any of Lion's peculiar looks anymore. That was one thing Max had done for her, stopped her from fussing about Lion's reactions. "I thought you hated Paris, Mother. Except for the time you played it during the war. You wouldn't even fly over with April, that time in London, when she was modeling the collections."

"That's true," his mother said amiably. "People change, you know. I'm looking forward to the city, to seeing old friends, and even a few old enemies." The smile she gave him was bright, teasing, a shutout, and the conversation moved on to something in the current news, but Mary was aware that Serena was watching her, puzzled, a little envious, as if she wished she could be like that with Lion, tease him, get his goat, perplex him, win his heart.

Aboard the overnight plane to Paris, suspended in the uneasy cloud softness of a berth in the sky, lulled by the drone of the engines, Mary tried to imagine the scene a few days hence. The darkbrowed, white haired man entering the salon of her suite at the Ritz, saying *well Mary, so here you are finally. You didn't make your impetuous and unsuitable marriage after all.* And she would say, *It was your fault, the whole business. Everything is always your fault, one way or another, so I decided to forgive you again. . . . After eight years*, he might say just before taking her in his arms, *there can't be anymore of these eight years.* But she couldn't imagine any further, lying alone and awake in that airplane berth. She could only hope, as the plane began bumping again, hope for a safe landing and another chance.

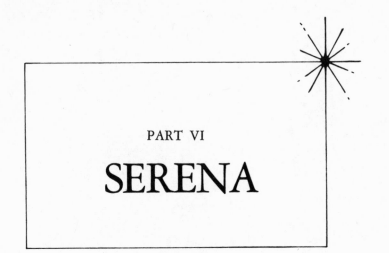

PART VI

SERENA

CHAPTER 15

1975

The doorbell rang. Serena stood alone, as she knew would happen if she let him go up there . . . for as things were in the beginning, so they would always be, for a love, a marriage, a party, a life. She had a vision, not very nice, as she moved toward the door: of all such evenings, such celebrations, beginning and ending with her alone. No presence beside her, in formal black or pin-striped navy or soft gray tweed; no hand lightly tapping her shoulder—you're on, Mrs. Grace—no voice whispering in her ear a provoking remark that she wouldn't be able to answer for another four hours; no Lion, no man. Only Serena hurrying down the bedroom corridor, through the sparkling decorated front hall, to welcome the first arrival. And four hours later, still alone, seeing out the last hanger-on, locking up, emptying ashtrays, a solitary woman in a dress like Christmas wrapping, shapeless and ageless, that had lasted for years.

That was her vision, not very nice for a married woman with two beautiful daughters and a husband she loved, as she opened the door to the first of the guests. Nearly twenty years they'd been man and wife—Serena Watkins and the son of Mary Gay—yet she'd never believed him securely hers; never believed he felt married, that the two of them were anything but an accident, a long-running improvisation.

God help her. It was Verna Michaels standing framed in the doorway with the elevator closing behind her. Verna, the bane of the leisure classes, the friend of the working man in ankle-length mink and diamond earbobs, with a hatchet face to match her tongue. The first. To be amused, to be placated. In her hand she held a small narrow box, an offering for her beloved buddy: a gold bracelet, perhaps diamonds—she could afford them.

"Miss Michaels! How wonderful you're so prompt! Lion has gone to get Mary and they aren't back. . . . Coats in there, second door to the left . . . and we're putting the presents here, on this table. Yes, aren't those roses magnificent. They must be a surprise from someone . . . they weren't ones we ordered. . . ." She could hear her hostess voice, the one Lion hated, private school girlish, nervous, affected, brought on by Mary's friends no matter how hard they tried, as Miss Michaels was trying now, returned from the bedroom, a perfumed battle-ax in lavender silk, saying, "What an attractive apartment! And call me Verna, dear. Now, aren't there daughters?"

As if in answer, right on cue, from beyond the pantry door came a cry; the sound of a crash; then the maidenly voice of Marjorie Grace: *God damn it,* Emma, can't you ever *watch* it.

"Indeed there are daughters," said Serena gaily, calling, Marjorie! Emma! Come out here! And which was the one, asked Verna gravely, as the girls appeared saying "Nothing important" when asked what broke—"Is this the impatient one, born on Mary's birthday . . . or was it early the next day?" She extended a thin spotted hand to Mary Gay's granddaughters, to Marjorie—the one, "and it was the next day"—and Emma, who followed, looking them over, up and down, not cracking a smile as if somehow they were still the competition, these shining-haired, long-limbed, high-breasted daughters in velvet sheaths; making such pleasant conversation, too, Marjorie telling of college where they put on Miss Michaels' plays. "That must cost you a great deal in royalties, dear," was Verna's single comment, as if she didn't realize what an honor it was to be talked to by girls these days, only turning back to Serena and asking in a flat voice if the Jacobses were coming and Harry Dresser—they were, they were—and if by any chance poor Max Brandel had been invited, she'd heard he was in town. It was Serena's turn to gleam her eyes and say in a flat voice, "Yes. At the last minute," and what would Verna like to drink?

Behind the bar stood Billy Potter, Mary's grandson, another introduction. "Whiskey, no ice, with a splash of soda, dear," said Verna to handsome Billy, the blond pirate, giving him a different look than she had the girls, though still unsmiling, as if somehow he was the one, there in all her plays, who'd done her dirt and was doing it still.

"Good idea on a night like this. I'll have one myself, Billy," said the hostess, wondering if maybe no one else was coming, if it would be her and Verna and Billy behind the bar for all eternity. "Isn't it foul? Don't you hate January?"

"No, I don't hate January. I love January and February and March," said Verna. "I hate June. All my plays closed in May or June. It's the end of the world."

"How interesting—how *original*—such a lovely month, June, though I suppose you are right, it's all association. Now me, I was married in June." Fortunately then for Serena the doorbell rang; the girls with loud, unladylike exclamations and laughs were letting in Walter Geylin—cousin Walter—the virtuoso, the merry widower, the pink-cheeked, clean-jowled dirty old man who radiated love of women with a relish undulled by his advancing years, Serena's favorite among all of Mary's swarming relatives.

"You eloped, didn't you?" Verna was saying with slight distaste, as if she could see those two young people of the fifties in their wet bathing suits in front of a justice of the peace. And then gemütlich Walter was upon them, embracing his dear Serena warmly, next Verna even more warmly; calling Verna "old friend," causing the long-faced lady finally to give a smile— ravenous, once started, that smile and rather beautiful—as she recalled a concert when his Brahms, such corn, such golden dough, had made her weep. "Wonderful, wonderful," Walter said, taking her arm, propelling her into the living room and out of Serena's way, "Wonderful": that they were the first and would have a chance to talk. He could remember Mary in 1910, on her tenth birthday, or was it '11, on her eleventh birthday, singing *Bohème*, in her family parlor, bold as brass and twice as bright, the scamp! How about Verna?

"I'd never think of calling Mary a scamp," said Verna dryly, though she could think of plenty of other more appropriate and interesting things to call her . . . such as?

Pausing a moment to light a cigarette and prepare her next greeting, hearing their old voices across her spotless, airy living room, Serena felt a pang: what was she like, Mary Gay—Mary Geylin she would have been then—in 1910 or '11, the birthday girl, so full of fire and beauty once, so overly vivacious now. What was the siren like as a child that her ancient cousin called her a scamp? Serena couldn't imagine—no more than she could remember anymore what Mary had been like in the Verna days, the *Lady Ruby* days, when a young Serena had thought Lion's mother the most dazzling—and most difficult—woman in the world. . . . Or in the post-*Ruby* days when she had stopped being dazzled, stopped being scared, and seen the prima donna turn before her very eyes into a human being, kind and thoughtful . . . a fellow woman.

But then what was Mary like at seventy-five, to that joyful group now at the door, Marjorie and Emma and the young couple they were greeting, Jennifer Potter and Nicholas Lumpkin. Youths so brilliant they chilled the marrow, yet Mary was amused, not frightened, by angel-faced Jenny, the oldest and most intelligent grandchild, and Nicholas her boyfriend, known as the Lump. There they stood with what appeared to be a forest of brown handles in their arms, asking, Where is Grandma? Where can we hide these?

"What *are* they? Mary's not here yet," said Serena.

"They're flags for the parade between salad and dessert."

"What parade?" And then they unfurled the banners so she could see: rainbow banners inscribed in gold like something from the second act of *Tannhäuser* or *Camelot*, designed by Jenny the medievalist and Nick whose specialty was quarks. *Mary is a Grand Old Dame . . . Toujours Gay . . . Mary, Mary, Quite Contrary . . . Say Hey, Mary Gay . . . Let Us Now All Say Grace . . . Tonight Is the Opening Night of the Rest of Your Life . . .* and the last unfurled with a double mast that listed all of Mary's hits from the very first, *The Divine Daisy*, the prelude, to the one after *Lady Ruby* that was a coda of sorts.

"In the pantry. Put them in the pantry, Nick," said Serena, laughing more uproariously than was her style, thinking what a great and risky idea, but they'd probably get away with it. After all, hadn't Mary said, "Dark Ages, black holes, it's all the same, too depressing. They'd better marry, the pets." Who else, besides her cat, did she call pet as though she meant it?

But then, fast taking care of the laughter, Jenny was asking —while there was still time, before Grandma came—if by any chance there had been a change concerning her mother. "No," said Serena tersely, a thought now coming into her mind too irritating even to consider. Or if her father, that monster, was likely—"I don't know," said Serena with sudden impatience, wondering why Jenny, so quiet and watchful ordinarily, who never asked questions—who claimed she had given up on her parents aged fourteen and turned to history—why sweet little Jenny, her favorite niece, had picked this night to begin; and why the Lump had bought himself such a terrible haircut, he looked better with his carrot afro, and why with his well-cut tuxedo he was wearing a ruffled shirt of such a pulsating shade of blue. (Not possible that Mary had persuaded Lion to take a quick ride over to Central Park West, to look in on April, just to see . . .)

"You know how Grandma hates a long cocktail hour," said Jenny, trying to be helpful, moving toward the bar set up by the living-room door; greeting her brother, Billy, who, waiting for customers, had just poured himself a third glass of Grandma's special champagne—his contribution to the evening. Billy, real name Hector William, thanks to his father's grandfather Hector was a rich young man, richer than either of his parents, yet gainfully employed and utterly pleasant: a moralist's despair.

And then, to distract everyone, the Dillons arrived, two generations of beloved nieces and nephews pouring through the door, all the damn Dillons at once and caught in their midst, a silver-haired dynamo with a big cigar, Mr. Harry Dresser himself, granddaddy of American composers, a look of panic and resentment in his round brown eyes, and who could blame him.

"Mr. Dresser!" Serena said, extricating him. "You came up with some of the cousins, I see." He gave her a look: Some of the cousins? How many more? "Have you met the Dillons, Kenny and Elizabeth, Ralph and Lorraine, this is Mr. Dresser, and another Ralph Dillon and . . ." Serena paused, barely—what was her name, little Mrs. Ralph, III, so pretty, so brave to come . . . Melinda, Melissa, Medora, Melanie . . . *Melody*, that was it. . . . "Melody, meet Mr. Dresser, who has written so many lovely ones," said Serena, pleased with her double save, "and tell me when the baby is due? When, angel? A week ago, was it?" Mr. Dresser was smiling now, finding her adorable, but Serena was less amused, thinking of the new slipcovers, remembering another birthday party for Mary, at the Dressers', herself enormous as Melody, in pleated turquoise.

On her second whiskey and soda without ice, Serena was even tempted to tell the story—as she looked to see who was arriving now, not Lion, not Mary, of course not, they were lingering—recall to Mr. Dresser, who after all was there, and overdue Melody, just for the hell of it, the mortification of Serena: the little trickle, then the major flood that presaged the too imminent birth of Marjorie. . . . But who had just arrived, speaking of the Dressers? Freddy and Maggie Lash, yes, excellent, the mixers who made any party go, the rich and charming and civic-minded ones who, though they hadn't been able to save Penn Station or the Roxy, had helped Mary Gay save the Grace Theater, and Aunt Belle, another mixer who would help with some of the family soreheads, but behind Belle, instead of Uncle Sasha, giving her mink to an awestruck Emma, an optical illusion, surely, a revenant, a mirage brought on by too hasty drinking and thoughts of just how exciting that other birthday party had been in all respects.

"Excuse me, Melody dear," said Serena in her own level everyday voice, "excuse me, Mr. Dresser, hi, Maggie, hi, Freddy, hi, Aunt Belle. Where's Uncle Sasha? On his way? Well, good, as long as he's not sick . . . well! speaking of sick . . . Jenny . . . Jenny dear, look who's just arrived. . . . Excuse me a minute while I . . ."

"Hello, Serena," said the vision in flame-red jersey, with the diamond earrings and the glittering combs in the tawny locks and the tricolor bracelet around the slim wrist. "I came after all. Aunt Belle tried to call, but the line was busy." So, that possibility was now eliminated, a stupid thought besides.

"Hello, April. Emma dear, you'd better go into the living room, please, and do your number, Helga will get the door now . . . go on, dear," Serena said to her younger daughter, who didn't miss a trick, and then to the unexpected guest who had once been her best friend, "Are you sober?"

"Quite sober, pal." April's eyes were amused. An eyebrow lifted. Clearly she found Serena funny still, that funny stiff girl who had run after Lion and finally caught him—1955 could be yesterday—and tried to be airy, saying only a half hour ago did she decide, because Aunt Belle had come, actually come, to get her, and unaccountably she was feeling better, the fever gone. . . . She smiled. Serena snorted: "Fever!"

"Aunt Belle forgives," April said, continuing to smile.

Serena continued to frown. "Wake's coming, you know," not to mention who else was coming.

"I know." The smile grew broader, opened, became Mary's smile. "You don't forgive, though, do you?" she added, the smile brilliant.

"Spoiled brat," Serena said as Helga the maid, trouble in a

black and white uniform, descended, saying, "It's the phone, your mother from Florida, Miss Serena, for Mrs. Grace senior, but will speak meantime to you for a moment."

For once, Serena was grateful that it was her mother on the phone at party time, enabling her to wave April into the living room, which was giving off a solid party roar now and the pleasant sound of Ralph Dillon at the piano, and be alone for a moment.

Hurrying down the hall, past a growing pile of brightly wrapped birthday packages, glancing at the moon-faced grandfather clock, Serena was now so furious she could feel herself trembling: furious at Mary, furious at April, most of all furious at Lion whose call this should have been. Even for Lion, who ran on his own clock, and had been known to disappear before a party and not return till long after the last guest had arrived, even for tricky Lion it was inexcusable, after an hour, neither to be here nor call, she thought, as she picked up the bedroom phone.

"Mother darling, we'll have to call you back. Isn't it typical, yes . . . yes, Helga is here, and Bridie's here. The flowers are spectacular, my apartment looks like the Bronx Botanical Garden, but I can't talk. . . ."

Into the bedroom now, a book-lined writer's retreat, a man-stamped boudoir no amount of flowers could make truly refined, dropping coats around the hostess as she tried to get her cosy ordinary mother off the phone, were arriving a succession of guests, stepping-stones in the life of Mary Gay, who was not ordinary or cosy, though most definitely a mother. Some waved, some blew little kisses, some looked at the hostess with puzzlement, never having met. There was Madame Clara Stoller, the retired prima donna, an acquaintance of Mary's Chicago youth, one of the notorious cows, rediscovered on a New York City opera board, swept up in one of Mary's whirlwind latter-day friendships; Madame Stoller blew a lot of kisses, then covered her face with her hands: she and the hostess wore identical dresses except Madame's was blue, silver, and purple instead of red, gold, and green. There was handsome white-haired George

Jacobs, Lion's godfather, co-owner of the Grace Theater, who for forty years had masterminded Mary's career, ever since Charles Grace's death, and fluttery blue-haired Loretta Jacobs, the tireless party giver whose mother had been Rose Hart; there were Perry Eldridge, the stuffy aristocratic publisher who had brought out Mary's memoirs, also Lion's novels—a big wave from Perry—and Donald Bascomb, in velvet tuxedo, silken turtleneck, and a Grecian gold cross, who dressed Mary—a blank look from Donald, even an imperceptible shudder; there was a large brunette in gypsy ruffles who had to be Denise Geylin, daughter of Walter, who helped Mary administer the Charles Grace awards at Juilliard, an overblown rose; and a poisonous little bud in a satin sheath who must be Julie Graves, winner of last year's scholarship, Mary's latest protégé. There was Roger Watkins, Serena's brother, whose firm handled Mary's investments, and his wife, Ann, a shy beauty in pink who hissed, "Where am I sitting, Serena? Not next to someone who will make me *nervous*, I hope." Finally, as Serena hung up the phone, there was that remarkable dowager Mathilda Vail, of the dyed red hair and diamond choker and myriad wrinkles, Lion's aunt, Mary's sister-in-law, flown from Chicago in a snowstorm for the occasion who murmured, hands on hips, "What an extraordinary collection of people—yes?"

"*Yes*," said Serena as the phone rang again, thinking of plump Mary's latest line about Tilly: "Across the room she still looks like the Statue of Liberty—but close up it's Gettysburg, an aerial view."

"You answer, I'll cope," said Great-Aunt Mathilda, who had recently celebrated her own eightieth. "Maybe that's them. I hope to God it's not the old maid dropped dead of stroke while lacing up Mary."

"The maid's in the hospital. It was Lion, Aunt Tilly, who would have done the lacing tonight," Serena said as she picked up the receiver.

"*Lion! Where the bloody hell . . .*"

But it wasn't Lion, only Wake Potter announcing his plane had got in, he was at the hotel changing and would be along shortly. "Where is that Lion?" he asked. "No kidding," he said when Serena told him. "Has he ever not been at Mary's. I wouldn't worry. Why not call and see if they've left? Or would that be too simple."

"I'm not worried. Just ready to kill, that's all. And say, Wake, I'd better tell you who just walked in. . . ." But when she told him, "Not come? It sounds to me like you need help, baby, see you," said Wake, ringing off.

Now she dialed, prepared to strike, as she hadn't dialed since the days of their courtship. SA 2-2468 . . . who do we appreciate . . . Lion, Lion, Lion. It was the oldest living unlisted number in New York, poetry that number, in her fingers like Braille for twenty-five years. She could hear her own voice, young, eager, feigning casualness in the winter of 1948 . . . and the spring of 1951 . . . though by the spring of 1952 he had his own place and another number. . . . "Is Lion Grace there?" Two to one, the times she'd called him to the times he'd called her, for what it was worth. Seven years of two to one till the night she dialed and, not so young and eager anymore, said, "Hello, Lion? I got a message you called. . . . So you're back, and at your mother's. . . . Tomorrow? . . . I guess tomorrow would be all right." "Well, don't sound so enthusiastic," he'd said, "what's your problem?" "A long winter," she'd replied, hating herself because his voice could still do it to her, though he didn't know that; her voice to him was just the voice of good old reliable Serena.

The line was busy. Why busy? She dialed the other number, the secret number nobody had, that wasn't poetry, that didn't scan, was simply a date. SA 2-1985, the year after 1984. A distant date, no longer distant. Also busy. Oh, to hell with it, she thought.

Into the mind of another woman at that moment might have come a picture, not pleasant: a picture of a game old lady slumped over her dressing table, the receiver of the dressing table phone dangling loose while on the other phone a man made an emergency call. Not into Serena's mind. Into Serena's mind came the picture of a coiffed and jeweled and scintillant woman on two phones at once, taking simultaneous long-distance birthday calls, as a man paced impatiently, pointing with no effect whatsoever to his watch.

In the living room all was merry now, and noisy and bright: Mary's tardiness called amusing, typical, a conversation piece— the phone one explanation, a gin—or gin game—for the road another, a gaggle of fans outside her front door another. More great old-timers had arrived, Cecile and Hugh Carlton, and Uncle Sasha, the noble Russian, the bon vivant prince, Aunt Belle's snappy septuagenarian bridegroom, and the not-so-old old-timer, with the sharp blue eyes and the boldly lifting brows though he'd aged dreadfully, had Max Brandel, and the hair once black as sin was a dull dirty gray. "So my darling Belle has retrieved haunted April from her lair," said the dapper White Russian, who like most men had a soft spot for the lovely and lunatic April, now also by the piano though singing was not her forte. "Oh, I can't be amused anymore, I can't be amused by such nonsense," Serena said. "Besides, you see who is here," fixing her eye on the ravaged dirty-haired Brandel, who was part of a happy group surrounding Emma in the arrangement of chairs around the fireplace they had named the conversation pit. Bless her, the child was certainly doing her number. What, Serena wondered, could her sixteen-year-old daughter possibly be telling Perry Eldridge, Madame Stoller, Verna Michaels, and Fitzhugh Stillman, second husband of Lucy Dillon, stuffiest man in New York, not to mention the horrid Max Brandel—now trying to catch Serena's eye—that they were so fascinated?

And then it was that Verna detached herself from the circle and stood before Serena, saying in a worried, almost maternal voice, "Was that Mary by chance on the phone? It seems odd, my dear, for her to be so late."

"Yes, it does," said Serena, grateful all of a sudden to this woman who had so put her off earlier, for now saying the right thing, for echoing her own growing sense of fear. Though all around them people were giving off a second- or third-drink radiance, a positive insouciance over the whereabouts of the host and the guest of honor, Verna Michael was sober and concerned. "Odd for both of them."

"Should we telephone?"

"I just did. The lines were busy. I'll try again."

There was someone else, she noted, also concerned. Max Brandel. He didn't move to join them but from where he was sitting caught Serena in a hard blue gaze, posed a question with his eyes in a way that recalled too sharply something the impossible April, in her cups, had once said to Mary, her own mother: "Oh yes, that look, Mother, when he looks at you, you *are* naked." Serena hadn't known what they were talking about; for all the times she had met him, Brandel had never looked once at Serena, only through her . . . which was not the reason, she swore, she detested the fellow.

Now she made a gesture, not bothering to analyze the reasons, in his direction: join us. He, after all, had talked to Mary last, just an hour or so before the party.

"And when you talked to her?" Serena asked.

"She sounded wonderful. So wonderful I scolded her a bit. I told her to knock on wood. I told her I hoped she'd done a lot of knocking on wood when she gave that birthday interview, for it was surely tempting the gods."

There went the phone again.

"Ah," said Serena, "you thought that also."

At that moment she saw Helga once again approaching, making a signal. "Maybe this is something," said Max, a hand on Serena's arm: not light that hand, no more than the blue eyes.

"Phone for me, Helga?" asked Serena. "Did you say Mrs. Grace or Mr. Grace?"

Which? But before the maid could answer, or she could hear the answer, Serena was off down the hall. It had to be him. Lion. Who always said things had their reason, there was a logical explanation for everything, but who also said bad news came from behind, over the left shoulder, when you least expected to receive it.

CHAPTER 16

1955

It was an afternoon in May, six months since the last time she had seen Lion, and Serena was in the library of the Grace house waiting; wondering how it was possible that once again she was early and he late. How many times, she thought bitterly, had she waited for that wretched boy—not even a boy anymore, a thirty-year-old man—had she sat in this library, looking at book titles, leafing through magazines, reminding herself of how much she detested yellow leather and coffee-colored walls; or in a bar, smoking a cigarette, thinking how much she detested maroon leather and Old King Cole; or in a restaurant reading a menu, thinking how much she detested Chinese food; until the day, finally, six months ago, she had been a half hour late herself, walked twenty blocks out of her way in a cold drizzle to fix him, only to be told upon arrival that Mr. Grace had left the Pink Lotus fifteen minutes before. He'd assumed, he said in their subsequent phone call, that she had forgotten; in that one phone call putting the relationship right where it belonged, just that casual.

And then he had been off to California for six months, to work in the Los Angeles bureau of his magazine. Now he was back, getting in touch with all his friends, including naturally her. And naturally, at his call, being just that sort of fool, she had come.

A new butler had let her in, a haughty fellow with a mustache and an accent not British, nor French, saying Mr. Grace had called and would be . . . "Of course," Serena said, stiff and stony-faced as the butler. "I'll wait upstairs," wondering why all of Mrs. Grace's servants, whatever their nationality, wore such a sour expression, except for Ninon, who always gave mademoiselle Serena a nice smile and a look of encouragement. But what good did it do to have the faithful old maid on your side when the lady of the house so obviously thought you were a bore and unworthy of her darling boy; when the mother, as far as you were concerned, was a block of ice, just like her servants, though the whole world called her magical?

Serena could hear Lady Mary now, coming out of her bedroom onto the upstairs landing, in a temper about something, speaking to Ninon in a way Serena had heard before that made her marvel at the powers to charm that Mary must possess, to keep the spirited little Frenchwoman all those years while talking to her so. Serena, who also spoke fluent French, winced at today's spiel. And then she heard Mary inquire about Lion's plans for the evening—the son of the house was currently apartment-hunting and living at home—and Ninon spoke the name of madamoiselle Serena, at which Mary said something so uncalled for, so unkind, that Serena thought she must surely have misheard. But before Ninon could get the further information across that the girl was downstairs at this very moment, Mary went on, elaborating on her unfortunate figure of speech, more of a pun in French than in English—*pauvre souris* . . . *chauve-souris*—about the mouse, the poor gray mouse who perhaps flew at night, till finally Ninon got out the words, *"En bas, elle est en bas, madame, dans la bibliothèque."*

At which point a very English "Oh, God" was sounded, and then the voice preceding Mary into the library, all phony warmth: "Serena! Serena! Where are you, dear? Where are you hiding?"

And as always, whatever Mary decided she was seeing, a bat, a mouse, a giraffe, a cow, seeing Mary was just that: seeing Mary. There was nothing you could do about that presence, that live presence coming at you—fresh and pink and perfumed from her bath —hair a perfect gleaming helmet under an invisible net, eyes dark, and glowing, smile turned on high, jaunty scarf around the neck. The torso, Serena noted acidly, sheathed in a sleeveless print dress, was thicker than it had been ten years ago; not much of a waist left these days; rather square, that torso. But there was no getting around the arms and legs, firm, smooth, insufferably shapely, nor the face, still that of a great beauty, from the mouth up, anyhow, with glowing skin that had profited from the extra pounds . . . and absolutely no sign of a face lift. (She'd know, given where she worked, if Mary Gay had had a face lift; the beauty department kept score.)

There she was, Mrs. Grace, Lion's mother, on her way to the theater where she would be transformed into the perdurably glamorous Mary Gay, this season playing, simply, herself in *An Evening with Mary Gay*—two dresses, two pianists, a few props, and forty years' worth of songs—a show that a few weeks earlier Serena had seen and found utterly enchanting. The bitch. How could such a winning creature be such a bitch? "Lovely, so lovely to see you, dear," she was saying now with an exaggerated friendliness that reeked of guilt.

"Hello, Mrs. Grace," Serena said, not getting up, though it hurt not to spring to her feet when an older person came into the room. But Mary didn't seem to notice the coolness, so absorbed was she in making the poor dear girl feel at home, offering her a drink, sitting down herself, looking at her watch, saying, "Lion is so bad, so naughty, but I don't have to go quite yet," smiling, actually patting Serena's hand, saying gaily, "I'd join you but I can't before the theater. No? Nothing, dear?"

Serena shook her head, not even saying, "No thank you," taking a deep breath, tensing her mouth, ordering herself not to dare to burst into tears in front of this woman who had finally got to her and didn't even know it, but was chatting on about the theater, the show, how lovely it had been a few weeks ago to see Serena and her parents backstage, how much their response had meant to her, how touched because she hadn't been sure, not sure at all, that she should be involved in such a, well, egotistical-seeming project, just her and those two pianists, but weren't they charming, the young musicians, stars of the future; except, "Not know it!" Mary would say a moment later. "Of course I knew you were upset, though I wasn't sure at first if it was that wretched son of mine or me, stupid me. Why do you think I went rattling on, giving you a chance to swallow those tears?"

Not till Mary said, "Well, it is my swan song, after all. I won't be singing in public, I don't believe, anymore after this year," did the tears get swallowed, the powers of speech turned on, and Serena finally opened her mouth to make—inevitably—one of her boring gaffes, only it wasn't a gaffe but a quite deliberate dig. "Oh no!" said Serena. "Don't say that, that this show is the last. What about the movie of *Ruby?*"—knowing full well, because as assistant feature editor of a fashion magazine she kept up with show business gossip, that Mary Gay was not going to play Ruby in the movie after all, that the role had gone to a younger (though not that much younger) actress whose last film had been one of the year's big money-makers.

And that was the moment when Mary had stopped her chatter and taken a hard look at the hostile young woman sitting on her library sofa and, not even bothering to answer the question about Ruby, said, "You heard, didn't you? You heard me talking about you to Ninon. I am a stinker, aren't I, and so is my son. But, my dear, you *are* a mouse. Yet you needn't be, that is the most exasperating part, as that last remark of yours made clear. We turn you into a mouse, Lion and I, and what's more, you let us."

Serena was too surprised by the suddenly honest outcry to do anything but stare. And now when the small exquisite hand with the ruby ring and ruby-red nails touched hers, and the exaggerated dark eyes scrutinized her face, and the enemy said, "Listen to me, child, listen," Serena didn't pull away or shake her head, she listened.

"Let me ask you a question I have wanted to ask you for a

long time now, but never quite dared, nor thought was my business to ask." A pause. A further focusing. "Do you love my son?" What sort of a question was that, Serena thought. Not even April would ask such a question. And what could she know about love, this golden gorgon who sang of it to break your heart but had no husband, no known lovers, no private life, it seemed, except to bother her children. Still, if Mary could throw the word around in such cosy fashion, so could Serena.

"Of course I love him. He's my friend."

"Friend! I'm not talking about friend! What nonsense to talk about a man being a *friend*. A man can be a colleague, yes, or a teacher, or a relative . . . or a lover . . . or a husband . . . or a convenience—but this modern business of a man being a *friend*. Folly! Though I suppose that's how you treat him—like a buddy—and have treated him for years, because you were scared to treat him any other way. To take the chance. Now I'll ask you again. . . ."

Serena was beginning to wriggle now, and in spite of herself, to laugh.

"Are you in love with that wretched boy?" Mary demanded.

And out it came: "Yes! Of course! Always! I loved him the first time I ever saw him, that day at school. Remember, *Romeo and Juliet?*"

Mary nodded. "You were in a black velvet doublet, shaking out your hair, taking off your mustache, and lighting a cigarette. You weren't a mouse that day. You looked smashing, that day. Smashing."

"He kept staring at me, you know that hard stare, and giving me the lopsided smile, and then he came over and sent another boy packing, in that way only Lion can send someone packing so you scarcely know what's happened. Then he said, 'Inspired touch, that mustache. I never would have known it was a girl. A beautiful girl.' And that was that. Later, remember, you took us out to dinner, and you and April and Wake were talking the whole time about plans for the wedding, and Lion was talking to me about me. I never knew before what people meant about love at first sight. But he thought he was making a friend."

"I know," Mary said after a pause. "I know all about love at first sight."

"Was that how you fell in love with Lion's father?" Serena asked, curious now and no longer bothered by how utterly peculiar the scene was becoming, as if the brown and yellow library had dissolved and she and Mary were strangers, met on an airplane, or snow-delayed train, or ocean liner; letting the scene flow.

Mary hesitated. Then, giving a faint smile, she said, "No." And then after another pause, "It was someone else, long ago, in Chicago. When I was a girl. Before I ever met Lion's father. The first time I laid eyes on this man I fell head over heels in love, but he saw me as a little friend, a little mouse. He even called me mouse, keyboard mouse. He was a young opera singer. I was the accompanist for his teacher, who later became my teacher— Pauline Selva. 'Friend,' he called me in the studio. 'Pal.' And one day I turned it. I made him look at me that other way. One afternoon and an evening. That was all it took. That's all it ever takes." The expression on her face was faraway, wistful and mischievous at the same time, and very young.

"And what happened?"

"Nothing good. But that was nobody's fault. That was the war."

And then, seeing the girl hesitate, swallow a question, "He wasn't killed, if that was what you wanted to ask. And after Mr. Grace died, he came back into my life again. But I turned back into a mouse. I didn't seize the chance. I've always regretted it. I can't explain. This man was my first love. My husband was my life . . . my whole life . . . the other was my *grand amour*. . . ."

She made a gesture: that's all. Finished. No more talking about it. Only, "Do you understand, Serena? You can make that bad boy of mine see you. You have the power. There's a vacuum in his life this month. We know that, you and I. That's why he called you. Fill the vacuum"—and widening her eyes, making them into the biggest eyes in the world—"and *don't* be so friendly. Instead of lending that pretty shoulder for him to cry on, or that pretty ear to bend, scratch a little! And then tell him how you feel! He may say, sorry, that is not how I feel. How embarrassing. But at least you've taken the chance. Told the truth."

Then Mary stood up and they were back in the brown and yellow library and she was putting a finger to her lips, giving Serena a look hypnotic in its brightness. "What I've told you by the way is *entre nous,* you understand? Women's talk, not for Lion's ears. Or April's. Ever."

"I understand," Serena said. It was a little present Mary had given her, to make up for years of snubs, a bit of knowledge she had no intention of sharing with anyone, only to put away with all the other bits of knowledge she had collected over the years about people that armed her and kept her amused so she could never be a victim. For that was Serena's small vice: always to know more than anyone. To know and guard secrets. Mary had guessed it.

"There's your friend now," said Mary. "Nobody else bangs the front door like that. And, dear . . ."

"Yes?"

"Just a little tip. Ponytails are for ballerinas. You need your hair to frame your face, dear, and it's such good hair, too. If you pull it back so tightly you'll begin to lose it." Another smile, so bright and mischievous it brought out the dimples, just like the one she gave her audience, at the end of the first act of *An Evening with Mary Gay,* that told people she'd be back, with even more treats, a new dress, the Grace ruby, the legendary eye of blood, around her neck, after the intermission.

And so it was that when Lion came into the library, decently breathless, full of apologies, of God, I'm sorry, and You have no idea, and I was sure you'd be gone, Serena was shaking out her hair, just as the first day they met; standing by the window, silhouetted against the delicate late afternoon sky, shaking out her hair and lighting a cigarette and smiling, saying, "I'm so glad you were late, I had a rare chance to spend some time with your mother."

"Oh, oh," he said, "should my ears be burning?" She continued to smile, and when he came over to give her the big awkward brotherly hug and kiss that was his inevitable greeting, she didn't return the hug with sisterly heartiness but held him off a little, continuing to smile, looking at him, pretending to size him up. Alas, his western stay had only improved his appearance: a regular beauty treatment, all those Hollywood months of swimming and tennis and open-air assignments and racing around in a convertible (or had it been a motorcycle, with a starlet in a kerchief at his back?). His hair was bleached as a boy's; his face no longer of that ghastly typewriter, or nightclub, pallor of the previous years, but attractively tanned. All he needed was a ten-gallon hat to look like a cowboy star, though his clothes were better than she remembered; along the way he'd picked up a good blue suit and a nice tie that brought out the color in his eyes. But she didn't say any of that, only continued to smile and stare, letting something come at him, that caused him to break away, as if puzzled or suddenly shy, and go to the bar and mix himself a gin and tonic. "You can make one for me, too," said Serena, who generally asked for a Coke or at most a sherry.

"You're different, old friend," Lion said, standing in front of the fireplace, scrutinizing the young woman in blue shantung on the library sofa. "What's different?"

"The hair, maybe. The dress. I don't usually wear blue."

"Yeah, that's it. The hair . . . the dress." But it was more than the hair, and the blue dress, he would say later, it was a whole . . . attitude . . . as when he told her his plan for dinner, a new place in Chinatown he wanted to try out, and she began to laugh. "Lion, Lion," she said, "I'm nearly twenty-seven years old and I have to tell you the truth. I *hate* Chinese food."

"Well," he said after a pause in which perhaps he had been trying to count up the number of Chinese dinners over the years he and she had shared. "So what sort of food would *you* like tonight?"

"Oh, French, or Italian, but it's not so much the food, it's the place. I'm in the mood for a *pretty* place, with music, entertainment, something to take my mind off my troubles. You know."

The sort of place, she thought, where you take those other

ones, the ones you see in the months when you aren't seeing me.

"You mean one of those awful hotel nightclubs?"

"That would be nice, yes."

"But I thought we'd talk. Get caught up. I thought you hated all those basement rooms with the red banquettes and dinky dance floors."

"Well . . . how about a roof for a change?"

Now he was grinning at her as if there was something about her, this evening, that tickled him. Really tickled him. "What the lady orders the lady shall have," he said, extending an arm. "A drink with a view, and then a cellar with music. As a matter of fact someone good is at the Maisonette this month, one of those French singers we like. Or are you going to tell me, now that you're nearly twenty-seven, that you can't stand Piaf and Greco?"

"No," she said, "it's just the company I hear them in," and let him interpret that as he saw fit.

"Old friend," Lion said after a thoughtful pause, "it's great to see you."

"Old friend," he said valiantly throughout the course of the evening: on a rooftop stained pink by the sunset, with a view of the park; on a velvet banquette over lobster and Rhine wine, followed by sherbet and champagne; on a crowded dance floor to a Latin beat and then to a set of old thirties fox-trots and while listening to a plainly dressed Frenchwoman with bruised eyes sing "Les Feuilles Mortes" and "La Vie en Rose"; till finally very late, walking up Fifth Avenue on the park side—it was that kind of warm soft night, the sort of night you wanted never to be over— she said, "No! No! No!" as if she were in her office and he was one of those terrible manuscripts that caused her to protest aloud.

"No what?"

"No more 'old friend.' I have too many friends, old and new. I'm sick of friends. Sick of being a pal, a good egg. All my life I've been a pal," she exploded. "I was a pal to the first boy I ever kissed, and a pal to the first boy I did more with than kiss. Even a pal to the first boy I slept with, who was drunk and abject and promised it would never happen again, only of course it happened again and he couldn't say it didn't count, only that it was confusing because there was someone else, someone in Philadelphia he was sort of engaged to. The second boy I slept with *was* a friend, and I was the one who walked away, bored, I'm afraid—"

"Serena! Don't tell me things like that."

"Well, what do you think, Lion?"

"Okay, okay, you're nearly twenty-seven years old now," getting quite upset, but also taking her hand.

"It's my fault. I encourage men to be friends. I pretend friendship, with sex or without, because it's safe. I don't dare to be romantic."

"You look romantic. Have I told you that? You look like Ninotchka, comrade. Garbo laughs."

"No *comrade.* I don't want to be your comrade. Romeo without his mustache. If you want to be a comrade say it now, and I'll never see you again."

And then she stopped, and stood there, and just as Mary said, made him look at her, finally, in a different way, and what could he do but take her in his arms, saying, "Oh, Serena, oh, Serena," and kiss her, and though there had been others on both sides, both would agree afterward that that was a kiss to wipe out all others, for him as well as for her.

Not too many weeks later, Serena and Lion drove off in his car one Saturday morning to Maryland and came back a few days later man and wife. It was the only way, they decided, to make it their wedding, truly theirs, given the families, the complications, their own natures; and in later years when things got rough as they do in any marriage that is destined to last, that was what Serena and Lion would look back on: the stillness, the privacy of that elopement; the jokes that were theirs alone; the details never photographed, never pasted into any album, only imprinted forever in their own minds; the fusty judge's parlor with the artificial flowers and the picture over the mantel of President Eisenhower; the slightly drunken judge who had been having a Saturday night poker game with the boys; the judge's wife and brother-in-law who were the witnesses; the wedding toasts in bourbon and ginger ale; the fact that the bride and groom both wore under their outer clothes, his seersucker suit and her linen dress and jacket, bathing suits.

They called his mother and her parents from a hotel bedroom. Mrs. Watkins wept copiously, what she insisted were tears of happiness, saying, "I thought you would never get married," though Serena knew her mother felt cheated, the only daughter and all, especially when her father made such a point of thanking them for saving him all that money. Mary wept also; "crocodile tears," Lion said. "She never weeps for happiness, but she is happy. Almost as if she'd had a hand in it." And Lion and Serena, the happiest of all, looked at each other bewildered, in love, not quite sure what had happened in a fortnight after so many years.

It wasn't till she saw Mary a few days later that the new Mrs. Grace—Mrs. Grace junior—thought again of her curious hour waiting for Lion; and knew she hadn't dreamed it; the change in the woman who greeted the newlyweds in her bright noontime living room was not in Serena's eye; it was a reality, that look of grudging respect and something else: affinity. Because more than convenience was in the air—that was what Mary's greeting telegraphed—more than good sense or "Why not?" or panic or a flashy impulse was in the air, or any of those considerations quite other than love. Love was in the air! Romance! Love slumbering in Lion, the difficult troubled Lion, love awakened in Serena, the mouse, the drink of water; the real thing. Love: a subject Mary knew about. "Darlings, darlings," said Mary, smiling, happy, enamored of the sight of them, tears in her eyes—real tears—because that worrisome boy had taken the step with this sensible girl who for a few weeks had not acted sensibly and had swept him off his feet. Serena smiled back. And then at a certain moment, when Lion was occupied elsewhere in the room, with Belle or April or whoever else had arrived to celebrate, her new mother-in-law gave Serena a look, a certain look of inquiry. Serena shook her head, giving a different sort of smile, faint, slightly conspiratorial, and blew Mary a little kiss of thanks.

"So, Mrs. Grace . . ." said Serena.

"So, Mrs. Grace . . . *darling* . . ." said Mary. "And no

more Mrs. Grace, when the whole world calls me Mary. It's Mary, darling Serena, Mary."

It was a short-lived intimacy, between those two, Mary and darling Serena, but one that had served its purpose. And no matter what the temptations in the years to come, Serena never betrayed Mary's confidence, such as it was. There were times—when Mary played the haughty grande dame or the demanding, mother-will-always-come-first parent, or simply the irresistible melting Mary Gay—and Lion squirmed—that the daughter-in-law was sorely tempted. But no. Nor did she try herself to play detective, to learn the identity of Mary's secret lover. For what else had the tête-à-tête meant than that the perfect impeccable Mary Gay was just that human, a fact frequently forgotten in the rush of the years?

CHAPTER 17

1965

And then one day her mother-in-law's secret lover died. There was no need for Serena, sleuthing, to discover the truth. It was all there in the obituary. The pieces fell into place. And something in Serena softened a little, as her heart went out once again to this woman who had so much and on the surface seemed so sure, so self-possessed, so superior, yet underneath had lived such a sad life, really, such an unresolved life, and seemed so bitter at times, so bewildered at the way life and the people she loved turned on her.

Gianna Amara actually had two obituaries, on succeeding days of that week in early October 1965. There was a small notice first, with a Paris dateline, that found its way into the *New York Times* and caught Serena's eye by accident.

Then the next morning—as if some friend and admirer had called to object or an editor with a folder of clips had said, "Wait a minute, this was quite a fellow, this fellow is a story"—there was a column-long obituary, which Serena found herself reading at the breakfast table with sudden attention: a salute to Giancarlo Amara, Chicago-born opera singer, dead in Paris at seventy-three after a long illness. For eighteen years this South Side Chicago boy, a pupil of the famed Pauline Selva, had been the leading lyric tenor of the Opéra-Comique, known for his way with Puccini, his magnetism, the persuasive sensuality of his big golden voice, his top notes, his ardor; there had been two acclaimed New York concerts in the middle thirties, but his career had been principally in Europe. And during the Second World War, unlike some others in the business of making a handsome living abroad, he had sent his family home to the States and stayed behind in his adopted homeland. That was the story, the nugget: that during the occupation the aging American-born tenor, well over military age, had turned into a real-life Cavaradossi, had been caught and sent away, and survived, though thanks to the hardship of his imprisonment would never sing again. Halfway down the column Serena began feeling uncomfortable, recognizing clues her mother-in-law had let drop over a dozen years. Pauline Selva. Paris. New York in the middle thirties. War. Paris again, where Mr. Amara had remained till his death, making a new reputation as a teacher, his popularity in his adopted city summed up in a tribute from a globe-trotting conductor who had known the tenor before the war: "Chicago should not be famous only for Capone or Carl Sandburg or Mary Gay, but for a tenor named Giancarlo Amara, a great singer and a great heart."

Chicago and Paris: two cities not generally linked in song and story.

Paris, where Mary had gone yearly since the summer of 1953.

Surviving were a wife, Mrs. Josephine Amara, three children, two sons and a daughter, five grandchildren . . . and—could it be?—someone else, not mentioned in the obituary, except that by a coincidence Mary Gay had found her way into that obituary, or was it coincidence? Serena was certain now, and with the knowledge she felt that yearning to see her mother-in-law, that desire to hold and comfort her husband's mother, the grandmother of her children, that she had felt only once or twice before: when Mary's mother had died; when her closest woman friend, the wife of Harry Dresser, had been killed in a plane crash. But Mary wasn't there. Mary was in Paris. Serena shivered with the realization of her mother-in-law's loss and her own discovery.

Now Serena remembered Mary as she had been the previous June, leaving for her annual trip abroad, not so cheerful as usual, only impatient and nervous; remembered how indifferent her mother-in-law had been, in the weeks before going abroad, to certain developments in the lives of her children: to Lion's announcement that he was taking a nine months' leave of absence from his job to write a novel; to April's announcement that she was planning to take the children to California—Santa Monica, Malibu, Santa Barbara—for their summer vacation, a much needed change for everyone, though Wake, it so happened, was headed in the opposite direction, to England on business and then to the Aegean, for a cruise with friends. "I don't want to get into it," the nervous indifferent Mary had said, to everyone's surprise, considering how loudly she had expressed herself in the past on the subject of separate vacations for husband and wife. "I hope that's good," she had said hesitantly of Lion's decision, though she had been the one urging him on, challenging him to take a chance, do it, for God's sake, before it was too late. "Mother is getting philosophical in her old age," April had said. "Mother is tired," Lion had said, "and has something on her mind, not us."

And then there was Mary's own announcement, relayed by Aunt Belle, with whom she'd been traveling, that she wasn't returning as planned right after Labor Day but was staying on in Paris for a while; and the fact that it was the second week in October and Mary was still over there . . . as April was back in California—but that was a whole other story, best put aside for the moment.

"Here is your mother again, one way or another she winds up on everybody's list," Serena said to Lion, who was reading books at breakfast nowadays, background for his novel, passing up the morning papers of 1965 in favor of the daily news of

1934, or thereabouts, though he allowed Serena to point out choice items. She handed him the *Times*, folded open to the story about Gianni Amara, gently swatting Marjorie in passing, who was making a mess with her eggs, and telling Emma her palm was not a butter plate, then smiling at them, because some days just to look at her little girls made her happy, Serena being "one of those awful people," her husband would say, "who wakes up cheerful; who loves the world at breakfast." But how loving, how good-natured, really, was she being that particular morning, to pass the paper to Lion, saying, "I wonder if that was someone Mary knew. Amara. From Chicago." Testing. Not for confirmation. She was already certain, but to find out how much her husband knew of his remarkable mother. "It's an interesting life. He studied with Pauline Selva, around the same time your mother did. And he lived in Paris."

"Amara." A shrug. "I think he came to our house once. When I was a kid. One of those fat Italian tenors. He took up half our garden. And I think Mother might have tried to find him in France, during the war. As you know, Mother is very loyal to old friends."

So, Serena thought. The *grand amour*. So.

Lion read in silence, his face inscrutable, that broad serious face framed by thick blond hair that still after ten years of marriage was the face she loved, though it maddened her sometimes, that cover-up Lion face, with its stock changes of expression, its set of frowns and smiles and grimaces and raised eyebrows that never let her know what he was really thinking; only a rare flicker in the frosty hazel eyes did that, and was gone faster than she could catch it. There was no flicker now, no expression whatsoever. But watching her husband read, Serena wished she had left the thing alone. For a moment something seemed to brush the sunlit blue and white breakfast table, set in a window, something dark and sad. But "Interesting, yes, touching," said Lion in an ordinary voice, returning the paper to Serena. "That bit about a great heart. Very old-fashioned coming from such a trendy fellow. Too sentimental not to be true."

Then, taking a last gulp of coffee, Lion stood up, telling the girls to get a move on, get the teeth brushed and the books collected, it was time to go. And they were off, the blond daddy and the tawny-haired little girls in their jumpers, a familiar week-day trio, except this year the daddy wore flannels and a sweater instead of a business suit and, having dropped the girls off at school, instead of proceeding downtown to the offices of a news magazine would return to his sunny, cluttered, side-street apart-ment and closet himself in the bedroom, muttering, Someday, someday, we are going to have space. And presently Serena would hear the typewriter, Lion making music; would know just from the beat and the pauses and the length of time the door stayed shut how it was going that day, rhapsody or dirge, and something as well about the mood of the man at the keys.

This day it was a copying beat she heard, steady and asser-tive, no clue in the rhythm of the typewriter, nor in the face of the man who emerged hours later, as to whether the breakfast scene for him had significance, whether he knew or really gave a damn.

But for Serena: alone for a moment, while Lion was walking the girls to school, reading the piece again, she found her eyes filling up in a totally uncharacteristic way. She wasn't accustomed to shedding tears over the obituaries of brave tenors. But she was remembering Mary, the day Mary had helped her, given her a kick when she needed and deserved one: remembering Mary say-ing so flatly, "I turned back into a mouse. I didn't seize the chance. I've always regretted it." And then that phrase—*grand amour* . . . my husband was my life but he was my *grand amour* —and Serena hadn't asked the question that was on the tip of her tongue: Aren't they the same? Can't they be the same?

Now the younger woman made a resolution: when Mary returned to New York, as she surely must in the next week or so, to see more of her, be more accessible and take the initiative for a change. Be a daughter to Mary whose own daughter had de-serted. To somehow communicate . . . what? Sympathy for a secret? For a loss? Some kind of woman's support such as Mary had given her that long-ago afternoon in May? A good impulse or simple curiosity? For once Serena gave herself the benefit of the doubt.

But no sooner had Mary returned to New York than she was off again, headed West, to Hollywood on business, said Lion, the only one in the family to have seen her. "I can't lunch, darling," Mary had told Serena, "not this week, but thank you, what a nice suggestion, I know how busy you are." The daughter-in-law could hear nothing out of the ordinary in Mary's telephone voice; nor get a picture from Lion of how his mother looked after so many months away, how she seemed. "Business," said Serena, the night Mary left for Hollywood. "What kind of business?"

"April business, what do you think?" Lion said harshly from his side of the bed, putting down his book, taking a sip of the drink he had made and brought back to bed with him. "Though there is some real business trumped up, some sort of a television show under discussion. You do know the latest about my sister?" Serena nodded. "She'll wind up on the cutting room floor, and out the beach house door. Out on her ear. But Mother should not meddle. She has no business meddling. People don't meddle with her."

And then he turned. For the first time in ten years of marriage Lion the loyal, the defender, the keeper of the legends and maker of the peace, gave, as he spoke of his mother, Mary Gay, the kind of sardonic laugh he generally reserved for people who were not his friends, who in some way had done him dirt. "She is about to make the most God-awful fool of herself," he said. "A fool of herself with April. A fool of herself with those smart operators out there who want to put her in an old-timers' TV spectacular; old-timers reliving their days of glory for three hours on prime time, giving their all for Anacin and A. C. Nielsen and Harry Dresser. Four decades in show business, the twenties, the thirties, the forties, and fifties . . . four great old troupers with Uncle Harry the fifth. After all these years of classy retirement, of doing things just the way my father would have wanted, including turning down offers for what she calls that coffin in the parlor, our wonderful Mary has chosen to die there. To die and be entombed for everybody to see, file by and cluck over."

"Why would she die? The fifties aren't that long ago."

"What makes you think she's got the fifties? They are giving her the twenties. Can't you see it? Broadway in the twenties on television. Mary Gay opening the show with a Charleston, in a headband and fringe . . . bee-stung lips . . . Merry Christmas eyes. . . . She's not thinking straight this year, of course," he added in a cold voice, "that sixty-fifth birthday, I suppose, but that's no excuse. And I won't weep."

And looking at Lion's grim face—no one could look grimmer than Lion—Serena thought: he knows. He knows all about his mother and that man. He put it together just like I did. Or maybe he's known for years. He must have known for years. Much more than I could ever know. And he's angry at her. He must have been angry at her for years. That's the really-well-kept secret. But at least he doesn't know I know.

"Because I don't give a damn," Lion was saying now, almost at a shout so she hushed him, reminding him there were little girls sleeping on the other side of the bedroom wall. "Really I don't. I don't give a damn if she makes a bloody fool of herself. Ever since I've been eight years old, except for the war, I've been worrying about those two, Mother and April. And even during the war, there Mother was, in her USO armband, for me to worry about, while back home April was starting to go out with the boys. And why for thirty long years have I worried? Because once we made a beautiful picture together. Because once we were nice together, Mary, Lion, and April, three against the world. Three for the world to stare at in wonder, the American beauty and her two darling kids."

If she hadn't known it to be impossible, because Lion had no tears, Serena would have sworn something glittered in his blond lashes. She reached for his hand. But he didn't want to take her hand and close the space between them in the bed. He wanted to go back to his book, immerse himself in a tome on the reign of FDR when, depression or not, the world seemed safe

and secure, before the petals began to fall . . . she loves me
. . . she loves me not . . . she loves me. . . .

"Is that what your novel is about, Lion?" she asked. "The
three of you against the world, long ago in the thirties?"

And Lion laughed. "There are no women in my story," he
said. "Not a one except for walk-ons. Not even you." And it was
almost as if for the moment she was one of those people who
had done him dirt, who were not his friends.

But the bad mood, whatever it was all about, soon passed.
He had no time for bad moods. He had work to do. By the time
Mary got home—saying nothing about April, April's movie,
April's unfortunate involvement, only talking about the show, the
Harry Dresser spectacular—Lion was his ordinary self: pleasant,
guarded, tactful, out of reach, only making the occasional caustic
remark, such as that April's staying out on the West Coast, though
hard on poor Wake, made New York rather restful for the family.
Nobody talked much about April that autumn and winter, as if
by not talking of the problem it might go away. She came and
went mysteriously, was in New York for Thanksgiving to see the
children, and for part of the Christmas holidays; Wake also came
and went mysteriously, his arrivals fitting April's departures, and
vice versa. Meantime the novel—that novel without women—was
going well, which was what mattered to Serena after all, whether
or not she played a part in it.

And in the spring there was Mary's television show, the
wonderful show that, rather than being the anticipated disaster,
the inevitable and perhaps overdue humiliation of Lady Mary,
proved yet again that the rest of the family, the rest of the world,
the cynics and carpers, didn't know what in hell they were talking
about, that no one would ever make a fool of Mary Gay, no more
at sixty-five than at twenty, at least not on a stage.

And that night no one was more pleased than Lion, his
broad-planed, handsome face caught in the flickering light of
the parlor television set, the expression hard at first, then gradually
softening when he realized someone—surely his mother, it had
to be Mary, who else would have had the gall—had insisted that

"Over the Years with Harry Dresser" go backward in time, with her not at the beginning but at the climax of the evening. And then when he saw her; when finally, after the other wonderful stars had performed the other wonderful but lesser numbers, and the final commercial, tasteful of course, had been played, and the curtains parted on a bare stage with Mary standing next to an old upright piano covered in mirrors; Mary in a classic, shimmering Worth evening dress, a copy of the very dress she had worn in the climactic scene of *American Beauty,* with the ruffled bangs and soft bob that for so many years had been her trademark; then Lion gave a big smile. Not a lopsided grin, but a rare open beaming smile such as Mary was giving now on the television, and you saw the resemblance, mirror image, between mother and son.

There she stood, silently waiting for the applause to subside because even on television, even in that phony West Coast barn that they had done up to resemble a West Forty-second Street theater, even aften ten years of retirement, or because of ten years' retirement, the applause was deafening. And then, "Okay, Harry, I'm ready if you are," Mary said, nodding to her accompanist, who was of course none other than Mr. Harry Dresser himself. He spun on the piano stool just far enough to intercept another wild wave of applause before turning back, and there was complete and utter silence, to-hear-a-pin-drop silence. And then the voice—that voice like pale honey, like silver candy, lilting, throbbing by turns—rose in the great old numbers: "You" . . . "I Never Speak to Strangers" . . . "He Doesn't Even See Me" . . . "Red, White, and Blue Girl"—rose in half the score of *American Beauty* . . . and the shouts began, the rebel yells, the whistles, the calls for encores, for songs that weren't even dreamed of in the twenties, that Harry Dresser didn't even write. Suddenly it was Mary Gay's night, and Mary Gay handed it back to Harry as only a great performer can, and the scene built, song after song . . . "Haunted April" . . . and half the score of *Lady Ruby* . . . and the young brash producer, the one Mary called the baby seal, and had fought with and needled and told how to do it, had the good sense to let it happen, cut somewhere else; and then it was over. The credits were rolling over a stage where Mary hugged Harry and a great wave of people came onstage and began hugging them both. And then once more to the commercial, as in the small crowded living room of Lion and Serena Grace there was silence, quite a long to-hear-a-pin-drop silence. And then suddenly everyone who'd come to watch with them began talking at once: sister, cousins, niece and nephew, children, grandchildren, all saying that she had done it again. That once more their Mary had done it, and so now millions, not just thousands, would know of the magic of Mary Gay, the legendary American Beauty who miraculously was a beauty still. But Serena sat in the darkness thinking of the two who weren't there, the two men responsible for this miracle, no longer alive, and said not a word. (Of the third, the one still alive, who might have had a hand in the proceedings, she thought nothing, nothing at all.)

And as nobody was more pleased than Lion with the program, the reviews, the ratings, the offers that followed, so nobody was more pleased than Mary, a year later, at the success of Lion's novel, *Remember the Future*: the reviews, the twelve weeks on the best-seller list, the book club sale, the paperback deal, the money, the new and grander apartment, the change success made in Lion and Serena's life. "Of course it wasn't very friendly of you, darling," Mary said lightly to her son, "to have the mother in your book run off with a cowboy before the story ever begins. But I understand. I always understand, you see. And that father and son . . . that is a very beautiful portrait of you and Charlie. As Charlie might have been. I'm glad you caught that much of him, and remembered that much of him though only eight when he died."

As for April, the daughter and sister, who had not shared in the good fortune of her mother and brother; who had returned from her California adventure in humiliation and fury; she tried. God knows she tried for a while, tried to take pleasure in their good fortune, so earned, so well deserved. But it was too hard, she would mutter to Serena, the night she stood up at a family dinner, at the moment of toasts (it was Lion's birthday), and weaving slightly said, "You are so wonderful, you and Serena, and Mother, and Aunt Belle . . . such Graces . . . such Geylins . . . you always land on your feet while little sister loses . . . even when she wins, loses . . ." and shrugged and walked out yet again.

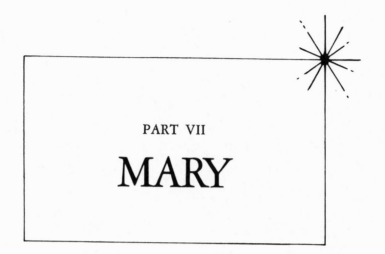

PART VII

MARY

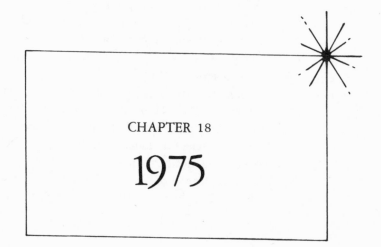

CHAPTER 18

1975

"Hurry up, old lady, quick, quick," said the robber.

Mary felt the clasp come free under her fingers. *Damn,* she said to herself, silently, vehemently, *damn,* as she had said before when she had been dealt a winning hand in a game where to win was to lose. *Damn.* And then suddenly—*thank God*—realizing that the loss of the jewel might possibly win her what she valued more than anything, what she would not admit was in danger: her son's life.

The gesture of relinquishment had already begun. The clenched fist that would tear the jewel free from her neck, and hand it over to the thief, telling him, *There. Take it and get out.* And then telling him how to get out, so there would be no possibility of an encounter with her poor chauffeur, who must at that very moment be waiting outside, or about to ring the bell. Telling him about the closed-up passageway with the door in the bathroom closet that, clever as he was, he didn't know about, that only Mary and Ninon knew about, that they had discovered after the war when work had been done on the house.

And then, even as her breath rose to form the words, she saw Lion. No ghost. Lion coming into the bedroom, not through the door in full view of the thief, but stealthily, beyond the dressing table, in the shadows at the far end of the room. The bathroom end. Cleverer than the thief, to have come in through that secret passageway that Mary thought only she and Ninon knew about, that was their joke. For through it, Madame and her maid had amused themselves by fantasizing, went Jean Archibald's lovers. Faithful to the death to the coarse and domineering Joseph Grace: so went the legend of the beautiful Jean Archibald, Charlie's mother; she never looked at another man. But Mary and Ninon, after finding the closed-up passageway, playfully imagined a different story. Ninon had even found, caught between two boards, a relic, a giveaway trinket, an old-fashioned shirt stud, and Mary had said, "Well, so much for the curse of the ruby." But how did Lion know about the passageway? How long had he known, her quiet snoopy boy? "There is nothing I don't know," Lion would say later, "only I don't let on till it comes in handy." "How nice for you," she would murmur. "How nice for me."

And seeing Lion was the cue to deliver the jewel, to hold it out to the intruder, who gave a little cry of pleasure and satisfaction.

As the thief reached to take it, the figure in the shadows behind him sprang forward.

How odd, Mary thought, looking at the thief, senseless on the floor, cut down by Charlie's son, wielding a bar from the brass towel rack that stood beside her tub. The mirror glasses were knocked off, and the hat and false beard that had made her think, first of Mr. Mercier, the florist's assistant, and then of Gianni Amara, costumed and wigged and bearded to play Rodolfo. Without his disguise there was something still that made her think of

Amara, a flickering resemblance in that dark-complexioned face, the curly black hair, the strong arched black brows. For a second a thought passed through her mind, not too amusing, not playful at all: that this man lying unconscious on her bedroom floor might be in fact Amara's youngest son, the one born in the thirties, the mother's baby, sent by poor crazy old Josephine (who was, that was no joke, back in New York, living out her last years with one of her children. Mary knew. Mary had sent money). But no. That was ridiculous. Johnny's last child would be over forty now, if one could believe it. A baby of forty-odd. And this was a much younger man. She looked back to her hand, where the necklace lay innocent of all this commotion, glowing, winking at her. She moved and stretched, aching everywhere. How unreal. How real. On the floor lay a thief, simply a professional thief, such as she had read about—clever, very clever indeed. But Lion had been more clever, more decisive, quicker. And she . . .

Lion, the clever, quick, decisive one, her son, was on the phone now, talking quietly, urgently, the gun that had pointed at her a moment earlier appropriated and now trained on its unconscious owner. Having kissed her, hugged her, released her, having helped her onto the chaise, fetched her a pill and a glass of water which she took with a surprisingly steady hand, and assured himself she was, amazingly, all right, Lion was calling the police. Then he was calling the doctor, these calls unimaginable as Mary listened.

"I don't need a doctor," she said, sounding like a child. "I want to go to my party."

The sequence in Mary's mind became a little muddled after that. Did the police come first, three or four men, or her doctor, who happened to live a few blocks away, and to be home that night, and who assured Lion there was no reason why she couldn't go to the party? Did Sergeant Lodi ask all those questions, or did she first persuade him not to make her go down to the station house that night to make a statement? When did she put on her dress and refasten the necklace? Did the thief start to regain consciousness and struggle before the police came? Did they start the questioning in the bedroom or in the living room, and was it after Lion brought her the drink, and when did they let out the poor cat? Was that before or after Lion remembered—*oh my God* —that he hadn't yet called Serena, and before or after they looked into the long white box that could have held four dozen American Beauty roses but was empty: cold, white, and empty.

She only knew two moments came into focus as sharply as anything in her life, one a moment of quiet casual terror, one a moment of happiness. The first moment had to do with the departure of the thief, the handcuffed departure of the criminal, who had been given a name now, an identity by the police. A known and nasty criminal indeed, a professional jewel thief with many aliases whose peculiarity was that he generally worked alone, picked a setup where this was possible, such as a rich old lady barricaded in a big old house.

"What if he comes back?" Mary asked.

"You won't have to worry about this guy again," the policeman said, so quietly and kindly, thinking to reassure her. "He'll go away . . . by the time they let him out . . ." He stopped, embarrassed. "By then you'll have proper locks and alarms," he went on lamely. But Mary knew what he meant. She was an old woman. A few years and she could well be gone and the ruby, whether she wanted to give it up or not, would belong to somebody else.

That was one moment.

The other, the moment of happiness, had to do with her departure, standing in the front hall of her house as Lion helped her into her coat. "Tell me one thing, Mother," he said. "Why did you put up such a fight? You could have been killed. That man was a killer."

"Because the ruby is your father. It is fourteen wonderful years," Mary said, feeling the jewel burn at her throat. "It is the only part of my life that was good. The part of my life I would not take back. It's the me I liked. It's you, it's April, it's *American Beauty*, it's who I am. No thief could be permitted to take that away."

"Yet it was only fourteen years," Lion said.

"The longest years, my darling, the ones that count," she said and turned, looking up at him, making him look at her.

"It's true, isn't it? You really meant that," he said.

"Of course it's true." It wasn't perhaps the whole truth, but almost, almost. "Of course I mean it."

Then something broke in him, broke up the ice of his eyes: the fear, the anxiety and question that had been there since those fourteen years had come to their tragic end. The evening had told him something. Mary didn't even want to examine what her foolish performance told her son, her gesture, his action: only wanted to observe the melting of the hardness of his eyes.

And then there was April.

Walking into Serena and Lion's apartment, into the foyer, almost empty, weirdly empty except for the woman in red waiting by the deserted bar, though from the dining room, invisible from the doorway, came the sounds of a dinner in progress; seeing that figure in flame-red jersey, Mary was bewildered for a moment. Dazed. Was that April? But April wasn't coming. April was sick. Could that really be April, that vision in red with the mane of tawny hair, April last seen at Christmastime, a nervous visitor in drab browns and grays, thrift shop Victoriana that didn't quite come off, with a shopping bag full of presents and shifty eyes? April back in red. "April should always wear red. . . ." Who was it had said that? A succession of Aprils came into Mary's mind, as her head spun and she sat down on the foyer settee, with this beautiful young woman in red leaning over her, kissing her, saying, "I'm sorry, Mother, you know, sorry I've been such a . . ." April at seven, backstage after *Rose*, in a lace-trimmed red velvet party dress and her mother's plumed hat . . . April in a red off the shoulder evening gown, in the Crystal Ballroom of the Blackstone Hotel, dancing with a handsome young marine, Lieutenant Wake Potter . . . April as Juliet at the ball, in red brocade . . . April at the opening of *Lady Ruby* in a gold and crimson sari . . . and then April in the living room of a Santa Monica beach house, thirty-seven though looking like a teenager, in a bikini and a red terry-cloth beach robe, the last time Mary had seen the child in her color, the last time she felt they had had a chance, she and April, to start all over, but she, Mary, had somehow muffed it again.

"Sit with me a moment," Mary said now, giving Lion her things, seeing him motion to someone else coming out of the dining room to go back, to give mother and daughter a moment together. And something must have caused April to think of that California afternoon also, for, taking her mother's hand, she said, "Remember, Mother, Santa Monica, Debbie's house?" Mary nodded. "Wake's here tonight, Mother. He thought I wasn't going to be. Waiting for you, going out of my mind waiting for you, I talked to him. I remembered what you said that day." Mary nodded again. "Tonight I could listen to you, if you said something like that. Do you remember?"

"I'm trying," Mary said, "I'm trying."

2

It was the fourth day Mary had been in the bad-luck place, the poisonous place called, collectively, "Hollywood," though it be Los Angeles, Beverly Hills, Bel Air, Glenwood, Culver City, Burbank, the San Fernando Valley, Santa Monica; always spelled "Hollywood," like that hundred-foot sign against the hills from which desperate starlets, in the old days, had sometimes jumped. Yet it had been the Garden of Eden, too, the first time she had been there with Charlie Grace in 1930, sun-drenched and utterly seductive: the mountains, the sea, the dazzling dry air, the pottery-blue skies, the orange groves and palm trees, the chalk-pink houses covered with purple vines, the flowers like flames, like birds, like bunches of grapes . . . and the views, the radiant, endless, cradle of the world views . . . she had cried out and clapped like a child.

Even now, she thought that afternoon in the fall of 1965, driving toward the sea from Beverly Hills, driving toward April, with the views hazed over, the once-dazzling air heavy with smog; with the blue skies mud-colored and the sun dim as the moon;

even now, as the car dropped down the plunging road from the Palisades to Santa Monica beach, Mary felt the thrill she had felt every time, at the sudden sight of the Pacific, gleaming, spread out before her. Never again, she had sworn, after the humiliation of 1954, of being wined and dined and cocktailed and conferenced, and then in the end passed over, rejected in favor of that year's "bankable" star. A disaster, that movie of *Lady Ruby*, but a disaster that gave her little satisfaction. Yet here she was again, on this fool's errand, slightly lunatic that bleak October—that would be her excuse to herself afterward—addled with grief, trying to accept the death of Gianni Amara and to undertsand the fact that this time there would be no reprieve. He was gone. She had seen him dead: dead as her father, dead as Charlie. And dead he was no longer hers. Even dying he had been no longer hers; he had been Josephine's. To see him at the end she had had to pass by Josephine, and the reality had been murky as this California landscape—that plump and faded woman with the carefully waved gray hair and stony blue eyes, that was the cow, the wife of nearly fifty years, nodding, letting Mary, the other woman, pass into the hospital room. And the man they both loved had been out of it, finally, only telegraphing with his dim eyes his thanks that the women had somehow arranged things, reconciled, pretended to reconcile, so that both could be there for him to bid farewell. *Addio . . . addio . . .* How many times had he sung that silly sad word to how many tunes, in how many costumes, plumed, bereted, helmeted, wigged . . . *addio . . . addio.* And then his lips were cold and gray, his eyes closed, his hands folded peacefully on his chest . . . and his wife and children beside him, on the far side of the bed as she, Mary Gay, the great star, the star of his life, walked away.

Anything to blank out that scene—drink, talk, rushing from place to place, sleeping pills, lunches, dinners, conferences about a television show—and now this, this reunion with the runaway April, who was at a crossroads, who might need her help. Only how could she think clearly, how could she have been expected to think clearly, she would say to herself later, and to the man who had died: *It is your fault, still, always your fault.*

So the rented limousine had stopped at a number, a blind
pink-walled entrance at the very center of the Santa Monica gold
coast, no longer so golden as it once had been—the gold had
moved north and south—but golden seeming still to Debbie
Vail, now Lohman, Mrs. Jack Lohman, married to a studio
lawyer. And the somber-faced, aging blonde in a Pucci print, the
fading star Mary Gay—six months before the Harry Dresser
show, the last burst of glory—being helped out of the car by a
chauffeur in gray livery, realized she had seen this house before,
been in it in the thirties with Charlie Grace, when it belonged to
a famous silent film star, also dead.

"I know this house," Mary said a moment later to April in
red, curled up on a beige linen sofa, reading a paperback. Gazing
around the glass-wrapped living room that gave onto a terrace and
swimming pool, and another pink wall, and beyond the lan-
guorous, then thundering Pacific, Mary let herself remember.
Briefly. "Your father used to call this room Coronado's revenge.
Of course in those days, as I recall, it was zebra stripes and mirrors and filled with what they used to call wampus baby stars and
the short bald men who paid their salaries. This is charming,
charming. Debbie has her mother's taste. Where is Debbie, by the
way?"

"Not here. I'm not hiding behind Debbie," said April,
standing up, kissing her mother, looking enigmatic.

"Hide? But why should you," said Mary. "You look wonderful. Oh, April, dear April . . ." How could she convey quickly
that she wasn't there to scold, though that might have been her
original intent, but to offer her help, her support? "Max told me
you were looking wonderful."

"Max? You saw Max? Max Brandel?"

"Well, of course. I'm here on business, dear. Max is the only
person in this town I can trust. These children I've been dealing
with, what do they know? I saw Max about me. Not you. You
aren't the only one who needs advice, you know." Mary smiled,
a smile she intended to be reassuring, but the dazzling young
woman opposite—she was dazzling that day, more than ever,
drawn finer, with an elegance Mary herself had never known—

this daughter she loved sat stiffly, frozen with caution, opposite her, not saying anything.

"But in the course of talking about me," Mary went on stubbornly, the smile permanent now, "he corrected some impressions I might have had about you. He told me how it came about, this bit in a movie as a lark. Most amusing. Max looking for a real-life young matron, blond and classy, to play in his movie, going through Debbie's playmates, the Beverly Hills tennis club crowd, offending one and all by picking you, the interloper. And how after seeing the rushes he understood it wasn't such a lark. That you were good."

You must encourage her, Max had said. *In a small part, no more than eight minutes on the screen, playing not herself, playing a cool, new-style nut in a summer dress and sunglasses, April after all these years on the shelf is right on. Focused. Absolutely professional. An actress. As if she'd been there all along. I have an agent interested. There's a screenplay making the rounds with a part that's tailored for her. . . . Isn't it too late*, Mary had said. *And what about her real life, Max, her life back in New York? Wake. The children. I don't approve. I can't approve. . . . With the right part, this could be her real life*, he said. *It's your second chance, Mary, as well as hers.*

"Max says there's something in the offing," said Mary now, continuing to talk, forcing herself to catch fire, although the dazzling stranger in her ridiculous outfit opposite sat motionless, unchanging, alert. "He thinks you have a future. You on that screen, he says, are alive, which is what I never was." Still no response from April, only a faint frown settling between her exquisite brows. "The children are launched, after all," Mary went on, convincing herself as she spoke. "Jenny off to college, Mary Beth and Billy both in boarding school. You've given them a fine foundation, nearly twenty years of your life. You started so young. But now you can do something for yourself. Wake. That's something, of course, you have to . . . only . . ." then stopping finally, realizing that April was still just sitting there, curled up on that beige sofa, staring at her mother, listening, waiting, waiting for something Mary wasn't saying, with that funny little look on her face, half amused, half anxious. *Wake loves you,* Mary wanted to say. *He's frantic. He'd commute from New York to Los Angeles if that would make you happy.*

"Only what, Mother," April said quietly, finally speaking. "What else did Max tell you?"

"What else? Nothing," Mary said uneasily, remembering a moment in the conversation when she had asked quite bluntly if there was something going on between Max and April—she was past the point of being shocked or disapproving, she just wanted to know, and Max had said, "You should be ashamed of yourself, Mary, ashamed of yourself."

"Only what?" April repeated.

"The only has to do with Wake. What's going on with you and Wake, April? Am I being stupid? Is there more to this movie, and the one in the works, than I know about?"

Now Mary was beginning to feel like a fool, catching something from April in her red wrapper, remembering a hint Lion had dropped, that didn't make sense to her, didn't register quite. She was feeling the old sinking sensation, that there was something else, something she could do nothing about whatever, that only April could deal with, and once again the decision would be . . . So, bluntly, she asked April the question she had asked Max. And April laughed, just as Max had laughed.

"I see you don't know, Mother," she said quietly. And then, giving a funny quizzical look, she picked up the book she had been reading, an early novel by Skip Hubbard, the one before the big best sellers and the quarter-of-a-million-dollar screenplays that had pleased the critics.

"About what?"

"About me and Skip. Max! Oh, I don't mind admitting that when I came out here last summer I had Max on my mind. I was desperate. After a long winter of me and Wake and no child left at home to referee. It was Eugene O'Neill, or Strindberg, every night at the Potter dinner table. I started dreaming about Max Brandel. Does that shock you? But I did, still, after all these years. I had some romantic notion that it was him and me, all along. Did Max tell you about that?" Mary shook her head. It was her turn now to stare in silence. "Well, he's his own form of gentleman. I threw myself at him. Made a total ass of myself. He wasn't interested. 'Once something is dead, it's dead, darling,' he said. But if I wanted it, the part was mine. You bet I wanted it, more than ever. And then I met Skip. Conferred with Skip about changing some of my lines. Met him again, I should say, except neither of us remembered we had met many times at Jenny Fawn's."

She held out the book, with the bronzed, rugged face on the back, the face of the man *Time* magazine had called the Balzac of Beverly Hills. "I want to marry him, Mother. *Marry him*. Work out here. Start over. A whole new life. You'll understand when you meet him. He'll be here in an hour."

Mary looked at her. Still didn't say anything for a moment. Then, "The brown people," she said. "He was another one of those brown people. That was your room, wasn't it, April? Your source. Your first chapter. As Pauline Selva's studio was mine." A pause. "April Grace. Mrs. Skip Hubbard." Another pause—an inflection that cut. "And nineteen years of April Potter down the drain. I never had nineteen years, so I wouldn't know, would I?" A long stare now, a bad stare. An exchange of bad stares. "I hope it will be Mrs. Skip Hubbard, darling, if that's what you want."

"It is what I want, Mother," April said, refusing to take offense.

"I won't throw those nineteen years of marriage in your face, nothing like that," Mary continued. "This is an age of divorce, after all. You're thirty-seven years old, though you look like one of your daughters today," staring dully at the beach house living room, at April in it, April the love object, April in love who could be about to pick up that guitar, over by the fireplace, property of Debbie's son, and start to play.

"I *hope* that's what happens," said Mary, winding up a bit. "Because you'll need a husband if you are going to work out here, start over. You'll never make it alone. It's too tough. This is a tough town, and not your town." Winding up, then letting out the spiel, and the living room of a Santa Monica beach house in 1965 could have been Mary's bedroom in 1945, and April seventeen again. "But if you think Wake Potter is a crude fellow, you've seen nothing till you've seen this Hollywood pack. Bully boys all, to whom women are nothing. Nothing! I've spent some time with them in the last week. Writers. Actors. Directors. Agents. Packagers. Warm as hell. And ice. Ice, April. The young ones who look like baby seals, with big round black eyes and sleek heads; the middle-aged ones who look like Max or him," pointing to the book jacket. "Even the old ones, the ones my age, the silver foxes, the snow leopards. I'm scared for you. Now I'm *really* scared for you," Mary said, standing up, delivering the volley of words, the new words that would haunt her, the wrong words.

"I could see you here, part of the year, married to Wake," the mother spoke the frantic words that were deceiving and true at the same time, "with his support, even if he wasn't with you every minute. And you *could* have his support. He's not the narrow boy he once was. I feel like such a fool. That was my picture when I walked in here of what might happen. What you've told me. I have nothing to say. It seems like a mess to me, that will end up nowhere. I must go. Really I must go."

But April in red didn't lash back; not then. April in red only said, with a bit of a smile, "Oh, Mother, must you? Must you leave like this? Come on, let's go outside. At least wait and meet him. He's not what you imagine. He's tough, yes, and brilliant, but very dear. Come on. It's cleared into a lovely afternoon. We don't get so many of them. Let's look at the ocean. You used to tell me about this stretch of beach when I was little, how beautiful you and Daddy thought it was, but how silly because the sun was on the wrong side, set behind the waves. No? . . . All right, I'll see you to your car, then."

"Your father," Mary said, "this wouldn't be happening if your father was alive. Not this way," and was gone.

And of course Mary was right. And found it unbearable to have been so right when April told her months later, with that same bit of a smile, but something irretrievably hurt and angry in the eyes behind the smile. Described how right she'd been. Described the scene in the Malibu beach house where April had moved after Christmas. Took a certain pleasure, even, this returned April, in describing a scene Mary couldn't possibly hear easily, a woman of her generation, when things were done in a certain way and discretion all; a scene, right out of one of his own novels, of Mr. Skip Hubbard, hairy-chested and bleary, coming out of the bedroom one morning, into the seaside kitchen that was also the dining room and living room, the hearth of the love nest, where April sat in the window, studying her script; taking a swig of milk, directly from the carton, then saying, "I don't think you are going to get the part, baby." Then a few days later, having let that sink in, he announced his own departure for New York and points east, London, Paris, Rome, Marrakesh, and it became clear that April wasn't part of his travel plans, though of course he hoped to find her still around on his return.

"You were right, Mother," April said, "you were right all the way. Only I wonder. If you hadn't said it. If you hadn't made me scared. If you hadn't lied even as you were telling the truth . . ."

3

"I remember too much, too much," said Mary in midnight blue and the ruby to April in flame jersey. "Nothing good. And afterward you said, *If you hadn't made me scared. If you hadn't lied even as you were telling the truth.* . . . That's what you've been trying to say all along.

"It would have come out the same. The only person who could have made a difference, like you said . . . that's what I was remembering. What you said about Wake. But I had to screw that up, didn't I, really screw that up. He's left Rosemary, you know, Mother, the wonderful second wife, the child bride."

"Of course," said Mary. "You didn't think he would be here, did you, if he hadn't left Rosemary. I am not that soft-headed or peculiar."

"But you are, Mother. What happened tonight was very peculiar, and a little soft-headed too. You're a little crazy, Mother, when you believe in something. I wish I'd understood that long ago. I wish you'd told me that, long ago. Are you steady now? Shall we go in?"

"Yes," said Mary, taking her daughter's hand, "I'm ready to go in now." As she walked toward the dining room she noticed, vaguely, the packages and the roses, the packages surrounding an enormous vase of American Beauty roses as if the roses were a Christmas tree . . . the roses that should have been at her house, the roses she had never quite believed did not in fact come from Gianni Amara. Who else would have kept it up all those years, such a gesture, such a joke to please her love of mysteries, and even left instructions for continuing the gesture after his death. Gianni Amara. Or. But the idea that had come into her mind in recent days, as she approached this particular birthday, that the anonymous admirer, the "crazy lovesick millionaire" had been Charlie Grace—Charlie Grace all along—was one Mary could not bear to think about. And now it was clear that if the roses were here, sent here, that meant . . . but who?

Which one of them, Mary wondered, seeing the group assembled at the table, already on the second course, for a moment frozen—the remains of her life—caught not in a blinding flare but in flickering candlelight, nonetheless clear and vivid. Not many at that table who for fifty-two years, ever since the opening of *American Beauty*, might have sent her, for her birthday, four dozen American Beauty roses with a card signed, simply, "an admirer." Her sister. Her cousin. Her sister-in-law. George. Hugh. Harry. "Darlings, darlings," she said softly to the remains of her life around that table, and took her place at the head, between Lion and Harry Dresser, who said, "Did you hire him, Mary, did you get that thief from central casting, so you could make the entrance of your life?" Not to make an entrance, she might have answered, but for something, yes, to put me through a last test, let me give a final performance . . . to make an exit . . . after which . . . But she said nothing, smiled and said nothing. The moment in the house with Lion, the moment here with April, had left her with nothing much to say.

And the dining room threw her, more than she wanted to admit. It was too accurate, too ghostly, too like her own dining room in the early days of her marriage—everybody's dining room then—before she'd swept the cobwebs out, and the stained glass, opened the room out toward the garden and painted everything that wasn't mirrored white.

The charm of Serena and Lion's dining room, she had always thought, was the mixture: they'd kept the dark woodwork and the stained glass that went with a building that dated from 1914, and used family furniture: but they set the table informally with bright Mexican linens and Italian pottery; had plants and trees in the windows and modern lighting. But tonight the family silver was out, the red Victorian glassware, the Georgian candelabra. Every Grace and Geylin and Watkins heirloom washed and polished, even the central fruit dish, and around the long table hired for the occasion, long enough to seat thirty-six people, were placed old-fashioned gilt ballroom chairs. They had used the cloth of silver damask, and the napkins big as shawls; they had used the dinner plates with the hand-painted scenes from Shakespeare that had belonged to Jean Archibald. There were even porcelain place cards and menus on silver easels at either end of the table, written in purple French script.

The dinner was from another age also, and the menu, as Mary peered mistily at the purple writing, oddly, eerily familiar.

"It was your thirtieth birthday menu," Lion said. "Aunt Belle told us once about that party."

"Belle, dear Belle," Mary murmured. That had not been happy, that thirtieth birthday party. January 1930. Not a happy month at all. A month to be quiet about if you'd lost as much money as Charlie Grace had in a matter of days; if your friend and broker had jumped out a window and you yourself had received the first set of lukewarm notices in ten years of unbroken successes and knew you wouldn't run past March. And then had come April, May, and June in Hollywood . . . and then . . . and then . . .

Down the table, as she tried to eat a little something, a small slice of chicken breast, a spoonful of vegetable, she noticed the way Wake Potter was staring at his ex-wife, the unexpected guest, who had stuck herself provocatively between Max Brandel and Aunt Mathilda; and the way April was returning his stare, with a mischievous smile, a little girl's look almost as if she was sticking her tongue out at him. But even that couldn't focus her attention. She kept slipping back. Tell me, Mary thought of asking Harry Dresser beside her, you didn't send me flowers by any chance, only here for this birthday instead of to my house, not the flowers you always send, that you and Theresa used to send together, but mysterious flowers, American Beauties with no name attached? But she didn't have the breath, the curiosity. It was enough to know she had been loved, that faithfully, by someone.

"Are you all right, Mother?" Lion asked. Again the smile, the nod. And finally the cake.

Through the swinging door came Serena with the masterpiece ablaze with candles. And around the table the grandchildren began marching with those extraordinary banners that made Mary want to weep or scream though she said, "How marvelous," and meant it. And then Marjorie started the singing. The singing was the trap door. Singing. Ruby glasses. Her ruby. The candles. It was her eleventh birthday. Sixty-four years of the person born that birthday, sixty-four years in a flash. Marching around the table like medieval banners. Flip flip flip flip flip flip gone in a flash. Puff. Imagined. Gone. The thirty-six people in the room reduced to herself, Isabelle and Walter Geylin who had been there the night Louis Geylin had said, "This girl will be an artist, a great star. This girl will scale the heights." This girl. The joke of the ruby. God bless you, may the night be yours. One to grow on. *Addio*.

From far away, at a very great distance, she saw the lovely painted birthday cake—where had they found anyone to do such a cake anymore—like the ones she used to order for the children when they were little. Scenes painted on glazed white icing, clowns, fairies, a skating pond, the Emerald City, a sunset, horses and Indians, every year a different scene for Lion and April till they got too old for birthday parties. Now, for Mary, who had never outgrown a birthday party, there was a stage painted on the cake, a golden proscenium with scarlet curtains. The curtains opened on a glittering number: 75. "But is the curtain going up?" she asked. "Or is it going down?"

"Up," Lion said. "Up. Of course!"

And then somebody cried, "Make a wish! And blow out the candles."

She wished. She blew. Then Lion made his toast, a charming toast telling what various people had done aged seventy-five: Verdi began *Falstaff*. . . . Queen Victoria started a war. . . . Sarah Bernhardt took a lover. . . . Madame Colette wrote a book. . . . Renoir painted his finest nudes. "What energy," Mary murmured, though not so Lion could hear, only Harry Dresser, her contemporary. A writer's toast, but not too long. "And at seventy-five Mary Gay"—and then he caught his mother's eye and if he had been about to say something of the evening's adventure . . . at seventy-five Mary Gay did battle with a thief . . . he understood she didn't want that, and finished simply, "Who knows what Mary Gay, my beloved mother, will do? Who has ever been able to say what comes next for Mary Gay?" And he raised his glass. Then Harry Dresser stood up, and after that it was Tilly Vail and Belle and George Jacobs, spaces between each toast to give Mary a chance, everyone waiting for Mary to answer Lion: What would she say? What words of wisdom? What classic, what unanswerable, or possibly unforgivable remark? But when finally she rang her glass, a perfect high B, she noted, Mary said nothing more than "Thank you." Thank you from a sitting position. "Thank you," she said, "thank you for being here. God bless you all." And even for that, that pathetic showing, everyone cheered, rang their glasses, stood up. Once again the grandchildren marched around the table fluttering their banners.

And after dinner, when people gathered around the piano, waiting for the moment when Mary would be unable to sit still a moment longer, would join them and burst into still-glorious song—"amazing for her age"—she remained where she had gone for coffee, seated on the sofa. After a moment of uncertainty, Harry Dresser had gone to the piano and Marjorie had followed him.

Mary was tired now, yet she sat up straight to listen, straight as Pauline Selva, when Marjorie, taking her cue from Harry, began singing. And rising sweet and strong, the voice of Marjorie Grace took off on the "Happy Birthday" song from Mary's first show. "That girl has talent," Mary said to Lion. "We must see about it. They say talent skips a generation." She was feeling better, she thought, nodding in time to the music, aware that people were watching her, aware of the blue eyes of Max Brandel, who was talking to Serena but looking at her; of April and Wake, standing side by side, leaning toward each other . . . maybe . . . of Verna Michaels, of dear Belle, of Walter Geylin, of all those eyes on her, watching her reactions, waiting for what she might say.

But she would say nothing more, only listen to her granddaughter sing *Happy Birthday to You . . . You . . .* and then take off on the *you*, like a bird, like a young girl a lifetime ago; and while her granddaughter sang, Mary mouthed the words, that was all, *no stars, no air, no blue, no me without you*, trying to remember what it had been like, what it was she had wanted so much, and that now she realized she had at last.